Patsy Barry was born in Dundee on 4th April 1936, Patsy lived through the war years. Even at the age of 84, she can still vividly recall that time of rationing, blackouts and shortages.

Patsy left school at the age of 14 and worked in the personnel office of Burndept, where she met Andy, a factory worker. Andy was called up for National Service and they married in 1956. Theirs was a happy marriage with five children, nine grandchildren, and eleven great grandchildren.

Sadly, after a two-year battle with prostate cancer, Andy died shortly before their 55th wedding anniversary.

For Andy, the love of my life.

Patsy Barry

OF TIME AND TIDE

AUSTIN MACAULEY PUBLISHERS™

LONDON ∗ CAMBRIDGE ∗ NEW YORK ∗ SHARJAH

A CIP catalogue record for this title is available from the British Library.

ISBN 9781788481571 (Paperback)
ISBN 9781788783194 (ePub e-book)

www.austinmacauley.com

First Published 2022
Austin Macauley Publishers Ltd®
1 Canada Square
Canary Wharf
London
E14 5AA

Thanks to my precious Granddaughter, Stacey and my sister-in-law Cathy for their belief in my writing.

Preface

It's all about money, isn't it? The compulsion that drives ambitious men with aspirations of greatness to do the things they do in order to gain wealth. For isn't it a known fact that the might and muscle of only wealthy men have the power and influence to hold authority and rule nations?

But not all wealthy men have hunger for that Machiavellian power where they alone hold the whiplash to control and dictate. Eddie Fraser was one such man; a unique breed of man with a down-to-earth love of life and cared nothing for a healthy bank balance. He deplored the idea of inherited wealth, for he would rather toil to earn than sit on an illustrious backside lazily enjoying a plush lifestyle and the supremacy which comes with it.

There are many facets of power and yet, the greatest of all, which should never be underestimated, is surely the power of fate. For instance, if fate ordains the union of two people, the mere detail that continents, oceans, deserts and forests separate them is of no consequence when destiny has decided.

Divine intervention brought Eddie and Tina together, yet the other merciless and much crueller hand of fate also ripped them apart. Somewhere along the way, their fairy-tale romance became a horror story when evil seeped in through the porthole of loneliness and carried with it a plague of wickedness and treachery which would last for decades.

Tina was indifferent as to whether or not the young Australian was a prince or a pauper. She fell in love with the man. Besides, since he displayed none of the trappings synonymous with wealth, how could she tell?

But in truth, Eddie Fraser was a man of means through both inheritance and his family's fortune. He had been born into money but money was of little importance to a man without greed for riches. Time alone would show the sad and bitter consequence of all this wealth he denied, yet others craved. Only after Eddie and Tina's passing would the memory of their love be marred by the stigma of corruption, greed and lust for what rightfully belonged to the outcome of their devotion to each other—their children.

Like every story, this story has a beginning, middle and an end…

Part One
A Time of Peace and Love

Chapter One

A cold February morning in 1907, that was when it all began.

Icicles formed on the ship's rails and frost clung to the deck as *The Rose* cut through the icy mist which covered the cold forbidding waters of the North Sea. Rising with the swell and heaving forward, tidal waves beating an anthem of the sea against the ship's hull as it moved through the Tay estuary towards the town of Dundee.

Sailing against the tide caused the ship to buck and roll, but it made—no never mind, since time and time alone was of the essence. Skipper Henry Jack had walked these decks many times before, his thoughts only of unloading, loading then enjoying a few days ashore before catching the tide. Today, this very morning, he felt only fist-clenching fervour watching and waiting for the sight of buildings and spires that were the town of Dundee. When he could almost reach out and touch them, they would only be minutes from docking.

The young Australian who had joined the ship as a deckhand some months ago had gone down with the fever, and Henry was sure the lad wasn't going to make it. He'd seen this before when his own brother died of the pneumonia and this deathly ill young man had the same symptoms. Laboured breath that rasped and gurgled and a body on fire; he barely clung to life. Time was running out but if they got him to a hospital soon, then God willing, he might just have a fighting chance.

With the heart of a true seafarer, Henry had always found it pleasant and relaxing to lean on the ship's rail, watching the foaming wake. That supreme sensation of moving, yet seeming to stand still in the middle of an empty ocean invigorated the senses, gave buoyancy to the soul and filled an old sea-dog with a spirit of wellbeing—usually. But today, there was no alleviation from the fear that gripped his heart; fear as icy as this handrail.

Henry brought his clenched fist heavily and painfully onto the metal rail. Why, Why this boy? For Eddie was no more than that, a boy on the threshold of life. The light spray was like cold sweat on his face as Henry tilted his head backwards, begging the heavens to hear his prayer and halt this damned unfairness.

Henry straightened and rubbed his smarting hand then paced the deck once more. 'Facts would have to be faced,' he muttered to himself. If the boy was ready to depart this life, a lesser mortal such as himself had no say in the matter. Only, this lad bore such an uncanny resemblance to the younger brother that was lost to him, the pain would be like losing him for a second time and that was the hurt. From the moment he set eyes on Eddie, with his easy-going manner and ready smile, it had struck a chord and brought back long-forgotten memories of a boy who had been just too weak to fight the fever.

The clang-clang of the ship's bell startled Henry momentarily, but it stirred another memory and a spontaneous smile replaced the worried frown. He remembered the day brashly confident Eddie Fraser had claimed a place in his heart. Like an old salt, he had swaggered into the bar and walked straight over to where Henry sat.

'I've heard tell you need a deckhand,' and then, like some arrogant brat uninvited, he pulled the chair opposite Henry from under the table and sat down without waiting for as much as a nod of the head. Leaning across the table, this stranger looked the skipper in the eye, 'I'm your man so you need look no further.' It was more of a command than a request.

'Is that a fact?' Henry answered sarcastically, but the sarcasm fell on deaf ears, for this lad obviously thought he was God's gift to any sea-going vessel.

'It is,' the boy answered with a confident nod of his head.

Henry leaned back in his chair and folded his arms over his chest. He thought to humour the boy by playing along with the charade but with no intention of actually taking him on. 'Tell me something,' he said, 'what makes you think I'd hire a greenhorn like you? I don't think you're even old enough to shave.'

'I'm no greenhorn!' Eddie was suddenly defensive. He might be young and inexperienced, but he knew when he was being taken for a fool. 'I'm a grafter and a damned good sailor; the sea's in my blood and for your information, I... I do shave... sometimes.' But the skipper's cold, discerning stare stifled Eddie's conceited self-confidence.

Through eyes that were slits in his weather-beaten face, Henry peered at the lad. He was beginning to see him in a different light because there weren't many who would stand up to Henry Jack. 'You'd have to work hard, harder than you've ever worked before,' he said gruffly. 'I'd expect that and more, because I tell you here and now, I don't entertain shirkers.'

'I can work as good, if not better than any man.'

You only had to look at him to know he wasn't the type to make an empty promise then lie down on the job. There was a truth about him. He wasn't boasting; he was giving a true account of his worth. Eddie Fraser, youthful and spirited, was like a young gorilla defiantly beating its chest to send out the message that he was worthy, he was the best and this kind of self-assurance had to be admired—and rewarded.

'Right then,' Henry almost choked on the laugh that was stuck in his throat: a great hee-haw that couldn't be held back for much longer. The boy certainly had faith in his own abilities, so why bring him down? Henry cleared his throat. 'You're hired,' he told him, 'but only on a trial basis mind. We'll soon see if you can work as well as you blow your own trumpet.'

Eddie grasped the outstretched hand; the contract was sealed and tomorrow, *The Rose* would set sail with a new deckhand on board.

The cocky, young Australian did prove he wasn't afraid of hard work and even managed to win the admiration of the hard-bitten, rum-swigging crew. The boson puffed on the old clay pipe that was forever clenched between gums that had long since discarded decayed teeth. The wise, beady eyes, that had seen so much of life, smiled at Henry. 'You picked a good 'un,' he cackled.

'I didn't pick him, boson... he picked me.'

'So, do we keep him?'

'Aye,' Henry answered, and that was the final seal.

The harbour lights twinkling in the distance brought him back to reality. Henry raised his eyes skywards and sent up one last, desperate prayer. 'Dear God, hold back the angel of death and let this boy live. He's a good lad who's harmed no man.'

The boy was fading faster by the minute as he was carried from the ship and Henry was aware of the fearful whispers among the crew. No one wanted to admit, even to themselves, that Eddie was done for. The only utterance of fading hope came in the form of an old adage, 'poor Eddie will never scratch an *old head*.' But the torment and pain of potential loss was there nevertheless.

The hospital corridor was clinically white; a cold, unfriendly place where Henry sat alone watching nurses come and go, passing him as if he were invisible. The tension of not knowing what was happening grew more and more unbearable. At last, a doctor came towards him.

Henry was aware of the bead of cold sweat that trickled down the side of his face as he rose unsteadily to his feet.

'What news, doctor? Will the lad survive?' His shaking hands clutched the well-worn skipper's cap as if it were a lifeline.

'Well, you were right about it being pneumonia, and we're hopeful you got him here in time. But I'd be failing in my duty if I didn't warn you he's going through the crisis and the next twenty four hours will be crucial. I'm sorry I can't be more specific. All I can tell you is that if he gets past that, then he has a chance.'

'Can I see him?'

'Only for a few minutes; he's very weak and barely conscious. I'll take you to him.'

The light blonde hair and deathly pallor against the crisp, white pillow made Eddie look so frail. The oxygen tent that held his almost lifeless body filled Henry with dread and this giant of a man shed unabashed tears. 'He isn't going to make it, is he?' Henry looked to the doctor for some sort of assurance. 'Please be truthful, for I've already lost someone dear to me in the same way, and this lad has become both a brother and the son I never had.'

'He's strong, and that's in his favour, but there are no guarantees.'

Henry bent over the oxygen tent. 'If you can hear me, son, hang in there,' he pleaded with the boy even though he was hardly aware of Henry's presence.

'Losing you would leave a great emptiness in my heart. Remember, it was *you* who made yourself a part of my life. Don't go thinking you can leave me now.'

For one brief second, Eddie's eyes flickered. He was aware; he had heard and his body although weak, still retained some fight.

After four days in dock and the cargo now loaded, *The Rose* was ready to sail. There was one last thing that had to be done.

The skipper's feet made an eerie, echoing sound as he walked the tiled corridor to Eddie's ward. He'd passed the crisis, but was still far from well. Henry sat uncomfortably by the bed, almost choking on the words that must be spoken.

'You're on the mend now, Eddie lad.' He wanted to sound cheery and positive but the little quiver in his voice let him down. 'Believe me; you're in the best place.'

'Skipper…'

Eddie's eyes were pleading, begging for reassurance that he wasn't going to be left behind when the ship took to the sea. His desperation was like an icy wind from the north, the kind that bites and brings a look of suffering to the face. Eddie had that look right now. Henry was aware of his need to be up and about and ready to leave, but he also knew it couldn't be.

The skipper spoke hurriedly, lest words failed him, 'I know what you want to say, but save your breath and your strength, and listen to me. You'll be laid up for weeks and we must sail tomorrow. Believe me; I don't want to leave you in this God forsaken place. If I had a choice, I would gladly wrap you in a blanket and carry you back to the ship myself.' A sad smile wrinkled Henry's weather-beaten face. 'Just keep in mind that I'll be back to collect you in twelve weeks.'

'Promise me, skipper,' Eddie grasped the sleeve of Henry's jacket, his eyes fearful and his voice anxious.

'I give you my sacred word and that's not something I do lightly.' Henry took a watch from his vest pocket and glanced at the dial, trying hard not to show his agitation. 'I have to go now, preparations to be made if we're to sail with the tide.' He walked quickly to the door before his spirit weakened.

This was the hardest thing Henry ever had to do and the worst part was that, to Eddie's mind, it must look like he was in a rush to leave without as much as a proper goodbye. Right now, Eddie must be thinking he was being abandoned and his skipper had no intention of returning. Henry did the only thing he could think of. He turned and raised his hand in a salute. Hopefully, this one gesture would leave the boy in no doubt the skipper was true to his word and would never cast him adrift in a strange land.

Eddie felt exhausted and drained. How he missed the sound of the ocean lapping against the ship's hull. He could estimate the time of day by the degree of light, but in here, he couldn't tell if it was dusk or dawn, not with green oilskin blinds pulled down over the windows. Oh, for the strength to leave this bed and flee like the wind to catch *The Rose* before she sailed from these shores, where he was without family or friends.

Days fled, but Eddie felt time had stood still, yet time was not infinite and knowing the day was coming when he would bid farewell to this place caused him no sorrow. He was getting better by the day. Eddie was a sturdy, well-built lad; hard work had made him strong and muscled. He had physical strength and coupled with strength of mind, these were the main factors in his recovery.

And then, came the rising of the sun on a new day that began with cheerful encouragement. The doctor gave his opinion on the state of Eddie's health. 'You're truly on the mend,' he said, 'now it's time to begin building up your strength.'

This was the most uplifting thing the doctor could have said. 'Just tell me what to do,' Eddie said eagerly. He was ready and willing to take this positive step towards a full recovery from the pneumonia.

'Start with slow walks at first,' was the advice given. 'Perhaps to the hospital shop, for a bar of chocolate or something a bit tastier than hospital food,'

The worst part of his confinement to bed had been the boredom, and now Eddie welcomed the chance to view the world from outside these four walls, even if it was only to walk the length and breadth of the corridor.

Weak and shaky, he began his sojourn to the shop before realising he didn't have much of an appetite, and the idea of devouring chocolate did nothing to excite the taste buds. So what was left? His legs were tired and aching after the spell of inactivity, oh, but it did feel good to stand on his own two feet again. If nothing else, a little harmless exploring would be less mundane than lying in bed.

Eddie was overawed by the vastness that lay beyond the ward door. The corridor long, wide and with so many doors: this must surely be the hospital's main artery. Eddie saw it as an ocean and all the doors were ports. He began walking as the adventurer in him took over.

The doors to the neighbouring ward lay open. It was like an invitation to enter so he did just that; he went in. Women in pretty bed jackets watched curiously, nodding to one another. The puzzled looks were questioning who this intruder was and then it struck him: this was a female ward and they were most likely thinking he was a peeping Tom. Red-faced, Eddie turned to make a hasty exit and that was the moment he saw her; a pale and very fragile looking young girl. Immediately, the sight of her conjured up a memory of a doll he had seen in the window of a toy shop. It was nestled in a box and had long, dark hair framing a porcelain face. Eddie couldn't remember ever seeing anyone so beautifully delicate. He was transfixed, unable to take his eyes off the vision. Had it not been for a nurse hurrying past and momentarily obscuring his view, who knows how long he would have stood there?

The girl had seen him staring and smiled as he turned to leave. Such a sweet smile; it left him with a dilemma. Should he return the smile or merely stride indifferently from the ward, hopefully leaving the impression he was a patient who had mistakenly walked through the wrong door? No, he wanted to speak to her. He had to speak to her. Eddie's feet began to move involuntarily across the polished floor.

'Hello,' he said, 'I'm Eddie, Eddie Fraser. I must have taken a wrong turning or something. I think I should be in the ward next door.' It was such a feeble excuse; the colour rose in his cheeks.

Her dark, questioning eyes scrutinised his face for a moment and then she held out a pale, delicate hand and said quite simply, 'Hello, Eddie. I'm Tina Morris.'

The sound of tittering that carried around the ward made Eddie's blush deepen.

'Somehow, I don't think it's the one thing for me to be here, I ought to go,' he said gruffly.

'Please, don't go yet, Eddie, stay for a few minutes and talk to me.'

How could he, how could anyone refuse such a plea? In an act of bravado, Eddie pulled over a chair and sat by the bed. He was no longer an intruder but a bona fide visitor, even though it was outside visiting hours. 'So, what's wrong with you then?' While trying to show masculinity and maturity, too late, Eddie realised the question was not only audacious, but very stupid.

The strange thing was, she didn't get angry or berate him and she didn't laugh at him either. Rather than taking exception, Tina salved Eddie's conscience by telling him not to feel bad about the faux pas and then she smiled, put her hand over his hand and in the softest, gentlest way explained the reason for her hospitalisation. 'I had rheumatic fever and it weakened my heart,' she told him without fuss or drama.

'Will you get better?' Too late, he'd opened his mouth again and spoke without thinking. Now, he felt really immature and very, very stupid.

Her reply was somewhere between brusque and whimsical, 'I'll be eighteen next month and I intend to live a long time and have lots of children. Does that answer your question?'

Eddie rose abruptly and replaced the chair. 'I think I've said enough! I'm sorry if I insulted you.' He walked hurriedly towards the door, every nerve in his body urging him to run and not look back.

But then, Tina called after him, 'Visit me again, Eddie Fraser.'

Eddie stopped, turned and walked back. He leaned so close to her, their faces were almost touching. 'Of course, I will,' he promised. 'That's what friends do, isn't it?'

'Oh, I hope so,' Tina answered, and there was the oddest fluttering sensation in her breast.

There had been an immediate attraction between them, an invisible bond. It wasn't just chance Eddie had wandered into that ward, it was fate. Tina lay back on her pillow, the encounter with the handsome, young Australian had left her breathless and yet, his vitality had somehow given her an inner strength. If there was such a thing as love at first sight…

For the next two weeks, they grasped every opportunity to be together. They would sit by the rose beds in the hospital garden and talk endlessly, yet never questioning the past. For them, there was no yesterday and no tomorrow; only the here and now. Every moment of the quality time they spent together was treasured, which made it all the more difficult to come to terms with the fact that one day, soon, he would sail out of the harbour, out of her life. More than that, there was a strong chance they might never meet again.

Eddie stretched out on the bed, hands clasped behind his head. He tried to banish from his thoughts, the words repeating over and over in his mind. 'Never see Tina again. Never see Tina again,' and suddenly, he saw the reality of his predicament. Parting was no longer a possibility, but a certainty, and they were plummeting towards that day.

'You've made a remarkable recovery.' That was the doctor's verdict on this day of days that Eddie had both longed for and dreaded. The doctor was confident enough of his recovery to say, 'no reason to keep you here.' How was he to know that these few words were like the quick thrust of a sword into Eddie's heart?

How many weeks were left before his ship returned to these shores? Was it eight or nine? He'd have to find a place to stay. Eddie asked the ward sister to write out directions to the Seaman's Mission. She handed him the rough drawing then began fussing over the bed, tucking, straightening, smoothing. Was it part of their training not to leave a single wrinkle on any bedcover? Someone should tell nurses that beds are supposed to be comfortable, not perpetually wrinkle-free.

There was no way to hold back the tide, just as there was no way to hold back tomorrow and the inevitable day when tearful farewells must be spoken. Eddie tried to coax his mind into believing that, for what were no more than a few moments in time, they had simply been ships that passed in the night, but for that he was grateful.

Tina was sitting on the bed, reading. The sunlight shone through the window, giving her hair a warm, burnished glow. Eddie stood for a moment to absorb the memory of the girl who was responsible for banishing despair and filling his life, albeit briefly, with happiness. As if sensing his presence, she raised her eyes and beckoned with a smile. Tina listened as he told her in the most matter-of-fact way that he was leaving hospital tomorrow. Gone was the boyish, good humour that made her laugh. In fact, he seemed almost indifferent.

What had she expected when this predictable day came?

'That's wonderful!' Tina's manner and posture feigned indifference. She picked up the book and held it in front of her face as a way to hide behind the pages so that Eddie couldn't see the hurt that wracked her entire being.

'I suppose you must be bored to death with my company,' she said, straining to maintain a lack of concern.

It was more than Eddie could bear. This charade had to end and the truth told. His heart was breaking at the thought of never seeing her again.

'Look at me, Tina,' he practically snatched the book from her hands. 'You don't know how wrong you are. I could spend eternity with you and never have one boring day.'

In that instant, Tina knew that what they had was much more than a fleeting friendship. 'But you seemed so… are you saying you're not relieved to bid a final farewell?' In a frail bid to expel her fear, Tina asked, 'Are you trying to tell me you feel as scared as I do?'

'I'm confused by what I feel, Tina, because I've never felt like this before. I love the travelling, I love my life and yet, without you in it, my life wouldn't have a meaning. Instead of seeking answers to what we don't understand, can't we take one day at a time and see what tomorrow brings?'

'Will you do something for me, Eddie?'

'Anything you ask.'

'My mother and cousin are visiting tonight. I've told them all about you and now, I'd like you to meet them.'

'If that's your wish then I'll be here, but for now, little one, I'd best head back to my own territory before matron has me shackled and forcibly removed from the premises.'

After lunch, Eddie wrote a letter to his parents, the first in a long time. He apologised for being remiss about putting pen to paper, and then told them briefly about the pneumonia but without being too graphic about how ill he had actually been. No sense in worrying them unduly.

Don't worry, Mum, the people here are sort of quaint but very friendly, and although they speak the King's English, they don't speak it like us, it's more like a foreign language, nevertheless, I'm learning. You and Dad would be proud of me.

The letter went on to assure them he had made a full recovery and under normal circumstances, these few hurried lines would have been enough, but now he went on to give a sublime description of Tina.

How do you describe an angel? She is the most beautiful and delicate creature God ever put on this earth. The doctors may have saved my life but this angel saved my sanity.

When they read this, Eddie Fraser's parents would be left in no doubt their son was besotted.

In the early evening, people began arriving with flowers and fruit. It was visiting time and Eddie was nervous about the promise he had to keep. It might be best to just take a brazen leap of faith into Tina's ward and hope her parents were as he had pictured them. Mrs Morris, a small, saintly lady, and her father, a kind, jolly man who adored the two ladies in his life. Then again, how had *they* pictured him? It would be something of an anti-climax if they saw him as a fly-by-night and warned him to keep his distance. There was so much to consider and only one way to find out.

Tina watched and waited until at last, Eddie was striding purposefully towards them. She whispered something to her mother who turned her head slowly. At first glance, Eddie was sure this stiffly upright woman wore a scowl, or was it only his imagination playing silly tricks? Mrs Morris smiled as she held out her hand, only the smile, like her voice, held no warmth.

'Nice to meet you at last, Eddie,' she said through pursed lips. 'I was beginning to think you were a myth since you didn't deem it necessary to introduce yourself—until now.' He could almost taste the resentment. This woman didn't fully trust him or his intentions. With a kind of cold insincerity, she said, 'Tina tells me they're throwing you out into the big, bad world tomorrow.'

Her presence somehow affected his speech. Eddie could only answer with a nod of the head. Mrs Morris wasn't at all what he had imagined. She wasn't in the least prim and gentle, but a stern, forceful character. Eddie struggled to find not only the words, but the courage to defy her very obvious intolerance of their friendship and then a sense of valour overcame indecision. 'Would you mind if...' He began a sentence that was silenced by a rather loud female voice.

'Well, look at you, sitting there as pretty as a picture. You certainly look much better than the last time I saw you and by the way, everyone at the mill sends their love and...' A torrent of information flowed from her lips. She obviously thought pausing for breath was a waste of time.

During the briefest break in the one-sided conversation, Tina managed to identify this human tornado. 'This is Agnes, my cousin and best friend,' she said proudly.

The round, pretty face beamed as they shook hands. Agnes was a big girl, not fat, just... big. Eddie would later discover she had a heart to match her size and the sweetest nature God ever bestowed on a human being. It was little wonder Tina adored her cousin when she had such an unmistakeable wholesome goodness. Eddie liked her immediately, but as far as Mrs Morris was concerned... that was, as yet, a very much undecided option.

No matter how earnestly we wish that time could stand still and give us the power to prolong a particular moment, life's pendulum swings relentlessly. As surely as the sun sets on one day, it will rise on another.

Chores began early in hospital, steaming cups of tea were handed out before six o'clock and this was the wake-up call. Bleary eyes had to be opened and patients were expected to be out of bed and bathed by six-thirty. Only the very ill were allowed the luxury of going back to sleep. Eddie dressed, packed his few possessions and made ready to face the outside world. But first, he must bid Tina a hasty farewell.

In the corridor, amid the bustle, they stood as close together as modesty allowed. 'Where will you live?' Tina asked.

'I'll go to the Seaman's Mission tonight, and tomorrow, I'll find a nice boarding house to stay in. I promise to see you on your birthday, little one.' Eddie felt the silent sob and tenderly, he kissed her cheek. It was Tina's nature to care, that much Eddie knew, but today, her concern was like a dagger to the heart. For Tina's sake he wanted, he had to sound jolly without being insensitive.

'If you're good, I may even bring you a present,' he said brightly.

'I won't mind one bit if you don't bring a present, all I want is for you to bring yourself. Promise you won't forget me, Eddie. Your friendship has meant a lot to me.'

'It's more than friendship, Tina. There's an everlasting bond between us, so how could I forget you? Time won't pass quickly enough until we meet again.'

'Then find your way to 22 Charles Street a week on Saturday, and I'll see you then.'

Chapter Two

The morning air was brisk as Eddie walked to the Seaman's Mission. Following directions on the rough map, he found Union Street and the Mission. It was just as he had imagined it would be. The unadorned walls were grimy with cigarette smoke that had clung to them over the years and it smelled musty. Iron bedsteads with thin mattresses and even thinner blankets lined the walls, and a strong smell of cheap pipe tobacco assaulted his nostrils. The awful stench came courtesy of the old sailor in the corner bed who silently watched Eddie while puffing on an old clay pipe. Had lack of funds and desperation, perhaps, forced him to smoke old socks? It certainly smelled like it.

Whatever happened, he mustn't allow his spirits to flag now that he had come this far. It was crucial to hold on to the thought that this page in his life would turn, and there were times he could virtually taste the brine and live the sensation of walking the decks. But there were also times he despaired of ever seeing his ship again. Troubled confusion didn't stop there; he had fallen in love and there was no point in refusing to acknowledge the fact. Leaving Tina forever would be like losing his right arm, yet she couldn't be expected to live a life of waiting, knowing their time together would be fleeting. It was a poser all right. A lot of soul searching was needed if he was to come up with an answer.

There was a park only a short walk from town, and Eddie learned that it was once the estate of a wealthy mill owner who had bequeathed the park and the small castle set in the centre to the people of the city as a refuge from the rigours of a hardworking week. It was a joy to walk beyond the gates where even the air was pleasantly different from the smoky grey of the industrial streets. Amidst the longing to escape back to the life he loved, Eddie also feared losing his grip on this beautiful place where he was surrounded by an abundance of spring flowers. The sensation of being in another world made it a deeply spiritual place, which was a tonic in itself, because here, Eddie could be alone to think his very private thoughts. With each passing day, he became more and more certain he could never let Tina go. On her eighteenth birthday, he would ask her to marry him, then if the answer was "no", Eddie Fraser would leave this country and never set eyes on Tina Morris ever again.

The city had some fine shops and while browsing for a birthday gift, Eddie wandered into a side street and discovered a small jewellers shop. He was immediately drawn to a gold locket that took pride of place in the front of the window. It was a beautiful piece with a rose carved on the front, but would it be the sort of gift that might please Tina? What he really wanted to buy was a ring, which all things considered, would be presumptuous and in bad taste. Eddie decided to settle on the locket; it was after all, the lesser of two evils.

A bell tinkled when he opened the door of the jewellers shop, bringing an elderly lady hurrying to the counter. She smiled and asked, 'How can I help you?'

'I'd like to buy that locket,' Eddie pointed, 'that one at the front of your window.'

She reached carefully into the window and retrieved the locket, placing it on a dark blue velvet pad.

'This has been greatly admired. You have excellent taste, but wouldn't you like to know the price first?'

'It's for my girlfriend's birthday and the price doesn't matter, I'll take it.' Eddie wondered why she was so hesitant until he realised, she was waiting to see the colour of his money. Once the locket was paid in full, before it was boxed and gift-wrapped, the assistant told Eddie it had a secret way of opening that only the owner must know, and then she gave up its secret.

It seemed so insignificant at the time, a gimmick of sorts, but in time the locket's secret *would* be of great significance, and the knowledge would result in this soon-to-be-treasured item being returned to its true owner. But right then, Eddie had no insight into what the future held. If only for one brief moment, he had that ability to see... At this moment in time, all he could think about was the look on Tina's face when she opened the box.

And then it was the morning of Tina's birthday. The streets bustled with Saturday morning shoppers, carrying message baskets over their arms. Queues of chattering women crowded every grocer, butcher and baker. A normal Saturday morning, Eddie navigated the busy streets until he found 22 Charles Street and then climbed the spiralling stairwell to the first landing, scrutinising every door until he found one with the polished, brass nameplate bearing the name, *Morris*.

Eddie rapped vigorously on the door. Tina gave such a squeal of delight when she opened the door to that familiar, smiling face. 'You came and I was so sure you wouldn't remember.'

'I've thought of nothing else for a week.' Eddie stepped into the narrow hallway and pulled her so close to him their lips all but touched. Before resolution waned, he whispered, 'Marry me.' He heard her gasp and felt her body tremble. 'If you say yes then I'll do the right thing by asking your father's permission.'

This was the moment Eddie discovered that they had talked so much yet never really spoken, at least not of the essential details that made up their lives. He had never spoken of his background or she of hers.

'We have so much in common and yet you know virtually nothing about me, just as I know nothing about you. I don't have a father, Eddie,' Tina said without malice for a simple mistake made. And then she explained briefly, but without sorrow or prejudice. It was merely a part of her life's history. 'My father was a dock worker and not long after I was born, a terrible accident took his life. I never knew him.'

Had the ruling power of infatuation been so strong it made everything else secondary? Tina only ever spoke of her mother and never a word about her father. Eddie remembered it had sparked in his mind a question that he never got around to asking. Only now, when engulfed by a flame of burning desire, there came the realisation that he had drifted along on a tide of ignorance where the question of her parentage was irrelevant. They had been like pebbles skipping over water, only seeing the surface and never the hidden depths.

'I suppose that's the kind of thing you talk about with someone who's a bit more than an acquaintance. And here I am, bold as brass asking you to marry me.' Eddie felt humiliated at his own arrogance. 'Did I mistake the hand of friendship for something else?'

'You really never realised, did you?'

'Realised what?'

'That I've been in love with you since the day we met! You see, Eddie, I thought all you felt for me was pity. There were times I wondered if all I meant to you was a way to forget your own troubles. I was twixt and tween then, but not anymore, and the answer is yes, I will marry you.'

The harshness of parental authority intervened, 'Are you bringing that young man inside or are you going to keep him standing on the doorstep all day?'

They had been summoned: it was the day of reckoning. Hand in hand, they walked inside and stood directly in front of Mrs Morris. It crossed Eddie's mind that having pins stuck in his eyes would be less painful than this. In fact, having teeth pulled would be a more desirable option right now.

'I have something to ask you… well, I'm not one to beat about the bush… what I mean is…'

'Do you normally ramble like this, Mr Fraser?'

If there was a time to be valiant and truthful, it was now. 'No, Mrs Morris, but then I've never asked permission to marry a girl before.' Eddie straightened his shoulders, stood tall and said, 'Tina and I would like your permission to marry.'

Like a scalded cat, Maggie Morris sprang to her feet. This was the last thing she expected. This was truly a body blow that left her gasping. 'Don't be so stupid,' she yelled, 'you've only known each other for a few weeks. Tina isn't aware of the implications.' She sniggered derisively. 'Somehow, I can't imagine you finding work in the local mill. Any day now, you'll sail away, then what?'

Ignoring the ungracious remark, Tina clasped Eddie's hand and calmly, without recrimination said, 'Isn't it time you stopped treating me like a silly, wee girl, Mum?'

'*What*!' Mrs Morris sat stiffly upright in the armchair. 'Alright, let's discuss this like rational *adults* and *I'll* be the one asking the questions, if you don't mind. Mr Fraser, why do you think I should give permission for you to wed my only daughter when you haven't even had a proper courtship?'

'Because I love her and she loves me.' The reply was short, but earnest.

The star-crossed pair stood side by side, stoically facing every objection. They refused to allow the brightness of their love to be made tarnished and tawdry by insinuations that they were motivated by some illicit desire rather than true affection. No! Their determination was not to be weakened.

What began as a birthday celebration had become a tour-de-force. Resistance was futile. Mrs Morris was forced to renege and so she gave her permission, but not her blessing. 'You take care of her or answer to me.' She pointed a warning finger at Eddie. 'My Tina's unworldly and I've spent my life protecting her.'

'And so will I,' Eddie answered with equal conviction.

It was done and for the rest of the afternoon they sat together—yet apart—because if Eddie edged across the sofa or made any physical contact with Tina, Mrs Morris glared malevolently. Finally, she said, 'I think you might be more comfortable in the armchair, Eddie,' which was as good a way as any of separating them. She was the rain on their parade, a shadow over their bright horizon, but Tina loved her mother and Eddie was willing to at least try to win her over.

The agonising silence was broken only by the sound of children playing outside. Outside, that's where Eddie wanted to be right this minute, away from the glare of those piercing eyes, but then he caught the reassurance in Tina's smile. Instead of making for the open door and freedom, as heart and mind urged him to do, Eddie conversed politely through gritted teeth.

'Will I meet the rest of your family, Tina?' The question—like the atmosphere—was stilted.

'Well you've already met Agnes so there's only her mum, my Auntie Lizzie, and that's all the family I have really—except for Joe.'

The drumming and tap-tap tapping of Mrs Morris's fingers on the highly waxed table was irritating in the extreme. She was making a statement and Eddie was well aware of it.

'I take it Joe is another piece of the jigsaw.'

Mrs Morris smirked irritably that the Australian knew so little about her daughter. The tapping finger gathered momentum.

Eddie ignored the rat-tap-tap and listened with the greatest interest as Tina related the saga of Agnes and Joe. They had been childhood sweethearts who would eventually marry, if they ever got around to naming the day. Because they were, and had always been an inseparable pair, everyone bet on a shotgun wedding. They had grown up together; she was the girl next door and he was her hero.

'Joe sounds like a great guy; I can't wait to meet him,' Eddie said.

There was an immediate rapport when Eddie and Joe met for the first time and shook hands. You could feel it in the warmth of their smiles and the easy way they talked when Tina made the introductions. Eddie and Joe were like best friends who hadn't seen each other in a long time, they even smiled the same contented smile just to be with Tina and Agnes and listen to their laughter.

'When do you two intend to marry?' Joe suddenly asked.

'Well it's like this, Joe, it's been a real battle with Tina's mother not taking too kindly to her little girl being betrothed, so I think it might be a good idea to let the dust settle first before I push my luck.'

'Will you take advice from someone a couple of years older and maybe a bit wiser than you?' Joe knew Agnes would support the advice he was about to offer. 'You two should make your own arrangements, *without* interference.'

'That's easier said than done, Joe. You forget I'm an interloper here. Mrs Morris is a nice lady, but where Tina's concerned,' Eddie made a whooshing sound through puckered lips, 'she does hold the reins a bit tight.'

'Don't think too badly of my mother, Eddie.' Tina looked hurt, and tears welled in eyes that were suddenly gloomy and sad. 'At the end of the day, she's still my Mum. If she is a pain in the backside sometimes, just stop and remind yourself that she brought me up all on her own and after all's said and done, she wants only the best for me.'

'I want the best for you too, so why can't she understand that I'm on her side? I have the means to shower you with everything you want. I'm not a pauper.'

'It's not about what you *can* give me, Eddie. It's about what you *can't* give. I know the way she thinks and she's worried that we'll be apart longer than we'll be together. In her eyes, ours wouldn't be a normal marriage, because you're already wed to the sea.'

'Then we have to make every day count. All last night, I went over and over in my head how we could make it work, so I have a proposition. I join my ship in May and return here in August… or would that be too soon for you to arrange a wedding?'

There was a sudden tightening of Joe's hand on his shoulder that Eddie was aware of. Maybe people from this part of the world didn't hold with spontaneity and this proposal was overstepping the mark, but Eddie had to say what was in his heart. He waited for a reaction.

For a moment, Tina was robbed of breath. It seemed like an eternity before she answered, 'Yes, yes,' and she threw herself into Eddie's arms. 'I would marry you tomorrow if I could, but an August wedding would be just dandy.' Tina's hand reached out for Agnes. 'No need to ask who my bridesmaid will be.'

This was the moment easy-going Joe pulled the rug from under Tina. 'I don't want Agnes to be your bridesmaid,' he said quite unexpectedly.

Tina's lip trembled and her eyes glistened with unshed tears. She was rightfully hurt and bewildered, for Joe had never given any inkling he felt this way. He was more or less forbidding Agnes from taking an active part in the most important day of Tina's life and it simply wasn't fair. On the face of it, this was the most callous behaviour from a man who Tina had always looked on as more of a brother. They were about to be even more astonished by Joe's motivation.

'The reason Agnes can't be your bridesmaid…'Joe grunted at the effort of getting down on one knee and without warning, he said, 'to hell with poverty, Agnes, why put off any longer the one thing we both want. Marry me and make it a double celebration in August.' For as long as he'd known her, Joe had never seen Agnes shocked into silence or speechless for such a length of time—until now. He winced painfully at the ache in his knee from the hard floor and Agnes still showed no sign of answering. 'Will you please say yes before I wear the knees out of my best trousers?' he begged.

Silence never reigned long, not with Agnes. She threw back her head, roared with laughter and then helped Joe to his feet. 'You're a right, daft buggar, Joseph O'Neill. Just when I'd given up hope you'd ever ask me, you go and do something like this. I suppose that means we're engaged—at last.'

'We've been engaged since we were in infant class, you dozy lass,' Joe answered smugly. 'We just never got 'round to making it official.'

Agnes ran a shaking hand over her now perspiring forehead. 'From now till August is only weeks away,' she mumbled, nervously biting her bottom lip. 'I don't want to start married life living with my mother, and I can't see Eddie taking kindly to living under the same roof as Auntie Maggie, but with so little time.'

All at once, Tina had an uncomfortable prickly sensation as the vision of married bliss suddenly became one of hell on earth. And then an idea took form amid her addled thoughts. 'On Monday, in the dinner break, why don't you and I jump on a tram into town and go see Coutts? There are two houses lying empty at number 26; we'll brazen it out and act like we're doing *him* a favour by renting them.'

Tina believed a problem was only a problem if there was no solution, and she was confident paying homage to the almighty Coutts was the answer.

Chapter Three

The weavers liked to clock in early. The short respite before turning on the looms gave them the chance to debate anything that grabbed the interest. This morning, Agnes had the piece-de-résistance and she was more than a bit eager to dramatically unfold events of the weekend in graphic detail. Unlike her shy cousin, Agnes enjoyed nothing more than standing in the limelight, revelling in having a captive audience that hung on her every word. Her pals on the neighbouring looms gathered like wasps around a honey pot, nudging and winking at the juicy details of how Agnes had snagged Joe.

The weavers were worldly-wise, their crude talk laden with suggestive overtones were enough to turn the air blue, but they were not wilfully malicious. The mill was no place for a Prima Donna and dishing out as good as you got was expected, which Agnes was quite adept at doing. Her best pal, Sadie, giggled wickedly when she openly hinted that Agnes hadn't saved herself for the wedding night.

'Where did he propose, Agnes?' Sadie asked with put-on innocence. 'Was it your bed or his?'

'Now, now, don't go judging everyone by yourself, Sadie Patterson,' Agnes pointed a stubby, calloused finger at Sadie. 'We don't all have the morals of an alley cat.' Agnes patted her hair and posed all prim and prudish then delivered her coup-de-grace. 'It's no secret that you *had* to make a rush for the altar because you were expecting.'

There was an impish grin beneath Sadie's expression of deep hurt. 'That's a downright lie. I'll have you know, my Colin was four months premature.'

'Oh, you don't say?' Agnes stood with hands on hips, a smile on her face and that familiar mischievous twinkle in her eye. 'Then he must be on record as the first ever, four months premature baby to weigh in at ten pounds.'

The buzzer signalling time to start cut into the sound of laughter and the amicable chatter about weddings and virginity was put on hold until dinner time.

Well, it had to with the clatter of the looms. But for once, Agnes was glad of the time to think her own thoughts without interruption. Imagining what it would be like to be referred to as, *Mrs O'Neill,* sent a strange shiver down her spine. She said the words aloud, 'Agnes O'Neill.' It was no longer a possibility but a certainty, and she loved her newly acquired status of an engaged to be married woman.

Tina hoped gossip hadn't reached the office before she had the chance to tell her closest friend, Maisie, but it would be a miracle if that happened, since Maisie was always ten minutes behind everyone and had been since primary school. They had started school on the same day; two lost little girls with the same characteristics, both gentle and caring. Like a magnet, they had been drawn to each other. This compassionate pair of little beings had sought to ease the others' distress at being cast into this strange place full of unruly children— the school playground.

Maisie had but one flaw (if it could be called a flaw) and that was her inability to see wrong in others. She constantly made excuses for everyone's indiscretions and had never been heard to say a bad word about anyone. Needless to say, she was well liked by all. Unfortunately, Maisie had one seriously irritating fault. She was never on time, which earned her the name, Late Maisie, but when it came to her bad time-keeping, Mr Meldrum, the office manager, turned a blind eye and a deaf ear. As far as he was concerned, any girl with such a sweet nature was entitled to one imperfection.

It was the locket Maisie saw first, resplendent against the austere grey of Tina's working dress. 'That's the most beautiful thing I've ever seen,' she gushed, gently drawing her finger across the engraving and then in true, unselfish Maisie-style, without a hint of envy, she added, 'Aw, Tina! I wish you good health to wear it.'

'It was a birthday present from Eddie. I'm going to put photographs of us on our wedding day inside.'

Maisie muttered, 'That's nice.' With her mind now back on the day's work, she opened her ledger. But then her mind began to puzzle over what Tina had said. 'You know, for a moment there, I thought you said you were going to put *your* wedding photographs…' And then it dawned. It hadn't been lack of interest, simply lack of understanding. 'That *was* what you said?'

'We're going to be married in August and what's more, it's going to be a double wedding. Joe finally popped the question to Agnes.'

As soon as twelve o'clock came, Tina and Agnes were racing to the offices of James Coutts & Son. Young James Coutts looked up in surprise to see them on a Monday, since they'd each paid their mother's rent on Saturday morning as they usually did. Still, this was an added bonus, another chance to openly flatter and flirt with the lovely Miss Morris. James Coutts's eager eyes were on Tina and transfixed, he asked, 'Can I help you with something?'

The leering stare repulsed Tina, but she forced herself to smile sweetly. 'There are two empty houses at 26 Charles Street that my cousin and myself are prepared to rent.' She had determined before even walking through the door that they must be demanding and not go pleading with cap in hand.

The way Tina looked straight at him flustered James, it was as if she could read his thoughts. Did she know he was picturing her body, milk-white and delicate in satins and silks? Beads of perspiration began to gather on his brow and he nervously ran a finger between his neck and the stiff, white collar.

'The houses you refer to, I am, shall we say, reserving for tenants who give the rent money to me, not the pub. I do hate having to evict.'

'And have either of our families ever given you cause to worry about the rent?'

'No, of course not,' Coutts said apologetically, 'but would it be presumptuous of me to ask why you would want to rent both these apartments?'

'Because my cousin, Agnes, and I are to be married this August, a double wedding,' Tina explained.

Without another word, Coutts took two sets of keys and laid them on the counter. 'One ground floor and one on the first landing,' he said. 'If they fit your needs, I'll draw up the letting agreement.'

'Thank you so much Mr Coutts, we are ever so grateful,' and almost haughtily, Tina picked up the keys and walked with Agnes, straight out the door without another word.

The lovely Miss Morris had been rather forceful, but it was the sweetness of her smile which would linger in his mind. James Coutts watched Tina walk away, she was almost regal and James had such a crush on her. Going to a ball with her on his arm would stir some envy. Unfortunately, he was expected to marry a lady of his own class. The Coutts were typically upper crust: they behaved and were treated like aristocracy in Dundee and like aristocrats, uniting wealthy families through marriage was considered obligatory. This was the reason James was courting Emily Brown, whose family owned the biggest and finest department store in town, but still, he salivated each time he saw Tina Morris.

It was impossible for Mrs Morris to participate in Tina's joy when she spoke about *her* house at number 26. She knew from personal experience how quickly happiness could be snatched away. Why couldn't Tina understand that a mother's protection of her daughter wasn't done out of malice? Tina was confusing the two and in so doing, failed to realise her mother was hurting.

'I only hope you know what you're doing because it's been done too hastily for my liking and without stating the obvious—I'm worried to death.' In a desperate effort to make Tina rethink, Mrs Morris cried out in panic, 'You know nothing of him or his background.'

Tina covered her ears and wailed at her mother's failure to accept. In total frustration, she cried out, 'Well, then I'll just have to learn.'

The misery on her daughter's face was more than Maggie Morris could bear. If she couldn't graciously accept the inevitable, then her pride and joy, her Tina would be alienated and lost to her.

'Very well, if you won't change your mind, at least I can help you financially.' Wearily, she faced Tina, the palms of her hands on the table for support. 'When your father was killed, I was paid a lot of money in compensation from the dock workers' fund along with a weekly wage. Blood money for the incompetence that caused his death and took him from me: but it did help me to give you a decent upbringing. Most of the money was put in a bank account for you, and now I think it's time you took charge of it yourself.'

'I can't take your money,' Tina gasped in a kind of outrage.

'It's not my money, it's yours.' Maggie Morris glowered doggedly. 'I can't see the sailor contributing much, so you'll need every penny since you're so determined to marry and set up your own home. Call it a dowry,' she huffed, throwing a bank book onto the table before turning away, embarrassed by the spontaneity of her tears, for Maggie Morris was of the opinion that only weak people cried. 'All I want, all I've ever wanted is for you to be happy. If you're prepared to commit yourself to Eddie in the knowledge that he'll be away oftener than he is here, I'll offer no objections. Frankly, I haven't the strength left.'

Like wings, Tina stretched out her arms and very softly said, 'look at me, Mum, can't you see I'm happier than I've ever been?'

'Just remember that twelve weeks may not sound all that long, but it's still three, long months no matter how it's said.'

After a few days, the first wave of speculation waned and there was only the occasional reference to the forthcoming double wedding. Was it lack of interest? Goodness no! Marriages and births were the two most favoured, *open* subjects that could be discussed freely. But there were always the taboo subjects which propriety declared must be discussed in whispers: infinitely more interesting things like drunken husbands, marital altercations and the favourite for serial gossips—infidelities. To be fair, the weavers did have occurrences in their own lives, which to them, were in context, every bit as important as a wedding— double or otherwise.

What Agnes loved most was describing in lavish detail how her house was being decorated like a little palace. She extolled Eddie's generous help because Joe could only pick up paint and brushes after a hard day's work.

How quickly can a house be made into a home? How much time is needed to make it habitable? The sea was calling him back and time-wise, Eddie was running on empty, but the home-making was almost at an end; this labour of love by two men for the two girls in their life.

As the days grew shorter, Joe got to thinking how much he would miss conversing with Eddie when he went back to sea. All the stories of places he could only imagine had been like riding on a magic carpet. Eddie had led such a full and colourful life for one so young, his tales fascinated Joe. The farthest he had ever travelled was on the ferry from Dundee to Tayport. As a boy, on his very first ride on the ferry, Joe remembered so well how, with childish imagination afire, he pictured himself with a telescope to one eye, calling out, 'Ahoy there,' in true sailor fashion. The mind's eye had visions of his trusty cutlass, gleaming in the sun as it cut and thrust, fighting off pirates as they tried to board. And then he had come over all queasy with sea-sickness.

'Do you ever get sea-sick?' Joe asked, remembering how his stomach had churned so much, his breakfast finished up in the Tay as he was held over the side, retching and roaring in the throes of that awful malady.

'I'm one of the lucky ones.' Eddie laughed at the question everyone seemed to ask.

'What's the worst place you've ever sailed?'

Eddie didn't hesitate. There was only one place where the contents of his stomach were at risk on his first encounter. 'Definitely the Cape, Cape Horn. There isn't a mariner who doesn't treat that place with respect. Oh yes, there's many a good ship gone down rounding the Horn.'

'It would scare the pants off me being in the middle of an ocean with nothing but water all 'round me and nowhere to go but down if anything happened.' Joe gave an involuntary shiver.

'You mean when the angel of death comes to call? She comes to us all in time, Joe. I've heard stories of how a man smiles and reaches for the angel's hand when his time's up.' Eddie was suddenly uncomfortable with a conversation that was getting too heavy, too morose. Death wasn't something you liked to think about. He had come close to an early demise with the pneumonia and didn't want or need to talk of such things. 'Actually,' he said, hastily changing the subject, 'what I fear most right now is the wrath of Agnes if your place isn't finished tonight—as promised. What about yourself, Joe? You must have met some odd characters in your time.'

'Och, the mill's full of them. Take hungry Harry for example. By the way, in Scotland, when a person's stingy, they get tagged with the name, hungry. Well, Harry is the salt of the earth and everyone likes him. Harry's always the first to offer a helping hand, but...' Joe went on to tell how Harry had earned the nickname because of his reluctance to reach into his pocket when it was his shout to get the drinks in. The many excuses he used were wearing thin, yet Harry still had a knack of infiltrating a company of men, and had become an expert at dodging his round after drinking all night at the expense of others. Harry was one of life's characters and his foible was a standing joke, yet while everyone admitted to a certain fondness for the man, no one wanted to be put in the same category. Telling someone they were just like Harry was an insult of the highest degree. By the time Joe had finished, they were both in fits of laughter and the final lick of paint had been applied.

'The light's going, mate, and so am I.' Eddie hurriedly took off the overalls he wore to paint. 'I put the finishing touches to our house this morning and I promised my girl that she could see it tonight. You look like your body's screaming out for rest, so I'll see you tomorrow. Get a good night's sleep, Joe, you've earned it.'

Tina smiled when she saw Eddie standing on the doorstep, then frowned as she reached up and cupped his face in her hands. 'You look overtired and it would kill me if you had a relapse,' she told him with deep concern.

'Ah, but it's not a sickly tiredness; it's a healthy tiredness and there's the difference. Now, would your majesty like to see her palace?' Eddie gave a mock bow and took the shawl that hung on a hook behind the door, wrapping it carefully around Tina's shoulders as protection from the cool night air before walking the short distance to their house.

The empty, freshly painted rooms seemed so grand, magnificent in the dimness of a gaslight. Lost for words, Tina could only make a gasping sound.

'It's up to you now, little one, to make the finishing touches.' This was Eddie's moment of glory, yet he was strangely solemn.

'Is something wrong?' she asked.

'Have you any idea how quickly time has passed? The last weeks have come and gone in a flash. *The Rose* is due any day now and we've had very little time on our own.' Eddie held her slight body in his arms. 'There's so much you need to know about me,' he said, 'but the important thing for now is to believe I will always do everything in my power to protect you and make you happy.'

'I know that, Eddie, and I promise to always be here waiting for you to come home to me.'

'I… I don't like talking about money. I've met too many people who make money their god.' The stumbling, awkward way he spoke was a stranger to her. 'But… but, how can I put this? The one thing you should know about me is that I'm not a poor man, not by any means. What I'm trying to say is… You'll always be well provided for.'

'I wouldn't care if you were a prince or a pauper, all I ask is that you come back to me and when your ship's due, I'll be there at the harbour, waiting.'

It was an innocent remark, but it sparked something in Eddie. He grabbed her shoulders in a vice-like grip and like an animal in pain yelled, 'No, no, Tina you must never go to the dock area. That's no place for a girl like you.'

'You're hurting me,' she looked terrified, 'I don't understand, Eddie, what have I said or done that was so wrong?'

He wrapped comforting arms around her shaking body, rocking gently to quell the fear. 'My sweet, innocent Tina, you just don't understand the ways of the world, do you? The area around the harbour is rough and the women who hang around there, well they earn a living by selling themselves to men. Now do you understand what I'm trying to tell you?'

'I think so,' she answered in a whisper.

Two days later, *The Rose* docked and when it sailed once more through the estuary to the ocean that lay beyond, Eddie was aboard, fully recovered and returned to his first love—the sea. He stood on the deck, looking back at the town that was to become his home, and wondered if his parents had received the self-explanatory letter. He grinned at the mental picture of them arguing over who was first to read the letter. Dad wouldn't win, he never did, but there was never any real contest anyway. The battle was lost before it had begun. It was inevitable. Mum always emerged the victor. Eddie closed his eyes and pictured the scene. For a brief time, it was as if he was a ghostly spectator, watching the letter written by his own hand reach its destination.

Chapter Four

'Was that the postman, Bill?' Helen Fraser hurried from the kitchen to the hall, rubbing flour covered hands on her apron. 'Any word from Eddie yet?' Her eyes shone with eager anticipation that her son's letter would be there and then for a brief moment, those few hurried words would unite mother and son.

'You ask me that same question every time the mail is delivered.' Bill shuffled through the mail then stopped abruptly, his eyebrows raised at the sight of the blue envelope with the familiar handwriting. 'Well I never… you'd better come here, old girl, your prayers have been answered. There is a letter from Ed.'

Caught between doubt and belief, Helen gave an agitated, little giggle and called back, 'If you're having me on, Bill Fraser, there'll be no freshly baked pies for tea tonight.'

'I'm not. Look,' he held up the pale blue envelope. 'Will I open it or would you like to do the honours?'

'Stop playing silly beggars and give it here.' Tiny in comparison to her husband, Helen stood on tiptoe to retrieve the envelope. Her face beamed like a child who had been handed the biggest lollipop as she glanced at the envelope and her eyes blinked rapidly in surprise. 'It's postmarked Scotland.'

'What the hell is he doing in a God forsaken place like Scotland?'

'If you give me a minute, I'll be able to tell you.' Her eyes quickly scanned the first sheet of paper. 'He's in a town called Dundee.'

'Never heard of it,' Bill said irritably, 'what else does he say?'

'Oh Bill,' she clasped a hand over her mouth to stifle a sob, 'our boy's been real sick, he was in hospital with pneumonia.'

Anxiety replaced irascibility and in a voice now quivering, Bill asked, 'is he alright?'

'Yes, yes, he's going to make a full recovery.' Her eyes darted across the paper. 'Well I never.'

'You're the most annoying Sheila I've ever known! Let me read the damned letter myself.'

'Stop swearing and give me a moment! I've waited a long time for this letter.' There was a hint of a smile, then she slapped her thigh and burst into laughter. 'Would you believe it? Our son's fallen for a Scot's girl.'

'Well, he can't have known her long enough to be all that serious about her.'

'Oh yes, I recognise serious when I see it, and I can read between the lines. Our Eddie's in love alright and she seems like a real nice girl. Well, she'd have to be, our boy wouldn't fall for just anybody.'

'As long as she isn't a gold digger, because you know how open-handed Eddie can be. He never did take money seriously.' Bill was suddenly struck by a not-too-irrational thought. 'You don't think he told her he has a small fortune in the bank? He hasn't touched a penny of his grandmother's money, but *she* might want to.'

'Don't let your imagination run riot just because he's at the other side of the world.' Suddenly, Helen crumpled the letter in her hand and began to cry, something she didn't do easily or openly.

'What is it, old girl?' Bill put a muscled, brown arm around her shoulder. 'What's wrong? It's not like you to shed tears.'

'I've just had an awful thought! We won't be there to see our only boy, our son, get hitched.'

'Well, you were the one who allowed him to be a free spirit. While other women would have tried to tie their only child to the apron strings, you let Eddie follow his dreams, and that was a brave thing to do: stupid maybe, but unselfish.' Bill took a handkerchief from his pocket and gently, almost reverently wiped the tears from her face. 'Now I'll tell you what we'll do, I'll bring the buggy 'round while you get one of those freshly baked pies, and we'll drive over to Dolly and Bruce to fill them in on our news. How does that sound?'

'You can be a cantankerous, old goat, Bill Fraser, but what would I do without you?' Helen reached for the brawn of her husband's arm to help her out of the chair.

'That's my girl, down but never out. I'll meet you out front in five minutes.'

The horse's hooves stirred up the dust as, obedient to the reins, it trotted along the path to Bruce and Dolly's house. Helen silently sat with the covered basket on her lap, mulling over the contents of the letter with conflicting emotions of sadness that she had lost her only son to another woman, and joy that he had found contentment and love. She had never believed that giving birth to a child gave any woman the right to dictate how that child should live his or her life. So why at this moment did she have an overpowering urge to order Eddie to come home?

Dolly stood in the front yard with arms folded over her ample bust. 'I saw the dust cloud from a mile back and had the feeling it was you.' She took the basket from Helen while Bill helped her from the buggy. 'I'll give Bruce a shout, and we'll all go inside and enjoy a nice cold beer.'

'This is an unexpected pleasure, but a pleasure nevertheless,' Bruce called to them from the back door where he was removing muddy boots. 'And I can tell from that delicate aroma, Helen's brought one of her famous pies.' They were two of a kind, Bruce and Dolly, likeable, good natured people. They were also Eddie's godparents. 'Now correct me if I'm wrong, but I don't think you dropped by just to bring us a pie. From that look on Helen's face, I get the feeling you're in some sort of strife.' Bruce looked from one to the other waiting for an explanation.

Gruffly serious, Bill answered. 'There's no pulling the wool over your eyes. There are times I believe, you know us better than we know ourselves.'

'I thought there was something when you turned up out of the blue like that.' Dolly patted Helen's hand and smiled reassuringly. 'Whatever it is, if it's some sort of trouble, you know we're here for you.'

'You've got the wrong end of the stick, Doll: we're not in any trouble.' Helen sighed and held out the letter. 'This came from Eddie today,'

Dolly was more confused than ever. 'So, is Eddie in trouble?' she asked.

'No, no, he's fine now, but he did have pneumonia and while he was in hospital, he met a little Scot's girl called Tina Morris,' Helen explained through trembling lips. 'Anyway, the crux of the story is, he intends to marry her.'

'We don't know that for sure! As usual, you're adding two and two and coming up with five.' Bill gently but firmly rebuked her. 'He's a sensible boy, so give him some credit.'

'I'm his mother, of course I know, and if you'd taken the trouble to read the letter properly, you'd see he obviously adores her.'

'Could I read it?' Dolly asked.

Without uttering another word, Helen handed over the crumpled blue envelope then waited silently while Dolly read and fully digested every word.

Dolly rested the letter on her lap. 'No doubt about it, he's hooked alright, but doesn't she sound the sweetest thing?'

'She has a dicky ticker,' Helen said disdainfully.

'Oh c'mon, Helen it's not like you to play the over possessive mother.' This whole scenario was beginning to remind Bruce of a time his family disapproved of his beloved Dolly and look how wrong they were. 'The way you're going on, anyone would think she was the devil's daughter,' he said contemptuously.

'I hate to say it,' Dolly's head shook slowly, meaningfully, 'but Bruce is right. You haven't even met the girl and I know for a fact, you'd be fighting mad if this Tina's parents put Eddie down for no reason.' Dolly was only being truthful. What she was basically telling Helen was, don't judge lest you be judged.

It was all too much for her, the floodgates opened and Helen wept bitterly. This resilient little woman had an Achilles heel—her only son. 'I'm sorry,' she said, 'I have this ache in my heart, a kind of premonition that I might never see my boy again. Why didn't I forbid him to go walk-about? I should have made him go to college like your Ralph instead of traipsing 'round the globe and now it's too late.' She blew her nose and wiped her eyes. 'Look at me, spoiling a lovely visit.' She sort of half-laughed then the natural humour returned. 'Get the shackles off the beer, Doll. A person could die of thirst here.'

Bill jumped to his feet. 'Beer,' he snorted as if Helen had just requested some awful beverage, 'forget the beer, I have a bottle of malt Scotch I've been keeping for a special occasion and it doesn't get any more special than this.' Bruce reached into a cupboard, and brought out a bottle and four, crystal glasses then poured the amber nectar into the glasses and passed them around.

'I'd like to propose a toast,' Bill stood and raised his glass. 'To our wandering son—wherever he is—and his bride to be. May they be blessed and happy as my Helen and I have been.'

'I would like to add to that.' Bruce raised his glass. 'To friendship, where would we be without friends like you?'

'I know where I would be.' They waited for Dolly to toast whatever she thought warranted a toast, but they were greeted with silence.

'Go on, Dolly. Finish what you started,' Bill urged, 'where would you be?'

'Why, I'd be in the kitchen making my own bloody pies.' Then she laughed such an infectious laugh, it was impossible to stay sad.

'Oh, you don't half do my heart good, Dolly.' This time the tears Helen wiped, were tears of laughter. 'You've made me realise I've only been thinking of myself. Tomorrow, I'll write to Eddie and tell him how happy we all are that he met someone as nice as Tina.' There was a momentary pang of conscience, but surely God would allow her this one little lie.

Chapter Five

The day Eddie left, time took on a different meaning for Tina. There was no longer that hustle and bustle of not enough hours in the day. Now, each day was an endless drag from morning till night, and one week seemed like an eternity, endless. It was something akin to her childhood days, awaiting Christmas. The way the hours stretched and the hands of the clock seemed to turn more slowly. And yet, when Eddie was here, there was so much to fill their time, they gave no thought to the next day or the days to come. The hours passed neither slowly nor rushed, they were simply cherished moments. Now, it was as if she were trapped inside a void that was surreal and without essence: almost as if she was yet to be born. How strange, she thought, that this may be how an unborn child felt while awaiting its birth.

This was the reality, and once she accepted that her life would be this way from now on, surely she would find the stamina to go forward and bear the life she had chosen with dignity, not despair. She must accustom herself to playing a waiting game while Eddie was at sea, for this was the existence he chose, the life he loved long before they met, and now that this love was divided, it would be a cruel and unreasonable thing to make demands. She had happily accepted his proposal of marriage with full understanding of the pitfalls, and now there must be no doubts or indecisions. It was all or nothing and she would rather share the briefest of intervals with Eddie than lose him forever.

In comparison to the ennui Tina suffered, Agnes and Joe were full of high spirits, preparing the home they were to share. They spent every spare moment together, which in itself was not unusual, so why for the first time in her life was Tina envious of her cousin? It wasn't so much a searing jealousy, just an odd feeling of resentment that they were preoccupied in their adoration for each other, happy to steal a kiss or share a secret smile. She could only hold Eddie in her heart and thoughts, but not in her arms.

Every evening, Tina went to the unfurnished house just to stand in the empty shell, trying to feel Eddie's presence around her. If she closed her eyes she could still sense him close by, hear his voice echo through the house, feel his touch, but just as the smell of paint had evaporated, so too had these sensations. It was sort of uncanny to know that soon, she would be coming here to this, her own home, instead of the house she had grown up in and shared with her mother for eighteen years. But these four walls wouldn't be just a house; they would be a haven, a retreat where she and Eddie could hide from the outside world and spend what little time they had together in each other's arms. They were to be wed, and what went on behind closed doors would carry no shame or sin. This concept was all that salved her aching loneliness.

Mrs Morris remained uncommunicative, making no reference to Eddie, the wedding or the house until finally, frustrated by this unreasonable stubbornness, Tina decided that no matter how bitter the taste of reality, it was time her mother faced up to the changes that were about to be made.

'Wouldn't you like to see the house, Mum?' It was more than an invitation, it was an entreaty, but she was greeted with silent indifference. The deliberate snub only made Tina more determined to end this farce. 'I really want your help and advice, and I honestly would like you to share decisions with me.' There was still no reaction and in a moment of utter vexation, Tina wailed, '*Please,* will you help me, Mum?'

A spark returned to the bright, blue eyes that for weeks had been lacklustre and at last, Maggie Morris smiled. 'Well, what can a body say when you put it like that? Now, if you'd had the gumption to say something earlier, I could have been making myself useful: but you know me, never one to push myself where I'm not wanted.' She swung a shawl around her shoulders, meticulously folding it across her chest and all the while, impatiently clicking her tongue. 'We'll go now and see what needs done. Bring the measuring tape and I'll get started making curtains tomorrow.'

Like a charging bull responding to a red rag, there was no stopping her. This was a mission of great importance, her daughter required help. These past weeks of friction could so easily have been avoided if Tina had used common sense and understood that all her mother wanted was to feel needed.

It was the short walk to number 26 that finally brought home to Maggie that her daughter wasn't lost to her. Perhaps it was an idea that had taken root somewhere in the back of her mind and spread like a weed. The idea that Eddie

46

would one day whisk her only child off to the other side of the world was so darkly frightening; she had allowed all the fears, doubts and jealousy to mar Tina's happiness. It was now time to make amends.

As yet, the house was a vacuous structure, but soon it would be filled with light, warmth and love. Tina watched, anxious and uncertain now, about bringing her mother here to criticise, but Maggie sniffed the air and pronounced, 'Smells clean.'

Tina made no effort to disguise her deep pride. 'Eddie scrubbed every inch with bleach and carbolic soap before he painted.'

'I can tell! He most likely picked up how to clean thoroughly from his mother,' Maggie said with open admiration. 'It's pretty.'

Praise at last, the ultimate acceptance. Tina wondered why she hadn't thought of this before now. All the tension could have been avoided if, instead of excluding her mother, she had offered the simple courtesy of an invitation.

When they left the house, there was no longer a strained silence; in fact, there was a significant change in Maggie's demeanour. She even hummed to herself as she filled the kettle. 'I'll give you one good piece of advice,' she looked her daughter straight in the eye. It may have been the soft glow of the firelight or it may have been wishful thinking, but there was a definite softness about Maggie Morris, as if a happy memory had surfaced to obliterate her natural severity. Her voice even became—melodic.

'I welcome any advice you give, Mum,' Tina said, diligently.

'Always remember, when you're furnishing the house, be as conservative as you like with the living room,' Maggie said, and her lined face was all at once almost youthful. 'But make the bedroom a special place that's sacred to you and your husband,' she said with a twist of nostalgia.

A statement so openly referring to marital relations from a woman who gave the appearance of being positively virginal was perturbing. It was strangely unsettling to think, that at some time in her life, she must have had these same feelings Tina experienced when she simply thought about Eddie. Feelings she could never ever talk about. Tina lowered her head to hide the fluster. This was so embarrassing, almost as if her privacy had been invaded, so she hurriedly changed the subject. 'There's something I want to do. Only, you may not like it.'

'I'm listening,' Maggie said warily.

'I want to give Agnes some of the money.'

Tina hesitated, expecting to hear some sort of opposition, but instead, this frugal woman who had always believed that charity began at home and giving too freely was more foolhardy than admirable, reached for Tina's shaking hand, smiled and slowly nodded her head.

'Of course, I wouldn't give Agnes the money if it made you angry for me to do this…'

'You're doing exactly what I expected, so why should I be angry?' Maggie cooed softly. 'Don't you know I'm proud of your giving nature?'

The breath Tina had been holding came out in a long, thankful sigh.

Maggie suddenly sat straight and rigid, her hands clasped in her lap, the way she did when something needed to be said. 'You'll no doubt be going into town on Saturday as usual, so I'll say this and get it off my chest. Stop flirting with James Coutts when you pay the rent. You know perfectly well he's marrying Barton Brown's daughter next month, and old Barton won't take kindly to his intended son-in-law making eyes at another girl.'

'That's… that's,' Tina stammered in disbelief at what she was hearing.

'Don't try to deny it either. Agnes said you wrapped him around your little finger and inveigled him into renting you those houses.' Maggie's censuring was harsh.

The verbal attack, for that's what it felt like, staggered Tina. The allegation was without substance and it was without provocation. No more than a moment ago, her mother had been so understanding and compassionate, and now here she was pitilessly accusing.

'I… didn't… I wouldn't,' Tina wailed defensively. 'Agnes jokes about Coutts having a crush on me but that's all it is, a silly joke, and you should know me better than to believe I would flirt with the likes of James Coutts.' The cry in her voice was real. 'I love Eddie and never want to be with anyone but him.'

It was time to eat humble pie, for at this moment, Maggie was shamefaced. *She* was responsible for all this distress and the ruination of what until a few minutes ago, was a happy turning point in her lonely life.

'Then will you listen and give me the chance to explain?' Maggie's head drooped to hide her shame at making a wrongful assumption.

'I'll listen.'

'Oh, I'm sorry for ever doubting you, Tina, but it's been burning in me ever since that day you came back from Coutts with those keys. It was the thought of that… that,' she squirmed with disgust. 'I never could stand young James. Oh, I always knew he had a fancy for you and I had this fear, a sort of premonition that one day, he'd turn your head. It was the idea of him ever laying a finger on you. Will you forgive and forget the ravings of a silly, old woman who let her imagination run wild?'

How one person perceives a situation can have dramatic and often drastic effects if these perceptions are discussed offhand, as Agnes had obviously done. So many ugly rumours begin, not with malicious talk, but with idle gossip, or in this case a silly, thoughtless joke.

It was dinner time on Friday when Tina walked tentatively into the bank. She felt very ill at ease. For all she knew, the teller might question the validity of her claim to so much money. With this in mind, she carried her birth certificate and the new rent book in the hope it was sufficient proof that the bank book was hers.

'I wish to withdraw the sum of £100 please.' Shyly, Tina pushed the book through the metal grill.

The look of utter shock on the teller's face when he looked up to see one so young requesting the withdrawal of such a large sum of money brought a nervous smile to her face and Tina shifted uneasily.

There seemed to be some confusion when the clerk opened the book. There was only one single deposit and nothing more, only blank pages. 'This is an old account opened almost seventeen years ago.' He seemed so taken aback, the teller only muttered his confusion. 'Could you give me a few moments please?' then without further ado, he put the pencil behind his ear, picked up the book and hurried away.

'Excuse me,' Tina called through the grill, 'is there a problem?'

He smiled reassuringly. 'It's not a problem as such, Miss Morris, but like I said, the original deposit was made years ago and a large amount of interest would have accrued in that time. It may take me some time to bring the account up to date, but you can leave the book to be made up, unless of course, you prefer to wait.'

Interest, now that was something she hadn't considered. Tina began to tremble as a host of what ifs, coursed through her brain, and then, in a voice she hardly recognised, Tina told the clerk, 'I don't mind waiting.' As an afterthought, she added, 'but this is only my dinner break and I do need the money today.'

The flurry of activity on the other side of the counter was hypnotic. Ledgers were opened and closed, the scraping of pen on parchment, the hum of voices as they checked and double checked the figures and then finally, Tina was invited back to the counter where the book was passed to her through the dividing grill.

'I'm sorry to have kept you waiting, Miss Morris,' the teller said apologetically, 'but seventeen years—what can I say? The original investment has nearly doubled.'

Tina looked at what was no longer a single entry, but pages of entries so neatly written in bold, black ink. She stifled a gasp and swayed slightly. 'On second thoughts,' she said with a tremble in her voice, 'could I make the withdrawal £150?'

The teller made a choking sound, but retained a business-like posture. 'With such a large sum of money on your person, it might be advisable to have someone accompany you to your home.'

'I have a friend waiting,' Tina lied.

He began counting out the crisp, white notes that were Tina's legacy from the father she could barely remember. For Agnes, this would be a gift of deliverance from debt, but the extraordinary sense of wellbeing was Tina's reward for *her* benevolence.

This was a day of days, but there was still one more hurdle. Agnes may be scatty, but like Joe, she was proud and it would be demeaning for them to think they were on the receiving end of charity. With this in mind, Tina put the money in a large, brown envelope and sealed it with sealing wax before tying it up with a blue ribbon. She wrote on the front: *To Agnes and Joe, a wedding present from Tina and Eddie.* This way, they couldn't refuse a gift that had been given with love and gratitude for the devotion they had bestowed on her. As far as Tina was concerned, this money was nothing in comparison to the affection she had received from these two wonderful people.

It was so tiresome having to wait for the working day to end before she could see that round, smiling face light up. In fact, it would be a wonder if Tina's patience held out till then. She undoubtedly worshipped her cousin, but more than this, Tina admired the strength of character that never allowed adversity to crush her love of life. How wonderful it was to have the means in her grasp to reward her mentor, the heroine, who for years had wrapped her in an invisible, protective cloak. It was impossible to take her eyes and her mind off the clock.

Agnes took pride in her status as a weaver standing alongside friends, the air filled with the smell of raw jute and the click-clack of a hundred looms. There was no denying it was hard work, but was there any other place on earth where people could sing loudly at the pitch of their voices and without restraint chorus to the joy of simply being alive? It was acceptable for the less talented and the tone-deaf to give vent to song without being threatened with the madhouse. What's more, this was Friday and there was always more singing on Fridays. Perhaps a full wage packet in the apron pocket had a lot to do with it.

At last, there was the blessed sound of silence as looms were switched off, and in a rush to make their way homeward, the teaming hoards of careworn, hardworking dreamers poured through the mill gates like birds freed from a coop. It was the best day of the week—pay day.

Now, whether or not mill workers' hard earned cash was spent in the local bars, depended on the individual. There were those who worked hard and played hard, preferring to stay in a drunken stupor for the entire weekend. Then there were the others, who preferred to use their sweat and tears earnings perfecting their living conditions; it was simply a matter of choice.

Chapter Six

Mill workers weren't all that well-paid, at least not well enough to save much for clothes and household goods. The normal practice was to shop at the Co-op and put the cost 'on the back of the book.' The debt was reduced by paying a little each week, and there was a certain prestige in telling the assistant to, 'Take two shillings off the back of the book.'

Agnes assumed she would enter into just such an agreement with the Co-op if they were to buy essentials for the new home. Table and chairs, settee, a bed of course, and Joe accepted there would be hardship while the debt was being paid.

There was nothing out of the ordinary about Tina asking Agnes to come down to number 22 after tea. Excitedly making wedding plans had become their favourite pastime: heads together, pencils and notepads at the ready. Agnes could never even imagine in her wildest dreams the windfall which was about to fall into her lap.

The brown envelope with the neatly printed message puzzled Agnes. Slowly, she broke the seal and then opened the flap to reveal the contents. 'Lord Almighty, I've never seen so many real five-pound notes!' Shaking hands fingered the notes. 'Are… are they real?' Agnes asked, her eyes daring to believe what she was seeing.

'Read the message! These is your wedding present and believe me, every note is genuine.' Tina's soft, velvet eyes watched intently. Agnes never had much money to spare; most of what she earned went to her mother, but she was proud to pay her way. How would she react to such an ostentatious gift? 'I came into a big inheritance,' Tina explained. 'There's £60. It should be enough to help you and Joe buy furniture without going into debt.'

'But… but,' Agnes sniffled.

'It's settled,' Tina said decisively. 'Tomorrow, we pay the rent then go shopping.'

It was the shock of seeing all that money, touching it and thinking, 'I'll never be poor again.' Every nerve in Agnes's body was seized in a kind of spasm, as if her flesh were being spiked by the stings of a hundred bees. And then, all of a sudden, the full understanding of what this precious gift meant to her and Joe was like being softly caressed. She couldn't find the words to express her gratitude other than to keep repeating, 'Thank you, thank you, thank you.'

The summer sun shone bright on this beautiful Saturday morning. This wasn't a day for merely window shopping; this day, Agnes would cast aside silent longing and look with pride at labels bearing that wonderful word *sold* alongside her name. This was a day for the fulfilling of dreams and aspirations thanks to a generous and loving heart. She and Joe might not be in debt to the Co-op, but they would forever be indebted to Tina and Eddie.

'My goodness, is it that time already?' Tina pointed to the big, round clock that hung in the furniture department of the Co-op.

Agnes laughed in such a frivolously excited way, heads turn to stare. 'Do you realise we've spent half the day in here?' And then, wide-eyed, she gasped, 'The Co-op's going to need at least three cartloads to deliver all this and sure as hell, there's going to be heads out every window for an eyeful.'

For some reason, Tina didn't lapse into the giggles, in fact, she was almost apologetic. 'I do have one more thing to get, but not here.'

'Like what and where, for instance?'

'A wise, old lady told me to buy something special for the bedroom, something so extravagant it would make my eyes water. I'm going to buy the finest quilt B. L. Browns have in their store.'

That was when Agnes fell short on frivolity, but she followed Tina to the exit without complaint or question.

For quality and choice, there was no other department store like Brown's. The soft furnishings were exquisite, but so too was the price. Barton Brown began trading as a boy with only a handcart and a head for business. It was through sheer hard work and a burning ambition to drag his self out of poverty, that the boy, who didn't even own a decent pair of shoes, was now one of the wealthiest men in town. This store was his flagship, frequented by affluent ladies who spent freely so that they could be seen carrying packages with the distinctive logo that was itself a status symbol.

'Does it have to be Brown's?' Agnes couldn't hide her dismay a moment longer. 'It's only well-off and well-heeled folk that shop there. I always feel out of place, Tina,' she wailed. 'Even the assistants' working clothes are better than my best, *and* they look down their noses at folk like me.'

Tina didn't brindle or snap angrily, she just silently kept striding towards the big department store. It was the purpose and determination in her step that made Agnes think it might be better to bite her tongue and say no more.

The display was awesome! Luxurious quilts and bedcovers in floral and pastels were displayed on pedestals all around the department, but Tina had already seen what she wanted. She was captivated by a satin quilt with matching spread. It was the colour of mulled wine, richly red. Her hand reached out and touched the soft, silky material, and Tina could just imagine it on the new, brass bed; silky folds of the luxurious cover draping to the floor and the sumptuous quilt in all its splendour lying regally atop. This was definitely the one. She visualised the room and Eddie's face when he saw it. Like her mother said, this was one room that had to be special; for they would spend their wedding night beneath this luxurious mantle.

'That one's fit for a queen. It wouldn't surprise me if there was one just like it in Buckingham Palace.' Agnes put her arm around Tina's shoulder and whispered, 'I think you've made your mind up.'

'Oh yes, Agnes, this is what I want. I'm not even going to look at the price ticket in case I change my mind and run for the door.' Tina beckoned to the assistant. 'Miss, could you please have this wrapped and delivered?'

The young woman glided towards them and ran a soft, white hand with polished fingernails over the quilt. It occurred to Tina that these hands had probably never been in dishwater. 'You've chosen *Fantasy*,' she said in an ever so cultured voice. 'This is new to our collection and quite, quite beautiful. Shall I charge it to your account?'

'I prefer to pay cash,' Tina answered in her most superior tone.

There was something exhilarating about buying an outrageously expensive item without counting the cost, but the best part of all was the way that girl, who obviously didn't come from working-class stock, took it for granted that Tina was not unaccustomed to making purchases like this. Right at that moment, Tina felt seven feet tall and she was overcome by the oddest, tingling sensation.

Did well-off people feel like this when they bought preposterously expensive items, like her quilt for example, without considering the cost? Did rich ladies of leisure simply dip into their little, beaded purses to pay for whatever took their fancy, or was that too plebeian? Did they merely charge the goods then wait for the final reminder before paying up?

This must have been the moment a flight of fancy became a real aspiration. Right there and then, surrounded by this display of affluence, Tina had a conscious resolve to one day, join the ranks of the well-off. Not those high and mighty buffoons with more money than sense, or the so called, *ladies* who charged what they couldn't afford even when times were hard. Her mother referred to them as the fur-coat, no-bloomers brigade. Spending on the frivolous with giddy disregard for cost wasn't for Tina, oh no, she had acquired a taste for money *in* the bank.

She didn't know it at the time, but this was the day her fate was sealed, and if only Tina could have glimpsed into the future to see the evil money attracted, then perhaps being wealthy would not have been such a tantalising ambition. One day, a hard lesson would be learned that there was more decency in those underprivileged, needy but honest, hardworking people who were her friends and neighbours.

Outside, the fine drizzle that had started when they went in had become a torrent. They huddled under a single umbrella and dashed along the rain-soaked pavements to reach Charles Street.

'You get out of those wet clothes and have a cup of tea,' Agnes ordered. 'I'll see you tomorrow.' Her feet seemed to only lightly touch the pavement as Agnes danced up the deserted street, leaving Tina in awe of her vitality while she felt fit to drop.

Saturated shoes and stockings were first to be removed. The sopping hem of her pale blue dress was cold against her bare ankles. Puddles had done their worst in the rush to get home. Tina stood by the fire and pulled the dress over her head, then she took the flannel nightdress that was warming over the brass fireguard and slipped into it. The warm flannel felt comforting against her shivering body. Wearily, she got into bed and for the first time that day, relaxed with a glass of warm milk.

The wedding dress her mother wore on her wedding day, hung on the front of the wardrobe. It had been lovingly and carefully preserved, and looked as new as the day it was bought. Tina marvelled at the delicate and exquisite bead work. This dress, the one she too would wear on her wedding day, was the last thing Tina saw before drifting into a dreamless sleep. She was another day closer to Eddie's homecoming.

Chapter Seven

On the fourth of August, Tina answered a rapid knock knocking on the door and Eddie swept her into his arms. 'I've come home to you, little one,' he whispered.

The waiting was over. Tina closed her eyes and clung to Eddie. 'I gave up believing this day would ever come and now you're here, I can't, I just can't believe it.' When she dared open her eyes again to make sure this wasn't a dream, Tina saw that Eddie wasn't alone.

Following her gaze, Eddie announced, 'Tina, I would like you to meet Henry Jack, my skipper, best friend and best man.'

Henry took the small, delicate hand offered to him in greeting and held it gently. 'You're exactly as Eddie described.' He bent down, smiled and looked deeply into her eyes. 'I feel I know you already—well—when you consider he's spoken of no other for the past three months.'

'When we first met, Eddie spoke constantly of you, but you're nothing like I had imagined.' Once she'd said it, Tina worried slightly that Henry might misinterpret the remark. 'I mean that in the nicest possible way,' she rushed to add.

Henry Jack smiled, even though he was standing in the somewhat uncomfortable position of trying to fit into the doorway with knees bent and shoulders stooped.

When Eddie said he looked up to his skipper, she took it he meant metaphorically and not physically. Eddie was tall, but Henry was a giant in comparison. 'Where are my manners?' Tina said, trying to appear a little less infantile. 'Come in and I'll make us some tea.' It occurred to Tina that if they were sitting down, then at least she wouldn't have to crick her neck to talk to Henry.

At first, the conversation was stilted, polite but formal. Tina was loathe to discuss wedding arrangements in front of a man who was a total stranger to herself and then, bit by bit, Henry's natural charm had her laughing at his seafaring stories and Tina felt an affinity with this man whose face was etched with a thousand adventures. Looking at Eddie, any fool could see it in his face; the hero worship for this larger-than-life man who had protected and cared for him.

As if reading her thoughts, Henry said, 'He's the son I never had, you know, that's why I'm happy to give a special wedding present to both of you; a fifteen-day honeymoon, no less.' And then, as Eddie's brow furrowed questioningly, he explained, '*The Rose* is going into dry dock. This is as good a time as any for the old lady to have her barnacles removed.'

'You didn't say anything to me, skipper.'

'Didn't want to spoil the surprise; even warned the men, not a word was to pass anyone's lips unless the guilty party wanted to find another ship. Besides,' he said gruffly, 'I wanted to tell both of you together, nothing wrong with that, is there?'

All at once, Tina felt such a rush of affection for this man who, until now, had been no more than a shadowy figure in the background. She kissed the weather-beaten brow and said, 'If no one ever told you before, Henry, I want you to know that you are the nicest, kindest friend anyone could hope for.'

'It surely is the best present anyone could have given us,' Eddie said with the broadest smile.

On the sixth of August, 1907, the little chapel, where Tina and Agnes regularly attended Mass, was filled to capacity as both brides walked down the aisle. Any misgivings Maggie Morris felt, vanished when she saw her daughter's beautiful face, normally so pale, now glowing with happiness. Reluctantly, Maggie admitted to herself that it was Eddie she had to thank for being this architect of her daughter's recovery and wellbeing.

Vows were exchanged before family and friends, and then Mr and Mrs Fraser, and Mr and Mrs O'Neill received congratulations in the church hall before celebrations proper got under way.

The hall quickly filled with guests, men in best suits and ladies, pristine in their prettiest dresses, all eager to let their hair down and enjoy the kind of reception hardworking mill employees appreciated. It was a night of singing, dancing and drinking, and this was one party that would not be forgotten in a long time. No expense had been spared to make it memorable, so much so in fact, that there was a distinct reluctance to leave when time came to clear the hall.

Tired but happy, the newlyweds made their way to Charles Street and the homes that had been so proudly and lovingly prepared. As they neared number 26, Tina suppressed a shiver.

'Are you cold?' Agnes asked.

'No… not at all… I'm just; well it's been a long day.' After all the weeks longing for Eddie to return, how could she admit to being shy at the thought of being alone with him on this special night?

'I know what it is,' Agnes whispered, 'wedding night nerves, and you're not the only one. I just hide mine better than you.'

Now there was a thing you didn't hear every day, Agnes admitting to being nervous. Oddly enough, it was this confession that had a calming effect on Tina. Fears that something would go wrong on the day had made her tense, but now, that tension was giving way to fatigue.

Eddie opened the door and effortlessly lifted Tina into his arms to carry her into the sitting room where he gently sat her on the sofa while he lit the oil lamp. 'Happy?' he asked.

'Nervous,' she answered. 'You know how I was supposed to be back to work in four days, Eddie?'

'Don't worry, little one, we'll just have to make the best of what we've got.'

'But four days doesn't give us much time together, so I've taken two weeks' unpaid leave of absence. There are so many things I need to tell you about myself and so many things I need to know about you.'

'We'll make each day an adventure,' Eddie said enthusiastically. 'Just finding out how much sugar you take in your tea will be an exciting fact. We'll gather memories for when we're parted and I'm going to make sure all your memories are happy.'

'What if you suddenly get homesick for Australia?' This was the one worry that had agonised Tina, but now she found the courage to broach the question.

It was the fear in her voice that perturbed Eddie. Did she really believe that one day he would tire of her and simply walk away? 'This is my home now, and as long as you're waiting for me, it's the only home I'll ever want to come back to,' he assured her. 'You must never doubt that I love you, little one.'

Apprehension came and went like a phantom. Tina smiled contentedly and snuggled closer. 'I know so little about you; what food you like, what your life was like before we met. I want to learn about the home of your birth and I don't feel the least bit tired now, so tell me about Australia.'

'Well, if you're sure.' Eddie watched Tina nod enthusiastically: only then did he begin to relate a chapter in his life she knew nothing about. 'Australia's beautiful, Tina, vast, but it isn't all deserts like some people imagine. There are so many green and lush places, and lots of sheep farms. In fact, meat and wool are two of our major exports,' he said proudly. 'But the outback, that's something else. To describe it, you'd have to think about the most deserted place imaginable, then picture it a thousand times bigger. In the outback, a man can walk all day without meeting another living soul.'

'Did you ever live in this outback place, Eddie?'

'Oh yes, I spent some time there working on a ranch. And then, I made friends with an Aborigine family and lived with them for a while. The Aborigines are great people, friendly, clever, inventive. A true Aborigine can survive on things that would turn most people's stomach.'

'Did you eat with them too?'

'Of course I did! They took me into their family and their hearts with no questions asked. It's the so called civilised folk who worry me, not the Abos. Even their religion is simple, they call it *The Dreaming*, because it's their belief, that through dreams, they come into contact with the spiritual world and it gives them strength. There isn't a cave that doesn't hold their sacred art, cave paintings that tell of their myths and legends over centuries.'

'I thought Aborigines were savages.'

'Aw, you've been reading the wrong books, Tina, they're gentle people.'

Well, that was one error in judgement put right. Tina changed the subject. 'What was your favourite place?'

'If you mean in my travels around Australia, well, I suppose Sydney was the place I liked most,' Eddie said without hesitation. 'Sydney harbour and the big ships…' he halted in mid-sentence at Tina's stifled yawn. The day had been exhausting mentally, as well as physically and had obviously taken its toll. 'C'mon, my little one, I made a promise to your mother that I would look after you, and here I am prattling on while you're practically asleep on your feet. You can listen to my life story another time.'

The crisp, white sheets against the deep red splendour of the quilt looked so inviting, and the bed seemed to scream at her to lie down and rest. She told herself there was no harm in putting her head on the pillow, just for a few minutes until Eddie came back. Her cheek touched the cool, soft pillow, exhaustion took its toll and Tina fell asleep almost immediately.

When Eddie came back into the room, he sat on the edge of the bed and tenderly stroked her head as she slept, so peaceful and comfortable, almost like a child at rest and that was what she needed right now, to rest. Consummation of their marriage could wait.

It was a chink of light shining through the drawn curtains that woke Tina, and she blinked until her eyes came into focus. She was unable to even hazard a guess at the time, but knew it must be quite early and this was the first morning of their married life. For a few minutes, she watched Eddie sleeping soundly beside her before slipping tentatively from the bed, tiptoeing through the sitting room and into the scullery to begin preparing their first meal together, their wedding breakfast.

'Breakfast time, sleepy head,' Tina stood by the bed holding the tray. She was cheerful, wide-awake and completely rested. 'I hope you're hungry.'

Eddie pushed himself into a sitting position and rubbed his eyes. 'You look bright as a button,' he said through a yawn. 'What time is it anyway?'

'It's still quite early, but we made a promise last night to make the most of the time we have, remember?'

Eddie stretched, smiled impishly and pulled back the covers. 'Then, Mrs Fraser, why don't we begin right here?' He patted the mattress, 'It's still early, Tina, come back to bed.'

She hesitated a moment, then laid the tray on the floor and climbed into the warm bed. 'I'm sorry about last night Eddie. I only meant to close my eyes for a moment but the next thing I knew, it was morning. I'd fallen asleep before I could tell you...'

'Tell me what?'

'That any doubts I had—and believe me, there were plenty of what ifs—are gone. Yesterday was the happiest day of my life.'

They awoke to the sound of someone banging on the door. Tina sat bolt upright. 'Who can that be at this time in the morning?'

Eddie drew open the curtains and sunlight flooded the room. 'Morning's come and gone,' he said. 'It must be nearly noon! We've really overslept.'

'Who's there?' Tina called out.

'It's only me, lazybones.'

Agnes stood on the doorstep, arms akimbo and a cheeky grin on her face. Tina blushed and blustered over the feeble excuse for still being in her night attire so late in the day. 'We were so tired, we must have fallen asleep again,' she said, somewhat unconvincingly.

'Oh, I know what you mean,' Agnes answered, and the cheeky grin turned into a not so innocent giggle. 'Joe and I were that dead beat this morning, would you believe we slept until nearly eight o'clock?'

The reply was more than just tongue in cheek, it was almost mocking. Agnes was, by no means, one of those nudging and winking, smarmy types, but that grin on her face, sort of finger-pointing and knowing, unnerved Tina. Or maybe, it was simply guilty conscience. Anyway, with obvious reluctance, she asked, 'Do you want to come in for a minute?'

'Better not, I'd rather get back upstairs.' Agnes lapsed into another spate of silly giggling. 'I only wanted to see if you were alright. You looked so tired last night.' Her eyes were full of fun and laughter. 'I told Joe I'd have dragged him to the altar years ago if I'd known honeymoons were so much fun.' And then, she was gone like a greyhound out of the trap.

Tina called, 'Bye Agnes,' but having taken the stairs two at a time, Agnes was already at her own door.

'That was Agnes playing mother hen,' Tina announced coldly. It was more than embarrassment. She was irritated that Agnes felt the need to not so much visit as to check up on her and on this particular morning too. It was nothing short of unwelcome prying.

'And you're angry with her for caring about you?' For the first time since they met, Eddie was critical of her. 'Agnes is a lot more than just your cousin. She's a good, dependable friend who, by your own admission, is only interested in your wellbeing. Maybe you should bear that in mind when I'm at sea and you're glad of her company.'

Tina looked like a little girl who had stamped her feet in a tantrum then begged to be hugged. It was this child-like bashfulness that made her so endearing and also made it impossible for Eddie to remain annoyed when she did behave childishly. One smile was all it took for his heart to melt and his arms to reach for her.

'I still have to give you my wedding present,' Eddie said, changing the subject. He pulled her onto the sofa beside him, reached for his jacket, took a bulky envelope from the pocket and handed it to Tina.

The envelope was turned over and over in her hands as she excitedly tried to identify the contents by touch until eventually, she ran out of guesses. 'I can't fathom it, so you'll just have to tell me what it is.' Tina held out the package, but Eddie eased it back.

'It's for you to open it and see.'

The wedding band Eddie had placed on her finger only a day ago glistened in the shaft of sunlight that shone through the window as Tina tore open the envelope. A shocked tremble started in her toes and rushed to her hands. 'How much is here?' she gasped as if the breath had been sucked out of her. In that moment, she understood how Agnes must have felt the day she opened their wedding present to her and Joe.

'It's almost all the money I earned over the past year. I never bothered much about spending my wages because I never had anything to spend them on, until now.'

That was the first time Tina saw Eddie's intense pride in providing for her. A whole year's pay! All the people she knew lived, worked and survived from week to week because that's the way things were, a way of life and she couldn't imagine anyone from the mill leaving their wages untouched for a week, let alone a year. 'I... I don't know what to say.'

'You don't have to say anything. I don't want you to worry about finances while I'm gone. Put this in the bank, it's a nest egg so that you'll always feel secure.'

The dream she had of being well-off was no longer a dream. This would most certainly be put safely in the bank with what was left of her inheritance and now, Tina Fraser was a woman of means. She wasn't to know it at the time, but this security Eddie so desperately wanted her to have would one day become a curse instead of the blessing it was meant to be. This was the beginning, the first linkage in a chain of events, which right then were meticulously being put together by the hand of Lady Serendipity herself and once begun, it could never be halted. But there was a tiny, unnoticeable rent in the invisible mantle of security that protected Tina and one day, it would eventually give way, allowing horror to rain on her.

They had two whole weeks to be together, walking to the park, talking endlessly about their lives, their likes and dislikes, but most of all, just being together to live and love.

And then in times whittling way, days became hours, hours became minutes and all too soon, the honeymoon ended, leaving only memories of laughter and passion. The inevitable time had come for Eddie to join his ship. Sobbing like her heart would break, Tina clung to her new husband, but her feeble threat to never let him go was like a candle in the wind; fragile, flimsy and without any real hope. This was the day: this was the hour when goodbyes must be said.

The second parting was more heart-rending than the first. The testing time had begun. How she would cope with the long wait for his return remained to be seen.

Chapter Eight

It was Tina's job at the mill, which became the staff she clung to for support. Without a reason to get up in the morning, she might simply have lain in bed wallowing in self-pity. The yearning for Eddie was painful. Not a physical pain, but an intense longing like a thirst that couldn't be quenched. It was important for her, at all costs, to disguise this longing lest others ridiculed her for being soft.

There was no shortage of well-meaning people who openly showed pity for the young bride, alone for so long without a husband to warm her bed and hold her when nights grew cold. She couldn't make up her mind what was worse, this misplaced compassion or the indiscreet remarks bandied about in her presence, as though marriage had somehow made her deaf to the remarks and blind to the pitying looks she wasn't supposed to see.

Outwardly, she was still quiet, serene little Tina, yet beneath the calm exterior, she hid a crushing loneliness that tested the limits of her endurance and haunted long, solitary nights. Nights when she would sit alone by the fire with the lamps unlit, watching the flickering flames make the strangest images that danced back and forth across the polished, brass fender.

Saturday was the one day of respite that revived her flagging spirits with the breath of life. The Saturday routine never differed, but oh how Tina looked forward to that leisurely day of freedom from the regimental tedium of a working week. She had made eleven vertical lines in a notebook and every Saturday, she crossed a line through each one in turn to show that Eddie's voyage home was growing ever closer. It was all in the mind of course, but it did seem to make the weeks go faster and today, she crossed off week six.

Coutts's office was busier than normal this particular Saturday, but Tina and Agnes passed the time by chatting idly about this and that while patiently awaiting their turn. The stories from the mill that Agnes told with zest and humour were what Tina looked forward to most. Agnes did have the knack of storytelling. Not in any way was she a malicious gossip. Agnes O'Neill, her tongue going nineteen to the dozen, only enjoyed the passing on of profoundly interesting titbits that inevitably began with a whispered, "By the way" and today was no exception.

'By the way, did you hear about Lorna Dunn?' When Agnes was angry, she had a way of tapping her toe and right then, she must have been furious because the toe tapping was extra rapid.

'Don't tell me Bert hit her again.' Tina was one of the many who didn't understand why a hardworking weaver like Lorna took such violent abuse from that brutish husband of hers.

'She came into work on Thursday with a black eye that went all the way down to her chin. Walked into a door, she said. Well, Sadie asked if it was the same door she walked into last week. I can't understand why she keeps on defending that animal. I told her straight she'd wake up dead one morning if she stayed with him.'

It wasn't actual surprise that brought a sharp intake of breath; Tina was only trying hard not to laugh at the contradiction in terms of *waking up dead*. Everyone knew Bert Dunn was a thug whose idea of masculinity was beating the living daylights out of his wife, and it was everyone's sorrowful prediction that Lorna would—as Agnes so eloquently put it—wake up dead one morning.

The queue had cleared and they were next. Tina took a step forward then suddenly reached out to grasp Agnes as her knees buckled. Agnes only just managed to catch her before she fell to the floor. 'Help me, somebody please help me.' Her hysterical scream brought James Coutts running from behind the counter.

'What on earth happened to her?' Coutts asked in alarm, which was odd in itself, since concern for others was a rare quality in him.

'One minute we were talking and the next she was falling down. Is my cousin dead, Mr Coutts?'

Agnes knelt on the floor and wept fearfully as she held Tina's lifeless body in her arms and nuzzled her deathly pale face. James Coutts patted Tina's wrists in an effort to bring her around.

And then, Tina's eyes flickered. 'What happened?' she asked in a voice so weak. 'I suddenly felt dizzy and there was a whooshing sound in my ears. That's the last I remember.'

'You had a seizure of some sort, Mrs Fraser. I think perhaps you should see a doctor.'

'Oh, I'll make sure she does, Mr Coutts,' Agnes assured him.

'Please don't fuss! I'll be fine after a cup of tea.' Tina forced a smile and tried to pass it off as a slight swoon brought on by standing so long. Only, this wasn't just a swoon, it was a dead faint.

'What, did you do lace your corset too tight?' Agnes made the half-hearted attempt at levity to hide the fact she was scared witless. Wasn't it only a few months ago her frail little cousin was in hospital with a heart condition bad enough to worry the physicians?

'I think maybe I should go home.' Her voice was hollow and weak, and she was as floppy as a rag doll. Tina was anything but alright.

'I don't think you should be on your own. I'm taking you to your mother, and don't try to argue.'

The moment they walked through the door, Mrs Morris knew something was far wrong. These two would never come back from town this early on a Saturday unless there was a real problem. Tina was like a limp lettuce, wan and looking like her legs couldn't hold her a minute longer. In her usual curt manner, Maggie asked, 'What happened?'

'She fainted in Coutts's office. We were standing there talking when down she went and almost frightened me to death.' Agnes held out her hands. 'Look, Aunt Maggie, I can't stop shaking.'

'Thanks all the same, Agnes, but you can leave her with me now. I'll take care of this.' The dismissal was polite, but a dismissal nevertheless.

'I don't mind staying a while longer.'

Agnes didn't want to leave; although it was clear her presence was neither needed nor wanted. She had been told rather brusquely there was no need for her to stay, practically ordered to leave. With the greatest reluctance, she did just that. There was no point attempting to cross this invisible barrier Aunt Maggie put around Tina.

When the door closed, Mrs Morris said, 'Tell me what happened to you, Tina.'

'I must be coming down with something.'

'Oh, you're coming down with something alright, in about eight months, if I'm not mistaken and I very rarely am. For the past week, you've had the look.'

'What look?'

'The look women get when they're expecting.'

'That's plain silly, Mum! I've only been married a few weeks.' It was easy to pooh-pooh these old wives' tales when the mind refuses to admit to the obvious.

'Stop burying your head in the sand, Tina. It's not a matter of how many weeks or months. Once is all it takes. Or did you think babies were made to order?'

Her mind went back to the first morning of their married life. They had spent that entire morning in bed and not once had Tina given a thought to the outcome. Her mind was perhaps just too feeble to understand that passion came at a price.

Sunday, the day of rest, rejuvenated Tina in body and spirit but still, her mind refused to believe. She preferred to accept as true that a simple malady had caused the faint. 'Leave diagnosis to medical people instead of jumping to the wrong conclusions,' she told her mother.

She didn't argue that matter, but as far as leaving well alone, that's exactly what Maggie Morris did—for today at least. The following day, she was waiting outside the mill for Tina to finish work.

'Protest all you like, but you and I are going to pay Doctor Jackson a visit.' Maggie took Tina's arm and practically dragged her. 'I'm only doing what Eddie would do if he were here.' Her pinched lips accentuated the, *don't dare argue with me,* look. She'd been around long enough to recognise the first signs when a baby was on the way, and she was going to make damned sure the doctor confirmed *her* diagnosis.

At the surgery door, Tina stopped and told her mother to sit in the waiting room. 'I can do this myself,' she said defiantly and barred Maggie's entry by holding onto the door handle.

'But… but shouldn't I…' Mrs Morris was unprepared for rebellion. Tina had always been so pliant and biddable, and now here she was, dishing out the order for her to sit in the waiting room. When that door closed in Maggie's face, a lifetime of lonely moments didn't compare with the loneliness she felt right then.

'Come in, Tina, or I should say, Mrs Fraser, now that you're a married lady.' Doctor Jackson watched her closely. A good doctor could tell so much by the way a patient walked into the room, or the lustre of the eyes and hair. Tina seemed a bit anxious but other than that, she looked well. 'You seem much better than the last time we met. Marriage must agree with you. Take a seat, Tina and tell me what's on your mind.'

'It's something or nothing, silly really.' She had intended to sound offhand but under his piercing stare, Tina became like a frightened little girl. 'I had a bit of a fainting spell on Saturday and you know what my mother's like. She's not happy unless there's something to worry about. She even worries when there's nothing to worry about.'

He took in the slight twitch at the corner of her mouth and the nervous, mirthless laugh. She was certainly ill at ease. 'Well, you're not sick like you were before, but something is definitely ailing you. Don't be afraid or embarrassed to speak your mind. Tell me, Tina, were you by any chance late last month?'

She lowered her head and almost inaudibly answered, 'yes.'

'What I want you to do now, is loosen your skirt and lie on the couch. It's just a little examination and I promise to preserve your dignity. All I want is to confirm my own suspicions.' He gently pressed her tummy and moved a stethoscope over her abdomen before helping her to a sitting position. This young lady wasn't just in denial; she genuinely had no idea about her condition. 'That's fine, Tina,' he said, 'you adjust your clothing and I'll be back in a minute.'

He smiled and asked if Mrs Morris could come through to the surgery. Maggie struggled to control the terror that was building up inside her. She had predicted a new life, but what if she was wrong? What if it was something pernicious? If that smile was meant to quell her fears, it wasn't working, yet, would a doctor be so relaxed if he was about to give bad news?

The door creaked shut behind them. 'I thought you might like your mother here for support, Tina,' he explained. 'You're not ill as such, but I heard the faintest little heartbeat and I'm quite sure you're pregnant.'

Tina sat motionless. The only thought on her mind was that she couldn't even share this with Eddie or reach out to him for consolation. She vaguely heard the doctor tell her to get plenty rest and something about a midwife, but Tina was too shocked to take everything in.

As far as Maggie Morris was concerned, this diagnosis was less than comforting. A grandchild on the way should have been cause for celebration. Instead, it had quite the opposite effect since she still looked on her daughter as a sickly child who needed to be protected. But even she could do nothing about this, and carrying a baby could have a devastating effect on Tina's health. As for Tina herself, instead of contemplating her own health, she was more concerned about Eddie's reaction. By the time he returned, she would be three months gone and if he saw a change in her, he may not like or accept it. What if she was one of those women who grew grotesquely fat when they were expecting? If this happened, Eddie might be repulsed and turn away in disgust.

'Do you want to come home with me and I'll make you a bite to eat?'

Her mother's voice seemed to come from afar and jolted Tina from shocked disbelief to the hard-hitting truth of her actual condition. Words tumbled from her mouth before she took time to think. 'Would you mind not treating me like an invalid?' The harsh retort was uncalled for and immediately regretted.

'Well, madam! I'm sorry if you're upset because I care about you more than you obviously care about my feelings. You seem to forget this has been a shock for me too. I'm the one who looked after you for eighteen years and whether you like it or not, you're still my wee girl.' She didn't speak in anger. She didn't even bear any look of anger. Maggie Morris was simply sad and hurt.

Tina wrapped her arms around the stiffly prim body. 'I'm sorry for being so horrible,' she said in her most apologetic voice. 'I'm not hungry; all I need right now is to go home and gather my thoughts.'

When her mother was out of sight and sound, Tina looked to the window above hers and called to Agnes. Her happy face looked over the window sill, smiling comfortingly. 'What did the doctor say?' And then Agnes grimaced, 'bet he gave you one of them vile-tasting tonics.'

'Come down, Agnes, I don't want to shout and let half the street know my business.' The window closed immediately. Tina turned the key in the latch, opened her door and waited.

If ever Tina needed her ever-faithful cousin, it was now. Agnes was the one she looked to for comfort, a hand to hold and a shoulder to cry on, but this was one of the rare occasions when Agnes was lost for words. Her mouth moved but no sound came out. It had just never occurred to Agnes that her little cousin was now a married woman who might possibly be in the family way.

'I said I'm expecting,' Tina repeated.

'You daft bitch, letting this happen! I can't make up my mind whether to hit you or hug you. Have you any idea what everyone's going to think with the ink not even dry on the marriage licence? That lot at the mill love a scandal, so you'd better pray it's not premature. That's all I'm saying, because when your time comes, folk are going to be counting the months since you met Eddie.'

Tina shuddered that people might assume she got pregnant out of wedlock. 'They wouldn't,' she almost screamed at the horror of such an idea.

'Oh, don't you worry. If I hear one person spreading gossip, they'll find out the hard way what real trouble is. Mark my words, Tina; they won't know what's hit them.'

Had the autumn sun suddenly become brighter? Had a warm, fragrant breeze filled the air? All at once, Tina felt as if a weight had been lifted from her shoulders and in truth, she was glad. With the secret out, Agnes would soon silence the gossips, but that was the least of her problems, there was one more hurdle. How would Eddie take the news that he was to become a father?

Chapter Nine

Autumn was almost at an end. Trees within the park had begun to scatter their rich, gold leafage and the bright, floral colours of this season were fading. Too soon, the warm hues would be replaced by cold white, as austere winter claimed its place amid the seasons.

Treading ever so gingerly along snow-covered streets or manoeuvring a safe path on pavements could be the most fearsome exercise. Victims of winter could be seen hobbling around on crutches or with arms sheathed in plaster of paris. Streets could be hazardous and extremely treacherous for unsuspecting pedestrians, and the main perpetrators of the many accidents were just playful children having fun in the game of sliding on pavements until they were polished into sheets of ice. Without a doubt, this cold harsh season was the one Tina simply couldn't abide. Her frailty and vulnerability to icy temperatures made her that much more susceptible to the cold.

This Saturday was biting, but Tina was regardless of the chill. What she felt was as though her body had been cocooned in soft, warm fleece. The cause of this sensation was, because today, with one definitive stroke, she had crossed off the final line in her little notebook. Eddie was on his way home, and according to Joe, his ship was expected to dock on the twelfth of November. She was only days away from holding him in her arms again.

Joe had eagerly, if perhaps a tad too eagerly offered to check the docking schedule with Ronnie McBride, the harbour master. Ronnie's sparse, wooden booth had but one embellishment, the word *Sanctuary* hand-painted on the side by the man himself. A somewhat facetious act on Ronnie's part; but as harbour master, he felt entitled to make the little booth a home from home, where he could sit awhile and pass the time of day with any friend who just happened to be passing.

It was no mean feat visiting Ronnie in his little booth, as any one of his pals could testify to. Grateful sailors, seeking help and advice on the best place to go in the city for friendly, female company after weeks at sea, contributed bottles of whiskey and rum in exchange for information on the whereabouts to make for. Ronnie had directed so many appreciative sailors to the local prostitutes hangout that one corner of the booth was like a distillery.

Escaping to the *Sanctuary* had been the saviour of many a marriage. When a wife's nagging raised a man's temper, Ronnie was the councillor, barman and peacemaker who listened over a few nips, dished out sound advice, then sent the half-cut husband home in a more peaceable mood to make up with his wife.

Joe had no need of marriage guidance. It was basically a good, old chin-wag with Ronnie he enjoyed. Although it had to be admitted, sharing a drink with his old classmate did make talking over old times tad bit more pleasant. Recalling schoolboy exploits and acts of daredevil over more than a few tots of whiskey, made the recollections of days gone by decidedly more amusing. Then, after an hour or so of amiable reminiscing and the expected date for Eddie's ship to dock known, Joe returned from the harbour, happily inebriated. His quest for knowledge having been completed, the cheery job of telling her cousin the glad tidings he left to Agnes.

'Dear oh dear, the state that man of mine was in when he finally got back from the harbour. It took him three hours to find out Eddie's ship is due on the twelfth.' Agnes could only chuckle at what would have sent most women into a frenzied rage. Then again, Agnes wasn't most women, just as Joe wasn't a habitual drunk. 'Well now, thanks to McBride, he'll have a buggar of a hangover and expect me to mop his fevered brow.'

As Agnes made to leave, having passed on the information, Tina clutched her arm. 'Don't rush off yet,' she begged. 'Please, Agnes, stay awhile. I'll put the kettle on and we can blether for a bit.' Tina had a desperate need for company and Agnes had such a unique way of telling things; it always gave her a reason to laugh.

Agnes happily planked herself onto the settee. 'Aw, Tina, you should have seen the comical way he staggered through the door and bounced off every wall. When he called me his dream girl, I said, "Joseph O'Neill, if you don't sober up, I'll be your worst nightmare." And then, the daft arse suddenly went all romantic and turned into the world's greatest lover.' Agnes winked knowingly. 'It's not that I mind, but he's that clumsy. He tried to grab me for a kiss and cuddle, missed and fell at my feet. Well, I'm standing there supposed to be furious and trying my best not to laugh.'

'So what did you do?'

'I came down here lest he got it into his head he'd been forgiven a mite too easily.' By the time she had finished telling the story of Joe's fall from grace, their sides ached with laughter. 'I'd better go before I burst a gusset,' Agnes said. At the door, she turned and smiled, but not her normal, eye-crinkling grin. It was a sad sort of smile and then she said a very strange thing. 'You know, Tina, my heart aches that the day might come when I have to live without Joe, so for now, I'll welcome each day I wake with him by my side. If all he's guilty of is enjoying an afternoon here and there with an old pal and getting tipsy, who am I to grumble?'

Many times, Tina had this same feeling, a fear of losing her beloved Eddie. Wasn't it strange that the dread of something so awful happening didn't belong to her alone? Perhaps it was a condition that came with loving someone too much.

The fire crackled in the hearth, the flames flickered and danced, and the glowing coals were warm and comforting on this cold November evening. The time had come for Eddie to find out he was to be a father. But how could she put it? 'Good to have you home and by the way, I'm expecting.' Not very subtle; poking a finger in his eye would have the same effect. In retrospect, it might be best if she just played it by ear.

And then it was the afternoon of the twelfth! Tina fluttered and fidgeted like the nervous, young bride she was. One minute she was trembling with anticipation and the next, shaking with apprehension. Conflicting emotions were very confusing, and her impatience didn't help. Then, in an instant, the weeks of forlorn waiting melted into oblivion at the sound of Eddie's voice. Tina ran into his arms and the tears of joy were kissed away.

'You need a shave,' she winced and screwed up her face. 'Your chin feels like a scrubbing brush.' It was then she stood back and saw him, really saw him for the first time in three months. 'You look different, older and so much broader in the shoulders than I remember.' She walked around him, running her hands across his shoulders and down his arms. An awesome change had occurred in such a short space of time. Three months ago, she wed a mere youth, but a remarkable metamorphosis had taken place and now the good-looking boy had become a ruggedly handsome man. Breathlessly, she asked, 'Are you hungry?' So much to say and this was all she could think of?

'Starving,' Eddie was oblivious to Tina's amazement and blind to the fact she couldn't take her eyes off him, even as she filled a basin with water.

'Take this,' she said handing him the basin, 'wash and change while I'm making the tea. Oh, and please remember to shave, Eddie.' Tina indicated the necessity by rubbing her cheek.

They spoke little during the meal, although their eyes constantly met. They were together again and that was all that mattered. Tonight, they would curl up on the sofa together in front of the roaring fire, in their own home behind closed doors and then at Tina's insistence, Eddie would recount every detail of his last trip while she ravenously devoured every word. It was her belief that when Eddie was away, remembering these stories in vivid detail was like taking part, being there with him in spirit at least, and Eddie indulged her whim.

It was exciting to put faces to the names of his shipmates and they took substance. The escapades of Sean Sullivan were her favourite. Eddie's fleeting references had caught her imagination. The fighting Irishman was in a kindly, but more realistically way known as Slugger, because after a drop or two of the hard stuff, he had a tendency to brawl with anyone who would oblige. Yet according to Eddie, in sobriety, Sean was actually quite meek and amiable. Tina imagined Slugger as a big, brawny Irishman, although that was completely different from the small, somewhat weedy and mild-mannered little man Eddie described. She preferred her own mental image of Sean Sullivan, which was far more swashbuckling and exhilarating. It occurred to Tina, that if the demon drink could turn a passive little man like Sean into an aggressive monster, then drink had a lot to answer for. Thank God Eddie wasn't a drinking man.

When the fire was reduced to a few glowing embers, Tina went to the bedroom and turned down the bedcovers carefully smoothing her precious quilt, then she pulled on a crisp, lawn nightdress and slipped between the cold sheets, shivering a little until she felt Eddie's warm body behind her and his arm encircle her waist. Tina took the big, course yet tender hand and pressed it against her belly. If he felt any change in her girth, Eddie said nothing. Perhaps he thought she had put on weight and was too considerate to say anything.

'I have something to tell you, Eddie.' The whispered words seemed to echo in the darkness. 'Only, I have this terrible notion you may not like it.' Tina held her breath.

With the inborn mirth that came naturally to Eddie, he said, 'Let me guess, you're fed up of me and you've found another man.'

If it was that simple, he would probably cope and even accept it, although he may not be so jaunty when he heard what had to be said and that was the hard truth of the matter. It was dark, but the darkness couldn't hide Tina's guilty thought that she was somehow responsible for a calamity.

Eddie was aware of the tentative bracing in her body and he could feel the rapid beating of her heart. 'You're scaring me, little one,' he told her, 'tell me what's wrong.'

Tina turned to face him and the dark of the unlit room hid her dilemma. 'Since the day we met, you have always called me, *little one*, and it makes me feel special and protected,' she said softly. 'But Eddie, what if… in a few months I won't be… little?'

'There is something wrong with you. It's serious, isn't it?' They were talking at cross purposes and Eddie was misinterpreting Tina's anxiety to mean she had a health crisis of some sort.

Perhaps this inability to communicate was a reflection of how little time they had spent together. Tina was becoming exasperated by her own failure to explain and his failure to understand. 'Oh Eddie!' she cried, 'I'm trying to tell you we're expecting a baby.' She heard a shocked gasp that seemed to reverberate around the darkened room. 'You're angry! I knew you would be angry.'

'You think I'm angry? I'm just the opposite, my precious little Tina. This is the best news I've ever had in my life.' He held her tightly in his arms for only seconds then suddenly slackened his grip. 'Am I hurting you?' he asked with undisguised concern.

'Good heavens, no! I haven't suddenly become breakable, so you just put those arms back where they belong.'

Tina nestled in the warmth and security of Eddie's arms and told of her anguish and fear, the agony of trying to anticipate his reaction, hoping for favour, fearing denial. In the darkness, a single tear trickled down his face to know, that for all these weeks, Tina had been haunted by a spectre of doom and all because she was aware of the fact that not every man rejoiced in the prospect of fatherhood. Many men would rather up and leave than face the responsibility.

With all the passion of a man who had been given the most precious of gifts, Eddie's pronounced joy at the magnificence of this news echoed in the darkness. With the sum of all her fears now ceasing to exist, Tina fell into a deeply contented, totally relaxed sleep and when the morning sun rose in the sky, silently so as not to disturb her sleeping husband, she dressed and left for work.

When the long day finally ended, Tina hurried home happy in the knowledge that Eddie would be waiting for her. They had ten whole days, and she was determined to make the most of every precious minute by gathering memories to cling to and sustain her during the long winter.

Tomorrow was Saturday and there would be no jaunt into town with the girls. Instead, she would walk arm in arm with her husband, buy provisions and then go home and close their door on the outside world. On Sunday, they would spend the day by the fire examining the past and planning the future. Her cheeks nipped and Tina shivered so much, her teeth chattered. Perhaps under the circumstances, it might be best to forego a shopping trip. Spending the entire weekend in the comfort of their home, by the fire, was a better option.

By the time she reached Charles Street, Tina's fingers and toes had lost all feeling. But tonight, she wouldn't be going home to a cold house, there would be a welcoming fire lit. 'I'm home,' she called, hurriedly closing the door to keep out the cold.

Eddie came from the scullery with an apron around his waist and a tea towel over his arm. There are moments in life when a word or a look touches the heart and becomes a precious memory, and this was the moment Tina would lock away in her heart. The sight of Eddie obviously cooking a meal, caring for her: this was the moment she was engulfed by an overwhelming love for this man.

'Come and sit here by the fire, you look frozen to the bone.' He guided her to the armchair. 'Supper's almost ready.'

'You don't have to do this, Eddie, there's no need to spoil me.'

He bent over the chair until their faces were within kissing distance. 'I want to spoil you for the rest of my life,' he said, 'because you are my life.' His voice was husky and charged with emotion, almost as if he were about to cry. Then he cleared his throat and said, 'You have a little rest until its ready.'

If truth be told, it was a blessed relief to close her eyes if only for a few minutes. An envelope being placed in her hand made Tina open them again. 'Did I nod off?' she asked.

Eddie smiled kind of sadly. 'I know you love your job, Tina, but I can see that you're tired. Please give up working for my sake, it's the only way I'll have peace of mind. I don't mean right away, but promise you will, as soon as it gets too much for you.' He pointed to the envelope, 'This is your security. You don't have to work for a living.'

The smallest of pleasures can be the most fulfilling. Tina and Eddie found contentment simply by being within reach of one another, hidden where prying eyes could neither judge nor make assumptions. 'Would you like a boy or a girl?' Tina asked.

'You mean I have a choice?' Eddie quipped.

'Now you're being silly.' She pretended to be annoyed.

'Does it matter all that much? The miracle is, we're having a baby, our baby. I often think about that day in the hospital when I almost turned and walked in the other direction until something stopped me. If I had, then we might never have met and that's the real miracle.'

They spent the weekend in near seclusion, grasping the precious moments alone together like greedy children before Monday commanded Tina's attendance at the mill. She fought the temptation to stay cocooned within the warm blankets, snuggled next to Eddie's sleeping body, but loyalty to her employer prevailed, and she reluctantly dressed and left for work with a woollen shawl covering her head and shoulders as protection from the cold November air.

As breath formed like mist before her face, Tina covered her mouth with the shawl and bent her head against the icy wind. Christmas was around the corner and soon, it would be time to write greeting cards and buy presents. How Tina loved Christmas, the season of goodwill. How her heart leapt with joy that this year, there was the added thrill that they would be decorating their very own home with holly and mistletoe. She stopped abruptly and her heart sank into the pit of her stomach. *They* wouldn't be sharing all this, because Eddie would be at sea and she would be alone on their first Christmas. This was the day she looked truth in the eye and faced the fact, that there were to be many things she would have to face alone.

The days were fleeting and Tina now looked on time as her enemy. The hours passed so quickly. If only, by some magic, there was a way to make time stand still, stop all the clocks, but the clocks ticked on and time relentlessly pushed forward to the day when Eddie had to leave—and that day had arrived.

Eddie tenderly held her in his arms. He had such an overpowering need to protect the small, fragile girl from everything harmful, to defend her with his life if need be. Gently yet firmly, he held her at arm's length. 'You must look to the future now, little one and take care of yourself.' He pulled her to him again so that she couldn't see the pain on his face.

Tina tilted her head to look up at him. 'Listen to me, Eddie Fraser,' she said, fighting to hold back the gathering tears, 'I'm stronger than I look. It was you who gave me this strength through your love and by God, we're going to have a beautiful baby.'

He forced a smile and kissed her one last time, then without hesitating or looking back, he was gone and she was alone again. Tina knew she had to come to terms with being a sailor's wife. She couldn't spend her life depending on other people to ease her loneliness. It was time to stand squarely and strongly on her two feet before people, with lives of their own, were tired of this self-pity.

Chapter Ten

Into the sixth month of her pregnancy, Tina looked well. The morning sickness had abated, there were no more fainting spells and her normally pale cheeks were now rosy pink, bringing countless remarks about the unmistakably healthy glow that had settled on Tina Fraser. On the downside, she had become unusually irascible. An innocent remark was all it took for an ill-tempered dragon to emerge. Agnes had commented on how neat Tina's figure was. The only evidence of her pregnancy was a slight bump. 'If it was me expecting, I'd probably be bloated and ugly and as big as a house,' Agnes said as a joke, her figure and height being so big compared to Tina's. Never in her wildest dreams did she expect a tongue lashing, but Tina started yelling at her for no good reason.

'Why do you have to put yourself down all the time? You could never be ugly and if you were as big as a house, Joe would love you even more—*if that was possible*,' she screamed. And then, like a summer shower, the bout of temper was gone as quickly as it came. Tina was embarrassed and apologetic.

'Forget about it—I have. Let's just say, you needed to let off some steam on account of your condition.' Without wrath or pique, Agnes dismissed the incident and in her own inimitable way, pointed out to Tina that pregnancy did nothing for her manners. They laughed and the silly words spoken in haste were forgotten.

How strange the passing of time was; one week could pass like the blinking of an eye, yet one day could feel like an eternity. Tina would never miss Eddie more than she did at this crucial time. She wanted so much for him to feel the new life growing and moving inside her. The longing for him was always there, yet she no longer felt totally alone, there was an odd sort of contentment in clasping her hands over *the bump*.

And then THE day arrived once more. In the early hours of the morning, Tina was awakened by a kiss so gentle. Eddie's lips simply brushed across her face, but it was enough to banish sleep and she held him as if she would never let go. Burying her face in the soft, nap coat, she smelled the brine and knew she wasn't dreaming.

'I'm sorry, it was stupid to wake you, but you were lying there so peaceful and I've missed you so much, I couldn't help myself. It's very early, Tina, go back to sleep and I'll wake you later.'

'Not on your life, Eddie Fraser.' Tina tossed back her hair and almost leapt from the bed. 'I want to spend every waking minute with you. There's plenty time for sleep.' She tiptoed across the cold floor into the sitting room where the morning sun shone through the window, filling the room with light: that was when Eddie saw the fullness of her body and the blush of her cheeks.

'You look wonderful!' He could only stand and stare, for there was every reason to be astounded. 'You're positively radiant and here I was, plagued by doubts and fears, but this is the best surprise ever. Obviously, you've given up the job, you couldn't look this well and still be working.'

'I haven't given up my job, not yet anyway.' Tina watched his face cloud. 'You have to understand, Eddie. I might just die of loneliness if it wasn't for my job.'

'I'm not condemning you, Tina. All I'm asking is that you keep your promise and rest.' Eddie realised it wasn't purely selfishness on Tina's part, for if positions were reversed, he might not be too happy about giving up his work either. It was just that her failure to uphold a pledge had overshadowed the initial gladness.

'You worry too much.' She brushed past him sulkily and walked into the scullery. 'I'll make breakfast while you tell me all about your trip.' It was a distinctly impolite way of telling him to end the discussion on her work.

Respectfully, as well as to preserve harmony, Eddie chose to ignore the clash of opinions. He ignored the sulk and said, 'We took on a new deckhand,' and the relaxed smile returned to her face, now that the subject of work had been dropped. 'Everyone took one look at him and right away, he was nicknamed *Redbush* on account of his beard. It's the biggest, bushiest, red beard you've ever seen and…'

'No,' she interrupted, 'tell me what Slugger got up to, so that I can make Agnes laugh.'

The tales of Slugger and his misdemeanours, which Tina passed on to Agnes, had circulated around the mill and he had become something of a cult figure. To the weavers, young and old, Slugger was a hero whose exploits brought a little glamour and excitement into their otherwise dull lives. The infamous Irishman didn't know it, but he was a star.

'Well the thing is, he's the reason we needed a new deckhand. You see, Slugger went ashore when we were in port and got drunk as usual, only this time, he didn't want to fight, and it took us all by surprise. No one knows to this day what went on in that crazy head of his, but he suddenly got maudlin and homesick, told everyone he was going back to Ireland to marry Maureen, his childhood sweetheart. Next morning, he was gone and that's the last we saw of him.'

'Didn't he even give as much as an explanation or a goodbye?' Now this was a sad and unexpected turn of events, the end of an epoch. Tina felt she had lost an old and dear friend.

'Sean was one of life's characters, a pain in the neck at times, but all in all, a good man. To quote Henry, "our loss is Ireland's gain." I can see you're disappointed, we all were, but here's something to cheer you up.' Eddie handed her the now familiar envelope and said proudly, 'A little something to add to your nest egg.'

There was a moment's silence and then the flicker of a smile crossed Tina's face. 'Today, I'm going to do something I've never done before,' she said, tapping her thoughtfully-puckered mouth with the envelope. 'I'm going to tell a deliberate fib, and say I'm poorly and have to go home.'

And that's exactly what she did, in fact, she feigned illness so well, Mr Meldrum practically begged her to go home, although everyone else knew the only malady Tina Fraser was suffering from was love sickness. She felt guilty about lying, yet it was worth it to spend a few, extra hours with Eddie, but first, she had to stop off at the bank.

She was greeted with an extra polite, 'Nice to see you, Mrs Fraser.' The teller smiled when she pushed the envelope and bank book through the grill, and amiably enquired, 'how are you this fine morning?'

'I'm quite well, thank you.' She returned his smile and held back a spluttering laugh at the way this man bowed to her. His eyes bulged in that purple face and his hands visibly shook at the sight and touch of so many banknotes. If she had but a few shillings in her account, it was doubtful if he would even raise his head.

It amused Eddie, the way Tina mimicked the teller. 'Yes Mrs Fraser, no Mrs Fraser, nice to have your money Mrs Fraser.' He sat in the armchair and laughed heartily at her antics. She minced around the room with one hand on her hip and in her most posh voice, said, 'I'm Lady Muck, you know.'

'I want people to treat you like a lady and that's what money in the bank does. I've travelled far and wide, and it's the same the world over. There's a certain power in having wealth: you gain respect. That's what you deserve and that's what you'll have.'

'Respect, financial security, I have it all, don't I?' Her mood was so erratic, that in an instant, all the facetious larking about came to an abrupt end and Tina lapsed into what was more or less rock-bottom despair.

Did an icy blast suddenly sweep across the room? That was how Eddie felt seeing Tina so solemn and unsmiling. Pain clouded the dark eyes that were bright with laughter only a moment ago. 'What is it?' he asked fearfully.

In a softly pleading way, Tina said, 'Do you know what I really deserve? More than all the money in the world, I would rather have you here to hold our baby the moment he or she is born.'

'Don't you think I want that too? I'll move heaven and earth to be here, but I will not make a promise I may not be able to keep. Babies don't always arrive on the date they're expected.' He held her in his arms and felt the life they had made, squirm and kick as if in protest at being sandwiched between them. 'I *will* try,' he promised.

'Doctor Jackson says the end of May or early June.'

Eddie made a solemn vow, 'Then God willing, I'll be here.'

Chapter Eleven

Showery April arrived with thunderstorms, the like of which Tina had never seen before. Perhaps it was a sign from God that the time had come for her to leave the job at the mill where she had worked for the past four years. A promise had been given and a promise must be honoured. If only she could reach Eddie by calling out across the vast ocean to ease his troubled mind by letting him know his wishes were being carried out. Besides, she was overcome by an indescribable fatigue, and every little task had become a stupendous effort.

It was inevitable this day would come sooner or later, but leaving behind the people, who had become like a family to her, was both distressing and painful.

By mid-afternoon, tears streaked her face. There had been so many kind wishes: so many goodbyes. But the most heartfelt thing of all was a single, newly cut, red rose, which had been placed on her desk and no one knew who put it there. How sad it would be to leave this office for the last time. Mr Meldrum, kind and considerate as ever, said, 'It's been a fraught day for you, Tina. It might be a good idea for you to go home now, rather than wait for the five o'clock buzzer.'

Having gladly accepted Mr Meldrum's kind offer, final farewells were made and promises were given to stay in touch. Maisie fought back tears when she reminded Tina, 'Too often, friends seem to drift apart when the circle's broken by one person leaving.'

Firmly yet kindly, Tina scolded her for being silly. 'I'm leaving work, not Scotland,' she told her. 'We'll still be friends after I walk through these doors for the last time, so stop blubbering and I'll see you Saturday.' But Tina had begun to feel at breaking point and all she wanted now was to make a hasty retreat before she broke down completely. The fuss, the strain and the sorrow of parting, had left her completely exhausted.

Misgivings faded into a kind of relief as she walked through the mill gates for the last time. Bringing her working days to a conclusion was for the best and

Tina didn't need anyone to tell her that. She was tired and her ankles were painfully swollen, which of course, was nature's way of reminding her it was time to rest and prepare for the birth of her first child.

The pledge had been fulfilled and when Eddie came back, there would be no more creeping from bed so as not to wake him. In fact, she could stay in his arms all day if that was her want. It was a thought-provoking concept and not one that would bode well with her mother. Maggie Morris considered anyone staying in bed instead of being up and about by six o'clock on a weekday had to be in league with the devil.

There was one drawback about becoming a lady in waiting. If she was to escape being bored witless, Tina *had* to find a distraction from her temporary solitude. With this thought in mind, she made a decision to spend the long, wearisome hours working on the baby's layette. She did have what her mother described as, 'a good pair of hands,' so what better way of using them. Besides, passing time productively appealed to the frugal side of her nature.

Over the next three weeks, Tina was consumed by an overpowering urge to work on the layette. In that short space of time, she had knitted a dozen matinee coats, countless bootees and mittens, and a gossamer lace shawl. She had also filled drawers with baby gowns, nappies and all kinds of things akin to a baby's needs.

Mrs Morris referred to this obsession as, 'feathering the nest.'

Until now, Tina's mind hadn't really accepted that soon, she would bring a small living being into the world. She had been negative about the whole thing, almost as if for the past months, she had been on the outside looking in. It was handling these tiny garments that brought everything into perspective and the negativity was replaced by a sense of wonder. On Saturday, she would buy the final item on her list of baby things… a crib.

Saturday was bright, sunny and hot, exceptionally hot for May. In this heat, Tina became overcome by the exhaustion of trailing the shops and her feet dragged wearily. But more than just wearied, she seemed unusually apathetic and distant. When Maisie expressed concern about this lack of energy, they made for the tea room where Tina thankfully eased her tired body onto a chair.

'Are you sure you're alright?' Agnes tilted Tina's chin with her forefinger. 'You would tell me if you didn't feel right?'

It wasn't the concern in her voice; it was the gloom Tina saw in those eyes that shook her. For the past few weeks, she had sensed a difference in Agnes, but until this very minute, to her fault, she had ignored the signs that all was not well with her cousin. How long was it since she had heard that infectious laugh or even seen Agnes smile? She'd overheard a comment that something was biting Agnes. If others had been quick to notice this, why then did it take her cousin and best friend so long to become aware of that persistently worried frown?

'I'm alright, Agnes. It's only this heat making me tired, so stop fussing,' Tina said.

'Are you sure that's all it is, Tina? Quite frankly, even Joe's noticed a change in you of late. Eddie's the bee's knees, but where is he at a time when you need him? Be honest, because we won't think any less of you if you admit to having a wee bit of regret about rushing into marriage with a man already married to the sea.'

This was a remark Tina fiercely reacted to with a snappy retort. 'And why exactly should I have regrets?' The snub was undisciplined, uncalled for, and an explanation along with an apology was due. 'I'm sorry, Agnes,' and she forced a sorry smile. 'Maybe you just got the wrong end of the stick, but I couldn't be happier. It's simply that…' She paused, as if formulating in her own mind how best to explain. 'Have you ever turned two pages of a book without realising it and missed part of the story? I don't know if this makes sense, but that's what I feel happened to me. I've turned two pages of my life. A year ago, I hadn't even heard of Eddie Fraser, and now we're married and about to have a baby. It's like I haven't had time to draw breath.'

They were interrupted by the sound of rattling crockery and the tea was served. Tina breathed a sigh of relief. She shouldn't have to justify herself to anyone. Wasn't her life complex enough without having it called into question?

The tea refreshed, but the real relief was leaving the swarming town centre to trudge wearily home. Tina had begun to feel quite claustrophobic caught in the mingling masses of crowded, jam-packed streets in this heat. Still, there was one consolation, when the baby did decide to make an appearance; he or she would have a crib and a layette.

'You look worn out,' Agnes told her. 'Put your feet up when you get home, rest awhile and don't worry if you fall asleep, I'll take the crib in when it's delivered and pop down later to see how you are.'

The big armchair was a sight to gladden any tired heart. Tina slipped off her shoes and snuggled into the deep comfort, but she couldn't relax. Maybe she hadn't seen how lethargically Agnes had walked upstairs just now, yet all that day, a niggling worry like a fearsome shadow had stealthily crept its way into her mind. Something had to be fretting Agnes, for her eyes no longer held mirth and mischief, and that in itself was scary. Today, Tina had taken stock of the worried frown. Until today, it had never entered her mind that her plucky cousin might actually herself be in need of a little, sound advice over some problems or other. It certainly never crossed her mind that someone as mentally and physically robust as her cousin wasn't immune to trials and tribulations.

These were tiring thoughts and when the fatigue of agonising overcame her, Tina fell into a much-needed slumber. The sound of her door opening lifted the veil of sleep and brought her to awareness. It was Agnes.

'Good, you look much chirpier,' Agnes said in a kind of solemn and vacant way. 'I said a rest was all you needed.'

Tina took a long hard look at her cousin and it suddenly hit her how fearfully strange that the one thing lacking in her voice was that familiar giggle. No cheeky quip to make her laugh, just an anxious wringing of those hardworking hands. It wasn't normal, not for her.

Tina forced herself into a sitting position. 'Never mind me! You look ready to burst into tears. Tell me what's ailing you, Agnes?'

The floodgates opened at the warmth of Tina's concern and she handed Agnes a handkerchief. Tina waited until the fierce sobbing was no more than a whimper, then hesitantly, she ventured advice. 'Aw, Agnes, if you've just had a falling out with Joe, think what fun you'll have making up.' But whatever misery had befallen Agnes, humour wasn't going to fix it.

'If only it was that simple, Tina.'

'Then tell me!'

'There was Joe going on about how lucky we were with both of us earning and how we could manage to put a little by, maybe even have a holiday by the seaside.'

'What's so bad about that?'

'I've been burying my head in the sand, Tina. I'm expecting and I don't know how to tell Joe. I kept thinking I'd wake up one morning and see I'd been wrong, but Dr Jackson says that isn't going to happen and I can't bring myself to shatter all Joe's dreams.'

'Stop that crying this minute and stop feeling sorry for your own self. You're always dishing out advice to everyone else, so it's time you were on the receiving end for a change. You didn't make this baby on your own, so tell Joe, because when you do, I guarantee he'll be like a dog with two tails to wag.' There were times when being harsh was more effective than being sympathetic and this was one of those times. 'Anyway, what a stupid idea to get into your head,' Tina scolded. 'Imagine believing Joe of all people would be disappointed.'

All she'd looked for was tea and sympathy, but a tirade like that from a gentle being such as Tina? Strangely enough, it had a calming effect on Agnes. 'Do you really believe, heart and soul, that he'll be happy about this, Tina?' At last, a smile crept over her face as she chewed nervously on her fingernails, 'even though it means only one wage coming in for a while?'

'What, a good man like Joe? He'd never put money before a baby and there'll be no holding him now that he's going to be a dad.' It was Tina's turn to offer a shoulder to cry on to the one person who had always helped and protected her, and it felt completely and utterly satisfying to be needed.

Not long after Agnes left, a loud whoop of joy coming from upstairs shattered the silence in a street that was probably preparing for a restful night before the daily graft. Agnes now had a good and valid reason to let go of her fears. Tina smiled. Strange how pregnancy made women weep and men celebrate. There must be a moral in there somewhere.

All in all, it had been quite a full to the brim Saturday that had left her drained and all Tina wanted now was an early night.

Chapter Twelve

In the early hours of Sunday morning, Tina awoke with such an aching back and could find no relief in turning this way or that. This was pain the like of which brought perspiration to the brow and tears to the eyes, subsiding for a while, then returning with such a vengeance. After almost two hours and the pain continuing to worsen, Tina rose to make a cup of tea and take aspirin, but by now, the fear that something must be wrong with her unborn brought on a fit of panic. She didn't take time to dress, just threw a shawl over her nightie and made for her mother's house.

The door opened no more than a crack and Mrs Morris, still in her flannel nightdress, peeked warily through the opening. 'Good grief, it's not yet seven o'clock on a Sunday morning, Tina,' she said sleepily before opening the door wide as Tina almost collapsed into her arms.

'Something's far wrong, Mum, I've had a terrible pain in my back all night and it's getting worse.' She was crying hard by this time, for the pain was nothing compared to the fear that this could be a sign of something bad.

'Well, first we'll get you as comfortable as possible in your own bed and then I'll fetch the midwife.'

'It's not a midwife I need,' Tina wailed, 'I'm not due for another two weeks.'

'Ah, but the baby doesn't know that, does it? Whether you like it or not, your labour's started.' Mrs Morris had the kind of wisdom that comes with age. She had seen the onset of labour more times than she could recall.

'I want to wait until Eddie comes home,' Tina cried frantically, 'can't you stop it?'

'Dear oh dear, Tina, you should know by now nature can't be halted. If my grandchild's in a hurry to enter this world, there's nothing you or anyone else can do to stop it, so let's get you home.' Even as Tina was being settled into the bed where she would soon give birth to her first child, she continued to protest. 'Hush now,' Mrs Morris told her, 'I'll be as quick as I can.'

The district midwife was well known and respected. She was a rosy-faced, little lady with greying hair, and most of the children in the area could attribute their safe delivery to none other than Nurse Lily.

She bustled briskly into the house, and Lily removed her cape and donned a crisp, white apron while giving orders to Mrs Morris. 'I'll just go in and have a look at Tina, and while I'm doing that, you can start heating water.' Maggie nodded and hurried to the scullery. 'When you've done that, Maggie, get me some clean towels, preferably white and also a bar of carbolic soap.'

Nurse Lily believed in the importance of first things first, like giving reassurance to first-time mothers with gentle words to calm and soothe the fear of childbirth. In her experience, they were invariably nervous and frightened, so the first priority was putting them at ease.

Following orders to the letter, Mrs Morris brought what Lily had asked for. 'Is everything going as it should?' she asked, nervously wringing her hands. Being present at countless births was one thing, but this was her own child, and she was powerless to do anything other than watch and wait. 'The baby isn't due for another two weeks, you know.' Maggie sat on the bed and gently wiped Tina's perspiring forehead with a soft flannel.

'If babies came by appointment, I'd get a full-night's sleep instead of being called out at all hours.' Lily said drolly, and then she smiled confidently. 'Don't worry, Maggie, things are going exactly as they should. From my experience, I'd say Tina's going to have a brief labour and it shouldn't be much longer now.'

Lily was right, it was a brief and comparatively easy labour, and on the fourteenth day of May, 1908, Eddie and Tina's daughter entered the world screaming and kicking. Maybe she sensed from the moment of birth that her life was going to be one long fight.

'My, she's a feisty little mite, full of fight and ready to take on the world.' Lily looked down at the tiny, new life she held in her arms. 'Lord, help anyone who tries to do her wrong.' It was only words, an observation, yet she had no idea how significant they were or how true this prediction would be.

When the midwife handed that tiny infant to her grandmother to be bathed and dressed, all the agonising doubts faded into oblivion. Maggie proudly carried the child into the bedroom. 'Are you ready to meet your new daughter now?' Tina held out her trembling arms to hold her newborn baby for the first time. Carefully, she inspected every finger and every toe with the wondrous joy that only comes through giving birth.

'She's beautiful! Isn't she beautiful, Mum?'

It was the most emotional moment of her life and Maggie Morris silently thanked God for this wonderful gift that had been bestowed on them. 'It seems like only yesterday I held you in my arms for the first time.' Maggie sat on the bed and wrapped her frail arm around her daughter. She had never been one to talk of intimate moments in her life but today was different. Today, she wanted to tell Tina just how precious her birth had been. 'Did I ever tell you how tiny you were? So tiny cradled there in your father's big hands. He held you so gently and safely. Your Daddy just couldn't take in what had happened, then out of the blue, he said, "She's so tiny we ought to call her, Tina." You were much smaller than this one.'

'Maggie… her name's Maggie after her grandmother.'

'Oh Tina, you're acting in haste; give yourself time and speak to Eddie before you give her such a common name. I'm flattered, but Eddie might feel his toes have been stepped on.'

'It's my choice! Eddie can name our first boy,' Tina said adamantly. 'Now, I need you to do something for me. Ask Agnes to come down, but not a word about this one. Just say I'm having a lie-in after yesterday and need to see her.'

'Before I do, there's something I want to say.' Mrs Morris smiled contentedly. 'I have an extra room that I've no longer a need of, but you're going to need the extra space. On Monday, I'll go to Coutts and tell him we're swapping houses and please don't argue when you know it makes sense, Tina.'

Who could tell how long this idea had been rumbling around in that lady's systematic brain or how long she had rehearsed the speech, but it was a perfect solution to the problem of overcrowding, and Tina was only too grateful to accept.

Agnes rapped on the bedroom door a couple of times before entering, it was propriety after all. 'Get up lazybones, it's a beautiful…' She was totally unprepared for the sight that met her eyes, and pointing at the baby, she stammered, 'Who's that?'

'This is my daughter, her name's Maggie and she arrived quite unexpectedly early this morning. It seems, she was the reason I wasn't myself yesterday.' With the explanation given, Tina handed the small bundle to her cousin.

The sleeping baby nestled contentedly in her aunt's arms, as if she knew already that the person holding her was to be an important part of her life. Agnes cooed, 'She's so perfect! But more to the point, Tina, how are you?'

'Never better: now look at Maggie and tell me truthfully, after all the doubts, are you still worried about having your own baby?'

'Are you kidding? How could I have any doubts when I'm holding this perfect little girl in my arms? Oh I hope and pray I have a baby girl as perfect as this, a little girl of my own.'

Mrs Morris peeked around the door. 'Lily's coming back later to check on you and Maggie, so I'm sure Agnes wouldn't mind coming back later too.'

This was the voice of authority. She, who must be obeyed, had spoken. Agnes put the baby in the crib that had been delivered at the most opportune time and left.

In the days following the birth, Tina's strength began to return, mainly because Maggie was such a contented and good-natured baby. She didn't constantly cry in a way that demanded attention like babies do. Of course, there was no shortage of fussing and caring friends who were only too happy to offer help. Agnes was there at every opportunity. She adored Maggie, and there were times Tina practically had to pry the child from her arms.

Agnes no longer feared what lay ahead but now, looked forward zealously to the birth of her own child, who she referred to as, 'my little Pearl,' the name she had chosen, so convinced was she that it was a daughter she carried.

Eddie was due on the twenty fifth but of course, there was no exact time for his arrival other than, according to the tide, it could be sometime late afternoon. Many times, more times than she cared to admit, Tina allowed herself the pleasure of speculating what it must be like to have her husband in a seven till five job. Not to look at the calendar, but to the clock and watch with all the confidence in the world as the minute hand ticked around to the exact time of his homecoming. No guesswork, no tense anticipation of waiting and wondering, only the heart-swelling pleasure of *knowing* that at the same time every evening, he'd walk through the door.

The morning had been taken up busily preparing everything and by midday, with her energy flagging, Tina fed and changed Maggie, then curled up in the armchair, the intention being to nurse the baby to sleep then lay her in the crib while she prepared the evening meal. But lethargy and the need to close her tired eyes took precedence and within minutes, she had drifted into sleep.

Tina had no awareness of the door opening, only the welcome sound of Eddie's voice calling to her, 'It's your husband, little one.' There was the thump of Eddie's canvas bag as it dropped to the floor and then a gasping, 'what the…'

Roused so suddenly and unceremoniously from sleep and still in a drowsy haze, Tina was caught completely off guard. All she could say was, 'This is our baby, Eddie.'

'But I thought…When?'

Tina was all at once wide awake. 'Eleven days ago! She arrived just a bit early, but isn't she beautiful?' She had accomplished this mighty feat of childbirth and now, with the greatest pride, Tina held out the sleeping infant and simply said, 'Would you like to hold your daughter?'

'She's so small.' A little awkwardly, Eddie took the child from her mother's arms and all at once, an indescribable emotion, that went way beyond anything he had ever experienced, swelled inside him as he held his baby daughter for the first time.

Tina whispered, 'This is our Maggie.'

'Oh, she's a healthy baby, that's for sure, but how are you?' There was no sign Tina was ailing, but looks could be deceptive. 'Truthfully, Tina, are you well?'

'Better than I've been for a long time,' she answered with the honesty Eddie needed. 'I'm still a bit tired, that's only to be expected. It took everyone by surprise when she decided to make an early appearance. Aw, but she's such a good baby, Eddie.'

With a brief look around the room, Eddie's eyes rested on the crib and he laid the sleeping baby inside. 'I need to hold you to make sure I'm not dreaming,' the wounded cry in Eddie's voice gave away the remorse in his heart that he had failed her. 'I let you down, didn't I? You depended on me and I wasn't there when I was needed most.' The kick from a mule would have been less painful than this weight of guilt Eddie felt right that minute.

'There's no blame to be laid, Eddie. You're not a Spey-wife, you couldn't have foreseen.'

'I really have a family of my own,' he said, 'a complete, wonderful family,' and with Tina's arms wrapped around him, the guilt faded.

'And you're not the only one, Agnes is expecting: they're going to have a baby too in the New Year. Our little Maggie is going to have a cousin to stand by her, just like Agnes and me.

Chapter Thirteen

The warm summer blended into autumn almost unnoticeably. The humid evenings were all at once chilly nights. Naked branches seemed to reach for the golden leaves that once adorned their boughs and now lay moulding on the cold earth. The need for scarf and gloves during walks in the park were the first tell-tale signs that winter was well on its way.

Tina had glowed with health during her pregnancy, while Agnes, on the other hand, was the exact opposite. She was poorly and growing more unwell by the day. Failing health gave rise to worry and doubts about both her and the baby she carried. Her own prediction that she would be as big as a house was sadly true, and she was forced to give in to the bitter truth that she could no longer carry on working the looms. The job itself was hard enough, but Agnes was so distended, it was almost impossible not to do herself harm. With her forced to quit and bills to be paid, Joe was obliged to work double shifts to compensate for the loss of earnings from their household.

By late November, unable to walk any distance, Agnes became totally housebound. Her attire consisted of long baggy nightdresses and slippers, mainly because she spent most of her time in bed since being on her feet made her swell even more. This pregnancy would be memorable for all the wrong reasons. For the first time in her life, Agnes became dependant on Tina's help with the shopping, cooking and cleaning the house, but more importantly to watch over her while Joe worked long hours. Concern for Agnes mounted, but Doctor Jackson could find no cause and merely put the condition down to a bad pregnancy. One thing was sure, something was far wrong, and as her cousin's health and vigour deteriorated by the day, it grieved Tina that nothing could be done to halt whatever malfunction was causing this.

Maggie was growing rapidly and looked every inch the happy, contented baby that she was. When Eddie was home at the beginning of September, he couldn't believe the difference in no more than weeks. 'Little mushroom,' was how he referred to this tiny being, his daughter, and he showered her with the kind of adoration and protective love that only another father could understand. His joy in proudly pushing the pram to the park every day to show Maggie off to anyone who was prepared to stop and pass the time of day, overwhelmed Tina with pride.

They were now counting the days till Christmas, Maggie's first Christmas, although she was still too young to fully understand. Strange to think, that last year Tina was fraught with anxiety because Eddie couldn't share with her the satisfaction of preparing the season's festivities.

But that was never going to happen again. Eddie vowed, that if the schedules couldn't be arranged to let him spend Christmas with his family, well then, Henry would just have to manage without him. Henry agreed, because he said that he too would rather spend Christmas in Dundee than anywhere else. Tina never thought to question what ties Henry had with Dundee.

Not all that long ago, this would have—it should have been the most enthralling time of the year, if only she was less troubled about Agnes. Doctor Jackson had assured them the baby was normal and healthy with a good, strong heartbeat. Why then had Agnes' health suddenly begun to fail when she had always been so robust?

On the twenty second of December, *The Rose* docked in a harbour glistening with snow and ice, picturesque maybe, but a dangerous place to lose your footing and plunge into the icy waters. Henry urged his crew to use caution on the gangplank.

Eddie arrived home cold and hungry, but grateful for the welcoming fire that blazed in the hearth. As young as Maggie was, she recognised her father immediately and squealed with delight at his appearance while Tina clung to her husband, laughing and crying at the same time. There was so much to tell him.

'It's always good to be home, but this time it's even better.' Eddie hugged the two most important girls in his life, Tina and his baby daughter. 'We are going to have the most special Christmas and before I forget, Henry sends his love and a present for Maggie.'

'That was kind of him! Maybe you should have invited him to spend Christmas with us. I'd hate to think he was alone and lonely at this time of year.'

The corners of Eddie's mouth lifted in a smile and he sort of choked back a gruff hee-haw. 'You don't have to worry about Henry being lonely or alone,' he told Tina. 'Henry stays with a friend when he's in Dundee, and to be honest, I think he would prefer to spend Christmas with her.'

So, Henry had a friendly landlady at the place he lodged. But what was so funny about that? Eddie was laughing in that secret way folk do when a smutty joke is being whispered in their ear. This confused Tina. 'I just don't understand why that's so funny,' she said.

'Think about it, Tina. A man like Henry… celibate?'

'You mean…' Tina put a hand over her mouth in shocked surprise.

'That's exactly what I mean!' Once he knew she had caught his drift, Eddie said, 'Let's just say, Henry's a man who enjoys the comfort of a woman's arms.'

From that moment, the subject of Henry and his lady friend was dropped. It had shocked Tina that this elderly man, who was a father figure to them, had an on-going affair with a woman. Not another word about Henry's amorous side passed Tina's lips. In her opinion, that was nothing more than prying and an invasion of his privacy.

When Maggie was asleep for the night, they settled by the fire and Tina told about the terrible time Agnes was going through. 'Try not to look shocked when you see her, Eddie. I have to warn you what to expect, because she looks really ill and we're all worried to death. To be perfectly honest, I'm very afraid we're losing her.'

'She looked alright last time I was home. When did all this start and what does the doctor have to say about it?'

'He says it's a big baby and Agnes is simply having a bad pregnancy. Poor Joe works every hour possible and he certainly doesn't get nearly enough sleep. The fact is, Eddie, I'm worried about both of them, and the way things stand, they won't have much of a Christmas.'

'But surely, we can help in some way.'

'What way can we help, Eddie, when they won't accept any kind of charity?'

'You think I'd treat them like beggars by offering charity?' Eddie said with a shrewd and cunning wink. 'What's wrong with inviting them to share our Christmas dinner? A pleasing family get-together can't be called charity now, can it? We can insist, that allowing us to do all the cooking while Agnes and Joe relax by the fire, is our Christmas gift to them: an offer they couldn't possibly refuse because it would hurt our feelings.'

How alike they were, as if their two minds had become a single thought. Tina had mused over this idea but couldn't find a way to put it to Eddie since this was supposed to be a special time for them. Bless him. She should have known her man's generous nature would prevail. Wasn't that why she had fallen in love with him in the first place?

The solution delighted Tina and she was all at once very animated, almost child-like in a way. 'I'll make a shopping list of everything we need to buy,' she trilled excitedly, and her eyes began to brim with tears, but they were happy tears. And then she pointed a finger meaningfully at Eddie and said, 'Of course, *one* of us will have to do a bit of shopping for all the Christmas fare.'

'And this *one* is only too happy to oblige,' Eddie answered with a smile and a courteous bow.

It was immensely satisfying for both Eddie and Tina to show their affection in this way, especially when the offer was grasped not with question or hesitation, but with glee… and a few grateful tears.

On Christmas day, Agnes was too incapacitated to do anything and Joe was simply too exhausted. Eddie gave strict instructions for both to put their feet up and enjoy the day because this was their treat. No objections there. It was the first time for weeks Joe had been at ease, the malt whiskey Eddie brought helped enormously of course. Perhaps it didn't drown Joe's sorrows, but it gave them a good soaking. For a while at least, it dulled the pain of his hands tied, helpless inability to ease this misery Agnes was steeped in and once again, see her chirpy as the birds in May.

For the first time in so long, Agnes actually managed a smile. She was happy and content just to see Joe relax more and more with each sip of the smooth, pleasant malt.

The Christmas dinner was a great success and a supreme delight. The four of them sat by the fire, sated and content to just idle away the time with pleasant conversation while listening to the comforting crackle of logs and coal burning in the hearth. It was a time of peace and love. Time also for the O'Neills to let go of uncertainties, for in the New Year, they *would* see the birth of the new life Agnes carried, and hopefully restoration of health for her.

Maggie was cuddled up beside the aunt she adored, her head nestling on the sad, bloated body while she slept. Christmas had turned out to be not only memorable, but it had been *so* enjoyable with good food and good friends that Agnes seemed to lose the awful, waxen, worried look she'd had of late and kind of… glowed. This in itself raised Tina's spirits. This was a gift that money couldn't buy. But the best present of all: Eddie's trips were to be shortened by three weeks, since some of the smaller ports of call had been removed from their schedule.

This day really had been a merry Christmas.

One short week and only one more day before Eddie's departure, the bells rang in the New Year, and Eddie and Tina drank a toast to 1909, gave thanks for the gift of their daughter, then offered a heartfelt toast for Agnes and Joe that soon their fortunes would change for the better.

On the second of January, with his canvas bag packed, Eddie bade his family a reluctant goodbye. *The Rose* was ready to take to the sea once more.

Before leaving, Eddie confessed to a deep concern for Agnes. All the warnings hadn't prepared him for the shock, not just her size, how gravely ill she looked. But it wasn't only Agnes that troubled him. Eddie was fearful about Tina. Her constant tiredness and lack of energy was proof that in an effort to help Agnes, she was draining her own self.

'The worry and torment is written all over your face,' Eddie told Tina, 'and I know you want to do everything in your power to help. I understand how you feel, little one, honest I do.' Eddie's face scrunched with the pain of having to say what had to be said. 'You feel a duty to look after Agnes and I get that, but you also have a duty to look after yourself and Maggie too.'

How do you curb the natural protection a woman like Tina had for her kin? Eddie wasn't trying to be an overbearing husband and he certainly had no wish to be the heavy-handed husband. He was quite simply a man torn apart with fears for his own wife.

'It's true I'm tired, Eddie,' Tina finally admitted. 'But soon, things will go back to how they were before Agnes got sick. Nothing lasts forever. Hold the thought that time will heal.'

Sympathy for her cousin had backed Tina into an emotional corner and the promises she made at their parting sent Eddie away with some relief. But then, once Eddie was gone, the promises she made were forgotten. In her effort to help Agnes, Tina became so listless, she seemed on the brink of collapse, and the sorry sight brought her mother's wrath.

'No matter how devoted you are to Agnes, your own child should be your first priority.' It was a strain for Maggie Morris to stay her natural impulse to speak as she found, but by the power of sheer will, she kept what had to be said to an opinion rather than a warning. 'Don't try to deny you're worn out. There are black circles under your eyes and if you don't watch out, you'll land in hospital again.' There was the merest tremble in her voice and Maggie's eyes became moist. 'You need to think long and hard, Tina, if not about yourself, then think about that poor, little infant.'

For weeks, Maggie Morris had watched in silence until she was unable to stand by and watch a second longer. The verbal ear-bashing finally forced Tina to take heed.

'You're right as usual, I am tired.' Tina had admitted it to Eddie and now, she was repeating it to her mother. Besides, the mirror told no lies and it showed that fatigue really was beginning to tell on her.

This was the day she made a genuine promise to rest more, a promise that was kept and if truth be told, she did feel better for it. With winter at its height, Tina didn't have much of an urge to stray for too long from the blazing heat of her own fireside anyway. She devoted mornings, but *only* a few hours of the morning, to helping Agnes with each and every chore which were a near nigh impossibility for her. They were the morning duties, but in the afternoon, Tina used the time of her baby's afternoon nap for her own rest and respite.

Chapter Fourteen

Snow lay thick on the ground and icicles hung from the roans as Tina carefully made her way up the street. She enveloped Maggie in the thick, woollen shawl that covered her head down to her midriff and gave both of them protection from the cold morning air.

The house was freezing and Agnes was still in bed. Tina handed her the baby. 'Take Maggie beside you and keep her warm under the blankets while I get a fire going before I get you something to eat,' Tina said through chattering teeth.

'I would love a cup of tea, but leave the fire and I'll light it later. I've made my mind up to get out of this bed and if it kills me, I'm going to clean out the bloody ashes myself. You've no idea how it hurts to have you skivvy for me.' Agnes made an attempt to get out of bed but the effort made her wince and she fell back onto the pillow.

'Just you stay where you are and keep warm, I'll have a fire going before the kettle boils.' Tina rubbed her hands together and shivered. 'It's so cold in here, there's ice inside the windows.'

'Joe slept in this morning and didn't have time to light the fire.'

Within minutes, the fire was blazing and the very glow made the room feel cosier. Tina brought a cup of tea and sat on the edge of the bed. 'How do you feel now?' she asked.

'You must think me a right lazy cow, still in bed at this time. I'm sorry, Tina, but I feel so bad this morning.' Suddenly, she screwed up her face. 'There's that pain again, it's been coming and going all night and it gets worse by the minute. What's wrong with me? I must have done something so bad; this is the punishment I deserve.'

'Listen to me, Agnes: you've never done a bad thing in your life. If the pain keeps coming and going, it could mean your time's come. How long ago was the last one?'

'Maybe about ten minutes, I'm not sure.'

'It looks like your labour's started. Stay calm. Keep Maggie tucked in beside you while I fetch the midwife.'

Ten minutes that seemed like ten hours passed before Lily arrived, full of business and ready to deliver another precious being into the world. 'Now,' Lily said, handing Maggie back to her mother, 'remember on the way here I told you all the things I would need? If you get everything ready, I'll have a wee look at Mrs O'Neill to see how she's progressing.'

The house had to be kept warm, so Tina busied herself by building up the fire and putting pots of water on the stove to heat. She was anxious and unable to shake off the feeling that all wasn't well. Finally the door opened, but the midwife was unsmiling.

'You were right to come for me,' Lily said, 'poor thing hasn't had an easy time carrying the bairn and I'm afraid she isn't going to have an easy birth either.' She was fidgety and didn't look Tina straight in the eye. 'Something's definitely amiss,' she muttered with an anxious frown.

This was the most fearful moment of Tina's life. Dying in childbirth wasn't uncommon and by tomorrow, Agnes could be gone forever. Tina bolted from the house to find her mother and tell her to fetch Aunt Lizzie.

Lily was an expert midwife, the best, but she knew birthing wasn't as easy and natural as some liked to make out. When midday came with little progress, she was forced to admit to never attending a confinement this bad. If she had to call the doctor, it would be the first time in her career.

Joe had taken to hurrying home during the short dinner break, although there was hardly time to grab a sandwich before he had to leave. Seeing Agnes was the important thing. This afternoon, Joe came in, took one look at everyone gathered in his sitting room and knew right away there was some mishap. 'What's happened?' he asked, his face white with fear at the solemnity that filled the room. 'Where's my Agnes?'

The midwife came hurrying from the bedroom. 'Agnes heard your voice, Mr O'Neill, she asked me to tell you this is the day you'll become a father.' The smile that was meant to be comforting did nothing to allay Joe's fears. He may not be an educated man, but he wasn't stupid either and instinctively in his heart, he knew there was a crisis.

Joe didn't return to the mill that afternoon. It would have been impossible for him to concentrate on work so instead, he sat by the bed. Never before had he felt so inadequate and powerless. He could do nothing to ease the pain Agnes was suffering. As the contractions grew stronger, he could only hold her hand and whisper words of comfort.

It was late afternoon when her waters finally broke. Lily ordered Joe into the sitting room and told him to stay there until he was called. They waited and waited with only a silent prayer on all their lips.

'I can't understand why she hasn't sailed through this,' Lizzie said woefully. 'Tina was the fragile one and look how easy Maggie's birth was. My Agnes was always a big, strong girl, so why can't she get this baby out? I've known women to have a hard time but this is the worst I've ever seen.'

Joe sat with his head in his hands, covering his ears, not wanting to hear these words of doom. He didn't believe God would allow a girl, as kind and caring as his Agnes, to die in childbirth. A sound that was music to their ears, the sound of a baby crying came from the room and minutes later, the midwife brought the newborn wrapped in a towel. 'You have a son, Joe, and a right little bruiser he is too, close to ten pounds I'd say.'

'What about Agnes, can I see her now?'

'She was asking for you, so go in and tell her how clever she is. I'll bathe the little O'Neill and bring him to meet his parents.'

'He's perfect, sweetheart.' Joe kissed Agnes and held her tired body in a gentle embrace. 'I'm so proud of you...' He was suddenly aware of the beads of perspiration gathering on her brow as her face crumpled in pain.

'Oh Joe, get the nurse,' she cried, writhing in agony, 'hurry—oh the pain—something's not right.'

Anguish sliced through his heart and Joe's frantic plea echoed around the house, gripped in fear. 'Quick, nurse, help her. Something's wrong, please help her.'

Nurse Lily was at the bedside in less than a heartbeat. Joe was unceremoniously pushed from the room with a warning to stay out. The moment that door closed in his face, Joe felt more frightened and alone than he had ever been in his entire life.

The midwife took one look at the distress Agnes was in and folded back the bedcovers. 'Let's see what the trouble is.' Her eyebrows rose in shocked surprise. 'Well, I never,' she said, 'I don't know where this tiny one was hiding, but it seems your son has a twin.' A few minutes later, the second child was born, only this time; there was no flaying of little arms, no kicking of little legs in eagerness to greet the world—and no crying. This ever so tiny little being wasn't a healthy pink: she was deep blue from head to toe. Lily let out a small sob, it was apparent now why Agnes had been unwell for the past months. 'I'm so sorry, Mrs O'Neill, but the baby girl… I'm afraid she's stillborn.'

'NO!' Agnes's screams brought Joe running into the room. Lily briefly explained that there had been two separate babies, but whereas the boy was big and healthy, his tiny, underdeveloped, twin sister had died in the womb and that was why only one heartbeat was heard. It also explained why Agnes had been so ill. The stillborn infant was wrapped in a towel and Lily rushed her away. This wasn't a pretty sight for a new mother to see.

'Why can't I see my baby?' Close to hysteria and completely inconsolable, Agnes sobbed her heartbreak. 'Where's my wee girl? Where's my Pearl?'

'My poor, poor darling, our wee girl was so tiny and weak, she didn't stand a chance.' Joe tried to give solace as well as some kind of credence to this incredibly cruel thing that had happened to them. 'Lily says she died weeks ago. Aw, sweet Jesus, it's not right after all you went through,' and their tears mingled as Joe and Agnes wept their despair.

Eventually, the crying stopped and an unnatural calm took over. Lily brought their new son and handed him to Joe, but Agnes turned her head away and refused to look at the baby. 'Please look at him,' Joe begged. 'This is *our* son, Connor Joseph O'Neill and he needs his mother.'

Slowly, Agnes turned her head, then before she could make any objections, Joe put the baby in her arms. The little, round face, so like Joe's, screwed up and the open mouth searched for sustenance.

'He's hungry after such a long battle to come into the world. Try feeding him,' Lily urged.

Connor suckled greedily and Agnes smiled. Her expression softened as she ran a finger over the contours of the baby's face. 'He looks like you, Joe,' she said dreamily.

'I'd rather he was good-looking like his mother.' Joe fought to contain the terrible sorrow. It was so difficult to act casual, but if ever there was a time to be brave, this was that time. He couldn't show the sadness that crushed his heart.

'I'll be off now; it's been a long day.' Lily threw her red cape around shoulders that were bent with fatigue. 'Get some rest, Agnes. I'll see you and this handsome, young man tomorrow.'

Joe walked with her to the door. 'I'll be eternally grateful to you for the life of my son,' he said through a torrent of silent tears, 'but more so for pulling Agnes from the jaws of death.'

The exhausted midwife buried her face in her hands. 'I feared it was going to end that way,' she said. 'You certainly have a beautiful boy, aw but I'm so sorry about the baby girl. There was absolutely no indication of twins, and the boy was that big, he obscured the littlest one. I didn't want to say anything in front of Agnes, but there's something very painful to discuss: the baby's burial. I can arrange for her to be buried at no expense to you and it will be a Christian burial.'

'I… we would be grateful.' Joe knew that it was usual for stillborn infants to be put in the coffin of someone about to be buried. 'Will Agnes get over this?' Joe asked, for in the back of his mind, there was the worry that her mind could be damaged.

'Time's a great healer and your wife has the constitution of an ox. A weaker woman couldn't have survived this day or the weeks leading up to it.'

The house emptied, Agnes slept and Joe sat alone with his thoughts. He was saddened by the loss of their baby girl, yet thankful God had spared his wife and son.

Chapter Fifteen

The winter of 1908 had been a pitiful time for the O'Neil's. It was in the past, but the sadness of that time couldn't be changed and would never be forgotten. The springtime of 1909 may have been somewhat inconspicuous within the dull industrial streets, but in the park where Tina and Agnes walked each day with Maggie and Connor, they were surrounded by glorious colour. It somehow gladdened heart and spirit to walk among the hosts of spring flowers. Daffodils, crocuses and snowdrops, revived by the warming sun, pushed forth from the earth to greet the season of birth and new beginnings.

Outwardly, Agnes appeared to be fully recovered from the difficult pregnancy which, were it not for her strength of body, would surely have taken her from them, and although she never spoke openly about the loss of her baby daughter, there was always an aura of sadness when she held little Maggie. Many times, Tina caught her wiping a secret tear from her eye. Connor had become the centre of her existence. Her fear of losing another child was so great, she constantly fussed over her baby son to fiercely protect him from the world at large.

Tina gloried in the companionship that made her solitude easier to bear. She was happy to drift along on a cloud of contentment with life as it was. It never entered her mind that Agnes was living on a shoestring, and being in this work or want situation would eventually demand her return to the mill to earn. A grasping need to hold onto the companionship her cousin gave never struck Tina as selfish.

Agnes was aware, that other than Eddie, she was the one person who made Tina's lonely existence tolerable and this fact made what had to be done, the most painful thing she ever had to do.

Connor was now four months old, and Agnes had fully recovered her health and strength. She was well enough to return to work and her anguish at having to break the news to Tina was immeasurable. 'It's time I pulled my weight,' she explained gently, but firmly. 'You have to understand, Tina, I need to earn. Joe can't be expected to work night and day while I take walks in the park.' It hurt so much to crush Tina this way after all that she'd done.

The utter despair was like a great, black veil that fell over Tina. She had settled into a way of life that contented her and now… 'You can't,' she cried woefully, 'what about Connor?'

'Mum's going to look after him for me.'

As kindly as possible under the circumstances, Agnes made it clear she didn't invite criticism over this issue that was for her a necessity, not an indulgence. But for Tina, left with the prospect of being alone once more, the anguish was too much to bear.

'If it's money you need, I can help.' Her eyes shone with hope and Tina insisted, 'You wouldn't have to go back to the mill, not just yet anyway.' Surely, this was the solution to both their problems. Or was Tina grasping a last straw that was about to snap?

'Be reasonable, Tina. You know full well I would never take handouts from you or anyone else. I have to *earn* a living and that's an end to it. Please, don't drench me in this guilt.'

'Then will you at least leave going back for a few weeks yet?'

'I can't do that, Tina, because I've already arranged to start back on Monday. You might think I'm a selfish cow after all you did for us, but you've no idea how much I need to do this, or how it tore my heart out having to tell you.'

The discussion was ended: Agnes was willing and able to return to the mill and on Monday, she was going to do just that.

There was only one day of the week to look forward to now, Saturday. That would, as always, remain the day of paying their way and getting in the weekend groceries.

As the months passed, Tina saw Agnes return to the jolly, fun-loving person she used to be and accepted that work was the best therapy after all. For a time, they had been two links in the same chain and now, that chain had been broken. It was difficult not to be envious when Agnes related in graphic detail all the day-to-day happenings at the mill. Tina listened, but she was no longer a part of that world, and the stories only provoked a feeling of isolation and depravation. Meanwhile, a bond was growing between Maggie and Connor that would eventually become as strong as the bond between their mothers.

Maggie and Tina were the beacons that guided Eddie home. They were the sun, the moon and the stars. They were the centre of his universe. The fourteenth of May, 1910, was Maggie's second birthday and Eddie planned a party to remember.

That Saturday, there was a cake, complete with pink icing and candles. All the neighbouring children were there for jelly and ice cream, sticky buns and of course—games. The children were enthralled by the conjuring tricks Eddie had learned on his travels and little Connor, who obviously worshipped and adored his Uncle Eddie, toddled closely behind him wherever he went.

The house was filled with the sound of happy children at play. It had been a day of fun and frolics, for Eddie, as well as the assortment of little girls and boys. His proficiency at entertaining the children had also earned him a certain amount of hero worship.

With the party almost at an end, Tina whispered to Agnes to help her cut the cake, and they left Eddie to carry on with the games and tricks that held the children in awe and brought peals of laughter. The day had been a complete and utter success. Eddie could hear the buzz of conversation and laughter coming from the scullery as Tina and Agnes made up goody bags for the children to take home. Suddenly there was a crashing sound followed by Agnes's heart-stopping scream, '*Eddie*, come quick.'

The blood drained from Eddie's face at the sight of Tina lying on the floor with Agnes bending over her. He was so frozen with fear; it was all he could do to ask what happened.

'We were just talking and then I heard the thud, when I looked...' In that instant, Agnes had a vision of the first time this happened, the fainting spell that morning in Coutts's office. Her mind didn't want to believe, but her heart knew this was the first tell-tale sign. Tina had to be expecting again.

Eddie lifted the small, inert body and carried her into the bedroom. Gradually, consciousness returned and Tina made a half-hearted joke about children's parties sapping the strength. Eddie was in no mood to make light of an episode that had frightened the living daylights out of him and he told Tina point blank he was taking her to see the doctor, even if it meant carrying her there himself.

Doctor Jackson reclined in his chair and indicated the two chairs in front of his desk with a flourish of the hand. He asked them to take a seat and tell him what the trouble was. There was no response to the question. Tina maintained an irritating silence.

Eddie had no alternative but to answer for her. 'My wife had a fainting spell and…'

Suddenly, Tina regained the power of speech. 'My husband is overreacting! We had a few children in to celebrate Maggie's second birthday and I got overtired, that's all there is to it.'

Doctor Jackson peered sourly at Eddie over his gold-rimmed glasses then smiled fondly at Tina. 'I remember the last time you came to see me about a fainting spell, it turned out you were pregnant. Let's see what caused this one, shall we?' He examined her briefly, then glowered acidly and accusingly at Eddie. 'It's a bit early to be one hundred percent positive, but I think it's safe to say you're having another baby.' His jaw was set and his tone was hostile when the doctor turned to Eddie. 'What I can't understand is why *you* let this happen. You were aware of Tina's heart condition, therefore, under the circumstances, I would have expected you to take some kind of precaution to make sure this didn't happen.'

The not too subtle reprimand left Eddie reeling and angry. How dare this man make recriminations? This so-called doctor was more or less accusing him of harming the one person he loved more than life itself. Eddie looked at Tina and the anger faded. What point was there arguing when, in his heart of hearts, he knew the doctor was only speaking the truth?

They walked in silence from the surgery until Tina could no longer contain herself. 'You're angry, aren't you, Eddie?' She felt guilty. 'You're angry about me expecting again.'

Eddie stopped abruptly in the quiet lane that led to Charles Street and wrapped his arms around Tina. 'I could never be angry with you when the blame rests with me. Oh little one, I worry so much about you, then go and let this happen. How could I have been this stupid?'

'There's no need to worry! I was fine with Maggie and I'll be the same with this one, you'll see.' She reached for Eddie's hand and laid her head against his chest. There was great anxiety in the rapid thump, thump of his heart. 'Maybe I'll give you a son this time,' she said to lightly soothe the minute.

A son, *his* son: Eddie smiled at a prospect that appealed to him. He loved Maggie, but you couldn't play rough games with a little girl. Whereas a little tough guy like Connor; the rougher the game, the more he laughed. In an instant, the marvel of it was spent and a kind of bleakness set in. Tina's mother still had to be told and one very painful thought outweighed Eddie's initial joy. It was a foregone conclusion, that if she didn't like him before, she would like him even less now. But pregnancy wasn't something which could be hid for very long, therefore, putting off wasn't an option.

Mrs Morris listened as they enthused about the second child Tina was carrying. And then, with a look that could turn anyone to stone, she uttered her verdict. 'I don't think either one of you has the brains you were born with,' she said icily. Maggie had a particular foible if she was angry or upset and today, she was both, so like a Titan, she marched around the room with her trusty feather duster, boisterously flicking dust from ornaments. But even this didn't hold back her boiling temper. The mask of composure slipped and she screamed at Eddie. '*You* should have known better than to let this happen.'

'It wasn't all Eddie's fault,' Tina cried in defence of her husband. 'It… it just happened.' She wanted to scream at her mother, "You've been alone so long, you've forgotten what love and passion is." Then Tina reminded herself that words spoken in a moment of anger would haunt for a lifetime.

Perhaps the austere Mrs Morris did remember what loving and being loved was like. She put aside the feather duster and said, 'Well, what's done can't be undone unless the Good Lord himself sanctions it.' Maggie sat like a queen on her throne, hands clasped in reluctant acceptance of what was simply the consequence of a tragic error in a moment when passion ruled.

The next six months were like a leap in time; they went so quickly. Mrs Morris rose above the initial dissention and even looked forward to the birth of her second grandchild, which she predicted to be a boy.

Tina kept reasonably well, but tired easily. She also expanded more than she had done with the first pregnancy and her girth didn't go unnoticed by Maggie. She prodded her mother curiously when the baby kicked and innocently asked if Tina had butterflies in her tummy. Tina explained to the child that she was to have a little brother or sister and would be relied upon to help with the new baby, a prospect that pleased and excited the little girl. Although no more than a baby herself, Maggie was developing a strong-willed, independent nature, just as Nurse Lily had predicted the day she was born.

Billy came into the world two days after Connor's second birthday. It was another short labour and relatively easy birth without complications. 'It seems you're one of those women who can give birth as easily as shelling peas,' the midwife commented, 'and beautiful, healthy babies too.'

Eddie's unbounded joy at the birth of his son delighted Tina and gave her a feeling of supremacy and such pride, the like of which she had never before known. There was something magical about watching Eddie with his new son, the way he gently held the tiny hands and stroked the baby's face as if he couldn't believe this miracle. Oh he adored Maggie, there was no doubt about that and he made a point of never excluding her in favour of the new baby, but it was obvious little Billy was the apple of his father's eye. Eddie also glowed with pride to write home with the news that their second child, his son, had been named after his grandfather.

The easy, uncomplicated birth lulled Eddie into a sense of complacency. And then Doctor Jackson called to check on Tina and the new baby. Eddie spoke with him at the door as he was leaving, gratefully enthusing over how well Tina was, thanks to the doctor's diligence. 'All that worry for nothing, eh,' Eddie said light-heartedly.

'I didn't realise you were worried about your wife. You certainly never showed any sign of fretting over her health,' the doctor said sarcastically. He didn't know Eddie all that well, but he did know Tina. He'd been present at her birth and seen her through her illness, which may have contributed to his prejudice against this foreigner.

'Of course I worry,' Eddie answered indignantly to the slur.

'Then come to the surgery tomorrow—if it's not too much bother,' Doctor Jackson said crisply. 'I need to have a private word with you, but alone, if you don't mind.' He spoke in such a low whisper, Eddie had to lean closer to hear him.

The door closed and Eddie stood for a moment, musing over the order that had dripped like acid from the doctor's tongue. What was it all about? He probably wanted to give advice on birth control to protect Tina from further *accidents.* But then, given Tina's natural shyness, this kind of delicate advice would have been embarrassing and awkward for her, and excluding her from all the descriptive guidance was no more than a saving grace gesture for Tina's sake.

The following day, Eddie felt no sense of foreboding when he went along to the surgery, fully believing he had been summoned for nothing more than a man-to-man pep talk.

With both hands clasped under his chin, Doctor Jackson leaned across the desk. 'About Billy's birth,' he began, 'like Maggie's, it was straightforward with no complications.' He heard the deep, audible sigh and watched Eddie relax in the chair. 'Unfortunately, it's not all good news,' he continued. 'Your wife's health, her heart to be precise, is giving me cause for concern.'

Eddie paled. 'Now, hold on, doc,' he interrupted, 'I thought this little meeting was only for you to dish out some do's and don'ts? Tina says she feels fine and she looks so well, I took it for granted there was no cause for worry. Now you're telling me there is? I don't understand.'

'There most assuredly is cause for worry.' Doctor Jackson reached for a glass of water that sat on his desk and took a couple of gulps before continuing. 'From a medical viewpoint, things aren't as well as you seem to think. The fact is, giving birth was no easy matter and it put her heart under considerable strain. Right now, Tina thinks the worst is over, and tiredness is part and parcel of childbirth, but I assure you, she will become more and more lethargic with time. I *urge* you to ensure she rests as much as possible. Think of it as building a temporary dam; the deterioration can't be stopped, but with proper care, it can be held back for a time.'

This wasn't happening! Dark terror wrapped itself around Eddie until he could hardly breathe. He couldn't accept the possibility that he might lose Tina, but a failing heart was a death sentence and if anything happened to her…

'There's no telling how rapidly the condition will worsen. I've given you my prognosis and my advice, the rest is up to you.'

Walking cleared his mind, and Eddie made a decision to speak to Mrs Morris. It wasn't going to be easy and it wasn't going to be pleasant, but it was something that had to be done. She was after all, Tina's mother and by definition, was entitled to know the truth. If necessary, he would beg her help on bended knee.

It may not have been the most painful thing in his life Eddie had ever done, but it was certainly in the top two. Mrs Morris wept bitterly that her worst fear had been realised.

'Tina's independent and proud to stand on her own two feet,' Eddie said with a kind of quiet admiration. 'She probably hasn't told you about her financial situation because it would be too much like bragging.'

'My girl doesn't show off because she's a saver, not a squanderer,' Mrs Morris answered haughtily.

Eddie matched her arrogance. 'And I make sure she has money to save,' he told her bluntly. 'Now, on the domestic side, will you make sure Tina has all the help she needs? I'm more than willing to pay, no matter what the cost.'

'I beg your pardon!' Mrs Morris frowned and glowered indignantly. 'Do you think I would take payment for helping my own daughter? I took care of her for eighteen years before *you* came along. I didn't need payment then and I don't need it now,' she bristled.

The absolute frustration of trying to break through this barrier of prejudice was too much to handle. She waved her bigotry like a flag of war. Eddie said, 'You don't like me very much, do you?' There was a hint of misery in the question.

It may have been the desperation on his face, but at that moment, something touched the heart of Maggie Morris. 'Oh Eddie, when will you stop thinking of me as your enemy? How could I possibly dislike someone who loves my daughter so much?'

All at once, the air in that room seemed to clear and it felt so good. An omen, that's what Eddie took it to be: a portent that all would be well. His mother-in-law, the one person he wanted to be his friend and ally, had been distinctly wary of him from the first minute she clapped eyes on him and Eddie had an immediate sense of it. But he accepted her harshly critical and suspicious nature. And now, on this night, when sadness and fear gripped both their hearts, came the realisation that she wasn't the supreme witch Eddie took her to be. All that was left now was to go home and make pretences.

Eddie stood at the door for a moment or two before going in to face Tina. He must be strong and give no inkling that he had spoken to Doctor Jackson. And he now had to do the one thing he swore never to do—lie to her.

When Tina laughingly asked, 'Where have you been? I began to think you'd deserted me,' that sweet, loving smile chipped another tiny piece from his heart.

She mustn't see his face, Eddie couldn't allow that. His arms encircled the petite body and he held her so close, she couldn't see into his eyes when he lied. 'I was just walking past your Mum's house when I got to thinking, that with my time ashore so limited, I don't visit her nearly as often I should. It was all on a whim really, the thought that it would be nice to thank her personally for helping you with my two beautiful babies.' Eddie salved his conscience by telling himself it wasn't really a lie, more a half truth.

The house was peacefully quiet while the children slept. It was one of those rare, golden moments when the opportunity presented itself to snatch some precious time alone together. Tina squeezed herself into the armchair beside Eddie and rested her head on his shoulder. Her breathing was steady and even. Her body was slender, but firm. Was it possible the doctor had made the wrong diagnosis? Doctors were only human and they weren't infallible. It may have been no more than wishful thinking, but he preferred to grasp at hope rather than give up hope completely. It seemed quite logical to Eddie, that if Tina was cosseted and shielded from stress and strain, her health would improve.

In the most matter-of-fact way, he said, 'I asked your Mum to find someone reliable to help you with the children. We can afford it.'

'I will not!' Tina jumped up and stamped her foot in abhorrence at the suggestion. 'I resent the idea of squandering the money you've worked so hard to earn and I am not helpless, Eddie, so please change the subject.'

Eddie did just that. He smiled apologetically, as if to convey the message that this subject was forgotten… finite, dropped from his vocabulary… for the time being at least. In retrospect, perhaps the best tactic would be to let her think that it had been no more than a suggestion, but since she was so vehemently against the idea, that was an end to it.

Having her bidding readily-accepted coaxed Tina into a kind of lull and she settled back in the chair beside Eddie. Afternoons spent like this were what Tina called their catching up time, and a more relaxed frame of mind banished her resentment. 'Talk to me about Australia,' she said. 'You told me all about what a wonderful place it was, but you never did tell me why you left.'

'Australia!' Eddie said fondly. 'So much still to tell about that part of my life, and here we are married three years: sort of puts things into perspective, doesn't it? How little time we've actually spent together, I mean. There are things I've never spoken about, things you have a right to know.'

Tina may have been naïve, but she was astute enough to pick up on guilt. From the day they met, she had taken Eddie at face value. She fell in love with the man, not some idealistic dream. As far as Tina had been led to believe, he was a hardworking sailor who toiled to earn good money. Didn't she have the bank book to prove it? Today, she would find out the full extent of Eddie's wealth.

'Then tell me what you think I have a right to know.'

'To begin with, when I chose to become a mariner, it was about my love of the sea. You have to take into consideration that I was an only child who could have anything I wanted… regardless of cost.'

'You say that like you were rich or something.'

Eddie laughed wryly. 'My parents were already loaded when my grandmother died and then we inherited all her money too.' He struggled to explain without sounding like a braggart. Inherited wealth had always been an embarrassment to him.

'So what if your parents had a bit of money?'

'Not just a bit of money, Tina, more money than you could ever imagine. The only reason I never told you about the money waiting for me in Australia is because we were happy and it didn't seem relevant. Do you understand what I'm trying to say? I won't acknowledge wealth handed to me on a plate, because I didn't earn it through my own sweat and tears.'

Tina brushed her lips across his cheek. 'It's called having principles,' she whispered in his ear.

'Money can't buy happiness or love, and that's what matters most in life, not material things. My mother used to say I'd be happy sleeping on a bed of straw, provided I'd worked for the straw. I thought about telling you when you agreed to marry me but be honest, little one, would it have made a blind bit of difference to the way you felt about me?'

'Money isn't a disease, Eddie, it's not catching and it wouldn't have made any difference. What I can't understand is why you found it so difficult to be truthful in the first place.'

'That's what I'm trying to explain! I wanted to be independent and make my own way in life, so please don't condemn me. I *earned* my keep and that's what was important.'

'That day you walked into the ward, I just had the feeling you were different: now I see why.' Tina rubbed her face against his shoulder. The touch and smell of his soft, clean flannel shirt always felt comforting and safe.

'The point I'm trying to make is that money was never an issue with me until I met you. I never needed or even wanted it, but there's more than me to think about now. Your little nest egg is just small change compared to what my family is worth. All you have to do is say the word.'

'I didn't marry you for money! It was *you* I wanted. Being happy and respected means more than wealth to me, so leave your money in Australia,

Eddie. One day, our children might benefit from it, but as for me, I have everything I want right here.'

'You have no idea what a relief it is to know you share my views, Tina. There are some things money can't buy, like the love I have for you, or the feeling I get just walking through that door and seeing you standing there. You'd love my parents, Tina. They have that down-to-earth goodness. Dad still works the land and Mum just loves being in her kitchen doing her own cooking and baking. They don't give a damn about wealth. All they want, all they've ever wanted is to just live for each other.'

For so long, Eddie had wanted to tell Tina of his true financial standing. How she would react was all that stopped him. Now, it was done and Tina had lived up to his expectations. She was without avarice and he had worried needlessly.

They stayed silently in each other's arms until Billy stirred and his crying reminded Tina that he was due to be fed. Almost simultaneously, Maggie woke from her nap and their brief time alone together was over. As she fed Billy, Tina smiled at the picture of Eddie holding his daughter and telling her stories she couldn't possibly understand. Her heart swelled with pride and love for this exceptional man whose concept of life was itself extraordinary.

Part Two
The Tides of War

Chapter Sixteen

In the three years following Billy's birth, Tina became serene, almost noble in her outward appearance. She had taken Doctor Jackson's council to live life at a leisurely pace and against all odds, her health actually improved.

The day Eddie told her their children would always have financial security was a milestone in her life. Eddie, wanting only the best for his family, tried and tried to coerce Tina into moving away from Charles Street: what he had in mind was a posh, little bungalow with their own garden. Tina herself had no desire to change how or where she lived, this being her true habitat, and she told Eddie in no uncertain terms that he could go on beseeching till the cows came home but it didn't matter how much persuasion he used, she would never leave Charles Street. Eventually, he accepted that a wealth of friendship was more important to her than the wealth to buy a bungalow out-with the grimy streets lined with tenement buildings.

Maggie and Connor were more like twins than cousins; walking to school every day, hand in hand. Anyone who tried to bully one or other of them, met with a force to be reckoned with. And then, in what seemed like the blinking of an eye, Billy changed from a beautiful baby to a handsome little boy.

The summer of 1914 was warm and pleasant, and although there was unrest in Europe, most people blinkered their eyes to the signs that this world was on the verge of war. It was easier and a lot less fretful to believe that whatever problems there were, would be dealt with and eventually go away.

In conversation, people assured one another that all the talk of war was plain and simple scaremongering. The idea that Britain might go into battle with Germany was scoffed at. Didn't our own royal family have ties with Germany? And a disbelieving nation settled back and put their trust in God and politicians. But the announcement came one warm day in August that the unthinkable had happened. Britain had declared war on Germany.

The news was cataclysmic, yet even as armies gathered, many still refused to believe the problem was that serious. And then the news blazed over the airways that King George had renounced all German titles and changed the royal name to *Windsor*: this was not what you'd call a storm in a teacup. The world was about to be plunged into a war to end all wars and go down in history as— "The Great War."

Posters proclaiming, *Your King and Country need you,* were everywhere, and Kitchener's pointing finger prompted men, both young and old, to enlist for service. Swashbuckling, young men who only saw the glamour, rushed to the recruitment centres, ready and willing to fight for king and country. Many, no more than boys who, fully believing they were as invincible as heroes of the silent screen, falsified their age in order to pick up a rifle and join the ranks. While many rushed to enlist, a great many remained insistent that it wouldn't last and waited to be called into action.

Joe wasn't a man who was motivated by patriotism. Although he loved his country, he just didn't see the point of rushing to get into uniform. 'I'm not taking the king's shilling,' he told Agnes, 'I'll wait until I'm called. Everyone knows it won't last six months and I'm certainly in no hurry to get to the front, only to be turned round and sent home.' It was a declaration made with the ease of an unconvinced man.

'But men are running around like headless chickens,' said Agnes kind of fearfully. 'Every morning, there are queues outside the recruitment centres.'

'If they're daft enough to enlist, that's their choice, but I'm staying put. Wait and see, Agnes, and mark my words, it'll all be over by Christmas. Everyone says so.'

Only it wasn't, and the war everyone thought would end quickly, went on. While the staggering death toll mounted, sceptics such as Joe, who never really believed the day would come when *war* would no longer be a word but a way of life, were conscripted to fight for their country.

The train station was filled with uniformed men carrying kit-bags, herded together on the platform, bidding what for many would be a final goodbye to loved ones, for according to daily bulletins, there had already been massive losses on the Western Front. So many heartbroken women gathered together, united by a common grief as husbands and sons readied themselves to go off to fight on the already blood-soaked fields of France. The anguished sound of sobbing hung on the air like a death knell.

Weeping and begging him to return safely, Agnes clung to Joe. 'You've never made me a promise you didn't keep, so now I want you to give your solemn promise right here this minute that you'll come back to Connor and me.' Her eyes were red rimmed with prolonged crying and her voice was hoarse with all the pleading for Joe to stay safe. 'If you never came back to me, I couldn't go on living and then Connor would be an orphan, so don't you *dare* get killed.' She was totally incoherent and fear had robbed Agnes of the natural optimism that Joe had forever known and loved.

Joe held her pretty, round face in his hands and silenced the anguished pleading with one long kiss. 'I love you too much never to see you again. Oh my dear Agnes, we've been together too long to let a war separate us. Just you concentrate on looking after yourself and Connor until I come home and trust me, my sweet lass; I will do my utmost to come home.' His eyes were fervently pleading with her to understand that he too was afraid this might be the last time he would ever hold her. 'I won't make you a promise I may not be able to keep, the best I can say is, I'll try not to get killed because I've too much to live for.'

Many men gave the same promise that day, standing on grimy platforms, waiting on trains that would transport them into a nightmare. There was hardly a man or boy who could or would believe that death on foreign soil or a foreign beach was a possibility. These heroic men had no way of knowing the carnage that lay ahead of them—or how few would keep the promises that had been made.

When the signal came to board, the sound of wailing and despair echoed loudly around the station as frantic women clung to their men, desperately trying to prolong the departure. Slowly, the train began to fill and carriage windows framed the faces of servicemen, all trying to catch one last glimpse of the loved ones they had been torn from.

'All aboard,' the station master waved the red lantern. It was the final call and one by one, the stragglers boarded and the carriage doors slammed shut. The train jerked into motion as the great, iron wheels turned and the train pulled out of the station.

The platform was a sea of hands held aloft, silently waving until the last carriage had disappeared out of sight. Only then did a reluctant exodus of women and children file from the station, going home to an uncertain future without the keystone of their existence.

Up to the time Agnes walked arm in arm into the station with Joe, she had never really allowed herself to believe this moment would come and now, leaving without him by her side, there was only numbness and the sorrow of withered hope. For the first time, she was forced to face the ugly truth that Joe had gone to war and she may never see him again.

The daily bulletins told of a bloodbath on the Western Front and spirits flagged as news filtered through of what now seemed to be a fruitless conflict. Kitchener's army was met by horrors they could never have imagined. Thousands of corpses littered the battlefields and the trenches.

Like many other women, Agnes worked on munitions. Christmas had come and gone with little cause for celebration, but in the munitions factory, spirits were uplifted through the power of song. The favourite of the day and the most prophetic was, "Keep the home fires burning," being sung in a chorus which could be heard even above the din and grind of machines as they turned out more and more elements of destruction. Keeping hope alive and spirits high were the things that counted most, and courage in the face of adversity became a way of life. If tears were shed, they were shed in private.

Every evening after work, Agnes made a pilgrimage to the Chapel to pray for Joe's safe return and that the telegram boy never stopped at her door. Those with men at the front held this silent prayer in their heart that they would never be handed the fateful telegram which made a wife a widow.

Everyone joined in the war effort and Eddie was no exception. Merchant seamen were an important factor in bringing much-needed supplies and may have believed they were exempt from shelling by German warships, but in May of 1915, the sinking of the neutral American liner, *Lusitania,* brought a new awareness to the dangers of Germany's lack of recognition and respect for non-military shipping.

Eddie considered himself fortunate compared to most seafarers. *The Rose* docked only briefly, but he could at least spend that brief stay with his family.

The war everyone thought wouldn't last six months, raged on with no end in sight. Now, every home had family members either at the front or working in the munitions factories. What used to be the local jute mills now produced ammunition and arms for the forces.

Agnes wrapped a shawl around her shoulders as she left the old mill and hurried to catch up with Sadie. 'I'm going to St Mary's Chapel before I go home, how about you?' Agnes put on the same old show of that cheery face she kept for the sake of friends and family. Rather this than an outright display of the gnawing fear she actually felt: the terror that Joe's existence on this earth was hanging by a thread which might snap at any given moment.

'Does praying help, Agnes? Do you honestly believe it makes a difference?'

There was a strange emptiness in Sadie's voice and Agnes felt a cold shiver rattle through her spine, although she didn't quite know why. 'Now, what's all this about? Of course, it makes a difference,' she answered with a comforting arm around those sad, drooping shoulders while keeping up the cheery charade. 'Don't let go, Sadie, you need to have faith and hold onto hope because without that, we have nothing.'

'Do you ever have the feeling you'll never see Joe again? There's like a cold hand clutching my heart and I have this dread that Len's never coming home. There are times I can't even remember his face or his voice and that can't be normal.' Sadie choked back unshed tears. 'I think it's some kind of premonition and it scares the hell out of me.'

'Everyone fears the worst, it's only natural, but you're letting your imagination run riot, Sadie.'

How do you give consolation to someone when you can't feel what they're feeling? Could it be that Len was dead and this was what it was like to lose someone? Even before the news comes, you know, for it's like a light has been dimmed. They might still be in your mind, but in the darkness, you can't see their face. Agnes had a memory of Joe so vivid, she felt she could reach out and touch him. She never let go of the trust and belief that when this war ended, he was coming back to her.

Sadie was all at once abashed. Maybe it was just her silliness. 'I'm sorry! I shouldn't be upsetting you like this. Put it down to the ravings of a lunatic.' She hesitated at this point as if wanting, yet couldn't say what was on her mind. The need to share her fears won. 'Christ Almighty, Agnes, it was the terrible dream I had last night that Len had been killed. It was so real I woke in a sweat, but I tell you what, tonight I'll burn two bloody candles in the window just to be sure.'

Candles burned in so many windows, lit and tended by women who believed that the light would guide a husband or son home. Of course, it was nothing more than superstition, a straw to grasp, yet so many were still left heartbroken by the news that a husband or son was never coming home. Only then was the candle extinguished.

When the telegram boy cycled into any street, women with fear in their hearts gathered to see where the fateful telegram would be delivered. The young cyclist on the red bicycle was the first person Agnes and Sadie saw when they turned into Charles Street and hardly daring to breathe, they watched him stop outside the block where Sadie lived.

'I know that telegram's for me,' Sadie gripped her arm so hard; it was all Agnes could do not to yelp with pain. 'I've been haunted all day with the feeling something bad had happened to Len.' Her pace quickened and she called to the boy as he walked towards the close. 'Who are you looking for?'

He glanced at the small buff envelope and answered, 'this one's for Patterson.'

'Oh dear God no, please, not my Len.' Sadie's hysteria, her shrieks of despair carried throughout Charles Street and Agnes had to lend a steadying hand as shock overcame Sadie and her legs buckled.

The statutory message was cruelly short. *Regret to inform you that Private Leonard Patterson was killed in action.* How could so few words have so much meaning? How many lives had been decimated and hearts broken by this one short message?

There had to be a bond, a link that distance couldn't break. How else did Sadie instinctively know that Len was dead? It was of paramount importance now for Agnes to sustain her belief that Joe was alive and **would** come back to them. She could see his face clearly in her mind's eye; the contour of his cheeks and the cleft in his chin. Agnes was so afraid to lose this vision, for if like Sadie she couldn't remember… if a time came when his face faded from her memory, she would never see Joe again.

Chapter Seventeen

At the battle of the Somme, where so many gave their lives, Joe was almost fatally injured and spent many weeks in a field hospital fighting for his life while doctors fought to save his shattered leg. He later swore that through the haze of pain, he had heard Agnes call out to him, 'stay alive,' and it was this that pulled him back from the brink of death.

Joe returned home a cripple, but alive. The day he limped through the door on crutches, Agnes wept with joy that her prayers had been answered. She went to the Chapel to kneel in prayer and thank God that the man she had loved since childhood was with her once more.

The horrors of the battlefield manifested themselves in nightmares and it was a fearsome thing to see a man like Joe terrified to the brink of madness. Finally, Agnes shook him awake from another nightmare. She rocked her broken man in her arms and sadly told him, 'I think it's time you talked about it, Joe. The only way to cast out them demons from your mind is through your mouth.'

She watched Joe ease his shaking body into the armchair, his head bowed with shame, for he was ashamed of his own frailty. Agnes knelt before him and held both his hands in hers, and the shaking ceased. He had the need to tell of the horrors he had witnessed. And now, with his brave wife's ears willing and ready to listen, the story of unspeakable terror would be spoken.

Joe wiped away a tear with the back of his hand and the saddest of stories began.

'Some battalions were all but wiped out and the stench of death was all around us,' and his trembling intensified with every word. 'Every time we were ordered over the top... I can't describe the fear, the way my heart pounded so hard inside my chest, for there was only two options; either die in the field or be shot as a coward.'

Joe stared wide-eyed into space, silent, as a fresh wave of horror swept through his heart, mind and soul. With words of comfort softly spoken, Agnes gently led him from the grim place where his mind had taken him. 'I'm here with you now, my darling Joe,' she told him.

His eyes flickered and at last, Joe let go the words that told of his ordeal. 'The flash of gunfire, the whining of a thousand bullets, agonised screams. Sights and sounds of slaughter, and all you can do is carry on firing your gun and wait for the bullet that ends it for you.' Big, strong hands that had always been used to hard work now covered his face to blot out those memories.

Agnes gently took his hands away from his face. 'Go on, Joe,' she said, 'let it out.'

'There was little time to eat or sleep, and all you could think about was home and those you might never see again. I kept telling myself that the promise made to you must be kept. And then, it was the searing pain that took me by surprise and I realised I'd been shot. I must have fallen back into the trench and then when I came to, the first thing I remember was hardly being able to breathe. There were bodies all around and the body on top of me was this kid, little Christie Smith. He was just a boy, not yet fifteen, a kid whose only sin was nicking an apple from the greengrocers. His face was almost touching mine, his eyes were staring. I can still see the terror in those eyes. I remember telling him that I'd been shot, but he didn't move so I shoved him aside and his… his…' Joe rocked back and forward in an effort to ease the mental agony. 'Oh Agnes, his guts were all over me and the trench ran with a river of blood.'

Guttural sounds came from Agnes's mouth. The words that she tried to speak were throaty and slurred through the weeping and the heartbroken sobs, and all she could do was cling tightly to Joe and bear the misery with him.

Joe's eyes brimmed with pain as he resurrected all the hurt of that time. 'My mates were all dead or dying and we were like pigs in the mire,' he muttered with all the hostility that battle instils in a man. 'I don't remember much more after that. I don't even remember how I got to the hospital. It must have been during a ceasefire when stretcher-bearers were allowed to collect wounded. And with these memories that will haunt me till the day I die, they say I'm one of the lucky ones.'

Finally, Agnes managed to speak. 'Those bloody awful memories *will* fade, Joe,' she promised. 'Hang onto that thought and we'll get through this— together.'

Agnes lay awake that night. As she watched Joe sleep soundly for the first time since his homecoming, she wept silently.

'His injuries will mend in time,' Agnes told Tina. 'We can live with that. It's the nightmares that are the worst. I worry that they'll never really go away.'

'I have a nightmare too that won't go away.' Tina clasped her hands over her belly. 'I'm expecting again,' she said woefully.

'You're what? Christ Almighty, this is no time to be expecting.' Agnes was well aware that not only the carrying, but giving birth to another child could have a seriously life-threatening effect on Tina. The last thing she wanted was to upset her further, but it was so hard to hide her angst. 'You poor wee soul, and I suppose you haven't even had the chance to tell Eddie.'

Scared and alone, Tina must have agonised over her predicament. How could she burden Agnes even further when she had enough problems of her own to contend with? So she kept it to herself and nursed her woe. It was her cousin's heartfelt compassion that let loose the bitter fears.

'What if I never get the chance to tell him? There are German ships out there and anything could happen. Look what happened to the *Lusitania*. I don't think I could bear it if Eddie never came back.'

'Now, you've got to stop thinking like that, you've got to keep telling yourself Eddie's coming home and he will. You must keep on believing he's going to walk through that door any day now.'

Perhaps it was easier for Agnes to keep a positive attitude and blank out the horrors of war. She was one of the lucky ones; her husband was a survivor.

'I don't feel well, Agnes, and there's not an ounce of energy in my body. When I was expecting Maggie and Billy, you used to say I positively glowed, and I could see it myself when I looked in the mirror. Now this white face with great, dark shadows under the eyes stares back at me. Something's gone badly wrong this time and I'm afraid.'

'It's me who should have paid more attention to you instead of being so wrapped up in my own little world. I looked at you but couldn't see what was staring me in the face, blind bitch that I am.' Anger took over from empathy, a rage that she had failed the one person who should have been a priority. 'I thought you were just fretting about Eddie and not sleeping very well. Why, oh why didn't you say something?'

'I wanted to, but you had been through so much already with Joe's injuries and everything. All I want is for Eddie to come home, hold me and tell me everything's going to be fine.'

'And he will,' said Agnes as reassuringly as she could manage.

'Do you really think so, Agnes?'

'Of course, I do,' Agnes lied, but with fingers crossed nevertheless.

Five weeks later, *The Rose* docked and the work of unloading the cargo of much-needed supplies began immediately. There was no time for dallying while people's needs were great and in a few short hours, they must take to the sea once more.

Eddie took the opportunity to hurry home to Charles Street. Tina and the children, they were the mainstay of his life, the stars by which he plotted his way back. And then the news that he was to become a father for the third time, instead of filling him with elation and joy, had the exact opposite effect. It fuelled the tormenting worries and plunged him into the deepest despair. There was no commanding the oceans to give calm waters to sail, just as there was no commanding the beast that was war to cease while he spent time with his wife. In fact, there was all probability that Eddie wouldn't see Tina again between now and the time of the birth. She looked ghastly and he dreaded to think what the effects of carrying this child would have on her in the weeks to come.

'This damned war,' he spat the words through clenched teeth, 'it should have been over by now. They said it wouldn't last,' he roared. 'Didn't they *promise* the conflict would be short term? Always lies, lies and more lies.' Such uncommon vehemence in one as mild-mannered and good-natured as Eddie was evidence the war had robbed him of laughter and reduced him to an intensely bitter man. He was bitter now, not because Tina was pregnant, it was at himself for letting it happen.

'I wish now that I hadn't told you. I'm sorry Eddie,' Tina said mournfully. 'I *shouldn't* have said anything. As if it wasn't bad enough for you being at sea at a time like this, now I've gone and given you another millstone to bear.'

'You had every right to tell me, just as I had every right to know.' Eddie glanced briefly at his pocket watch and grimaced. 'It's like ripping my heart out leaving you here, but I have to get back.'

'Then go, Eddie, before I make demands you can't answer to.'

He held her to him, fearful of the moment his arms must let go. And then, Eddie rose above the bitterness of parting and confessed his guilt. 'I should be ashamed. Here am I complaining because we only see each other for a matter of hours every now and then when there are men at the front who will never see their families again. It's a humbling thought and I must learn to be more tolerant and thank God for small mercies.'

The brief interlude had left them with hardly enough time to catch their breath. On hearing of Eddie's predicament at having to leave his wife in such a fearful state of health, Henry offered him a stay on shore until the next time they docked. But these were hard times, so Eddie put duty before self and reluctantly declined the offer.

'Don't think I'm not grateful, Henry,' he told the skipper, 'but think what it would be like for Tina having to face the ugly things people would say. They'd criticise and condemn her for needing her man there for something as simple as a birth while their men are still fighting and dying in France. I'd be branded a coward, and Tina could never live with all the hate and name-calling. So you see, as much as I'm tempted, I can't.'

As they sailed through the estuary and out towards the open sea, Eddie looked back at the city that had become his home and wondered when or if he would ever return.

In a way, it was fortunate that Eddie didn't make it back to Dundee over the weeks to come. He would have been horrified to see Tina look so desperately ill and discover that his fears had not been unfounded. She looked at death's door by the time Eve was born. It had all been too much for her ailing heart.

While Maggie had her father's looks but her mother's dark hair, Eve was born with Tina's doll-like features and Eddie's blonde, curly locks. Her proud father wept the first time he saw this perfect, little human being. 'She's a miniature of you, Tina,' he said rapturously, 'so beautiful.' Eddie loved all his children but there was something special about this tiny symbol of hope born into a world of strife, a world torn apart by war. He was filled with wonder at how someone so small could be so perfect.

'Joe says she's going to be a head-turner and Agnes just adores her, but Billy doesn't pay much attention. Well, he's only a little boy and little boys aren't all that interested in babies.'

'What does Maggie think of her little sister?'

'She makes me feel so proud, Eddie. Oh the way she tries to mother Eve all the time. Our Maggie's only a child herself, yet she helps me in every way possible. I wish I didn't have to depend on her so much, although she does enjoy the importance.'

'And your Mum, does she help?'

'Well, her contribution to the war effort is working six days a week in the Co-op so I couldn't ask her. Then again, I have Mrs Smart coming in every day to wash and iron the children's clothes then tidy up. She's grateful for the extra money. So you see Eddie, there's no reason to worry about me.'

'I hope the war doesn't last much longer.' Eddie looked at Tina propped up in the bed and it reminded him of the first time he set eyes on her in the hospital. The beautiful face almost as white as the pillows that rested her head: dark hair tumbling around her shoulders and in that moment, Eddie made a decision. 'When it's over, I'm going to seriously consider not just taking a few months off, but packing it in altogether.' Tenderly he stroked her face. 'I'm worried about you, little one, you don't look well.'

Having Eddie with her every day was an appealing prospect—if he really meant it. This was the one thing she hadn't reckoned on. Still, it gave her a dream to cling to while he was gone. Tina's voice was barely an echo, she was so weak. 'Who would have believed it would last this long?' she said sorrowfully. 'Here we are, after three years and still no end in sight. I suppose we just have to keep on waiting and praying.'

With Tina's warning to watch out for, "those damned German boats," ringing in his ears, Eddie returned to his ship.

Chapter Eighteen

Maggie and Connor took Billy to school every morning to relieve Tina of stress and strain. It allowed her to ease gently into the day ahead. Doctor Jackson had warned her health would worsen, but even he couldn't have foreseen how rapidly it would happen. The doctor didn't vilify Eddie for this pregnancy when all he had done was snatch a few moments of comfort in his wife's arms and at a time like this, who could blame him? Eve was simply the product of their love. Tina was always lethargic and tired at the least exertion. Where once, resting in the afternoon was a luxury, it was now an essential part of the day's routine.

Weekends were the biggest headache. With no school, the children were under her feet most of the time and were it not for Maggie, it would have been impossible to snatch even a few minutes rest. Thankfully, Maggie was at an age where she enjoyed helping around the house and had even learned to feed and change Eve. Wise, little Maggie could even amuse her when she was awake and lull her to sleep by pushing the pram up and down the street. Billy was more of a problem. Being a typical little boy, all he wanted was to run wild with the other children, and Tina didn't have the energy to watch over him every minute of the day.

Saturday was the most exhausting day of the week, for regardless of how tired she was; the weekly shopping had to be done. How strange it was to think back to a time when Saturday was the one day Tina zealously looked forward to, and now it was her worst nightmare. So little time had passed, but so much had changed. Gone were the days of leisurely browsing around stores then sipping tea and nibbling scones while excitedly sharing secrets. If only, by some magic, she could relive just one of those wonderful, carefree Saturday afternoons with friends. But Maisie had married a vicar and was now so caught up in church work. Poor Sadie had simply lost interest in life since Len was killed. Even Agnes had more important business. Working on Saturday paid well and that was too good to turn down.

Tina took the children shopping all on her own now with promises of goodies if they behaved. As a reward for being mummy's little helper, she bought Maggie pretty, blue, satin ribbons for her hair and the brightly-coloured ball Billy had craved for weeks became his proud possession: his reward for being a good little boy.

Queuing in each and every shop took its toll and by midday, Tina was so exhausted, she was helpless to do anything but stretch out on the sofa, leaving Maggie to coax and cajole Eve into taking a nap. Billy was simply bored waiting around the house for his mother to wake. It was no fun, so he did what any other little boy would do, he ran into the street to find someone eager to seize an opportunity to play with the shiny, new ball.

Lots of children were left to their own devices on Saturday. It wasn't unusual for errant parents to spend the day in the local pub while their boys ran wild and grew street-wise and crafty. Boys like Andy Nelson and Terry Hunter who were older in mind than they were in years. As fate would have it, they were the first two Billy met.

'Want a game of football?' Proudly, Billy held up the new ball. He had every reason to feel magnanimous, after all, this was an offer too good to refuse, therefore, it came as quite a shock when they appeared disinterested and even looked at him with contempt.

'Fool,' Andy sniffed, 'call that a football?'

Terry stuck his hands in his pockets and sneered at the little boy.

'We have better things to do. *We're* going to the docks to see the big ships.' It was only an afterthought, but in a moment of generosity, he said, 'You can tag along, if you want.'

This was an offer that, in all probability, would never be repeated. Billy was actually being asked to join in a big boy's adventure. There was only one not so slight problem. His mother had always warned Billy that the docks were a forbidden place full of unseen dangers for small children, and that was the dilemma which now tugged his conscience. Still, Andy and Terry were older, so by his reasoning, it would surely be alright.

'Well, are you coming or not?'

The indecision was almost painful: to go or not to go? Billy had an overwhelming need to impress these older boys and show them *he* wasn't afraid to go exploring, but on the other hand, he was reluctant to upset his mother. 'I'll have to ask my Mum first,' he told them.

'You're a little sissy.' Both boys made faces at him as they walked away.

'I am not a sissy, I can go to the docks if I want,' Billy called out defiantly. By now, he was more afraid of losing face than suffering his mother's wrath, besides which, doing something his mother would never allow was strangely exciting and she need never know if he got back before she woke. In a moment of folly, Billy chased after the boys.

Walking to the forbidden place seemed to take an eternity but at last, the unmistakable smell of brine told him they had arrived. Billy looked for the wondrous things he had expected to see but this bleak, empty place surrounded by a dark and empty river held nothing to catch the imagination: nothing that seemed even vaguely dangerous anyway. The fascinating vessels he had hoped to see didn't exist. Overcome by disappointment, he wished now he hadn't been so gullible. Totally downhearted, he asked, 'Where are the ships?'

'This way, follow us.' The way Andy and Terry appeared to know their way around the docks, it was obvious they'd been here many times before.

In his haste to follow, Billy dropped the ball and it rolled towards Terry, he kicked it to Andy who in turn kicked it back to Billy. The ball rolled past him and disappeared.

'Oh no, it's gone into the dry dock,' Terry called out. 'If you want it back, you'll have to get it yourself because I'm not going down there.'

Slowly, Billy walked over to where the ball had gone then jumped back in terror when he saw the great abyss below him. 'I can't get down there. It must be a mile to the bottom.' His lips trembled and Billy fought back tears that would only fuel their contempt and worse still, he now had to admit to his mother that the ball he had so desperately begged to have, now lay at the bottom of the dry dock and then he would have to explain what he was doing there in the first place.

'I told you not to bring the little sissy.' Andy sneered contemptuously at Billy's predicament.

Children never see the danger before them when bravado overcomes fear. 'I told you I'm not a sissy and I'll show you.' Without hesitating to think, Billy scrambled over the side. His hands clung to the edge as his small body dangled over the first lengthy step of the dry dock. Too late he realised the steepness of that first step, and his little legs kicked and threshed the air in an effort to find any surface where his feet could reach and take the weight off his aching hands. Suddenly, his grip slackened, and Billy tumbled and bounced before his poor, battered body reached the bottom.

The two boys moved stealthily to the edge and peered into the great pit in open-mouthed horror. They were unable to take their eyes off the lifeless child lying at the bottom of the dry dock: all they could do was shout to him, but Billy didn't move.

Ronnie McBride had heard children's voices and was on his way to warn them out of the docks. 'What are you doing here?' he yelled. 'That's a dangerous place to play, so get off home before I flay the pair of you.'

Stirred into motion, they turned and ran like the wind straight into the policeman who patrolled the dock area. 'What mischief have you been up to then?' He gripped each boy firmly by the arm as they tried to flee.

'Billy Fraser fell down there.' By now, they were sobbing hysterically. 'It wasn't our fault, honest, he was trying to get his ball and he fell, we had nothing to do with it.'

The policeman let go of the boys and ran towards the dry dock where McBride was already staring unbelievingly over the edge. 'Get help, there's a kid down there,' he screamed.

In Charles Street, Tina was looking everywhere for Billy and becoming more and more frantic as her efforts to find him failed. A neighbour said he was last seen leaving the street with Andy Nelson and Terry Hunter. Given the reputation these two had acquired, this was little consolation. Billy was too young and innocent to understand that of all the children to play with, these two were the worst, for whenever there was any trouble, you could be sure Andy and Terry were the ones at the heart of any wrongdoing.

Running into every back yard, Tina kept calling out his name, knocking on doors as she went. Asking if anyone had seen her Billy only met with blank looks. Then when the local bobby walked into the street, she breathed a sigh of relief. He was the one who could find her little boy. She should have thought of asking a policeman in the first place.

The bobby stopped and spoke to a woman. She pointed to Tina then hurried into number 26. Moments later, Agnes came charging headlong down the street.

Her face contorted with anguish and Tina grasped the policeman's arm. 'Help me find my little boy,' she pleaded, 'his name's Billy, he was playing right here and now he's gone.'

'Mrs Fraser, I need to have a word with you about Billy, but not out here in the street, let's go inside.'

Of all the duties a policeman has to perform, this must surely be the most heart-rending, and this bobby was clearly emotional. He was about to tell this poor woman the one thing that was every mother's worst nightmare.

Agnes arrived breathless. 'What's happened?' Her eyes were frantic.

'Perhaps you should sit down, because I'm afraid I have bad news and there's no easy way to tell you.' The policeman drew a long, painful breath, then said, 'Billy fell into the dry dock, and I'm sorry to be the one to bring you the sad news that he didn't survive the fall. He died before anyone could reach him.'

'No, no you're wrong! You've obviously made a mistake.' Tina began to laugh, not a normal, happy laugh but a shrill, hysterical sound. 'My Billy would never go to the docks, because I've always forbidden him to go anywhere near there and he's such a good little boy, he would never disobey me.' Tina grasped Agnes by the hand so tightly, her nails dug painfully into the flesh. 'Tell him it must be someone else, Agnes.'

It was purely emotional instability that made Tina's mind refuse to accept what her heart knew was true. When she finally did take in the tragedy that had befallen them, Tina's agonised screams ripped through the length and breadth of Charles Street.

Word of the tragedy spread within the close-knit community. The death of a child was bad enough, aw but the manner in which wee Billy had died, that's what was so frightening to mothers. It could so easily have been one of their own. Every child was emphatically forbidden to go anywhere near the docks from now on if they wanted to avoid a good thrashing. Only foolhardy boys with a misplaced sense of adventure and a ghoulish curiosity to see for their own self the place where Billy Fraser met his death would rather risk a beating than stay away.

Unable to accept or come to terms with Billy's death, Tina entered into a state of near catalepsy, until the funeral forced her to realise that her little boy was gone forever. And then she struggled to understand why the God she worshipped could allow this to happen. How was she going to tell Eddie that their precious, little son had died in such a horrific accident? His dear, kind heart would surely break and he would forever blame her.

On a bleak February morning, *The Rose* and her crew, wearied by war, sailed into the Tay estuary. At the point in the voyage where the harbour was only just in sight, Eddie would stand at the bow of the ship and watch the city lights twinkle in the distance. He was nearly home. In an hour or so, he would be back with his family, if only for the briefest of visits. Eddie closed his eyes and could almost smell the scent of lavender that surrounded Tina. This morning, he would take her in his arms and assure her, that just as night follows day, these hard times were sure to pass and when they did, he would be staying at home with her. When the war ended so too would his travelling days. Eddie now knew that his love for Tina far outweighed his love for the sea.

'It won't be long now, son, until you see your family again.'

He had been so wrapped up in his own thoughts and plans for the future, Eddie couldn't even tell how long Henry had been standing there. 'I was just thinking, well, it's more of a wish really, that maybe Tina will be stronger than the last time I saw her. She's so frail, Henry, it frightens me to death.'

The anxiety and worry that lined Eddie's face now was so different from the happy, carefree face that had confronted Henry that day in Sydney when he pleaded to be part of the crew. Eyes, that at one time seemed to permanently smile, were now clouded by an inner pain that never eased.

'I know it hasn't been easy for her, but it's been no picnic for you either.' Henry wasn't being cruel and unsympathetic. The kind of love Eddie had for Tina was what poets wrote about. It was pure and unblemished. But it pained the skipper to watch Eddie tear himself apart with guilt because this same love had resulted in Tina's health failing through giving birth.

'You must come and see the new baby, Henry. She's the image of Tina.' Eddie always glowed with love and pride when he spoke of his family.

'I'll take an hour before we sail to pay a visit,' Henry promised. 'There's an envelope in my pocket with two gold sovereigns for Eve. I want to give it to Tina before we leave.'

Eddie had made the difficult decision to tell Henry of his intention to give up the sea and stay at home to nurse Tina, only there never seemed to be an opportune moment, until now. 'I've been meaning to speak to you, skipper, there's something I have to tell you.'

Henry knew instinctively what Eddie was about to say. He'd known for some time this day had to come, because when a man is torn between two loves, the greater love must take precedence. Henry had already determined to make it easy for Eddie to do what had to be done.

The most difficult words Eddie believed he would ever have to speak were to forever remain unspoken. At the moment of truth, their conversation was cut short by the intervention of an enemy submarine lurking beneath the surface of the dark North Sea.

When the first torpedo hit, causing panic and chaos, Henry was bewildered and unsure of what exactly had happened. 'Did we strike a mine?' he asked Eddie. Seconds later, another torpedo ripped through the ship's hull and the air was filled with the frightened screams of injured and dying men. *The Rose,* in her death throes, creaked and groaned as she was engulfed by the cruel, merciless water and rapidly sank with all hands. They had been unprepared for a sneak attack so close to home.

Fate had once more taken an unkind hand, and now Eddie would never know the pain of losing his little boy. He would never have to endure the horror of being told the details of how his son had died. The icy North Sea pulled him down into its depths, yet even as the sea he loved at last claimed him as her own, Eddie's last thoughts were of his beloved Tina and their children. In the final moments of life, Eddie prayed, not for his own salvation, but that God would watch over and protect his family.

When news came of the sinking of *The Rose* with the loss of all hands, Tina's grief was insurmountable. There was once a time when she seemed to others to be the one person who had it all. A handsome husband, lovely family and according to rumours, a small fortune in the bank. Now, she was just another war widow, alone with her two remaining children.

Chapter Nineteen

On the eleventh of November, 1918, an armistice was signed. The guns fell silent and the Great War, one of the bloodiest wars in history, was ended. But the aftermath would be felt long after, for many thousands lost lives and limbs on battlefields along the Western Front, while thousands more were broken in spirit. So many families had suffered the loss of loved ones, yet among the despair, there were also tearfully happy reunions as the casualties of war returned home.

Tina kept in touch with Eddie's parents in Australia. She sent a photograph of Maggie, Eve and herself, and her letters always expressed the wish that one day they could meet Eddie's children—their grandchildren.

In every one of their letters, Eddie's parents reiterated the same wish but assured Tina it was unlikely that this would ever happen. It was the distance you see: the other side of the world to be exact. Had they been able to make the journey by horse and carriage or motor car just to another town, fine, but flying through the sky on an aeroplane was too daring a feat. The kind of journey their generation just didn't care to make. Were it possible, how grand it would be if they were able to make a pilgrimage to see with their own eyes the country and the girl their only son had given his heart to.

There was also the matter of his grandmother's inheritance which Eddie had reluctantly spoken about. Tina was adamant she couldn't accept great wealth which she didn't consider to be hers. Nevertheless, Eddie's parents insisted that if not all, then a large amount would be made at hand for Tina and the children. It would ensure they wanted for nothing. The money they transferred into her account, along with the money she had saved over the years, made Tina a woman of substance, even though she refused to spend one penny piece of the money.

Tina had surpassed her own youthful dreams of being simply *well-off*. She was wealthy. But was it worth the price she had to pay? Life itself had lost all meaning. The zest was gone and nothing mattered to her any more. Without Eddie, her one true love, there was no life, only existence. Back in the days, when she longed for him to come home, it was no more than that, a yearning ache that disappeared the moment he walked through the door. Now, it was a pain that never ceased.

The children, Maggie and Eve, were now the centre of Tina's universe. They alone preserved her sanity and made life bearable. Tina was never seen to shed a tear: it was as if the icicle, which was her heart, had no room for pity. In fact, the closest she came to crying was on hearing of the tragic death of James Coutts's wife. Tina wiped away a solitary tear and said to Agnes, 'Poor man, he must be feeling awfully lost and alone.'

The mind is so delicately balanced; there were times, had Tina allowed herself to dwell on the past and think about what happened to Eddie and Billy, she could easily have descended into madness. Perhaps the irrational fear she had developed of losing another child was a form of insanity that manifested itself in her overpowering protectiveness towards the children. Maggie was now eleven and had matured beyond her years. She sensed Tina's turmoil and made sure Eve was with her at all times in an effort to calm her mother's fears.

Bit by bit, the munitions machinery disappeared and looms took their place once more in the mill. Although for many, life would never be the same. Lives had to be re-built. There was no longer the threat of invasion or the heart-stopping sight of the telegram boy on his red bicycle—thank God. The sameness of a week to week routine was accepted with gratitude and thanks that the world was now at peace.

Tina's routine was almost robotic in a life that was methodically precise. Every weekday, she made the short walk to the shops for fresh milk and bread, meat or fish, but leisurely, never in a rush that could be hazardous to her weak heart. Sunday was the one day she and the children spent with her mother. Mrs Morris had enjoyed the sociality of serving in the Co-op and decided to stay on working there five days a week. Life had changed in so many ways since the war. The one and only thing which never changed was the ritualistic paying of the weekly rent every Saturday morning. Little did Tina know that one particular Saturday was destined to change her life forever.

'Good morning, Mrs Fraser.' James Coutts still made a point of hurrying to the counter as soon as Tina walked into the office, and this action didn't go entirely unnoticed either. More than one person commented on his fondness for the widow and it was rather maliciously whispered that this had been going on even before his own wife's death.

Tina mumbled an ill at ease, 'good morning,' as she tried to avoid the piercing stare. His attention, being both unwanted and uncalled for, still flustered her. 'It's in here, somewhere,' she stammered and her hands fumbled within the large satchel Tina always carried with her for the wallet which contained her rent book.

Agnes shook her head and laughingly quipped, 'No wonder you can't find it, there's everything in that bag except the kitchen sink.'

'Ah, here it is!' Tina brought out the leather wallet which held all her important documents. She had no idea that the much smaller bank book had somehow managed to slip between the pages of the larger rent book, and while taken up with nattering to Agnes, she unconsciously handed over both.

The rumours about Tina's wealth had also reached Coutts's ears via the *reliable information* passed on in conversations within the businessman's club. But her reluctance to spend money led many, and that included Coutts himself, to believe the rumours were no more than a fairy tale. And then, as though heaven-sent, the simple, little, green book that could tell all, fell onto the floor and at his feet when James opened the rent book.

James Coutts's guilty eyes rested on Tina Fraser for a moment. Fortunately for him, evidently neither she nor Mrs O'Neill had seen the bank book, mistakenly concealed within the rent book, fall out. He covered it with his foot while glancing quickly around to make sure that no one else had noticed. On the pretence of bending to tie a shoelace, he retrieved the bank book and unobtrusively slipped it into a drawer. The perfect occasion had presented itself to find out exactly what she was worth. This was a chance too good to miss.

A plan was already forming in his mind. It was an opportunity for James to finally dot all the i's and cross all the t's to solve the mystery of Tina Fraser's alleged wealth. A scheme stirred every nerve in his body and made his mouth salivate with delight. Only after an underhand peek inside the pages naturally, he would deliver it to her personally rather than return it by post with the excuse that she had dropped it in the office and had left by the time it was found. With undeniable candour, he'd say, 'whenever I saw the name on the front of the book, I did what any gentleman would do. I immediately sealed it in an envelope to preserve your privacy.'

When the office had closed for business and he was completely alone, that was the time to see with his own eyes whether or not there was any truth in the rumours about Mrs Fraser's mythical wealth. Coutts took the book from the drawer and slowly opened it, savouring the moment when he could know the truth once and for all.

The contents shocked him and left his mouth agape and his hands shaking. This was way beyond his wildest expectations. He had been thinking in terms of a few hundred pounds, but this much! It didn't make sense to him that she was still living in a rented house in Charles Street when she could be rubbing shoulders with the cream of society. She could even be a society icon if she gave up mourning the Australian, who it seemed, now had been something of a dark horse moneywise.

It would soon be two years since Emily Coutts's death and since then, every business venture James entered into had all been failures. He had taken over the family business after his marriage but was more intent on socialising and womanising. Emily was the real power, she was the one who had inherited her father's business acumen and like Barton Brown, had the know-how and a flair for investing wisely and well. James, on the other hand, was neither prudent nor clever. He squandered shamelessly and without Emily's intervention, their financial situation would have been dire.

Now Emily was dead, and since her untimely death, James had made even more bad investments, which meant he had to keep his wits about him to stop the truth from becoming public knowledge. In truth, he was becoming increasingly desperate, not only to regain his financial standing, but to stop members of the local businessman's club from learning of his problems. Perhaps a solution to all his monetary problems was now fortuitously within reach.

'Yes,' he thought aloud, 'I think it's time I wooed the pretty, little widow. If I play my cards right, this might be a very profitable merger.'

The sound of the doorbell startled Tina. She laid down her knitting and hurried to the door, wondering who or why someone had cause to ring her doorbell on a Saturday evening. She was taken completely by surprise to open the door to none other than James Coutts.

'Sorry to disturb your evening, Mrs Fraser, and I do hope I didn't startle you, but you dropped this in the office earlier today. I sealed it in an envelope and thought it might be best to return it back to you personally. I apologise if my taking this liberty offends you.' The well-rehearsed speech was perfectly delivered in such a quiet, respectful tone of voice; even the shrewdest of shrewd would never have suspected a hidden agenda.

Hesitantly, Tina opened the envelope and partly withdrew the book then quickly pushed it back into the envelope. 'Oh dear,' her face grew a shade paler, 'I hadn't even realised I'd dropped this. Thank you so much for taking the time and trouble to return it. I hope you didn't have to go out of your way.'

'Not at all, it was my pleasure,' James gushed. He wore the gracious smile of one who had just performed a good deed, yet still made no move to leave.

There was an awkward silence. Tina didn't want to appear rude in rewarding Coutts's generous gesture by closing the door in his face. Left with no option, she reluctantly invited the man inside with the offer of tea and freshly baked scones.

Everything was going according to plan. James was confident he could eventually break through the invisible barrier which kept all except her family and trusted friends at bay. Maybe he'd never win her heart since that still belonged to the Australian, but he'd willingly settle for what was convenient to him—her hand in marriage.

Plausible and smarmy, that was James Coutts, and he had carefully practised saying the right words if and when this moment arose. On entering the sitting room, James drew in his breath in a surprised gasp. 'You have a lovely home, Mrs Fraser,' he said in such an approving way. 'Your décor is extremely tasteful and so like my late wife's, it's… it's uncanny. Why, I could almost be in my own sitting room.'

The nicety, the flattery, it all masked the innately evil and greedy side to his nature and now, with the stage set and this lonely widow hanging on his every word, like a snake hypnotising its prey, James entranced Tina with all the skill of a deceitful seducer.

'Thank you, Mr Coutts,' Tina said and her eyes glowed with pride. 'That's praise indeed. I'm flattered, considering your wife was well known for her style.' Tina began to feel more at ease in his presence. Perhaps it was being within the comfort and security of her home, her own four walls, and not the dull and dreary office where she simply exchanged small talk with the polite but stern Mr Coutts. In person, James seemed quite pleasant really. This was the moment Tina let down her guard.

They spent the evening talking. Tina talked about her beloved Eddie's seafaring and Coutts related the sad story of how a freak accident robbed him of his wife and Millicent of her mother. Then in a moment of feigned grief, he said,

'I never realised how much we have in common,' and the sad actuality of that one statement began to melt the ice in Tina's heart.

'It must be a strain on your elderly parents,' Tina said in a more questioning rather than sympathising way. 'I mean to say, being left with a little girl to care for and at their age?'

As was the case with many more, Tina speculated as to why Millicent was never seen in public wearing pretty dresses, bonnets and shiny, patent shoes fit for a princess, just like other children of her class. It was strange too that her grandparents were never seen to proudly parade their granddaughter in town of a Saturday. The Coutts were seemingly also conspicuous by their absence at the Sunday Service. Rumours and fabrications circulated that Millie Coutts had never been quite right in the head since her mother died.

'Well, naturally, my parents dote on her and she isn't all that little now… is that the time already?' James hurriedly changed the subject. 'This has been the most pleasant evening I've spent in a long time, but I've intruded enough on your hospitality.'

As James was leaving, Tina found herself saying, 'If you'd like to come for tea next Saturday, we can talk some more.'

The plan was taking shape better than he had hoped. James smiled a sad sort of smile purely for Tina's benefit and raised her hand to his lips. 'It would be a pleasure,' he answered.

Although she was obviously still grief-stricken about the Australian, Tina Fraser was nevertheless vulnerable. She was a ripe berry waiting to be plucked and he was willing to bide his time until the time was right for him to convince her, money was useless lying in a bank when it could be put to good use. Of course, he would omit to tell her the full facts such as, where the money would actually go. Like any other empty-headed woman, she would grasp the opportunity to perhaps double her investment and then, when he had complete control of her finances…

Coutts's sojourns to number 22 became more and more frequent, but that family were still looked upon as upper class and James Coutts openly courting one of their own gave rise to crude gossip and speculation as to what actually went on behind closed doors. Tina used to be a common mill worker even if she did work in the office. Besides, she was born on the wrong side of the track to go getting romantic with a Coutts. It just wasn't seemly.

Curtains would twitch when James walked into the street. Tina was either oblivious to the interest she caused or she was past caring what anyone thought. Agnes was the one who felt most humiliated. Mill workers didn't use gentle criticism, they told it how it was and to all intents and purposes, Tina Fraser was as good as prostituting herself with the gentry whereas a widow woman '*having it off,*' as they indelicately put it, with someone of her own class, would have been acceptable. Eventually, Agnes gave up arguing Tina's innocence but she didn't give up watching her from a distance.

'Come away from the window,' Joe said, wearied by all the fuss about an affair that he was sure would inevitably fizzle out.

'*He* went in five minutes ago. Maybe I should go down and borrow a cup of sugar or something.' Agnes heard Joe groan and she reconsidered. 'No, I have a better idea. You go and stand on the corner with the men for a chinwag.' It was an order, not an option. 'Make out you're just having a cosy blether, but keep watching Tina's house, and if Coutts hasn't left by nine o'clock, I'll bloody well go in and see what's going on.'

'You want *me* to spy on your cousin?'

'It's not spying; it's looking after her interests. Please Joe,' she wheedled, 'Aunt Maggie's frantic. She thinks Tina's lost her marbles and you're bound to have heard the stories circulating around the mill. They're calling her Coutts's concubine.'

'There you are, getting yourself all a-dither again, woman. Stop listening to spiteful gossip and accept they've struck up a friendship because she lost Eddie and he lost his wife, both in tragic circumstances. I don't like it any more than you, but if that's the way it is, so be it.'

'Eddie's death was a tragic outcome of the war, but there are them that aren't so sure about Emily Brown's tragic *accident*.'

'There's no talking to you when you're on that high-horse.' Joe picked up his cap and walked to the door. 'I'm going for that chinwag with the boys and don't expect me home too early,' he growled. He protested by deliberately slamming the door behind him.

Shortly before nine o'clock, James Coutts strode high and mighty from number 22 and walked straight into Mrs Brady, one of his more unsavoury tenants.

'Good evening, your honour.' Jessie Brady made a little curtsey. 'Mrs Fraser isn't poorly *again*?' My, my, she's *so* lucky to have a kind-hearted gent like you to see to her, uh huh… needs.' Jessie made no effort to hide the innuendo or the mocking. She tittered and nudged her husband in a way that showed she'd got one over on Coutts.

Bill Brady stuck his chest out, smiled cunningly and called loud enough for the little gathering of men outside the pub to hear, 'Aye, isn't that the truth? Bonnie widows are like meat that's gone off; they attract all kinds of flies.'

James pushed past them, silently seething and unsmiling. The Brady's were weeks behind with their rent and not for the first time either, so let them have their jibes—for now. 'They'll be laughing on the other side of their faces on Monday when the bailiffs come knocking on their door,' James muttered to himself.

After a courtship of only five months, James proposed and Tina accepted without hesitation the companionship she longed for. 'I don't love you, James,' she told him, 'you know that, don't you? There's only room in my heart for one love and that was Eddie, but I've grown to like you and I think that's sufficient.'

'I have enough love for both of us,' he lied.

There was a sort of magnetism that drew her to him. Against all objections and advice, marrying James seemed like the right thing to do. He was here and *he* wouldn't leave her for weeks at a time, not like Eddie. For a time, a sort of outrage warped her reasoning. Tina had been angered at fate's cruelty by allowing Eddie to prefer the enchanting embrace of a cold ocean rather than her loving arms. But the anger was short-lived when she reminded herself of the promise he had made on what was to be their final parting.

Silently, Tina rebuked herself as guilty tears cascaded down her cheeks. Guilt that Eddie was gone and she had now given a promise to spend the rest of her life with a man who never would or could compare. How childish she had been to even make a comparison. 'Forgive me, my darling,' she whispered with eyes raised to the heavens, 'no man will ever take your place in my heart or my life.'

Maggie was spirited like her father and vehemently fought against her mother's forthcoming marriage. She was only a child, but one thing about children; they speak with a candour adults find hard to swallow. Wise beyond her years, Maggie had not only an intense distrust of Coutts, but a hatred Tina couldn't fathom. What a pity she didn't follow her daughter's intuition.

Three year old Eve, having never known her father and so different from the rebellious Maggie, was filled with excitement at the prospect of having a Daddy. Coutts used this childish adoration to the full. He bought the little girl's affection with sticks of candy, ribbons and cheap toys. How could a small child such as Eve possibly have understood the devious mind game this man was playing?

They were married quietly in the spring of 1920 and James moved into Charles Street, not through choice, but because Tina refused to leave the house that held all the memories of her precious Eddie.

'The people here may not be in your league, James,' she told him, 'but once you get to know them, you'll realise they're good, hardworking people.'

'Of course they are, my love, and I would live in a tent if it made you happy.' The lies dripped like honey from his lips, for James had no intention of living among these common working-class loons a minute longer than he had to and the lies kept coming. 'I'm proud to live in this lovely home, even if it is a bit cramped.'

Coutts just gritted his teeth and showered his bride with flowery words of love. But with the heart and mind of a true cad, he wondered how long he could stand keeping up this charade. The only thing that kept him going was the mental picture of Tina's bank book and the fortune that awaited him when his grand plan bore fruit. That was all that mattered.

There was only one thing which bothered Tina. 'I've been thinking, James, don't you think it's time Millicent met her new sisters? She and Maggie are about the same age and it would be nice if they became friends.'

None of James family had attended the marriage ceremony. It had irked Tina at the time, but she accepted the excuse James made that Millicent had a terrible, chesty cold and her grandparents felt it was inadvisable to take the child from her sick bed. She was sure to be over that particular malady now, ergo, there was no longer any reason to delay meeting her stepfamily.

'Well, my dear… the thing is…' James always became flustered at the mention of his daughter. He always managed some sort of diversion when Tina asked questions about her. It was obvious she wasn't going to be put off any longer. 'Millie isn't like girls her age,' he gave a nervous, little laugh. 'She witnessed her mother's poor dead body.' He held a handkerchief to his mouth and stifled a sob. 'It was too much for her to get over and I'm afraid her grandparents compensated by spoiling her rotten.'

'Then I insist you bring her for tea on Sunday. She's part of our family and we'll accept her as such.'

By the time Sunday came, even Maggie was enthusiastic about meeting her stepsister and spent the morning helping Tina prepare a special meal before dusting and polishing until the house gleamed. At the sound of a key in the latch, Maggie hugged Eve and excitedly told her, 'She's here.'

That first meeting with Millie Coutts was something Maggie would never forget. She had expected a slim, little girl in a pretty dress, but instead was confronted by a large and rather hideous girl in a quite garish cotton smock that was meant to conceal her bulk. Millie Coutts sniffed the air and said, 'I hope that's chicken I smell because I love chicken. It's my favourite and you'd better have cakes too.' A large, pink tongue licked lips that were almost obscured by the fleshy cheeks.

James cringed with embarrassment and snapped a caustic command at his ill-mannered daughter, 'Behave, Millicent.'

'But I'm hungry, Daddy,' she whinged in an overly-emphasised, childish voice.

'Tea isn't quite ready yet, dear. I thought it would be nice if you and your sisters got to know each other first.' For James's sake, Tina tried to play down the situation. Now, she understood why he had been so loathe and backward about introducing his daughter to her new family.

Millie glowered and in a ludicrously infantile way, began noisily sucking her thumb. The atmosphere, to say the least, was tense.

Suddenly, Maggie clasped a hand over her face and yelled, 'Ugh, what's that smell?'

Millicent had farted freely and without the least embarrassment. 'Grammy says it's natural to fart. Grandy said its better out than in,' and she stood there smirking at the utter disgust on Maggie's face.

It was the last straw: the embarrassment was too much for James to take. He made his apologies, grabbed Millie's hand and dragged her away.

The whole sorry business upset Eve. She cried for the rest of the day, but Maggie was more angry than anything, that this, 'ignorant fat snob,' as she called Millie, had ruined what was supposed to be a special day after all the work they'd put into it. Only when Tina begged her children to be a little more humanitarian and explained that Millie's trouble was… glandular (which was simply a polite way of saying she was a greedy pig who was prepared to eat until she burst), the girls accepted this and calmed down.

Although Tina couldn't take to Millie, she persuaded James to bring her for another visit. 'We got off on the wrong foot, but it'll be different this time,' she promised. Only it wasn't, and whatever warnings her grandparents had filled her head with, Millie now regarded them with suspicion.

'Would you like to come into our room; mine and Eve's that is? I have some nice toys and books you might like.' Maggie tried so hard to show that she at least had good manners. More than could be said for this hostile being who had more or less invaded their home on her last visit and not only insulted them with her snobbery, the filthy brat had filled the room with her stink.

When Millie followed willingly, even eagerly, Tina smiled at James as if to say, 'I told you there was no need to worry.' The tension lifted, but only momentarily. There was the sound of raised voices and Maggie came storming back into the sitting room screaming her fury. 'She says I've not to get too close because her daft *Grammy* told her she'll get nits.'

There was no rebuke, no chastisement, only blind anger written all over his face as James hurriedly, and without another word, left with his daughter. And that was the last time Millicent Coutts ever set foot in Charles Street.

Chapter Twenty

The first few months of marriage were… amiable, even although Coutts was more demanding than accepting. Their union certainly wasn't the kind of ecstatic passion she and Eddie had shared, but affable in the respect they sat by the fire in the evenings talking of everyday things the way contented couples do. Tina may not have felt any great adoration for James, but there was a charismatic side to his normally austere nature which blunted the edge of any misgivings she had.

And then little by little, a nudge here and a wink there, James began introducing finances into the conversation. To begin with, they were no more than fleeting references to his business interests, so casual and fleeting in fact, Tina had no idea where they were leading. Slyly, he would say just enough to give her food for thought. Had she recognised the signs, Tina might have been alerted to the dangers. At first, he simply implied that anyone with funds would be ill-advised *not* to invest. 'Gilt edged,' was how he described these investments in an effort to grab Tina's awareness.

Unfortunately for him, a reply of, 'hmm, really,' was about the most awareness Tina showed.

By the time their first anniversary came around, Tina knew she had made a terrible mistake in marrying James. His constant talk of finances were of little appeal to her, yet appeared to be the butt of his every conversation. Not only was it boring, Tina also sensed a certain belligerence, which now crept into his channel of communication. He may have been an ardent suitor, but he was a self-indulgent husband whose only thought was for him alone and it hurt her deeply, that on the day of their first anniversary, he forgot the significance of the date. She was lonelier now than she had ever been. Those who were once friends now gave her a wide berth. Even Agnes had grown short on visits and rarely set foot across her threshold.

Marrying for companionship had not been a good idea. James Coutts was certainly not the pipe and slippers type of husband he had professed to be. It was the elite businessman's club which claimed his presence every evening, not 22 Charles Street.

Sadly, Tina knelt by the fire and picked up the seashell that sat in the hearth. Eddie had brought this home to her as a token of their first anniversary. 'Put it to your ear whenever you're lonely,' he had said, 'listen to the sound of the ocean and I'll be right there beside you.' But Eddie was gone and no amount of jiggery-pokery could bring him back.

There were no more cosy nights by the fire, no tête-à-têtes and it didn't escape Tina's attention that James only took the time to speak to her when he enthralled over stocks and shares and some tip or other that would undoubtedly make an investor very rich when it came up trumps. That was usually the point where he'd slip the odd innuendo into the conversation. 'What a pity no one in your circle of friends has a few pounds to spare,' or 'there's many a rich man started as a poor man with the courage to invest a pound.' But much to his annoyance, Tina either ignored these insights into the world of finance or passed to another subject.

It was supposed to have been a short-term thing, a few months at the most. Just long enough for him to gain control of Tina's money, then James would have been out of Charles Street like a shot. But the grand plan had gone awry and now, after two wasted years of unsuccessful attempts to coax money out of her, desperation took over and James was forced to pay Barton Brown a supposedly friendly visit.

'It's been too long, Barton,' he said, warmly shaking the old man's hand. 'My fault entirely, I can't blame anyone but myself.'

'As long as you know where the blame lies.' Barton's bright, beady eyes took in every move James made, saw the tremble in his hands and the bead of sweat that ran down the side of his face. 'Is there something you need help with?' It was a leading question and he knew it. Barton was setting the lure because if his source of information was right—and he could bet his life on its accuracy, he knew exactly what this unexpected and long overdue visitation was all about. Barton had gotten wind that yet another of James's foolhardy investments went down the drain *again,* and this peacock of a man's feathers had been sorely ruffled. He kept an air of calm and waited.

With all the enthusiasm he could muster, James said, 'I need some help with a business venture which has come my way.'

Barton put on a show of interest. With an appreciative smile, purely for effect of course, he asked, 'What did you have in mind?'

'Well, to get things off the ground, I'd need a loan, short-term of course.'

'And will I be privy to what this loan is for?' The smile waned as the keen eye of a true businessman saw beyond the veil of a deceitful con artist.

'Suffice to say, it's a business opportunity too good to miss.'

'Well, James, the fact of the matter is, I've worked hard all my life and earned my fortune by the sweat of my brow. That, of course, is something you would know nothing about. Lending *you* money would be like throwing an anchor to a drowning man and watch him sink to the bottom with it.' Barton didn't blink or take his eyes off James for a second. 'When my Emily came crying to me that the once-thriving business you had taken over from your father was going under, I helped her find a way to pull you back from the brink of ruination and brought out what was already in her genes, the ability and the shrewdness to run a successful business. I have no idea what genes you inherited, but all you have is a knack of turning everything you touch to dust, therefore, I *will not* throw good money after bad. Whatever mess you've gotten yourself into this time, you can get yourself out of.'

'It's not for my sake alone, it's for Millicent,' James pleaded.

'You dare to use my granddaughter as a lever? When I asked—no, begged you to allow my wife and me to bring her up, you refused point-blank, even though we were prepared to give her a first-class education and send her to the finest finishing school money could buy. And then the final insult, for three years, she was spirited away by your parents each and every time we tried to see her.'

Barton shook with emotion when he remembered how, frustrated by this outright denial to allow them any contact with their only grandchild, he and his wife went to Coutts' family home and rather ungraciously bulldozed their way in. The sight of Millicent shocked and infuriated them. The terrible stories that had reached their ears were all too true. Their daughter's child was no longer a dainty little girl, but a monstrous creature with the manners of a pig.

All the agony and anger he had suffered over what had been done to his daughter's child was in Barton's refusal. 'You handed my Granddaughter to your parents and they turned her into a freak. Now get out, James and do what I had to do—earn a living.'

Weeks turned to months and seasons changed. Tina struggled to maintain equilibrium at home for the sake of the girls. She didn't want her folly to affect them and it had to be accepted, her marriage was folly.

Somehow, James managed to keep his head above water and escape bankruptcy. Unbeknown to him, Barton had called in a few favours to save his skin, which gave James the chance to start pulling himself out of the financial quagmire he had fallen into. Then again, James being James, he wasn't content to work and then wait until business boomed once more. He had set his sights on Tina's money. He drooled at the thought of what that kind of wealth could do. It was after all the reason he had married her. If only he had known how stubbornly she would dig her heels in... In retrospect, perhaps he should have pursued Margery Miller-Booth to the altar. Then again, she was quite ugly and her father was so mean, there was little chance of him parting with shillings, let alone pounds.

James Coutts was nothing but a parasite. He fed off Tina's purity and goodness. If only she didn't have such strength of will stinginess. If she did have a generous side to her nature, it might yet spill over... straight into his bank account. But there was little or no chance of that ever happening: he realised that now. Since it was never going to happen, other plans must be made.

The offices of James Coutts & Son had been busy all morning. By closing time, James had the chance to read the financial section of the newspaper, only to discover that the shares he had invested so heavily in had taken a nosedive. The anger and resentment flared again at Tina's stubbornness to part with the money, which would feed his addiction to gambling in stocks and shares.

Despondency hung over him as James slowly locked the office door, the same door he used to watch for Tina to walk through. How he had lusted after her in those days, even after she had married the Australian, who by all accounts worshipped the girl. Someone said he wouldn't let the wind blow on her and then it hit him. If she had been mollycoddled by the sailor, then perhaps that was what she expected from him. Perhaps a gift might turn the tables, nothing too expensive, a bouquet of flowers perhaps? He hurried to the florists before they closed for the day.

'I'd like a bouquet made up, five stems of pink lilies and I'll leave the finishing touches to you.' James handed money to the florist and, much to her surprise, told her to keep the change. He had every reason to feel generous. No woman could resist flowers and when he handed her these, Tina would be putty in his hands.

The look on Tina's face was somewhere between distrust and delight when she took the flowers. 'What's the occasion, James?' It was a natural question.

'It's simply an expression of my undying love and an apology for the way I've treated you over the past few months.'

'Not the past few months, James, the past three years.' Tina threw the flowers on the table. 'Now what's this *really* about?' she demanded.

'Alright, I'll tell you what it's about. The shares I bought, took a tumble and if they don't pick up, I stand to lose a hell of a lot of money. You didn't respond to hints so now, I'm asking you outright. Will you help me financially?'

'I've come to the conclusion that you're not as well-off as you'd like people to believe, James. What makes you think *I'm* in a position to help?' If he was going to question her, she had every right to question him.

'Come off it, Tina, you're bound to have realised by now that I know about the fortune you have tucked away. It's true I'm in temporary financial difficulties at the moment, but as your husband, aren't I entitled to share *your* wealth?'

He was through humouring her to achieve his goal, in fact, anymore and he might not be able to stop himself from wringing her pretty neck. Such was James's frustration at Tina's selective deafness every time he mentioned money.

The evil look in those cold, unfeeling eyes plummeted Tina into a state of fright. It was a scary thing to suddenly realise now what his true interest in her had been. Now, looking back to the night James had come to the house to return her bank book in a sealed envelope, she had been too trusting in assuming he had observed decorum and respected her privacy—as any reputable gentleman with noble regard for his honest reputation would. Assumption had been a grave mistake. This wasn't a decent man who would do the decent thing. He had obviously snooped. She had been ridiculously naïve, and it was sickening to discover that James Coutts hadn't married her for love or companionship. He had a hidden agenda. Tina shivered and shook with the awful thought that all he had ever wanted was to gain control of her children's inheritance. With hindsight, she should have seen how foolish it was to believe this creature could ever love anyone other than himself.

James broke into her train of thought. 'Answer me,' he arrogantly demanded.

Was it possible a woman could have two men in her life so utterly and completely different in character? One was the epitome of all things good, kind and compassionate and the other, twisted and selfish. 'Eddie's money is for his children,' she told him bluntly. 'No one—especially you—will have one brass farthing.'

'And what about *my* daughter, or did you conveniently forget you have a stepdaughter?' He wore that same sneer she had come to detest.

'I can't believe you have the cheek to say that when I tried so hard to get to know her and bring her into this family while you never even take the time to visit that poor, motherless child.' This was arrogance beyond belief, and it made Tina wonder what depths he would sink to next.

'Millie is still my daughter,' James argued.

'Then it's your place to take care of her, not mine,' Tina answered hotly.

But if truth be told, James never had much time for the girl. He had never really recovered from the disappointment of his wife producing a daughter instead of the son he needed to carry on the Coutts' name. This was a man so devoid of feelings for anyone other than himself; he refused to accept that the sex of his child wasn't entirely Emily's fault.

'You're scum, James! Oh, you may have been born with a silver spoon in your mouth, but you're still scum.' Tina spat the words with a passion that only comes from excessive love… or in her case excessive hate. She was suddenly very cold, but the shiver that ran through her was purely a mixture of emotions. What did the future hold now?

For weeks, the incessant arguments went on; still Tina refused to give in to Coutts's pretentious demands. As his frustration and debts mounted, James tried a different tactic. He planted seeds of terror.

'You know of course, that if anything happened to you, say for instance you had a fatal accident, then as your husband, I would have control over your finances.'

The menacing suggestion had been served without one ounce of compassion. James smiled in a sick, self-satisfied way that turned Tina's blood to ice and set every nerve in her body jangling. Difficult as it was, somehow, she maintained an air of dignified calm. Tina determined to show that his threat didn't have the effect James desired.

'Try it!' was all Tina said. Then slowly and deliberately, she walked from the room.

Coutts was nothing more than a predator that made the mistake of thinking he had married a quiet and passive woman who could be manipulated. Instead, he came face-to-face with a tigress protecting her cubs, and his lust for wealth failed to materialise.

The local businessman's club was still the place where James spent his evenings, for if there was anywhere he could claw his way back onto the ladder of success through association with other businessmen, this was the place. A word here, a handshake there, but even he couldn't pull the wool over eyes that had seen it all before. It was whispered that Coutts was in over his head and then rumours that his stocks and shares had plummeted, brought more than a few witty asides about "just deserts".

Nightly dalliances to the club took up not only Coutts's free time, but his rapidly diminishing cash. The members of that particular club were every bit as ruthless as Coutts, and if there was a fool willing to pick up the bar tab in return for a few scraps of information and a few empty promises, only a bigger fool would turn that down.

Amid the hearsay and speculation, James picked up a snippet that interested him greatly. He overheard a club member say, that because of his wife's worsening arthritis, he was contemplating moving to a warmer, sunnier climate to alleviate her pain and was toying with the idea of selling some of the property he owned before moving abroad. He gave every indication, that the property in question was an exclusive block of flats which housed only upper-middle class tenants with the means to rent these élite apartments.

This was the breakthrough James was looking for. All he had to do now was find the money somehow. The one good thing in his favour was that the vendor had made it clear he was in no particular hurry to put the property on the market. He also made it apparent that not being a man to drive a hard bargain, a private transaction—cash—would be extremely beneficial to any buyer.

'How would you like to become part-owner of a top-class property?' James put the question and then waited anxiously to see if Tina's reaction was favourable. 'Apart from the property itself, the rents alone could make you very rich,' he added with an urgency that bordered on panic.

Tina eyed him suspiciously for all of five seconds, and then gave an answer that was short, sharp and to the point. 'I neither need nor want to own property. Don't think for one minute I'm going to fall for one of your get rich quick schemes.'

But there was something about his desperation that frightened her. What if he did arrange for her to have an accident? Her health was failing so rapidly, maybe he wouldn't even have to arrange an accident. It was time to put her affairs in order. The game of cat and mouse had become one of life and death.

Chapter Twenty-One

Tina knew for certain that the man who now shared her bed was a monster. She could no longer deny that this marriage she had entered into was nothing more than a sham. The way she felt with Eddie was sweet: his touch was tender. Her relationship with Coutts was bitter and the coarseness of his touch filled her with revulsion. Far from being a blessed union, this was a living hell.

It was almost four years to the day since Tina ignored all the well-meaning advice offered by friends and family, and wed Coutts. Little wonder her pig-headedness had caused a great rift between her mother and herself: a rift that over the past four years had grown still wider. It was time to close that rift, end this conflict and beg not only her mother's help and ever-wise advice, but her forgiveness.

The old lady was agog when Tina told her the whole sorry tale and showed her the bank book, which had been the real reason for James Coutts's fervency to wed her. 'This is what he was after all along,' Tina sadly concluded.

Her mother grimaced angrily. Didn't she have every right to be angry? 'How did he find out you have this kind of money when *I* didn't even know?' Mrs Morris stormed. 'Did you use it as a kind of lure? Were you that desperate for a man in your bed, because that's what many a folk thought. I'm not deaf, Tina. I heard the whispers.'

The verbal whipping hurt and Tina's answer was a pathetic whimper. 'What a cruel thing to say! I'll tell you how it all came about.' Tina fought back the hot tears rising in her eyes. 'Think back,' she said. 'Do you remember when I told you he came to the house to return something I had dropped in the office?'

Maggie nodded slowly. 'Oh I remember alright! I was doolally with rage to think you actually invited him in.'

'This is what I dropped and that's how he found out, so please don't look at me as if I'd done a terrible thing. I never, ever looked on this money as mine.

155

This was Eddie's legacy for our children and I was happy to know their future was secure. Now I'm afraid, if James gets his hands on it…'

Maggie let loose the anguish and the fear for her daughter's safety which clutched her heart at that moment. Her intense hatred of the man was in the words she fumed. 'I'd say he was a rat, but that would be an insult to all rats.'

'If he got hold of this book, with his connections, James would find a way to get this money out of the bank and straight into his clutches. I have a plan to make sure that doesn't happen.'

'What kind of plan?' Maggie Morris asked warily.

'He believes I'd be too afraid to keep this kind of money in the house, and that's to my advantage. I'll do the one thing he would least expect.'

'Oh, Tina, please tell me you wouldn't do something that daft?' Mrs Morris was suddenly rigid with panic now that she fully grasped what Tina's desperate intentions were. 'You can't just throw caution to the wind. You're not thinking straight. I know now what you're planning on doing, so for God's sake, think again. Have you any idea what that weasel is capable of? Aw, Holy Mother of God,' she wailed, 'it's not like you can hide that kind of fortune in a sock. If he finds out… '

'Then I'll just have to make sure he never finds out. I know exactly what James is capable of, Mum. He's already hinted that if I happened to have an unfortunate accident then, as my husband, he'd have every right to gain access to my savings and that's why I have to do this.' Tina held her mother's hands firmly to stop them shaking. 'Can't you see that right under his nose is the last place he'd think of looking?'

Gradually, Maggie's trembling became less intense. The sadness that had flowed through her life was undeniable. It was there when she spoke, it was etched on her face and yet, right this minute, Maggie Morris was more bereft of faith and hope than she had ever been.

'I never liked him, you know?' Maggie's lined face was a picture of loathing and contempt. 'Even as a little boy, he was always sneaky. I remember old Coutts used to take James into the office with him every Saturday morning. He was so proud of his son and heir, and I know how terrible and unchristian this is going to sound, but he always reminded me of a slimy little toad with those fat cheeks and bulging eyes.' She stopped to catch her breath and stem the flow of tears with a handkerchief. 'I didn't interfere when you said you intended to marry him, because I thought when push came to shove, you wouldn't go through with it.

Now, I'll carry with me to the grave the shame of what I *didn't* do. I stood back and did nothing to force you into a change of heart.'

'I'm the one who should be ashamed. It was an act of idiocy I'll regret forever. The thing is, he seemed genuinely sincere when he told me how lonely life had been since Emily died.'

'Do you know there are more than a few who truly believe James Coutts killed his first wife? All that shit about Emily catching her foot on a worn piece of carpet at the top of the stairs was what caused her to fall and break her neck, huh. Lies, all lies.'

'That's the story he told me, but I've had my doubts lately. Maybe he doesn't realise it, or maybe he thinks I'm too stupid to notice, but when James speaks about his wife's death it's not with sadness, but always with a smirk on his face.'

'Alice Glenn's son was one of the policemen who went to the Coutts's house when it happened. He says little Millicent was in a right state since she was the one who found her mother. Anyway, Alice said her son told her they could find no worn part on the carpet and *he* suspected Emily Coutts didn't fall, she was pushed. Of course, being a Coutts, James was above suspicion and it was put down to a fatal accident. He's not a good man, Tina. I'd swear he's the devil's right-hand man and if he is in league with Satan, he'll know your thoughts.'

When Tina left, Mrs Morris leaned out the window and watched her daughter walk the road to number 22. They were on speaking terms again but the pity of it all was, Tina hadn't listened or taken heed of good advice. What would become of her?

If Tina's mind hadn't been so clouded by confusion, she might have listened to her mother and had second thoughts, only, she was beyond the point of thinking or acting rationally. If her mother had only suggested that the safest place to stash the money would be with her and not in the same house as Coutts, Tina might have been less reckless and more prudent by taking her advice and doing the sensible thing. Her mother's keep would have been the safest place… provided the brute never found out.

From the first day they set eyes on each other in that bleak place of ill health, Eddie deemed Tina to be a fragile innocent in a wicked world. A world he strived to protect her from. How pained he would be if he could see her damaged in mind and spirit by the schemer whose sole interest was relieving her of the money Eddie had lovingly bestowed on his family.

Once started, there was no turning back. Drastic situations required drastic actions. Tina began by making smallish withdrawals from the bank once or twice a week. She had an old canvas bag lined with sturdy cotton. It held all kinds of bric-a-brac that any good wife and mother kept to hand for the purpose of stitching and sewing, mending and making good again. She emptied it and slit open the bottom of the lining, slid the notes inside, then refilled the bag right to the top. Perfect. This way, as the bag filled with banknotes, it would just be a case of removing some of the bits and bobs so that the shape of the bag would always appear the same. At first, it was no more than an exercise to see if he suspected what she was doing and searched for her cache. Her greatest worry was that someone from the bank might break the rule of confidence and whisper in Coutts's ear what she was up to. But when James remained utterly oblivious to what she was doing, Tina relaxed in the confidence her secret was safe, fool-proof and this was the best course of action.

Over the next few weeks, requesting the withdrawal of only large denomination notes, Tina's bank balance diminished and so too did the manager's respect. No longer did the man smile gratefully for her custom or stop to pass the time of day. Although there must have been times he was tempted to ask exactly what she had done with so much cash.

There must never be a time when she was caught off guard and James must never suspect that there was more than just an assortment of darning wool, needles, thread and things sitting on the fortune hidden within the lining of that innocuous, old canvas bag. As wads of notes were crammed inside the now bulging lining, there was only just enough room left for oddments to cover the space she had left at the top: merely a crafty disguise for the true contents concealed within the canvas and cotton of her tatty, old needlework bag. She was confident James had neither interest nor suspicion in it, but there was one sure test.

It was said, the best place to hide something was out in the open. With this in mind, Tina sat the bag at her feet and innocently darned socks while James read his paper. Her heart pounded. She was sure that his evil eyes could see straight through the canvas and he could tell what was in the bag. Was he readying to pounce at any given moment? He just sat there without concern in her or her darning. The financial section was of more interest than a scruffy, old bag, which, for reasons of penny-pinching frugality apparently, had gathered and was now crammed full with haberdashery. Tina breathed again: he didn't have the slightest inkling or even suspect that those innocent bits and pieces used for mending and crocheting weren't as innocent as they seemed. They were actually there as camouflage for a secret.

When she was alone, Tina opened the lining and touched the crisp notes. They didn't give her a sense of great joy and neither did they quench a thirst or feed a hunger. They certainly didn't ease this tremendous pain in her chest at the least exertion or allow her to breathe easily rather than gasp at the effort of simply walking. If these pieces of paper could do any one of these things, then perhaps she could understand why they meant so much to the man she had taken as her husband. Would he really have no hesitation in harming her to possess them?

The bag was put back inside a cupboard and if James did happen to open the door, Tina was confident this inoffensive-looking container of needlework would appear to his mind's eye as simply part of the scenery he had become accustomed to. It was an inoffensive article, so what reason did it have to arouse suspicion? Tina picked up a skein of darning wool that had fallen to the floor and laughed. It had to be an omen. In a hushed whisper, she said, 'This really and truly is *pulling the wool* over your eyes, James,' and then she laid the skein expressly atop this mask of seemingly miscellaneous objects.

It was a Friday when the last of the money was withdrawn and the account closed. Now came the hardest part. The green, linen-covered book now showed only noughts at the end of a column and must be destroyed, for if he got his hands on that, James would see in black and white the cash she had obviously been withdrawing over the weeks and know it must be hidden somewhere. He would then tear the place apart to find it. Tina cried as she watched the flames consume this symbol of her pride and Eddie's love. When the last remnant was reduced to ashes, she silently asked Eddie to forgive her, even though she knew in her heart it was what he would have wanted her to do. Her only consolation now was in knowing, that with her health deteriorating so rapidly, she would join her darling Eddie sooner rather than later.

From that moment, the confusion and doubts were gone and so too was the will to live. For four years, she had been like a trapped bird, frenziedly flapping its wings yet unable to escape its confines. Now, her time on this earth was nearly over and she knew it. For the first time in so long, Tina had a sense of freedom. Her plan had seemed so perfect, except for one important thing she had given no thought to. In destroying the bank book, she had also destroyed proof of ownership.

Chapter Twenty-Two

It may have been the combination of distress, horror and uncertainty which inhibited Tina's maternal instinct and intuition, but she was oblivious to the change that had come over Eve. The happy little girl whose laughter once filled the house had become sullen and morose, and the only person who couldn't see it was her own mother.

Maggie was sixteen now and already had spent two years of her young life being the earner. Responsibility had given her wisdom. Sixteen going on sixty was how Agnes laughingly described her niece. Maggie had the sense to see something was far wrong with Eve, yet lacked the maturity to know the signs of a child in harm's way. But deep within, a strange nagging fear she didn't understand haunted her and there was only one person Maggie could turn to for advice. Agnes was the only one she could trust to listen while she gave vent and confided her fears.

'I just don't know what to do about Eve,' Maggie angrily admitted to Agnes. 'She's turned into a nasty, spiteful little buggar and I'm at my wits end.'

Agnes thought for a minute before giving her opinion. 'Maybe she's worried about Tina's illness and too frightened to say anything.'

'It's not that I don't have any sympathy for Mum. She can't help being ill,' Maggie bleated helplessly, 'but I can't be in two places at the same time. I have to work, since Coutts pays nothing other than the rent.'

'You don't have to go short. Joe and me, we don't have much but...'

'You've got the wrong end of the stick, Agnes,' Maggie interrupted. 'It's not a hand-out I'm looking for, its help. This phase Eve's going through has me wrecked. I've been seeing Tommy Stark and I like him a lot, but he's bound to get fed up of me being provider, housekeeper and mother all rolled into one. When do I have time for him?'

'You must set aside time for you and Tommy. Live your life. Just…all I'm saying is, make sure Eve's never left alone with Coutts. When you and Tommy go out, bring the bairn to me and I'll look after her.'

'You think he'd hit her or something?'

'Look Maggie, all I'm saying is, *do not* trust Coutts an inch.' Agnes shivered involuntarily. 'Ugh, there's something about that man, he… he makes my flesh crawl. Just don't leave Eve on her own with him because I wouldn't put anything past the swine.' There was a kind of accusation in the way she said it: more of a blaming than just her point of view.

Maggie was still too young to be worldly-wise, and not being too sure what Agnes was insinuating, she was loathe to allow her naiveté to show by asking for an explanation. It wasn't so much what she said, but the way she said it, that was scary, and without the benefit of fully grown up intellect, Maggie didn't understand the intimation. Maybe she'd picked Agnes up wrong. It sounded like she was suggesting that Coutts might harm Eve. He was a rat for sure, but it beggared belief that even he would sink so low as to hurt a little girl.

There was one fact of life Maggie was sure of, and that was her extreme hatred of Coutts. She detested the way he constantly made an excuse to walk into the bedroom while she was getting dressed, and without as much as a polite knock on the door first. It was embarrassing the way he always seemed to catch her in her underclothes. Perhaps this was the route of Eve's troubles, for whereas Maggie felt anger, a child Eve's age would feel guilt and humiliation. This must be what Agnes meant. Well, if spying on girls dressing was his game, he wouldn't get off so lightly next time. The next time Coutts walked into her bedroom uninvited, she'd scare the shit out of him. She'd tell him Tommy was onto his game and he could expect a couple of black eyes.

Life had one simple philosophy for Maggie: to gain respect, you must give respect, and it was obvious her stepfather didn't share this belief: otherwise he wouldn't keep invading her privacy. The hostility simmered inside her for the rest of the day and then in the evening, as she changed from her working clothes and reached for her dress, Maggie turned to see Coutts standing in the doorway leering at her. It was sheer instinct that made her pick up a heavy, silver-backed hairbrush and throw it with all the strength she could muster, screaming that she was going to tell Tommy. 'He'll get you for this, Coutts, you dirty, old bastard,' she yelled with no shame for her language.

It was something of a shock to hear a sort of whistling sound as the hairbrush whizzed past, narrowly missing his head. There was barely time to get out of the way of whatever missile Maggie chose next to pick up and throw at him. Coutts almost fell over his own feet in the rush to get out of the line of fire. From now on, he would leave this one alone. She was much too spirited for his liking and anyway, he preferred girls who could be manipulated. Girls like sweet little Eve.

The feeling of supremacy was like a drug, and all next day, Maggie kept visualising that twisted smile being replaced by a look of utter confusion as the bristled missile flew past his worthless head. Her only regret was that she had missed. 'If I live to be a hundred,' she told Agnes, 'I'll never forget the sight of that coward running like a scalded cat.'

'Sounds like you made enough of an uproar to wake the dead. What did Tina have to say about it all?'

A forlorn look dimmed the smile on Maggie's face and she answered in almost a whisper, 'Mum was asleep.'

'There must have been a hell of a racket, and she still slept through it?'

'It's not her fault! She... she does sleep like the dead on account of her heart being so weak.' On that note, Maggie made it perfectly clear that the subject was closed and other than a few choice remarks about her stepfather, she refused to utter another word about the incident.

With each passing day, Tina grew rapidly sicker and more fragile. She felt sapped of strength and her palpitating heartbeat was so faint and slow, she knew before long her ailing heart would stop beating altogether. She was nearing the end of her life, or as Eddie used to say, the Angel of death was close. Her biggest fear now was that she had told no one about her secret cache or where it was hidden and if she died, James would surely discover the hiding place and the children's inheritance would be lost to them.

The packed canvas bag was still in the cupboard under Coutts's very nose. He still suspected nothing untoward about the bag. But for Tina, time was running out quicker than she had anticipated. It was her own stupid fault, for instead of securing the money in a safer place, she had arrogantly turned it into a game of catch as catch can. She revelled in Coutts's pleading and demanding, knowing full well that what he wanted was actually within his reach, right under his piggy nose and he had no idea. It was time now to summon up every ounce of strength and do what should have been done weeks ago.

Tina watched and waited for the time school came out, praying Eve wouldn't find some distraction to hold her back. It was three-thirty before she deigned to come home. James wasn't usually home until after five. There was time to do what had to be done.

'You have to help Mummy, Eve,' Tina said frantically, 'so listen carefully, for this is very important. I want you to run to the shop and buy two large sheets of strong, brown wrapping paper and some string.'

It was a strange request that Eve felt must be questioned. 'What do you want brown paper and string for?' she asked.

'Please don't ask questions, child, there's not much time left. Just do as I ask and run like the wind to the shop. Hurry in case, *he* happens to get back early.'

Eve brought the paper and string then watched curiously as her mother made up two packages, forming the string into handles that would make them easier for a child to carry. When the parcels were completed, Tina looked at the clock: still a good half hour before James made an appearance. She gave Eve the packages with strict instructions that they must be given to none other than Agnes and Joe for safe keeping. 'Tell Maggie when she comes home, but on no account must you let Coutts know,' she sternly warned the child. 'Go now. Run as quick as you can.'

The effort drained Tina of what little energy she had left and she fell back onto the pillow gasping for breath, but contented in the knowledge that the money would now be safely out of Coutts's reach. It would have been better to wait until Maggie got home; only, time was a luxury Tina couldn't afford any longer. Some inner force was warning her there was no time to waste. This had to be done immediately.

It was a mammoth task Eve had been charged with. She was, after all, only eight and like any eight-year-old little girl, was easily distracted. It was asking a lot of a child to understand the importance of such an assignment. She wanted to question her mother about it, but she was fast asleep. Unaware of their value, Eve laid the parcels on the floor beside her while she got her doll. With the doll and her toy tea-set, she played house, completely forgetting that she had been ordered to do her mother's bidding *immediately.*

The sound of Coutts returning startled her and only then did Eve remember what she had been asked to do and the promise she had made to carry out her mother's wishes. She grabbed the parcels and made for the door. If only she had waited quietly until he was in the sitting room, she could have sneaked out without being seen and he would have been none the wiser. Only, common sense rarely prevails when fear is stronger and instead of waiting, she ran headlong straight into Coutts. All her mother asked was that she carried out one simple task to get the parcels to Agnes and Joe without Coutts knowing. Now she'd gone and let Coutts see the parcels he wasn't supposed to see.

'What have we here then?' The oppressive form towered over her.

'I have to give them to Agnes and Joe, *not you*.' Eve tried to push past him to reach the door and safety, but with that base malevolence he had been born with, Coutts barred the way. Escape was futile and all she could do was cower away from him.

'If you're not going to tell me what's in the parcels, then maybe we should just go to your bedroom like we usually do when Mummy's sleeping.' His mouth was drooling and he stank of whiskey.

'No, no, no.' Eve cried in terror and then, dropping the parcels, she ran from the house and the man whose very presence terrified her so much, she wet herself.

It was just like Tina to try something like this. Coutts knew before he opened the parcels what he'd find inside. How fortunate he'd come home early, otherwise she'd have gotten away with it. Shaking hands folded back the paper and sweat dripped from his brow as he savoured the moment, gasping at the contents: five, ten and… even twenty-pound notes. Coutts filled both hands with the notes and embraced them to his chest.

'At last,' he sighed, throwing back his head in jubilation. The battle was over and he had won.

'Give that back to me, James! It doesn't belong to you, it belongs to my children.'

He turned to see Tina standing in the doorway, her dark hair loose and damp with perspiration framed that deathly pale face. 'Oh no, my love, this is mine now, all mine,' he told her with a kind of madness. 'Besides, no one would ever believe you anyway if you claimed to have this much money, not when you've lived like a pauper for years. Surely you realise, they'd be bound to question where a poor widow like you got all this. Oh and one more thing, where's your proof of ownership?'

It was then it occurred to Tina that when he opened the parcels and saw what was inside, he would have realised she'd probably destroyed the bank book too.

164

Her mother had warned that he could see her thoughts. Since it had been her only proof...

She had been foolish in so many ways. Hate had robbed her of wisdom. Four years ago, when James offered a poisoned chalice, she had drunk willingly, but no more. Summoning up the last remnant of her strength, Tina lunged at him in a vain attempt to retrieve the money, but the effort proved too much for her and she fell to her knees clutching her chest as she collapsed in a heap at his feet.

Coutts stood over Tina's lifeless body for a few minutes before calmly lifting her from the floor and unceremoniously dumping her body onto the bed. He then took a satchel from the top of the wardrobe and stuffed the money inside. The bulging satchel could only be closed with the greatest difficulty. Coutts then seized a moment to stop and take one last look at Tina, but only to make sure there was no breath left in her body.

'What a pity, you fought so hard,' he said. And then with coarse and uncompromising smugness, he ran a hand along the contours of her still form. 'My first wife didn't put up half the fight you did, not even when I snapped her scrawny neck.'

Callously, James Coutts bent and kissed Tina's forehead before leaving to fetch the doctor, sauntering slowly as if he was out for a Sunday stroll instead of a supposedly life-saving mission. Coutts smiled complacently, safe in the knowledge that neither the doctor nor God Almighty could save Tina. She was already dead and he was once more affluent. Things couldn't have worked out better.

Maggie and Tommy had been to see a Charlie Chaplin film and they were still laughing as they walked into the sitting room. The smile on Maggie's face faded into deep concern to see her grandmother and Agnes, but not her mother. The deafening silence and the tear-stained faces filled her with a dread, the likes of which she'd never known. 'What's happened?' she asked, 'and where's Mum?' They didn't have to say it. They didn't have to speak the words. Sense alone whispered the awful truth and Maggie knew her mother was dead.

'She's gone, Maggie.' Agnes put an arm around the shocked girl's shoulders and sat her down on the sofa. 'Eve saw Coutts taking the doctor upstairs so she followed. They found Tina on the bed. Poor Eve: the wee soul was hysterical when she came to me and all she kept saying was that Mummy wouldn't wake up. I've left her with Joe and Connor looking after her. She doesn't have a clue what's happened.'

'My Tina's gone and so has that fiend.' Mrs Morris uttered the words with all the bitterness of a heartbroken old woman. 'The doctor said Coutts showed him into the bedroom then picked up a satchel and left without as much as a "by your leave." He didn't even wait around long enough to find out if she was dead or alive because he already knew. *He* killed your mother, Maggie and I'll bet my bottom dollar all her money was in that satchel.' She rocked back and forth in the chair, tears streaming down her face. 'I tried to warn her but she wouldn't listen. Why, oh why didn't she listen to me?'

Chapter Twenty-Three

On a cold January morning in 1925, Tina was laid to rest in a simple ceremony. She was only a few short weeks away from being thirty five years on this earth. James Coutts was conspicuous by his absence, and there were nudges and whispers around the graveside that the chief mourner was nowhere to be seen.

More than a few expressed their disgust that Coutts didn't even have the decency to attend his own wife's funeral. Of course, there were one or two of his esteemed associates who were prepared to give him the benefit of the doubt by pointing out that, as they were virtually newlyweds, wasn't it more likely he was too distraught to watch his beautiful, young wife being laid to rest beneath the cold, damp earth? Others made less polite, but more frank and honest comments about how he had also failed to attend his first wife's funeral.

A few close friends returned to the house in Charles Street to pay their condolences and receive hot refreshments after the coldness of the cemetery. Conversations were hushed amid little groups that huddled together sipping tea and debating the callous way Mr James Coutts had never turned up at the graveside or even sent a wreath. This cold-hearted act would never be forgotten or forgiven. Coutts's absence from the funeral service would be the topic of conversation on many lips for a long time to come.

The duties of a minister's wife were tying, but Maisie had never failed to make time for a flying visit once a week to see Tina and reminisce a little. Theirs was a bond of friendship that, over the years, had grown with them from childhood into adulthood. Now, there was such pain on Maisie's pale, tear-streaked face as she openly grieved the untimely loss of her best friend.

'If only we could turn the clock back, Agnes.' Maisie snuffed and sniffled sorrowfully. 'We all know Tina never enjoyed good health, but wasn't this a bit too sudden? Tina's death caused a big stir, and many folk believe their suspicions hold more truth than just ugly rumours.'

'Like what?' Agnes asked.

'The rumours and common gossip are that Coutts didn't even sit with Tina while she was ailing and then when she died, he just took off then vanished, and no one's seen hide nor hair of him near Charles Street since. You were closer than anyone to her, Agnes. Is it true he left her alone while he went traipsing every night, and in her hour of need, sick and alone, she had some kind of seizure?'

Agnes's brow gathered in a frown. 'Keep your voice down, Maisie,' she said in a hushed voice. 'We don't want to add fuel to the fire. Isn't it embarrassing enough for Maggie, having to listen to everyone picking over her mother's bones? And that pig didn't have enough in him to show his wife some respect by coming to the service to say a last goodbye.' Agnes clenched her fist until the knuckles showed white. 'Tina was too good for him and she didn't deserve this.'

'Look, Agnes,' Maisie moved closer and glanced quickly around to make sure she wasn't overheard. 'This may not be relevant, but you know that big block of flats in Milton Street?'

'Do you mean the posh building with tiled closes? What about them?'

'The Sinclair's are my Eric's parishioners. They own that building and Mr Sinclair confided in Eric that they're selling up to move abroad.' Maisie lowered her head a bit shamefully. Was passing on this information too much like breaking a confidence?

Without a qualm, Agnes questioned this deed. 'What's this got to do with Coutts?'

'Before I say another word, let me point out that this isn't idle gossip and neither was Eric sworn to secrecy. This was just a friendly conversation over a cup of tea with a parishioner.'

'For Christ's sake, Maisie, will you just get round to telling me what's so important about rich folk going to live abroad?'

'Well, the thing is, two days ago, Sinclair was made a cash offer for the entire block—by none other than James Coutts. He and Mr Sinclair are members of the same businessman's club. The strange thing about it is this. Sinclair also told Eric that the story bandied around by members was that Coutts didn't have two pennies to rub together. In fact, two weeks ago, he couldn't even afford to settle his bar tab.' Maisie raised her eyebrows and shook her head slowly. 'The question is, where did all that money suddenly appear from?'

They stood in a corner away from the main group of mourners who were too busy airing their own views to bother about two old friends having a quiet confab, but Maggie was close enough to get the gist of their conversation and she was stunned by the revelations. More than stunned, she was confused.

Agnes caught sight of Maggie, open-mouthed and a look of bewilderment on her paling face and she was all at once ashamed at what Maggie probably took to be some kind of maligning of her dead mother. 'It's Coutts we're talking about,' she said in a sorry voice. 'Maisie heard a story. All we're doing is trying to put two and two together.'

Maggie's concerned eyes settled on her mother's one-time best friend. 'I heard some of what you said, Maisie. There can't be truth in what you just told Agnes! You must have got it wrong about him buying property.' Maggie adamantly challenged this as some sort of misunderstanding. 'Quite frankly, Coutts didn't even have enough money to put food on our table.'

'It was Mr Sinclair himself who told my Eric,' Maisie argued in defence of her allegation, but keeping her voice to a hush. 'According to him, it's a done deal. Coutts handed over a leather valise full of cash.' A deep blush developed and Maisie began to fidget nervously. 'I've said enough! Actually I've said too much, but before I go, promise that you won't tell where you got your information because Eric would be so hurt and angry if he found out it was me. To him, it would be like betrayal of a sacred trust.'

It seemed ridiculous to Maggie when she remembered the all too frequent quarrels between Coutts and her mother about his financial difficulties. There was no way he could afford to buy a rundown garret, let alone the kind of property Maisie talked about: unless of course he had unexpectedly come into money.

Suddenly, it was there in front of her, like seeing a jigsaw take shape. Ever since the night her mother died, grandma had gone on and on about Coutts stealing all the money. They ignored what seemed to be only the ramblings of a heartbroken old woman. And yet, her insistence that Coutts had robbed them of their inheritance had to have come from somewhere.

Maggie thought back and remembered that once, in a sort of dreamy way, her mother spoke of some nest egg... and then she got all agitated and said no more. Maggie never gave it much thought at the time, but what if her frugal mother did have a few pounds tucked away somewhere? What if Coutts found her secret money and used it to stoke the dying embers of his financial furnace? Of course, Maggie didn't know (nor could she have guessed) just how much was involved, although now, she had food for thought. *If* there was a grain of truth in the story: *if* it wasn't such a tall tale after all and *if* he had taken what didn't belong to him, then as surely as night follows day, she would fight tooth and nail to have it returned. It was as simple as that.

'I wish I could have done more,' Maisie half-smiled apologetically as she hugged Maggie and said a final goodbye.

'You were a *true* friend to my mother! Just look around us. Half these people are only here for the tittle-tattle.'

When Maisie, left others followed suit and soon the room emptied. Maggie and Agnes were finally able to sit down and talk freely.

'Can *you* tell me why she did it, Agnes, why she wed a man like Coutts?' Maggie appealed for answers, reasons, anything that might explain her mother's madness. 'I've tried to fathom the depths of her mind, but she took her reasons to the grave.'

'How can I tell you what I don't know myself?'

'All I want is for somebody to explain why she went and married a monster like Coutts. It couldn't have been love. Not the kind of love you have for Joe or I have for Tommy, and I know she loved my Dad so much, she'd never let a stinker like Coutts take his place. Do *you* think Coutts killed her?'

'Leave it be, Maggie, for today at least. You just buried your mother.' But Agnes knew her niece was too feisty to drop it. With a deep sigh, Agnes settled back in the armchair. If it was Maggie's will to get it out of her system, then the best thing she could do was hear her. Agnes folded her arms over her chest and said, 'I'm listening.'

'Didn't I tell you something wasn't right, the way he used to shout at her?'

'Yes, and I agreed! But what you've got to remember is that Tina didn't take kindly to interference.'

'Oh, she stood up to him alright, but I could tell she was afraid. I hate him! That sorry excuse for a human being made my mother's life a misery and I swear, he was so desperate, he'd stop at nothing. I'd like to push him under a bus and kill him because he sure as hell had something to do with her death.'

Agnes sat nodding her head. 'I have my doubts too,' she said grimly.

'There were times when I'd walk into the room, and she'd be sitting there holding a worn and faded old bank book and talking to my Dad as if he were right there beside her,' Maggie solemnly told Agnes. 'I've searched the house from top to bottom but there's no sign of that bank book.'

'Your Mum told me Eddie made sure you and Eve were well-provided for, but I never actually questioned her about how much. Well, no matter how close you are to a person, isn't how much money they have in the bank still personal and private? But it *must* have been a tidy sum. She did say her children would never want for anything after she'd gone and to never want for anything takes more than just a bob or two.'

'I don't think she was spinning fairy tales when she said that Eve and I would never be poor. I believe Coutts got his hands on the money first. How else did he suddenly get back on the rich list one week after she died? Maybe she caught him stealing her money and the shock stopped her heart.'

Maggie had no idea how close she was to the truth.

The two of them had become so engrossed in their fathoming, they'd forgotten all about Eve quietly sitting in a corner drawing pictures with crayons Maggie had bought her. And then out of the blue, she said, 'There were lots and lots of money in the parcels,'

'What parcels?' they both asked.

'The ones Coutts took from me.' Eve put the crayons down and rested her chin in her hands. 'Mummy told me to go to the shop for brown paper and string, and then she wrapped up all the money and said I had to give it to Agnes and Joe for safe keeping.'

'You were a good girl, helping Mummy like that, but what did you do with the parcels?' Maggie had that clutching-at-the-heart sensation people get when they know something is very wrong.

'Well, I forgot to go right away like she said and *he* took them from me. He said if I told anyone, he'd come back and get me.' Confessing stirred the terror Eve felt that night. 'I was frightened, Maggie,' she wailed pitifully. 'I'm sorry if I did wrong but please, oh *please*, don't let him get me.'

'Never, I'd bloody kill him first. Don't be afraid, Evie, *you* didn't do anything wrong.' Holding her little sister and feeling that small body shake with fear, Maggie's temper overcame her reasoning and obscenities the likes of which she had never before allowed to pass through her lips, were suddenly a gusher for all her hatred. She screeched oaths that damned Coutts to hell. 'Shouldn't I have seen and believed there was more behind him taking off the way he did and not even showing face for the funeral?'

'There are times we see, yet can't believe. Is it really all that unbelievable that a man could be evil enough to fill a wee girl with so much fear, she pees herself at the mention of his name?' Agnes motioned with her eyes to the wet patch at Eve's feet. She wrapped Eve in her arms and held her protectively. 'Don't you worry,' she said, 'if he tries to touch you, Uncle Joe will knock that big, fat head right off his shoulders.'

Maggie's temper had mounted until now; it burned like a furnace in her belly. 'Why did she keep this secret to herself for so long?' More in anger than despair, she yelled, 'It gets my dander up to think that she had pots of money tucked away and never let on, not even to her nearest and dearest even when we had to scrimp and scrape.'

'She must have had her reasons. Maybe she'd come to mistrust everyone so much, she couldn't even talk to me. There was a time not so long ago, she would have been up that street like a shot, asking my help instead of nursing her wrath and fear.'

The agony of it all was there in Maggie's wan scowl and the faithless shake of the head. 'Poor Mum,' she said feebly. 'She must have tried to put things right when she parcelled up the money and told Eve to get it to you and Joe where it would be safe.' She brushed away an angry tear. 'This had to be the devil's doing, because God would never have let him get his slimy hands on it first. Now we'll never know how much there was.'

'Don't be so quick to give up without a fight, for that's not your style. There are laws against thieving. You and I are going to the cop shop tomorrow to make a formal complaint.'

'But what if...'

'Let the police handle it, Maggie. They'll prove he stole it and he'll have to hand back every penny.' All at once, Agnes grinned, 'Now there's the joy,' she said. 'Coutts is going to prison where he belongs and you know what? They might even do the world a favour and throw away the bloody key.'

Chapter Twenty-Four

It was the morning after the day of Tina's funeral. Maggie and Agnes sipped cups of tea thoughtfully. They stared silently at each other over the raised cups, each waiting for the other to speak first, to say aloud what had to be said. What best way to take an accusation as serious as this to that breed of men who call themselves "officers of the law?" For a start, if gossip was to be accepted as true, some earn more than is in their wage packet by doing favours here and there for certain well-off citizens with shady business interests. Coutts fell into this category, so what if…

The two women staunchly made their way to the police station. No matter what, they were determined to lodge a formal complaint against Coutts. Unfortunately, what they hoped would settle a score and see him behind bars for such an unscrupulous act of theft, wasn't to be the lawful and happy ending they expected. It was to be an insight into true corruption.

Her own belief in the validity of her accusation ebbed as Maggie hesitantly approached the desk where a tall, stern-looking policeman stood. Her legs felt leaden and confidence was replaced by uncertainty, for if no one believed her, what then? She shuddered as the cold, emotionless eyes met hers.

The desk sergeant was pitilessly unmoved by the girl's obvious anxiety. The pale face and almost audible hammering of her heart didn't bother him one iota. Anyway, why should it? She and her companion were only common mill workers with the smell of jute oozing from their pores and clinging to their hair. Now, he'd have to listen to whatever whinging tale this one had to tell. 'Yes,' he said with annoyance that was all too obvious.

'Could we talk to a senior police officer please?' Maggie breathed deeply and drew back her shoulders. 'I have to report the theft of a large sum of money.'

There was no turning back even if she wanted to. Now was the time to resolutely pursue the matter, while keeping in mind her grandmother's words of wisdom to never rest until a wrong was righted.

Those cold eyes never blinked and his malevolent stare sent shivers down her spine. 'Take a seat,' he snapped, 'you'll have to wait until an officer is free to see you.' There was no please, there was no thank you, just an impolite command to follow orders.

According to the wall clock, they'd now been kept waiting for the best part of an hour, sitting on a hard bench in this harsh, inhospitable place where common criminals were just part of a day's routine. Maggie was growing more and more fractious and impatient to end this ordeal. The sound of her feet echoed around the room as she angrily stamped back to the desk. They were honest citizens, not criminals and they deserved to be treated with at least a modicum of courtesy. 'Will we have to wait much longer?' She made no excuses for the clenched teeth anger in her question. She was done being servile to this ignorant fool. 'Surely, there's more than one officer on duty and I'd like to remind you, we've taken time off work to come here.'

He looked straight at her with the same unfriendly stare and a sneer twisted his mouth. 'You won't have to wait much longer,' he said with an indifferent shrug. The curl of his lip deepened and his wide turned-up nose wrinkled like the snout of a pig.

How did he know they wouldn't have to wait much longer anyway? He hadn't moved from that spot for the past half hour. Was it possible that the ability to communicate through mental telepathy was obligatory for all cops?

Agnes remained calm and in control, sitting there on that hard, wooden bench as if she were taking a tram ride into town. Maggie, on the other hand, was on tenterhooks and finding it harder to control her frustration. A blind man could see that they were being treated like second-class citizens and it was Coutts who should be treated like this. He was the thief.

Finally, an older policeman came and stood in front of them. Maggie looked up and saw a face from the past. This officer of the law used to patrol Charles Street as part of his beat. She remembered he was the one who came to the house when little Billy was killed. He smiled in recognition. He too remembered that day he had to inform a heartbroken young girl, her wee boy was dead. Silently, he ushered them into an office where a police sergeant, sitting regally behind a large desk, indicated with a mere flick of his hand for them to take a seat.

Had superiority robbed this man of manners? Without as much as a nodded response to their presence, he carried on reading, or at least pretending to read. It was only when Maggie gave a little cough that he raised his eyes briefly to look at them and in that moment, Maggie wondered if in this day and age, in order to join the police force, it was also statutory to have an obnoxious attitude and cold, unfeeling eyes like that of a dead fish.

'This matter of great importance you want to discuss, you told the desk sergeant it was some kind of fraud or theft.' He was offhand and too disinterested to even look up to see who he was speaking to.

As offensive as his manner was, Agnes quietly sat there and her reassuring smile urged Maggie to say her piece. She mouthed the words, 'tell him.'

'My mother died last week. We buried her yesterday morning,' Maggie paused momentarily for the normal expression of sympathy. Not surprisingly, none came. She ignored the ill-mannered snub. 'My stepfather has stolen the money she set aside for my sister and me.' Still, he never deigned to look her in the face and all Maggie could see of this man was the balding spot on the top of his head. What's more, her faith in the law was fast diminishing.

Suddenly, this righteous officer of the law irritably tapped a pencil on the notepad in front of him and shouted, 'Names first, if you please; I don't deal with anonymous complaints.'

The roaring command echoed like the clap of thunder around the sparse room. Incredibly, Maggie's weighty accusation had totally failed to move *him*, yet left *them* with the feeling they were by far nothing more than time wasters. Maggie held back the fearful sob in her throat and told him, 'My name's Fraser, Maggie Fraser.'

He looked up abruptly. 'You're James Coutts's stepdaughter?' Suddenly, they had his undivided attention.

'That's right and...'

Instead of politely allowing Maggie to finish what she started to say, he pointed a pencil threateningly at her and rudely interrupted. 'Before you go any further, are you aware you're making a very serious allegation against a prominent and respected member of the community? I hope for your sake, you have proof to back up this accusation.' He sniggered at the wide-eyed, taken-aback look on Maggie's face.

The nerve of the man to question her integrity: Maggie bristled with indignation. 'Of course, I have proof,' she said in her most snobbish voice, 'I wouldn't be here if I didn't.' She shifted uneasily in the chair, weighing up the situation. This was a serious complaint, yet this buffoon was treating her like the offender instead of the offended.

Maggie's lapse into thought appeared to aggravate him even more. 'Well then,' he narked forcefully.

She glowered contemptuously. Had it not been for the importance of this complaint, Maggie might just have stomped out to show *her* annoyance. Tight-lipped, she said, 'Coutts found out my mother had a fair bit of money tucked away. He wanted it: she refused to hand it over. The day she passed away, my little sister saw her put all the money into two packages, and then she cautioned the child to give them to my cousin and her husband for safekeeping so that Coutts didn't get his dirty paws on it.' At that point, Maggie had a vision of Coutts forcing Eve to hand them over while frightening the little girl witless and her temper erupted once more. 'But that thief...'

The officer halted the verbal onslaught by thumping his fist on the desk. 'I warn you,' he said angrily, 'be very careful what you say, because I will not sit here and listen to you maligning a fine man like James.'

'It's the truth!' Agnes jumped to her feet and leaned across the desk until she was so close, the stench of his stale sweat filled her nostrils. 'Ask anyone, or better still, get Coutts in here and ask him to deny that two weeks ago, he was almost penniless and this week, he was suddenly rich enough to buy a whole block of flats.'

With one wave of his hand, he rejected the allegation. 'What you say is ludicrous.' He leaned back in his chair, openly mocking them. 'The Coutts are a highly esteemed family. James may have been financially embarrassed, temporarily of course, but there are few businessmen who aren't in this position from time to time.'

'*Last* week, he couldn't pay his bar tab for goodness sake. *This* week, he bought an exclusive property—cash—and you don't think that's questionable?'

'What's questionable is where a poor widow, with two children to bring up, allegedly came by so much money?'

Because Tina had kept the matter of Eddie's inheritance to herself and Maggie knew nothing of its existence, she could give no viable explanation other than that her mother was a dedicated saver.

'And as a matter of interest, how much was in these mythical parcels?'

'I'm not sure of the exact amount,' she said hesitantly, 'but my little sister said the parcels were about this size.' Maggie held her hands apart to demonstrate.

'That big,' he said sarcastically, 'but as you didn't see them for yourself, all we have is the fantasising of an imaginative little girl. How old did you say your sister is?'

'Eve's eight, but she's very clever for her age.'

In a way, Maggie could see how he might find difficulty believing her story since she herself had no idea how her mother had amassed so much money. It hadn't escaped her attention either that this police officer was on friendly first-name terms with Coutts and it was highly unlikely he would take her word against his.

A look of controlled anger replaced the unpleasantly mocking smile that had irritated Maggie throughout the proceedings. 'I advise you to retract your statement, *Miss Fraser*,' he snarled, 'because quite frankly, I refuse to take the word of an eight-year-old against that of a prestigious man like James.' The cold eyes narrowed and the tone was threatening. This was a man to be feared. 'You have no idea how much trouble you could be letting yourself in for; slander being a serious crime in the eyes of the law.'

It was inconceivable that she should have to suffer this tongue lashing, yet Maggie forced herself to bite back her objection to his ill-mannered criticism. Given the stance this officer had taken, one more word of protest and she might even be handcuffed and thrown into a cell at any given moment. She hadn't expected unconditional acceptance, but he could at least have considered that she might just be telling the truth. There *were* two sides to every story.

One thought leapt into Maggie's mind. Was this justice? Was being working class sufficient reason to give her no rights, while an upper-class scoundrel like Coutts was above the law and protected by the very establishment that should be penalising him?

'Let's go, Maggie,' Agnes took her arm and pulled her towards the door. 'You'll get short shrift here. You only have to listen to him. No *Mr* Coutts, it's *James* this and *James* that. They're probably members of the same club, Lodge, whatever it's called.' It was a scathing and pointed insinuation that they were members of a Masonic group and as such, were duty-bound to protect one another, regardless of the crime.

Agnes had made the remark with little caution and it lit the touch-paper. The sergeant's face grew purple with rage. It was there in his eyes, the promise of a terrible penalty for not only insinuating, but actually accusing this supposedly keeper of law and order. He sprang to his feet. 'I warn you to watch your mouth, do you hear?' He all but poked Agnes in the eye with the warning finger he pointed at her. 'Your accusations are unfounded and without proof.'

'Maybe you think I'm in the wrong, but I think it's your own guilty conscience.' Agnes sneered contemptuously. 'Did you hear me accusing him of anything, Maggie?'

'I didn't hear a thing.' By now, a rage burned within Maggie. She was through bowing to this man's superiority. Instead of walking away fearful and apologetic, she spun on her heel and looked him squarely in the face. 'Your turn to listen here to me,' she wheezed furiously. 'I've had to sit here and tolerate threats, so now I'll give *you* a word of warning. Don't get too chummy with Coutts! He's an evil rat who wouldn't bat an eye in doing the dirty on you or anyone else standing in his way. But I'm pretty sure you already know that and only your stupid masonic laws stop you from admitting it.'

She was standing so close to this supposed upholder of the law, Maggie could see his pupils dilate to pinpoints. This standoff had somehow unnerved him. 'James... Mr Coutts,' he stammered, 'is a guiltless man,'

'Fool,' Maggie sniggered. 'I know about the cover-up over his first wife's *accident,* and I know he caused my mother's death then robbed her, so take this as a promise: one day I will prove it. When justice is served, we'll see who has the last laugh. He'll rot in prison along with them who covered up his crimes.' It was Maggie's turn to point an accusing finger straight at him, 'no matter who they are.'

Strangely enough, her guile seemed to actually succeed in blunting the razor sharpness of the aggressive policeman's tongue. Who knows, perhaps a few too many guilty thoughts over some of the illicit goings on he'd either been involved in or turned a blind eye to were doing cartwheels in his mind. He was momentarily lost for words and Maggie made a hurried retreat before he had time to gather his senses and retaliate.

That night, Maggie cried herself to sleep. They were penniless and there was nothing else for it, she would have to work to earn a living for herself and Eve. She struggled to control the anger and frustration which was tearing her apart, but if it were to be unleashed, well then, what she was capable of at that moment was anybody's guess.

Chapter Twenty-Five

One week after the travesty at the police station, a policeman stamped dutifully into Charles Street straight to number 22, and hammered in the most ungracious and hostile fashion on Maggie's door. The visitation of a dedicated member of law enforcement was a shock in itself, but what did Maggie have to fear? She was guiltless of any law-breaking and for that reason, she had no hesitation in inviting him into the sitting room. What she didn't expect was what could only be termed an interrogation.

'Can you tell me your whereabouts on Saturday evening?' The cold, hostile stare directed at Maggie seemed to even challenge her very right to exist.

'I was at the Odeon picture house with my boyfriend,' Maggie answered simply and honestly. 'Why do you want to know?'

All sorts of notions rampaged through her mind. That ill-natured officer, who interviewed her at the station, made it clear he was on very friendly terms with Coutts and didn't take too kindly to her calling him a thief. Had she riled him so much that fabricating some false allegation against her was his way of seeking revenge?

'Late on Saturday night, a brick was thrown through the office window of James Coutts, the house factor,' this unfriendly visitor explained. 'As you have been openly displaying animosity towards this gentleman, it makes you a suspect. Now, I'm not saying *you* did it, but it's my duty to ask questions in order to eliminate you from our enquiries,' he added icily.

It was just as she thought, and it was the last straw. That surly police officer at the station, who clearly didn't abide by the law he was paid to uphold, was now making sure that, by fair means or foul, she'd be made to pay for shooting her mouth off about Coutts. If that wasn't victimisation, she didn't know what was. Maggie jumped to her feet, stood with hands-on-hips defiance and bellowed loud enough to raise the rafters. 'I've never heard anything so ridiculous. I was with Tommy Stark all evening, ask him yourself. Oh and by the way, if I was to throw a brick, it wouldn't be at Coutts's window, it would be at his ugly, bloated face,' and she stamped her foot in temper.

The bobby couldn't stop a smile from creeping over his face. He dropped the coldly, officious attitude and said, 'well, I'm only doing my job and right now, that job is to question everyone with a grudge against Mr Coutts.'

'Then you'd best be ready to question half the folk in Dundee,' Maggie rudely quipped.

'No doubt, when I speak to Tommy Stark and people at the Odeon, they'll confirm you had nothing to do with the incident.' He offered a somewhat tongue in cheek, 'Thank you for your help, Miss Morris,' and left in what appeared to be obvious relief that she had an alibi.

The bobby's footsteps were still echoing down Charles Street when Maggie ran to tell Agnes and Joe the latest episode in the Coutts' saga. They listened in amusement as Maggie babbled on about the broken window and Agnes laughed so convulsively, her whole body shook. 'I wonder who did it,' she said, holding her aching sides. 'Whoever it was should be given a medal. The old fart deserves all he gets.'

A few days ago, Maggie thought she'd never feel good about anything ever again after that fiasco at the police station. Humiliation left a bitter taste in the mouth and there was nothing more humiliating than being treated as appallingly as she'd been. So appallingly in fact, she had despaired of the judicial system when the law not only failed to give credence to her allegations, but actually hailed Coutts like he was some kind of hero. Cynically, she said, 'Well, I'm one who won't lose sleep over Coutts's smashed window.'

Agnes crossed her arms over her bosom in that righteous way she had. 'This may be little comfort after all you've been through,' she said kindly, 'but believe me, there are people all over this town you don't even know and yet, they're on your side. People who are prepared to take the law into their own hands and dish out their own kind of justice.'

From the scullery, they heard Connor laughing over the sound of metal on glass as he fervently stirred his tea. 'It'll take them a year to question everyone who hates Coutts.' He stood in the doorway, nonchalantly sipping from the mug. 'I'd like to be a fly on the wall of the police station next week when the same happens to Coutts's nice, new window. They'll all be running around like headless chickens, trying to fathom out who the phantom brick-thrower really is.'

'It was you, Connor, weren't it?' Maggie drew in her breath sharply. Of course, the last person she thought of was the first person she should have suspected.

One thing Connor had inherited from his mother was her mannerisms and in particular, an infectious full-bodied laugh everyone recognised. He threw back his head and guffawed. 'They wanted proof from you, Maggie, well that goes both ways. They'll probably come knocking on this door, so just let them. Without proof, they've got nothing on me.'

'Please, Connor, don't get caught doing anything daft. You're dealing with a vindictive sod. He has a score to settle with this family and I'd hate anything to happen to you because of me.'

Right then, Maggie fell into a state of truly genuine worry. Coutts had regained a social standing and it was obvious he had the police in his pocket. This fact alone made his power far-reaching.

'Don't worry about me, cousin. He's not the only one with friends. Mine may not be as rich and influential as his, but they're a damned sight tougher.' Connor put his arm around Maggie's shoulder, protecting her the way he'd done since they were toddlers. 'Coutts may not be the most hated man in Dundee, but he's in the top two after what he did to you and Eve. We're going to make his life so miserable; he'll regret the day he was born.'

'What do you mean by, *we*? Who else are involved in this?'

'No offence, Maggie, but its best you don't know, that way there's no chance of you slipping up if the police come back. What you don't know, you can't tell.'

The following Saturday night, when the streets were deserted, Coutts's new window was smashed and on Sunday morning, James Coutts barged into Maggie's house like a raging bull. Eve went into such a state of fear and alarm, she crawled into a cupboard to escape from the terror of her once upon a time stepfather.

'You broke my window **again**,' Coutts yelled. 'I know you threw that brick. Or did you get some lackey to do it for you? I demand you stop this damned hate campaign against me, you hear. Stop it or you'll be sorry.'

His bloated face looked like it was about to burst. Maggie would never again see the colour blue without visualising Coutts at this moment. 'Get out of my house you... you half daft clown.' She stood her ground and stood up to him without showing any sign of fear. Maggie stared him in the eye and screamed, 'I don't need lackeys and thugs to do my dirty work: not like you. You're only good at fighting with women, but you won't find me as easy to bully as my mother.'

'I know you went to the police to make accusations against me.' He clenched his fists menacingly. 'Don't try to deny it, because *I* have friends in high places.'

'Yes, I met one of your *friends* a couple of weeks ago,' Maggie said facetiously. 'He was a big, cowardly pig too; only, he was all dressed up in the disguise of a policeman.'

'There's only so much a man can take. Your mother pushed me too far and…' In a moment of irrational panic, he raised a clenched fist to strike Maggie, but then he must have realised this could bring serious repercussions and stayed his temper.

Maggie stood toe to toe with him, hands defiantly on her hips. 'Go on, Coutts, try it, you sorry excuse for a man,' she goaded. 'Just remember you're not dealing with a little girl now. You like scaring little girls half to death, don't you? Well, let's just see how you stand up to real men,' and with that, she screeched a command to her sister, 'Eve, go now, run to fetch Joe and some of the men to get this filth out of my house.'

Ever the coward, Coutts ran faster than a greyhound out of the trap rather than face a hoard of angry men who he referred to as, 'self-styled vigilantes.' As he beat a path out of there, in a last gasp act of bravado, he called to Maggie, 'You've not seen the back of me.'

The last thing Coutts expected—or wanted—was for his hurried departure to coincide with Joe's arrival. But the devil wasn't doing him any favours this day, and Coutts collided headlong into Joe as he made a dash for the street.

'You spineless pig, it's time someone taught you a lesson about scaring the life out of girls with your gutless threats,' Joe growled and took Coutts by the scruff of the neck. Amid jeers from other residents of the street, Joe threw him bodily into the stinking gutter that had gathered around a blocked drain.

At the sound of a barney going on at number 22 between O'Neill and none other than Coutts, no less, an audience gathered to cheer Joe, the hero of the street. 'No mercy, give the bastard what he deserves,' they ranted.

Old Mrs Brady walked over to where Coutts was sprawled in the gutter and gave him a good, hard kick in the arse. 'I've been dying to do that for many a year,' she said gleefully.

Joe stood over the pathetic figure lying in the foul-smelling emission from the sewer. 'Take this as a warning, Coutts, come back near this street again and you'll be sorry. As you can see, there's a lot more than me after your worthless hide. If I were you, I'd run while I still had the use of my legs.'

Picking himself up from the gutter, Coutts made one last effort to save face. 'I'm warning all of you,' he yelled officiously, 'I'll see you all homeless by next week.'

Of course, they knew, just as Coutts knew, it was an empty promise that was blown away on that wind of stench from the gutter. Even he couldn't evict a whole street. It was useless trying to retaliate and hope to win against a community united.

Coutts never did carry out the vain threat of mass eviction, well, even he couldn't chance it once he realised it would not only be a totally impractical project, it would be commercial suicide. He never did show his cowardly face in Charles Street again either, but the bitter memory of that visit would haunt Maggie for a long time to come.

Part Three
The Tide Always Turns

Chapter Twenty-Six

'How can I carry on putting my dear Tommy through this turmoil?' Those were the frantic words on her lips and the hurting thought on Maggie's mind when she opened her eyes to a new day. She'd had little sleep in another night of restless tossing and turning. How could she sleep when it was impossible to close her tired eyes and rest? So many sleepless nights: too many tears on her pillow. It was this constant fretting over the terrible change that had come over Eve. What devilish thing had turned her from a sweet, angelic kid into a juvenile delinquent who made not only hers, but Tommy's life too, a living hell with the worry she caused them?

It was for the best to be candid and tell Tommy it was over between them. Oh he would be hurt, but when the pain went away, he'd thank her. Wasn't it kinder to do this now rather than have the poor lad hang around and for what, a quick cuddle maybe? A hurried kiss if they were lucky? Poor Tommy, he was so willing to throw his life away for a lost cause like her and Eve, and she couldn't let him do it. Tommy was willing to take on the thankless role of substitute father to Eve, and a heart as kind as that should be rewarded. Eve had become a troubled child. Whatever maze of nastiness she had gotten lost in had warped her mind. Tommy had such a kind and caring nature, he wanted so much to help and guide Eve through this muddle. The insolent, little horror only ever treated him with contempt and he didn't deserve that. She would tell him tonight to find someone who had the time and energy to be courted. He had to move on and forget about her.

A day's toil was long and hard-standing at a loom from dusk till dawn, working those extra hours just to make ends meet. Although Maggie was barely an adult herself, it had fallen on her to earn a living and provide for her and Eve, now that circumstances had forced her to become both mother and father to her little sister.

At the end of each shift, Maggie made her way home exhausted, fit to drop, and still, the laundry to be done and the evening meal to prepare. A meal she was usually too tired to eat. There were times she even imagined how good it would be, a blessing, to simply fall asleep and never wake up. There were times too when, wearied by the grit and toil of this hell on earth, she just wanted to float into oblivion and leave all those cares behind her. Maggie prayed to God for deliverance from hardship and suffering, even though she now found it hard to believe such a divine being full of supposed goodness, had treated her so cruelly. Only, she was a fighter and the will to survive was too strong.

It was after eight when she reached Charles Street and once again, walked into a deserted house. Where was Eve this time? Tommy would be here soon and he'd likely have to do what he did most nights; scour the back alleys and street corners looking for Eve. Oh how increasingly wayward and difficult to control she had become. She was rebellious and refused point-blank to help in any way with housework or other chores. Time and time again, Maggie tried to explain how hard it was for her to work long hours *and* run a home single-handed. Many times, she was reduced to tears, yet Eve was like some soulless creature, unresponsive and unmoved by all the anguish and sorrow that was of her making.

Listening for the sound of Tommy's footsteps, Maggie's stomach churned. How could she let go of the one person who was prepared to work with her shoulder-to-shoulder? How could she tell her tower of strength to go and not come back? But her patience was stretched to the limit, she was narky and no fun to be with. How could she expect Tommy to put up with that? He never quibbled, but this was asking too much of a wonderful young man who understood the importance of keeping what was left of her family together. A lesser man would have shied away from what other men referred to as woman's work: but not Tommy. He was only too willing to do everything in his power to relieve Maggie of some of the burden. Yet surely, even one as tolerant as Tommy had to have a breaking point?

'Guess where I found this one?' The door opened and Eve was thrust inside. 'I walked into the close and there she was, standing against the wall in the darkness with two boys,' Tommy said with spitting disgust. 'God knows what was going on, but with her gymslip hoisted and the guilty way they took off, I can guess. I asked if she'd done anything to help you. She said it was none of my business. Well, I told her it *was* my business.'

Maggie sighed deeply and her face crumpled in despair as her brain scrambled to take in what Tommy was trying to tell her. She had to face the sordid truth about her little sister. Maggie wasn't deaf to the whispers that Eve would end up selling herself on Dock Street because she was nothing more than a little trollop.

It was becoming more and more gut-wrenching for Tommy. His eyes could watch and his ears could hear, yet it was all he could do to hold back a growing rage at Eve's lack of respect for the sister who had been left with the thankless task of bringing her up. Rather than her idleness, it was this open defiance that infuriated him. But it wasn't about him, it was about Maggie. There were nights she looked close to collapse. An undisciplined brat who was rude to everyone around her, that's what Eve was and the strain was taking its toll.

'I can't stand to see you so tired when *she* should be helping you instead of hanging around street corners with boys.' There was no longer the smile that lifted the corners of Tommy's mouth and crinkled his eyes. 'People talk,' he told her fiercely, 'and she's too young to be making such a bad name for herself.'

'What bad names? What are they calling her now?'

Looking Maggie in the eye to tell her would be a sore thing to do, but better coming from him than some taunting toe-rag. 'Some young lads passed the word that she's a knickers-dropper and now, it's going 'round like wildfire. I'm sorry, Maggie, but folk are saying she's like a cat in heat.' Tommy held back his fury through clenched teeth.

It was so uncharacteristic of Tommy to speak in anger, but he was only speaking the truth and Maggie tearfully accepted that. Although she had done everything in her power to bring Eve up properly, the girl had neither moral nor family values and was well on her way to being taken into care. Yet, Maggie still made excuses for her.

'She's only weeks off her tenth birthday, no more than a bairn,' Maggie wept. 'How can I be hard on her after what she's been through? Just think what a terrible shock it must have been for her, finding Mum the way she did. I don't think she has or ever will get over the fright.'

It was incredible that anyone could be this tolerant! Tommy shook his head in disbelief. 'You'll be telling me next that it's all been a bed of roses for you,' he said. 'Open your eyes, Maggie. She's making you her dogsbody, letting you do everything for her as well as yourself while she swans around like little lady muck and believe me, muck's the right word for her. It's time to face facts. That little madam has no respect for me, for you, or for her mother's memory, and it's about time she realised you have feelings too.'

Deep, heart-breaking sobs racked Maggie's body. 'You don't know what it's like, Tommy. She'll never get over being the one responsible for Coutts taking the money, and there are the nightmares. She wakes screaming most nights and I haven't slept a full night in ages. It's a living hell and I don't know how long I can go on. Try and understand,' she pleaded. 'What terrible guilt for a wee girl to live with, knowing that if she'd done as Mum told her and took the money to Agnes and Joe, things would be so different now. Eve isn't a bad girl, Tommy, she just got lost in some dark place along the way and it's up to me to help her find the way out.'

'You are a beautiful person, Maggie Fraser, and you don't have a bad bone in your body,' Tommy said and gently wrapped her in his arms. 'Do you know what I think would be best for both of us?'

She looked at the honesty in his pale blue eyes and her heart filled with despair. The moment she'd dreaded had arrived. 'You think the same as I do, that we should go our separate ways? Now, before you say another word, Tommy: I don't blame you. You deserve to find someone without commitments.'

Tommy held her at arm's length and sighed deeply. 'I've no intention of giving you up if that's what you were thinking. Oh no, I'd rather we get married so that I can look after you properly,' he said with that honesty she'd come to love and bless, but never as much as right at this moment. 'What do you say we do just that?' It wasn't a hasty decision made on the spur of the moment. Tommy had been trying for weeks to summon up the courage. He just hadn't found the right time... until now.

A proposal of marriage wasn't at all what she'd expected to hear. Maggie felt she was climbing a great ladder to get to a happy place and didn't know whether she was halfway up or halfway down. She wanted so much to say 'yes' and climb to the top of that mythical ladder, but she would only succeed in pulling Tommy all the way straight down to the bottom, right back into this miserable existence.

Maggie gave her answer. 'No, Tommy! There's Eve to consider and you said yourself she's a handful. You'd be trapped, and I love you too much to do that.'

'Listen to me, Maggie. Eve won't be a bairn forever: she's growing up. Before you know it, she'll be working and probably thinking about getting married. One day soon, she'll be able to fend for herself, but until that day comes,

I promise to take care of you both. Please say yes then between us, we can help Eve get over her nightmares. Together, we'll wash away all that guilt.'

This wasn't some pathetic meaningless gesture. This truly was a plea from the heart and Maggie knew without doubt what she wanted to do. 'Marrying you would be the best thing that ever happened to me. I'd be a fool to lose you. Of course the answer is yes.'

The sitting room door was ajar and unknown to them, Eve had listened and heard *almost* every word. Unfortunately, she had only heard snippets of the conversation. The storm clouds were gathering as she walked slowly into the room and the look on her face was nothing short of demonic.

'So that's the plan, is it?' she hissed. 'You two get married and live happily ever after. But where does that leave me? I suppose I'll be put in a home for orphans. Well, you're not sending me to any orphanage, because I won't go, do you hear? I won't, I won't.'

There was something very frightening about a child displaying such instability. Eve was verging on hysteria and Maggie tried to put comforting arms around her but she lashed out and pulled away. It was this act of aggression that filled Maggie with more indignation than she felt even when Eve was sulky and brooding. Her cheek stung where Eve's hand had made contact, but it didn't hurt half as much as her feelings.

She didn't shout, nor raise her voice in the least. 'You ungrateful, little bitch,' Maggie snarled in disgust. There was only so much a person could take, and Maggie had crossed that invisible boundary between love and hate. She loved her sister, yet hated what she'd become. 'I'm worn out working my fingers to the bone for both of us,' she grabbed Eve by the shoulders and shook her until her teeth rattled. 'Look at me,' she shrieked. 'I'm old before my time and still you refuse to as much as tidy up or even wash your own stinking pissy knickers.'

'Don't lash out in anger, Maggie; you'll only regret it later.' Tommy got between them before the fists flew.

But by now, Maggie was verging on homicidal and she screamed, 'I'm sick and tired of her antics, Tommy. I can't take any more. Maybe, putting her in care wouldn't be such a bad idea after all.'

If Eve had shown some contrition, Maggie would probably have hugged her and said everything would be alright, but she simply yawned in a way that spoke volumes. Eve didn't give a damn for them or anyone. Insolent as ever, she muttered one word, 'huh,' and it was the last straw.

That was when Maggie gave up and gave in. She was jaded to the point of despair. 'What a pity you didn't eavesdrop a little earlier, then you would have heard Tommy promise to look after you and me both,' she said wearily. 'Only a good, kind man would be mad enough to take on a loathsome brat like you.' The words she had tried to suppress were out: painfully cruel words that Maggie immediately regretted but couldn't take back.

Eve burst into tears and crumpled into a cross-legged sitting position on the floor. For the first time in so long, this "loathsome brat", as her sister had called her, was showing real emotion. Maggie could only stand silent and motionless. When the flow of tears eventually ebbed, Eve appeared oddly submissive. It was almost as if she had been two people: a child and an ogre in the same body.

And then the ogre was suddenly gone and the true child whispered to Tommy, 'Did you mean it when you said that I could still stay here after you and Maggie get married?'

It was clear now what had been on her mind. The child had mistakenly believed there would be no place for her in their life after the marriage. Tommy's face creased in a smile. He was a hostage to his love for Maggie and accepted his roll of surrogate father to Eve. It wasn't a means test. He had a genuine affection for the troublesome little girl.

'Of course, you're going to stay here with us.' Tommy playfully and reassuringly pinched her chubby, pink cheek. 'Did you really think we'd put you out onto the street? This is your home too. Unless you'd rather go and live with your step-dad in his big house.'

It was meant to be nothing more than an innocuous remark to lighten the moment, but it opened an emotional hornet's nest and sent Eve into a violent rage. 'Never, never,' she screamed, throwing herself onto the floor and curling her small body into a ball as if she was protecting herself from invisible blows. She looked up at them through glazed eyes. The look on her face was one of blood-curdling terror and Eve peed in her pants… again.

It alarmed Tommy, frightened the hell out of him, for he'd never seen this side to Eve. She was rebellious for sure, downright insolent at times certainly, but this… 'What kind of fiend must Coutts be, Maggie?' Tommy said with sore concern. Gently, he tried to lift Eve to her feet, but she whimpered and curled up even tighter. 'Only a devil would have the power to put this much fear into her.'

At that moment, Tommy wanted to unceremoniously push Coutts's teeth down his throat and he might just have done that as well as a whole lot more had he known the whole truth.

'Now do you see what I've had to put up with, and you thought I was exaggerating, didn't you? I didn't make it all up, Tommy. How many times did I tell you Coutts was a devil in fine clothes? You never see wrong in anyone, but maybe now you've seen this for yourself, you'll believe me.'

It was never Maggie's intention to take her frustrations out on Tommy, but the evil that was Coutts's legacy still haunted this house. The very mention of his name petrified Eve.

How painful and disturbing to watch her sister's distress and be powerless to help. All Maggie could do was sit beside Eve and rock the child in her arms. She had to protect her until this evil could be exorcised before it became insanity, for it was only a matter of time before the fine line into madness was crossed and then she would be lost to them forever.

The cruel notion, that Eve might one day be locked away in a madhouse was the fearful, formidable anger and pain Maggie bore. But this was pain and anger unlike any other. This was a thrusting sword that sliced her soul and shred her reasoning.

Her very integrity and common decency had been invaded, and Maggie thundered, 'Oh, how I want to see that swine pay for what he's done. Damn him and all his kin. I will find a way to make him pay. Maybe not in this life, but I curse all him and his to roast in hell for all eternity.'

It was a rasping, hate-filled curse that tumbled bitterly from Maggie's lips and made Tommy wince. This pretty, young girl he adored, had become a she-devil, and the intensity of her hate was a frightening thing to witness.

Chapter Twenty-Seven

When the morning sun rose on a bright, brisk morning, Maggie felt no tiredness or struggle to leave her bed and ready for work. There was little fatigue, even though she had slept very little. Way into the small hours, she had lent comfort to Eve; talked to the distraught child in an effort to assure her Coutts was out of their lives. He could harm them no more and everything was going to be different from now on. Eve's mind was slow to open the door and allow trust in, but somewhere in that long night, Maggie felt that the murky waters of her sister's despair were at last beginning to clear.

She drew back the curtains and Maggie welcomed the light of this new day. For the first time in a while, she felt the ever-widening gap between her and Eve had been breached. Perhaps now the plague of demons that had infested and corrupted her mind could be sent back to whatever hell they arose from. The morning was as bright as her future, and Maggie couldn't wait to tell Agnes that she and Tommy were to marry.

When Maggie recounted every detail of Tommy's proposal, Agnes positively exuded delight. 'Well it's no surprise to me. I knew it was only a matter of time,' she said all-knowingly. 'Ah, but it's still the best news I've heard in a long time and it's gladdened my heart. Tommy's one of the best and he'll take good care of you.'

A strange thing happened just then. Maggie had expected a gushing stream of helpful advice, as well as a whole catalogue of pre-nuptial plans. But instead, Agnes grew strangely quiet. Under the circumstances, this wasn't quite normal. Right now, she should be so chatty; there would be little chance of getting a word in edgewise. This dreamy and vague wasn't natural. Not for Agnes. It was almost as if she had crossed the threshold into another dimension. She had a faraway smile on her face as they trod the cobbled street to work. Agnes was there in body alright, but certainly not in mind.

'Are you alright?' Maggie asked.

'Yes, yes of course.' She raised a hand to push back a stray wisp of hair that had fallen over her face and Agnes was shaking. 'You know that feeling you get when something happens and you'd swear it had happened before?'

'You mean déjà vu?'

'That's it,' Agnes said. Then she clasped a hand to her heart and kind of croaked, 'For a second or two, I was back to yesterday when your mother was telling me exactly the same thing. I felt she was walking right there beside me, her bonny face smiling and if I reached out, I could touch her.' A great sadness fell over her right then. 'But no, that bonny face wasn't there and never will be again.'

'Tell me about them… please,' Maggie begged. 'Tell me about my Mum and Dad when they were young and carefree… Were Mum and Dad ever young and carefree?' She let loose a sob for the pity of it all.

Agnes drew in her breath and said, 'Don't.'

But Maggie was deaf to the protest. 'All I seem to remember about Mum was her sadness and yet, she couldn't always have been sad. I need to know about them, Agnes, and then maybe I'll understand why she did what she did. My memory of Dad has faded so much, I can't even remember his face, and it makes me want to cry.'

This was a feeling Agnes knew only too well each time she allowed her mind to dwell on the past. She shrugged and in a grudging way asked, So, where do I begin?'

'At the beginning: start with how and where they met.'

Maggie couldn't explain the need to know all this now. Her situation was so different from other girls her age, Eve being the fly in this particular ointment. And yet, even under these circumstances, Tommy had still asked to marry her and she had agreed to wed him. Could that be what brought on this urgency to understand her parent's unconventional marriage? She remembered a sensation of being surrounded by love when her father was there, but beyond that, there was nothing. Although at times, she did recall being conscious of a terrible loneliness that seemed to envelop her mother when he was gone. Apart from these vague memories, Maggie knew virtually nothing of the two people who, through their deep love, were responsible for her being.

It had been so long since Agnes had allowed herself to remember, for in remembering came pain. But there was more to her pain than losing Tina. There was the hurt of not being able to stop the inevitable from happening when Coutts wormed his way into her life and her affection. She was torn between wanting and yet not wanting to go back to the beginning and talk about that happy time of budding youth and blossoming love. Was it time to tell the true love story about the first time Eddie and Tina set eyes upon each other? That was when Agnes put aside her reluctance.

'They met in hospital,' she said without all that much will to go on. 'It was one of those chance meetings: like in fairy tales. They took one look at each other across a crowded hospital ward and in that moment, they fell in love. Eddie was so big and so very handsome, with masses of blonde, curly hair.'

'Like Eve?'

'Yes, and Tina was so small and delicate with dark hair that fell all the way down to her waist.' She smiled at that particular vision which suddenly sprang to mind. Agnes remembered how she used to love brushing Tina's long hair. Maybe, that was when she came to realise that those were times that had no right to be locked away. They should be spoken about with lots of laughter… maybe a few tears. These were the happy times that should be remembered, not cast into a pit of silence and forgotten. The story of Tina and Eddie could inspire poets. With a sigh so profound, Agnes said, 'Eddie used to look at your Mum like he wanted to wrap her in his arms and protect her from every ill.'

All at once, as if a locked door to memories had been thrown open, her mind began turning back the pages of time. Agnes clutched every blissful recollection and reminisced, but silently and only within her own mind did she return to all those happy times of love and laughter that had belonged to them.

When Maggie could no longer stand this strange silence, she lightly prodded Agnes. 'Go on, tell me more,' she urged.

And so, the story of Eddie and Tina began. It was extraordinary how recollection incited enthusiasm. Agnes was swept along on an emotional tide of almost forgotten moments in time when youth and love was within their grasp.

'Aw, but Tina's birthday when she turned eighteen,' Agnes was all at once giggling and tears of laughter filled her eyes. 'Oh, I'll never, as long as I live and breathe, forget *that* day.'

'Why, what happened?'

'Eddie came to the house and asked your grandmother's permission to marry Tina. Well, she put her foot down because they'd only known each other a few weeks, and all hell broke loose. But they were determined to let nothing or no one stand in their way.' Agnes chuckled as the thought of Joe on his knees filled her mind. 'Did I ever tell you Joe proposed to me that very same day?'

'Joe actually proposed? I never took Uncle Joe for the proposing type. I always thought he just dragged you to the altar one day and that was that.'

'Ah well, that's how it might have been if their happiness hadn't rubbed off on the soppy, old devil and gave him the push he needed. Anyway, we agreed on a double wedding and with only weeks to arrange everything, we had to work against the clock. I can still almost taste the excitement. Oh, the way Tina and me shopped, giggled and fussed over our new homes.'

'You were very close, weren't you?'

'We shared everything, and everything was fun. In those days, even watching the paint dry was a wonderful experience. Joe and me, well, we didn't have much money and we knew getting started was going to be a struggle for us. And then… do you know what your mother did?'

'Something kind, generous and wonderful I bet.'

'She shared her inheritance with me. Money that had been put aside for *her,* because that was her way: generous to a fault. She said she didn't want me to worry.' This bittersweet memory was the most poignant and Agnes fought back deep sobs, took a hankie from her pocket and dabbed her eyes. 'There's not a day goes by that I don't bless her and till the day I die, I'll never stop missing her. Now would you look at me, crying like a big baby?' Agnes raised her tear-filled eyes towards the heavens, 'She's probably up there right now, laughing at me for being such a clown.'

'I'll understand if you don't want to go on. It's just that I can't imagine my parents ever having them kind of feelings or doing… you know? *That.* I never realised how much they must have loved each other. So what insanity possessed her to marry a man like Coutts?'

Sorrowfully, Agnes cast her eyes to the ground and slowly shook her head. 'That's the reason I can't let myself remember,' she said. 'It's this anger that comes over me.' Her shoulders lifted in one of those conclusive shrugs, as if this was treading on a no-go area and Agnes hastily changed the subject. 'Have you told your gran about you and Tommy?'

She understood *end of conversation,* so Maggie let it go and said, 'Tonight: we'll tell her tonight! I only hope she takes it well.' It was important to Maggie that her grandmother whole-heartedly approved her marriage. 'I often wonder what goes on in that head of hers, Agnes. She just sits there and hardly speaks a word.'

'I'll let you into a little secret. The last time I spoke to her, she said it was about time you and Tommy set a date,' Agnes winked impishly. 'She'll have plenty to say tonight, and that's a promise.'

There hadn't been much to smile about in her life, but tonight, Maggie Morris positively beamed and it was a beautiful sight to see. 'If anyone deserves someone to look after and care for them, it's you,' she said with the kind of joy that comes from the heart. 'While other lassies were playing with dolls, you were looking after the real thing: first Billy, then Eve. And now looking back, it's to my shame that I didn't do nearly enough to help.'

'You were working six days a week at that time, Gran. Mum used to say that was enough for any woman your age.'

'Your mother thought I was born fifty-years-old! She never could get it into her head that I was young once. Anyway, I'm happy for you, Maggie. God knows you've had enough heartache to last a lifetime, and you deserve to have love and laughter in your life. As for you, Tommy Stark,' she actually laughed at last and shook a warning finger at him. 'Never mind dragging out the engagement, you drag her to that altar quick as you can.'

'I intend doing just that on the fourteenth of May, Maggie's nineteenth birthday.' Tommy bent and whispered to Mrs Morris, 'I had that date in mind even before I proposed.'

She gave an exaggerated, open-mouthed gasp. 'Oh you great, big fibber, Tommy: you know full well I'd have had that day in mind too, because the day she was born was the happiest day in my life.' Her face lit in a cheery smile: it hadn't done that in a long time.

'Then lucky for me, I'm a mind reader,' Tommy joked.

The grand, old matriarch sighed nostalgically. 'My Tina met and married Eddie all within six months. They didn't get the chance to see any of you grow up, and that's the pity of it all. I pray if there's an afterlife, they're together again. For in ten years of marriage, what with Eddie at sea and then the war, they only got to spend a few precious months together. While not many women would have accepted that life, my Tina was content to wait for her husband to come home to her,' she said proudly.

'I know they were devoted to each other, Gran. Agnes told me all about it, but what even she couldn't tell me was why my mother married Coutts.'

Mrs Morris stamped her foot in a defiant way. 'Well, it wasn't because she wanted another husband! Companionship; that was all she wanted, and like the parasite he is, Coutts fed off her purity and goodness. I should have forced her to take heed of my warning not to do it. I'm the one to blame.'

'The guilt isn't yours, Gran! She was taken in, flattered and fooled by his attention.'

All at once, Tommy seemed possessed with the wisdom of ages. 'People make their *own* choices in life. That's *their* entitlement,' he said. 'You might never know why she did it, but it was her choice, and it's time you two cast off the sackcloth and ashes.' Tommy rested a reassuring hand on Mrs Morris's shoulder and the old lady relaxed in the comfort of his nearness.

The weight of conscience must have been an almost unbearable burden. Now, the long silence was broken and by opening her heart, this suffering was over and she felt cleansed of guilt. Maggie Morris was now able to talk freely, easily and at length about Tina and Eddie; smiling at one memory, weeping at another.

They listened in silence, as every emotion poured out of that frail old lady, and her Granddaughter, her namesake, felt humble. She had never stopped to consider that she and Eve were not the only ones to have lost. This poor, lonely woman had lost her daughter, son-in-law and grandson in tragedies that, by rights, would have creased the strongest human being. It was little wonder she had never fully recovered from the trauma and her mourning would never end.

This was the day secrets had been uncovered and revelations made. This was the day knowledge gained had fuelled Maggie's hatred of her step-father and strengthened her resolution to one day get even with him for every one of his evil deeds.

On her nineteenth birthday, Maggie married Tommy Stark in the same church where her parents were wed. Eve was still a very troubled child and with the greatest reluctance, acted as bridesmaid. By rights, she should have been happy on her sister's happy day. If anything, she was even more sullen than usual.

Heads turned to watch Maggie walk down the aisle to where Tommy waited at the altar, smiling proudly. Agnes slid closer to Joe and whispered, 'Doesn't this bring back memories? Makes you wonder where the last twenty years have gone. They seem to have disappeared faster than the morning mist.'

'I still have a clear picture of you and Tina walking down that aisle. Two of the bonniest brides anyone's ever seen.' Joe leaned over until his mouth was almost touching her ear. 'I've never told you this before, but when I turned and saw you that day, I almost broke down and cried. You were so beautiful. Here in my heart, I'll always carry that picture of you in your wedding dress to remind me of the happiest day of my life.'

A blush that matched the red rose Agnes wore on her dress, crept over her face. Considering that Joe had never been the most demonstrative of men and was rarely ever extravagant where words of love were concerned, she had been taken completely off guard. Agnes never looked for any great gesture of affection. She knew Joe loved her just as he knew she loved him. It was this impromptu confession that completely overwhelmed her.

'Well, Joseph O'Neill,' she whispered softly in his ear, 'what a fine pair we are. So much love between us, yet it takes a wedding in the same chapel where we were married for either of us to say the words. Even if I never say it again, I'll tell you this here and now. Never before, nor ever again, will I love any man the way I love you.'

He didn't turn his head, not Joe. He just sat there grinning from ear to ear. 'I've always known that, you silly woman,' he said from the side of his mouth. 'Don't you know you were put on this earth to give me a reason for living?' And this was the closest Joe would ever come to proclaiming his undying love.

How do you add to perfection? The truth is, you can't. Sitting there in the chapel next to Joe, Agnes felt she was surrounded by perfect love. She watched the girl, the one whose birth had eased the pain of losing her own little girl, become a bride.

Tonight, at the reception in the same church hall where they held theirs, she and Joe would laugh and dance as they did twenty years ago at their own wedding. Tonight, they were blissfully oblivious to the fact that youth had long since gone, snatched by the relentless, unstoppable march of time. For tonight only, the last twenty years would melt away and they would be young again.

Chapter Twenty-Eight

That first night in the seaside boarding house where their honeymoon began, they cuddled together in the rather antiquated bed. 'It's not as uncomfortable as you'd imagine for a cheap bed and breakfast place,' Maggie said and Tommy just sighed contentedly.

They weren't like mad, passionate lovers on honeymoon. They were simply two wearied people grateful to be alone together. Gathering the strength to face the uncertainties, which lay ahead, was of the utmost importance. But for now, this was their time; their perfect honeymoon.

After breakfast, they strolled hand in hand along the sea front. Maggie was radiant, serene and oh so happy. 'Isn't this lovely, Tommy? Just smell that brisk sea air.'

'Mm,' Tommy still wore a contented, secret smile on his face as his arm tightened around Maggie's waist and drew her closer to him.

They had three whole carefree days to enjoy the start of their life together as man and wife. The newlyweds still couldn't believe they were lucky enough to be spending such a wonderful honeymoon in a small seaside town with long walks on the beach taking in the sea air. It was even harder to believe they were walking in sunshine with a warm breeze ruffling the hair and only a relatively short train ride from the smoke and grime of industrial Dundee. The distance may not have been great, but the difference was immense.

Maggie squeezed Tommy's hand. 'I wish we could live here forever and ever,' she said, resting her head on his shoulder. 'Even a few more days would be fine.'

But the brief honeymoon had to end then it was back to 22 Charles Street and the reality of once more facing the on-going worry over Eve's behaviour. The breakthrough had been short-lived. Things had steadily worsened rather than bettered. Having to return and fight a battle they couldn't seem to win, wasn't a pleasing prospect.

The night Tommy proposed to Maggie, things reached boiling point. Many spiteful words were spoken and then came the calm after the storm. For a brief time, it seemed the battle was over, but the invisible shell in which Eve had cocooned herself hadn't as much as cracked. At the time, it seemed that they had made a giant leap forward. Maggie had been so sure they'd got to the root of her problems, but it wasn't to be. Eve reverted to type and once more, became the bane of their lives. There had been no breakthrough. All she had done was cleverly mask whatever badness had invaded her and in so doing, the once gentle child cunningly managed to lull them into a sense of relief that their troubles were over. They weren't. Woes were only simmering in a pot of dilemmas, which would surely boil over in time.

One look at Eve when they walked into the house and it was patently clear nothing had changed. Their absence hadn't made the heart grow fonder. If anything, she was even more ill-humoured. She ignored them completely, her attitude being, since they'd left *her* for three days, she'd now treat *them* with the contempt they deserve.

'Put the kettle on and I'll tell you all about our holiday over a nice cup of tea.' Maggie tried hard to keep a smile on her face... and her hands from shaking this aggression out of her sister. If only she'd open her eyes and take a good look, then she'd realise *they* were not her enemy.

Tommy battled the urge to yell, '*Enough.*' Instead, for his new wife's sake, he forced himself to smile when all the while, he felt more like weeping. In a last bid effort to bring a spark of interest to those angry eyes, he told Eve, 'There were ice cream carts and people selling candy floss on the beach. Imagine that.'

He tried so hard to put on a cheery face, smile and tell funny stories about how seagulls swooped on any bits of discarded food, but it was only too obvious his endeavour to thrill and delight Eve with tales of seagulls, ice cream and candy floss was dead in the water.

'There was even a fair,' Maggie added. Still, the silent treatment continued and dejectedly, Maggie asked, 'Don't you want to know all about the seaside?'

Eve griped, 'Why should I?' and her face twisted in a look of repugnance.

Maggie was at the end of her tether. 'Now look here you...' Just as she was on the verge of lashing out in fury, she caught sight of Tommy's shaking head warning her to draw rein on her temper.

Why couldn't Tommy see reality had to be faced? Why didn't he see Eve was nothing more than an unwelcome guest who made their life hell? In the space of a few minutes, she had even managed to wipe out the memory of those few happy days.

'We were going to save like mad and take you on holiday there next year. It was to be a surprise.' Maggie slammed her backside onto a chair so hard, the legs seemed in danger of giving way and tears of despair fell fast and free. 'We're just fighting one losing battle after another, Tommy, and I'm sick to death of it. What's the point of trying?'

They had stepped out of the sunshine and straight into a world of gloom. The honeymoon was truly over and now, Tommy despaired of Eve ever being a normal little girl, sweet and loving. He now had to accept there was a serious kink in her nature. 'No point at all,' Tommy said wryly.

The truth he hid from Maggie was that, Eve's increasingly bad attitude was telling on him. How could he tell her there were times he had reason to wonder if perhaps he'd bitten off more than he could chew? Was there any nice way to say that, thanks to the brat, married bliss wasn't the bed of roses it should have been? Their marriage was more like a bed of thorns; a living hell.

Given time, the inclination to move out and move on might be too hard for Tommy to ignore.

When the autumn chill brought leaves tumbling from the trees, leaving naked boughs, Maggie seemed to be filled with a strange kind of melancholy. She constantly wanted to weep but didn't know why. It wasn't Eve, because she'd given up crying over her. There were also changes coming over her that she didn't understand. Perhaps watching those dead and dying leaves wither and fall from the trees was a sorry reminder of all the hopes and dreams in her life that had also wilted and withered.

All hopes of peace and quiet were dashed as Eve became more unstable than ever now that Tommy was living under the same roof. It wasn't only their love that was put to the test: their marriage too was under so much strain, all the signs were there that it was deigned never to last.

Maggie would never dare confess to anyone other than Agnes that she secretly wished to be rid of Eve. 'I'm wracked with guilt. An awful guilt for wanting to throw her out onto the street,' she told Agnes. 'I don't think Tommy can stand much more, and it's a fight to stop myself lashing out and belting the life out of her.'

'Knowing the hell she's putting you through, there are times I feel like doing the same,' Agnes admitted. 'I can't blame you for wanting to lift your fists and bash her. Unfortunately, it might do more harm than good.'

Agnes was more than willing to give her honest opinion and douse Maggie's guilt. Only, it wasn't all that easy to give reassurance. The truth had to be faced. Although they loved the child, none of them liked Eve for the torment she piled onto her sister.

Agnes urged Maggie to err on the side of caution and bide her time. 'With a little luck and a lot of patience, she'll eventually grow out of whatever's bugging her.' It was the best advice, the only advice anyone could offer.

'But what if Tommy reaches the point where he can't take any more? I'm scared shitless, that one day, he'll pack a bag and leave. I wouldn't blame him, Agnes.'

'If things are that bad, then maybe it's time you put yourselves first and do the needful. You might have to make the choice of ending your marriage, or putting Eve into care.'

The snow was falling lightly when Maggie opened the curtains on Christmas morning and her inner excitement far exceeded the occasion, for she had a secret that was about to be shared. 'Merry Christmas, Tommy,' she said excitedly and thrust a small parcel into his hands.

'Hold on until I get your present....'

'No, no, you have to open mine first,' Maggie insisted.

'It must be a snowball that'll melt unless I open it quick,' Tommy kidded and flippantly tore apart the wrapping to reveal... a tiny pair of bootees nestling in tissue paper? It was one of those head-scratching, confused moments. He'd expected socks, just not like these. 'What are these for? Sorry to tell you, Maggie, but they're a wee bit on the small side for me.' He scratched his head and frowned. 'I know you're one for pranks, but I just don't get this one.'

'Can't you guess?' Maggie waited and willed the penny to drop. 'Surely, you must have some notion by now.' She couldn't believe how anyone as clever as Tommy could be so dim.

'Sorry, Maggie, I don't understand what exactly I'm supposed to do with them.' He laid them on the table in front of him and still Tommy's face remained a blank.

'Oh, Tommy,' Maggie wailed in exasperation, 'this is my way of telling you I'm expecting. We're going to have a baby. I found out two weeks ago and I've been biting my tongue ever since, so that I could wait until today to tell you and make this Christmas special.'

'It's not a prank and you're not joking, are you?' Tommy suddenly remembered how, over the past two weeks, he had caught Maggie smiling softly to herself in a sort of *'I know something you don't'* fashion, and then she'd gently rub her belly. Of course, the thought never crossed his mind that it couldn't be anything other than a windy tummy.

It was the season of peace and goodwill, and for Tommy, the best Christmas ever. This had to be a sign from God that the New Year would be a new beginning: an end at last to this topsy-turvy life of friction and the nerve-shredding continual cacophony of shrieking and shouting. He grabbed Maggie and playfully began to cover her face in kisses and telling her what a clever girl she was.

It was Maggie's squeals of laughter that brought Eve stamping into the room. Rubbing sleepy eyes, she irritably demanded to know what all the noise was about. 'You woke me up,' she yelled in anger.

This was a joyful day. It was a day for indifferences and bad feelings to be put aside. Tommy and Maggie happily chorused, 'Merry Christmas.'

Typically insolent and ignorant, Eve retorted, 'Oh really, is it?'

Maggie overlooked the snub and excitedly said, 'We have a special present for you.' She truly believed that this would be the decisive turning point. Surely, a girl's natural enthusiasm for her sister's impending motherhood would overcome all that aggression. Surely, this was the one thing that might oust the demon and give her back the little sister she knew and loved. 'You're going to have a little niece or nephew.' Maggie looked for... what? A bolt from the blue, a flash of light, some sign that Eve cared at least a little?

All she said was, 'What's for breakfast?'

The announcement had made not the least impact. They didn't expect her to jump for joy, hell, this was Eve after all, but she could at least have forced a smile. She simply glowered and pushed past them without as much as glancing at the Christmas stocking that hung over the mantelpiece or the parcels stacked by the hearth.

Tommy felt a churning in the pit of his stomach. 'Can't you pretend to be happy, just this once? Please, Eve, at least try to show some enthusiasm.' He tried to be kindly when, if truth be told, all Tommy felt like was slapping some sense into the senseless brat. 'Can you not see how much you're hurting

Maggie?' Bitterness burned like acid in his throat and that was hard to swallow. 'This is supposed to be a time for celebration and you still haven't wished either of us a happy Christmas or looked at your presents.'

Tommy's pleading was gentle, but to no avail. He had more chance of getting a pleasanter reaction from a block of wood than Eve's snotty look of indifference.

'Did I ask you for presents?' Eve made a point of kicking the parcels as she passed.

The joy and Christmas spirit had all been ruthlessly and callously ripped from their grasp and Tommy realised, as he watched the tears roll down Maggie's face, that this would never be a happy home as long as the young she-devil was under their roof: but what to do without breaking Maggie's heart?

The idea of a baby in the house was enough to make any little girl's heart flutter with excitement. Only, Eve wasn't a normal little girl and their happy chatter just sent her into an even worse temper. Maggie's despair hit rock-bottom, for now she feared the worst, her sister *was* succumbing to madness.

'Let's go and wish Agnes, Joe and Conner a merry Christmas.' Tommy fetched their coats. 'Just you and me,' he said pointedly, and then whispered to Maggie, 'once she's alone, maybe then she'll be tempted to unwrap her presents.' She didn't, and the hurt went on.

Chapter Twenty-Nine

It was in the seventh month of her pregnancy when matters came to a head. The police paid Maggie a visit dragging a frenzied, wild-eyed Eve with them. It stunned Maggie and all but made her faint with fear to open the door and be faced by two uniformed men standing on the doorstep with Eve between them, her arms tightly gripped to restrain her flaying fists from connecting with their faces.

'What's happened?' Maggie had to lean against the wall to stop from falling over.

It was obvious by the serious looks on their faces; she wasn't going to like what they had to say. Every nerve in her body stung. Every limb felt leaden and numb. Fear sent Maggie into a trembling seizure she couldn't control when, without waiting for a customary invite, they shoved the rebellious child forcefully over the threshold and into the house.

'A bit of a handful your sister,' the senior police officer said in a rather jovial and light-hearted way that Maggie supposed was for her benefit. 'Look at the state of me.' His tongue made a clicking sound as, with the palm of his hand, he began brushing the dusty footprints from his dark trousers. Little footprints left by Eve when she kicked out as they dragged her home. 'Your sister was caught red-handed throwing a brick through the office window of James Coutts & Son,' he explained, 'and before you ask, there's no mistake. She waited to be apprehended and of her own free will admitted that she was the perpetrator, but refused to explain why she did it.'

Maggie listened wearily to the allegation and the colour drained from her face. Shaking arms enfolded her unborn baby as if to protect it from all this hurt. She didn't show anger, only heartbreak and deep sorrow.

Until that moment, Eve had been reasonably subdued. Perhaps it was the pain on Maggie's ashen face or the way her work-worn hands guarded her child, but something triggered another verbal onslaught and unleashed an even greater fury.

'Go on, Maggie, you tell them why I did it,' Eve screamed. And then the harshest of oaths tumbled from her mouth and the pitch of her screams became so intense, it was almost as if it would bring the walls tumbling down around them. **'Tell them, fucking tell them,'** she roared at Maggie.

Maggie gasped and gurgled as if every breath of air had been forced from her body. This foul-mouthed creature couldn't possibly be the little sister who was once so sweet and pure.

Suddenly, Eve fell to the floor. Her whole body shook so violently that they feared she was in the grip of an epileptic fit. The policemen looked alarmed and the elder of the two tried to calm the distraught child with soothing words that seemed too soft and gentle for such a big, hardened man.

'No need for all this shouting now, is there? We're not here to hurt you or your sister. All we want is a reason for such senseless vandalism. Why, you didn't even try to run away. You're old enough to understand it's against the law to damage other people's property.'

In spite of the calming tone and the continuing assurances that she wouldn't be punished for her actions, Eve became increasingly agitated and shook her head so fiercely, it seemed in danger of separating from her delicate, little neck. 'Because, because, because,' she repeated over and over.

The senior officer had a gut-churning feeling in the pit of his stomach. This pretty, little, fair-haired child looked almost angelic. Whatever happened to change her into this demon had to be something sinister. He had to find out what. There was no way he could leave here without discovering the source of her torment, if only for his own peace of mind.

'Please child, whatever it is, you can tell us and I promise no harm will come to you.' When he gently laid a hand on Eve's shoulder, she leapt out of reach as if his hand had burned through sinew and bone.

'**No, no, no**. Keep him away, Maggie. Please don't let him touch me.' Her eyes were deep pools of horror, terror and despair.

Suddenly, Eve darted to a corner of the room and huddled on the floor with her knees under her chin, rocking back and forth and rambling incoherently. There was only the sound of the creak, creak, creak, from a loose floorboard as Eve rocked. And then all at once, silence. She became very still and the creaking stopped. Eve had never allowed a word of the terrible secret she kept to pass her lips for fear of the grave punishment which had been promised her if she told. The guilt she had borne in silence could no longer be contained. Maggie had called her insane and if that were the truth, then the only way to purge her soul was by letting go of the secret. Her head lolled forward and rested on her knees as if she were in a trance, and Eve's voice sounded strangely disembodied as she at last opened the door where unspoken horrors lurked. She laid bare her soul.

What unfolded, turned their blood to ice. The reason for her extreme behaviour wasn't inborn badness or demon spirits. It was a cry for help. A cry Maggie had ignored, not through lack of feeling, but through her own naivety and lack of knowledge. Now, she understood the problem hadn't stemmed from the day Eve was entrusted with the money. It had begun long before that. Not only had Coutts stolen their money, he had also stolen Eve's innocence when she was no more than a trusting child. She had been forced to keep to herself the vile acts Coutts had subjected her to.

The two hardened policeman, who thought they'd seen every horror, were visibly shaken by the tale of unspeakable filth and degradation this child told of being exposed to. They left the house with tears in their eyes and disgust in their hearts for the creature that had put this family through deprivation, anguish, and if whispers were to be believed, the robbing of some inheritance.

There was a lot to think about. The business of policing had soured and the two policemen strode slowly on their beat, discussing whether or not it would be good politics to raise questions back at the station as to why the claim of theft against him had never been investigated and James Coutts had been whitewashed. Maggie Fraser's allegation, that Coutts had stolen their money, was common knowledge. The subject of Coutts near bankruptcy, the coincidence of both his wives' tragic deaths and the unexplained fortune he came into had been raised many times over the years. But with who Coutts referred to as, *friends in high places* backing him, rumours were hastily quashed. No one was permitted to take Maggie Fraser's accusations seriously. Perhaps those who were nonbelievers that Coutts was an honest man should have stood up and been counted.

What a shame: it was too late now, mores' the pity. Coutts was surrounded by high-ranking, influential people who had the power to protect him against accusations and even prosecution.

As they walked and talked, the shocked policemen admitted to one chilling doubt. How many of these high-ranking, supposedly principled men, knew of

Coutts's penchant for little girls? More to the point, how many of these apparently honourable gentlemen believed that indulging in lecherous behaviour with children was an acceptable pastime?

After much thought, they agreed that the best, the only action they could take would be to report what they had witnessed and make it official. After that, they'd make damned sure word was spread throughout the station to let those involved in this kind of depravity know that their game was up.

Maggie held Eve gently in her arms and softly murmured assurances that she held no blame for past events. Eve clung to her sister and wept softly. The tears had been a long time coming. Hopefully now, they could wash away her misery and suffering.

This was the scene that met Tommy when he came home from work. With the same feeling of dread that filled his every waking hours, he stammered, 'Wh... what has she done this time?'

'Give me a minute, Tommy. I'll explain later.' Maggie took Eve's hand. 'Come on,' she said gently, 'lie down and rest easy, because no one will ever hurt you again.'

It was something of a shock for Tommy to see Eve follow obediently. He couldn't help but wonder what anomaly could have suddenly made this unbearable, little monster so goddamned saintly. For months, she had brought chaos into the home and made aggression a way of life and now... He waited on an explanation.

'The police brought Eve home after they caught her breaking Coutts's window!'

Tommy's hands covered his face and he let loose a string of raging expletives.

'Let me finish,' Maggie said. 'They wanted her to tell why she did it. I don't know if it was the fright of being arrested, but she broke down and told... everything.' And then, just when Maggie thought she had no tears left, the floodgates opened once more. 'Oh, Tommy, the things Coutts did to her, even the police were sickened.' She related every detail while Tommy sat with his hands clasped tightly to stop them from shaking.

'You mean to say, we've been treating her like... well, like she was really wicked or something, and the poor kid was only trying to hide her shame?' The revelation brought with it another terror for Tommy to face. 'Did that devil ever touch you?' He asked hoarsely. 'If he did, I swear I'll kill the sick son of a bitch.'

'He knew I'd probably scream it from the rooftops if he tried anything with me. He preferred little girls like Eve who would be too frightened to say anything.' Maggie shook her head in disbelief. 'I can't understand. Why didn't I see what was staring me in the face instead of jumping to all the wrong conclusions? Was I was that thick and stupid I couldn't even see what was going on under my own nose?' This was the thing that hurt Maggie the most.

'You were never stupid, Maggie! Maybe we were both too immature to believe anyone, including Coutts, could be capable of hurting a child in such a diabolical way.' Tommy held her to him. 'You're not to blame, my darling, he is. Right now, I want to go out and tell everyone there's a depraved monster loose among them, but we have to keep this to ourselves and tell no one.'

'No, no, we have to tell everyone what he did and see that he's punished.'

'That's the worst thing we could do! Think about it Maggie. How will Eve ever get over this when all the damned whisperers and gossips, who called her filthy names, point their bony fingers at her in blame? There's a stigma attached to things like this and right now, we have to protect her from them that would cause her even more hurt. We'll wrap her in cotton wool if that's what it takes.'

Tommy's logic overcame Maggie's compulsion to seek revenge. Instead, she looked to his inherent wisdom and patience to carry them through this time of anguish and pain.

From that day forth, they showered Eve with genuine love and affection, and instilled in her the belief that she was blameless for Coutts's wickedness. Maggie never allowed her to go to sleep without telling her that, although she had been touched by evil, it didn't make *her* an evil person. She was and always would be an angel in their eyes.

It's said that confession is good for the soul and there must be truth in this adage, for since the day Eve rid herself of the terrible secret, she slowly began the return journey from madness to normality. Now and again, she lapsed into the occasional outburst. It was soon quelled by a reassuring cuddle.

With her sister's help and guidance, Eve finally banished all thoughts of Coutts's bestiality to the deep, dark recesses of her mind where they belonged. Now, she even showed interest in the imminent birth of Maggie's baby, especially when it was pointed out to her that she would no longer be just Eve, but Auntie Eve. This special slot in life seemed to be the thing that put the finishing touches to her recovery. Eve Fraser now had a particular place in this family, a place that belonged only to her.

In July 1928, Maggie gave birth to a beautiful, healthy baby boy. The only problem was, that she had been so convinced their first child would be a girl, she and Tommy had only thought of girl's names.

'Well there's a surprise,' Tommy said when he saw his son for the first time. 'I thought you said we were having a daughter. We can't very well call this little man Tina, so what do you suggest?'

'Would you mind very much if we named him Billy?' she asked hesitantly. 'I'd like very much to name him after my grandfather in Australia who I've never met—and the little boy who never got the chance to grow up.'

Maggie watched as Tommy proudly held his son, waiting, fully expecting some kind of objection or fierce denial to her choice of name. Insistence that his first born should be named after himself was only natural. Maggie should have remembered what a sweet, kind nature Tommy had. Wasn't that why she had fallen in love with him in the first place?

'I'd like that,' he answered, with that crinkling smile Maggie adored, 'what better way to keep the memory of a loved one alive than to carry their name? I think William Edward suits him, and I know your parents would be so proud.' Tommy handed the baby back to his mother.

'It's settled then, this is our Billy.' Maggie looked lovingly at the tiny baby nestling in her arms, then smiled at her husband. 'You know something, Tommy Stark,' she said, 'I don't deserve you.'

Chapter Thirty

Mrs Morris passed away shortly after Billy was born, and was laid to rest beside her husband and her darling Tina. As the coffin was lowered, Maggie cast a glance around the friends who stood at the graveside to pay their last respects. She grimaced when one face from the past caught her eye.

'Is that who I think it is? It is Millie Coutts! What the hell is she doing here?' Maggie walked over to where the young woman stood aside from the other mourners. 'It would have been enough of a shock to see your father put on a show of caring and turn up for his mother-in-law's funeral, but I didn't expect you,' she said haughtily to her stepsister. 'What brought you here, Millie, *his* suggestion or your conscience?'

'I don't know what you mean.' Millie adjusted the silly hat she was wearing; a purple creation bedecked with pink roses and totally unsuitable for a funeral, or for that matter, someone of her immense build. It made her look garish perched on that head of over-permed, frizzy hair that bore a strong resemblance to a bird's nest.

'I think you know fine, Millie. The folk here came to pay their respects. Good, old daddy didn't bother paying his respects at your mother or my mother's funeral. We made you welcome in our home, you were treated like one of the family and you repaid us with insults. Tell me, what malice made you come to my grandmother's funeral? There's no more money for your father to steal, if that's what you were thinking.'

'It's nothing like that!' Millie yelped defensively. 'I was simply trying to be friendly. I wish now I hadn't bothered.'

'I remember offering you the hand of friendship and you bit it. Now if you don't mind, we have grieving to get on with. Thank you for paying your respects.' And then, in a moment of remorse for remarks that were unkind, Maggie grasped Millie's arm as she turned to leave. 'My mother was kind and loving, so why didn't you forget for a while you were a Coutts and accept the

213

affection that was freely offered instead of acting like queen bee? You would have found a good friend in me, Millie.'

'Whatever gave you the idea I was *looking* for a friend,' Millie said sarcastically, then she straightened her ridiculous hat and wobbled away.

Maggie and Eve clung together at the graveside after everyone else had gone. This final farewell was so difficult for them, yet there was also relief. For many months, the grand, old matriarch had slowly let go of the will to live. All that kept her going was the wish to witness the birth of her first great-grandchild, then, and only then, would she be free to leave behind her earthly domain and all the sorrow that went with it.

'We have to come to terms with this, Eve, and accept that she's gone. Her poor heart was broken when Mum died and the pain never left her. I remember the night me and Tommy told her we were to marry. She said some very strange things. Seeing Millie Coutts sort of brought them all back.'

'Grandma was always saying strange things, Maggie.'

'This wasn't just rambling, it was different. Our grandma always maintained, if Mum hadn't married Coutts, she would still be alive, and she had it on good authority that the police believes he threw his first wife down the stairs and broke her neck, only they couldn't prove it.'

'Don't open old wounds,' Tommy warned.

'You were there, Tommy, you heard her, so think about it and ask yourself, was it all that daft? **We** know full well what he's capable of. I'll tell you why someone so evil can live and thrive. He sold his miserable, black soul to the devil, that's why.'

'You buried your grandmother today and now, it's time to bury the past.' It worried Tommy to see the hate that contorted Maggie's face until she looked almost demonic and what was worse, that explosive anger was building up inside her again: an anger that only a Coutts could unleash. They were happy together and he wanted it to stay that way. Unfortunately, Coutts might forever be in their subconscious. But at least he was out of their lives. They made a pact a long time ago never to mention his name again and it never was, until now. Why, oh why did Millie Coutts have to show face today of all days? 'Please, love, don't put yourself through this again. Let it go,' Tommy pleaded.

It was like a summer storm that passed as quickly as it came. Maggie smiled and said, 'you're right, Tommy. If we let him spoil what we have together, then we really have lost everything.' She took his hand and held out the other to Eve. 'Let's go home,' she said with a last fleeting glance at the grave.

Their life was simple, but sublime nevertheless. Rich in love if not money, and that was what mattered. As they left the cemetery, Maggie vowed never to let Coutts creep back into their life, and like a cancer, eat away at this love.

In the same week Mrs Morris was buried, Connor proudly told his parents they were to become grandparents. It had always been Agnes and Joe's dearest wish to have more children themselves, only, Agnes was never able to conceive after the twin's difficult birth. Each month brought the torment of failure, but never once did she huff bitterly when those who knew how much she longed for another child raised questions about her barrenness. Agnes simply hid her anguish with jokes about the fun it was trying for another baby. No one saw the tears. After years of raised hopes and then bitter disappointments, they were forced to accept that Connor was fated to be an only child. And now at last, fate smiled on them; Connor and his wife, Ellen, were to give them a grandchild.

'I know how bad this might sound in the midst of your grief, Maggie, but would you be offended if we had a little celebration on Saturday night?' The way her eyes swept the floor rather than look Maggie in the eye, no one could mistake the discomfort Agnes felt. 'Mind you, it won't be nothing much, just a few friends round for a drink or two.'

'What makes you think I'd be offended, for heaven's sake?'

'It doesn't feel decent or respectful somehow, your gran not yet cold in her grave. We've so much to be happy about while you're... in mourning.' Agnes was suddenly regretful at her own elation while Maggie had just suffered the loss of her dear Gran.

'Well, my feelings will be hurt,' Maggie said in her best, indignant voice, then she laughed and jokingly poked her finger at Agnes, 'but only if we're not invited mind.'

'Are you sure, Maggie?'

'I think a good, old knee up is just what the doctor ordered.'

'Oh Maggie,' Agnes gave a great sigh of relief, 'thank God your feelings aren't hurt. I'm so happy today, I wouldn't change places with the Queen, and to think how I used to worry about Connor. Every week, a different girl on his arm and all I wanted was to see him settle down. But of course, being his mother, I didn't think there would ever be anyone good enough for him.

'There wasn't a weaver who didn't pant at the sight of Connor O'Neill and you used to get yourself in such a flap.' Maggie bit on her bottom lip and giggled. 'Mind you, I didn't think any girl was good enough for him either.'

'Until Ellen came to work at the mill,' Agnes said. 'When I first saw her, well, the thought that bobbed into my mind was, if I could choose a wife for my boy, she would be the one, and I got my wish.'

It was fortunate Agnes couldn't read Maggie's mind at that moment, because she was thinking that even the powers that be would never dare deny the autonomous Agnes her dearest wish.

Connor had been something of a worry to Agnes, although she strongly denied it. His altogether Bohemian attitude to life bothered her. Connor had this magnetism along with wildly-rugged good looks that made girls positively swoon at his feet. There was a string of broken hearts throughout the mill that were testimony to his popularity. Connor O'Neill was footloose and fancy free. Not one of the many beauties, who relentlessly pursued the handsome rogue, could tempt him to settle down—until the day he walked through the mill and saw Ellen Randall. From the moment Connor set eyes on Ellen, he was lost to all woman-kind and his heart was lost to the pretty, raven-haired girl.

Connor had been striding alongside the foreman, deep in discussion, when his head suddenly swivelled. 'I don't remember seeing her before,' he said, staring at Ellen and acting all couldn't-care-less. After all, he was used to being chased, not the chaser.

The foreman was aware that Conner's fast stride had become a slow crawl. 'Oh her,' he said casually. 'She started this morning as a trainee weaver.'

It was a straight answer to a straight question, but that was all the information he was getting. The foreman had seen that lustful look before. Connor had a reputation with girls in the mill, but Ellen Randall didn't act all rough and ready like them. She was different. She had a kind of quiet dignity that raised her above the others.

'At least tell me her name.' Connor was, if nothing else, persistent when a pretty girl caught his roving eye.

'Now look here, you've already left a trail of weeping women the length and breadth of this mill and it's not good for production. This one's just an innocent kid, so leave her alone.' The foreman walked away, fully aware Connor would follow with dogged determination.

'You know I'll find out anyway, Frank.'

'I'm sure you will, but not from me. Now go and do some work. Loom five needs seen to.' Frank smiled craftily to himself. Loom five was the one Ellen was training on, and he could just picture the mill's prize peacock strut his stuff for the benefit of the new girl.

To be heard above the clatter of the looms, Connor had to speak directly into Ellen's ear. Her hair, tied back with a blue ribbon, was soft against his cheek and she smelled of Pear's soap, clean and fresh. In that singular moment, Connor knew he would never want another girl as much as he wanted this one. He could charm the birds from the trees and knew he had the reputation of being a heartthrob. Connor also knew he was extremely attractive to the opposite sex, which gave him a self-confidence that was often taken as arrogance. Many times, Agnes warned him he would meet his match one day.

'You're new to the mill, aren't you?' Connor asked, deploying every ounce of charisma he possessed. 'What's your name?'

'Ellen, Ellen Randall.'

Her mouth was so close to his ear, if he turned quickly, their lips would be touching. Connor swallowed hard and fought the temptation. She looked at him with the biggest, brown eyes he had ever seen, and his fate was sealed. In that instant, Connor knew that one day, he would marry Ellen Randall. Oh yes, this was definitely the one to tame the infamous Connor O'Neill.

Before the end of her second week at the mill, Ellen succumbed to Connor's charm and persistent pleading to go out with him, in spite of all the dire warnings about Connor O'Neill's unfaithful ways and his *love them and leave them* policy. Bets were taken as to how long it would take Connor to tire of this one, considering the longest he had ever kept a steady girlfriend was four weeks.

It was no surprise to anyone that Connor was always on hand to repair loom five when it developed some mysterious fault or other, again and again and again. Joe just laughed at, what to him, was no more than some kind of daft mating ritual.

'If you can't find the fault, Connor, I'll be only too happy to give my expert advice,' Joe told him in a tongue-in-cheek sort of way.

'Come off it, Dad, you know as well as I do there's no fault. Ellen just wants to see me and make sure she's not dreaming.'

'Don't let your ego get too big, or you'll be in danger of losing her. You're not the only pebble on the beach, and that is one very pretty girl, a real head-turner.'

'I know, Dad, and I'm going to marry her one day,' Connor proudly announced.

'You're very sure of yourself! What if she doesn't want to marry youèor did that thought never enter your mind?'

Joe and Connor were more like best pals than father and son, and it was normal to see them scuffle in the passageway pretending to box. The weavers were used to these antics that made them laugh and shout out which O'Neill they'd put their shirt on. Agnes just smiled patiently and shook her head, although adoration was written in every line on her face.

'Look at me, Dad,' Conner stood with his arms outstretched. 'How could any woman resist?'

'You know what they say about pride, Son, it comes before a fall.'

'I've already fallen, Dad.' Suddenly, the brash façade was gone and Connor was just a boy telling his father he was in love with a girl. 'I fell for Ellen the minute I clapped eyes on her. I just plain love the girl and I think—I hope she loves me enough to say yes when I ask her to marry me. If she does say no, then I won't give up. I'll keep asking until she says yes.'

'Well, well,' and that shortest of statements was about the limit to Joe's vocabulary right at that minute.

'I know she's beautiful, Dad, but Ellen's a lot more than just good to look at. Jeez, I've gone out with lots of really good-looking girls, but she's different. Ellen Randall's warm and loving and... I worship the ground she walks on.'

It was as quick as that. Connor loved Ellen and he saw no point in beating about the bush. Within no more than just a few weeks, he asked her to marry him. She accepted and six months later, they were preparing a wedding.

Many hearts were broken the day Connor and Ellen—the new Mrs O'Neill—walked down the aisle. There was a veritable river of tears shed by girls, who at one time or another, thought they would be the one to take this most prestigious place. Girls had loved and lost, but as far as Connor was concerned, there was only one girl for him and he would never again have eyes for anyone but Ellen.

Eighteen months after their first meeting, Ellen gave birth to a beautiful baby boy who had all the makings of a heartthrob... just like his father.

Chapter Thirty-One

In the spring of 1930, James Coutts's obituary was reported in the Courier. Strangely enough, darkness didn't descend over the earth and thunder clouds didn't gather to show that the devil had claimed one of his own. Quite the opposite in fact; the sun shone brightly in a cloudless, blue sky. Perhaps it was God's way of showing that the world was rid of another evil.

The day began like any other Monday morning. Maggie made breakfast and saw Tommy off to work before dusting and polishing. It was a glorious day, so she took advantage of it by putting Billy in his pram and taking a walk into town. In the afternoon, with the shopping done, Maggie listened to the radio while preparing the tea. Just another ordinary day… and then the newspaper fell through the letterbox.

Softly humming the song that was playing on the radio, Maggie looked in the cot. Billy was still sleeping soundly, so there was time to sit down with a nice cup of tea and have a glance through the paper until the potatoes came to the boil. Suddenly, it was as if a thousand pins were piercing her body. It was there on the third page, the picture of a much younger Coutts alongside his obituary. Was it her imagination or was that sick smile on his face actually taunting her?

'So,' Maggie laughed mirthlessly and bitterly as she read aloud, 'after a short illness, James Coutts died peacefully in his sleep. Huh, peacefully! Well that's unfortunate.' She may have felt elated that her tormentor was gone from this earth forever, but the manner of his death gave no satisfaction. For years, Maggie had prayed he would suffer a slow, agonising death. How typically Coutts! He had even cheated her out of that pleasure. 'Still,' she muttered to herself, 'you won't escape the fires of hell, James Coutts.'

The crumpled newspaper lay open on her lap as she sipped the tea. Maggie didn't have the stomach to read all the codswallop they'd probably have written about him but the words teased her to read it all, so she laid down the cup and shook the creases from the paper. With a great deal of cynicism and stomach-churning disgust, she read what was nothing short of a glowing obituary.

The report bore no resemblance to the man she knew and hated. Millie had more than likely raved to a reporter that her Daddy was this wonderfully kind and generous man who was loved by all. Shit! According to this, James Coutts was a respected pillar of the community. More shit. Maggie ranted as she read this drivel that made the man seem almost saintly. Whoever wrote this trash, obviously didn't know the real Coutts. Then again, did reporters ever write the truth about wealthy people? Or was that more than their job was worth? If they'd wanted truth, they should have come to her. Maggie giggled to herself, for if she were asked to give an accurate account of the man, it would have been unprintable. Imagine people's faces if they read that James Coutts was a lying, thieving toad who killed both his wives for money. That was how the obituary should have read if the truth was told. Billy stirred just as the potatoes came to the boil, so Maggie folded the paper neatly and laid it on the arm of Tommy's chair.

After tea, there was the ironing to be done while Tommy settled down in the big armchair to read the paper. Tommy didn't just read a paper: he was like a sponge soaking up every word. She had deliberately failed to mention Coutts's obituary. It would be interesting to see if he pointed it out to her.

There was a kind of satisfaction, like taking a deep intake of breath just to know Coutts could no longer bring them grief, harm or destruction. He was gone for good. Gone from a world that would now be a better place without the likes of him and more importantly, he was gone from their lives forever. Now Eve could finally close the door on the awful memories, lock it and throw away the key that by now must be rusted with all the blood, sweat and tears she'd shed.

Ironing was a chore to most, but to Maggie, it was relaxing and quite mesmerising to watch creased material become smooth and crisp under the iron's heat. This was time needed to let her mind wander. She hadn't yet told Tommy, but there was a great need for her to see a doctor tomorrow morning. Lost in her own thoughts, it was the sound of choking that startled her, that and Tommy springing bolt upright in his chair. 'Did… did you see this?' he spluttered. 'What a bloody nerve and I suppose they hoped no one would notice.'

'I read it earlier. Hallelujah and amen, Coutts is dead. I couldn't believe all that claptrap they wrote about him either. Respected pillar of the community be damned.' She had taken it for granted Tommy was referring to the obituary.

Maggie's disgust was marked in the way she brandished the iron over Tommy's best shirt. Sullenly, she added, 'the headline should have read: *Rat shakes hands with the devil at last.*'

'Not the death notice! I wasn't even going to mention that.' Tommy folded back the page and pointed to a tiny article tucked away in the bottom corner, so small and insignificant, it might easily be overlooked by anyone other than an avid seeker of information about the world at large in the written word. He cleared his throat, 'Any person having a claim against the late James Coutts, please lodge their claim by no later than midday on Friday at the offices of Mather, Crumb & Dick, Solicitors.' Tommy made a growling sound. 'There's something very underhand going on here. This is normally done after the funeral, the reading of the will and all that palaver. Isn't that when creditor's accounts are settled from the estate?'

'I don't know enough about things like that, Tommy, but I imagine outstanding bills would have to be paid from the money he left.'

'Yeah, *if* he had money to leave, but you know what, Maggie, I wouldn't be surprised if Coutts knew he was dying and over the past months, he's been transferring all his assets into Millie's name so that he dies a poor man. That way, none of the people he owes money to get a penny.

'That wouldn't be surprising, it would be typical.' Maggie carried on ironing without further comment and her pretence that she was totally disinterested was so effective, Tommy gave up raging about the whole thing.

Outwardly, Maggie appeared cool, calm and collected, swaying to and fro with the iron as though nothing of any significance had happened. Yet inwardly, her stomach churned and her inner mind was riled and ridden with anger. She wasn't going to take this lying down, oh no! If Millie Coutts thought she was going to wallow in wealth that didn't belong to her, she had another think coming. After years of waiting, it was time for the Fraser sisters to claim what was rightfully theirs, even if it was a foregone conclusion that the quest would be futile. In all probability, Coutts would have prepared for this day. But it wasn't in her nature to complacently stand aside and let him win without putting up a fight, or at least drawing attention to his corrupt ways.

'You're very quiet.' Tommy had been watching her over the paper. 'Listen, Maggie, I'm sorry if my mouthing off upset you.'

'I'm not in the least upset, Tommy! In fact, now that he's gone, I feel as happy as a sandboy.' Maggie didn't dare let on about her intentions: he would only try and talk her out of it, and her mind was made up. Not even a raging bull could stop her, for this was more than carrying out one final task: this was a necessary call of duty.

The following morning, Maggie dressed Billy, then left to keep an appointment with the doctor. From there, she walked to the solicitors to lodge her claim, but the news, although exactly what she had expected, was nevertheless disappointing. The crafty devil had made sure there were no loopholes when he nominated Millie as his sole beneficiary, although his *assets* amounted to only a paltry few pounds, just as Tommy suspected. The Coutts Empire legally belonged to Millie and it had all been done by the letter of the law. Only weeks before his death, Coutts had *sold* all his goods and properties to Millie for the grand sum of £1, and it was a legitimate sale, legally binding. It would be at Millie's discretion whether or not she honoured her father's debts. There was but one problem. Like her father, she didn't have an honourable bone in her body.

There was worse to come. The will stated, that in view of the fact his stepdaughters had done so much to blight his good name, thereby causing him pain and suffering, Coutts categorically stated they, nor any of Tina Coutts's offspring by a former marriage, must ever lay claim to money or property held by any member of the Coutts's family. Maggie saw it in black and white, but her strong-willed determination refused to let go. There was still one more person to see.

Her heart pounded furiously as Maggie made her way along the crazy, paving path that led to the ornate front door with its highly polished solid brass fittings and the fancy nameplate with, *Coutts,* written in bold, italic letters. So this was Coutts's family home. Her eyes, somewhat enviously, took in the newly-mown lawn and the well-kept flower beds, and Maggie imagined how lovely it would be to have a garden like this for Billy to play in. The thought also crossed her mind that it was more than likely her mother's money had paid for most of this grandeur.

At the carved front door, Maggie raised her hand to the brass door knocker and then stopped to take a deep breath. Her heart was beating so fiercely and yet, it wasn't through fear: it was the enthusiasm of going into battle with a Coutts. Many times, Maggie had visualised this meeting and her mind was made up a long time ago that come hell or high water, she *would* have her say. This day had been a long time coming and she had no intention of leaving with words unspoken.

The rap, rap, rap of the door knocker was answered by Millie Coutts. She was openly shocked to find Maggie standing there, for this was one visitor she hadn't expected. The struggle to regain her composure was apparent by the fidgeting, but what was even more fascinating was the mound of fat under her chin that appeared to wobble in time to the spasmodic trembling of her bottom lip while beady, little eyes, so like her father's, blinked rapidly. Maggie silently waited on a response.

'Well…' it was obvious Millie's feeble mind was thinking hard what to say. 'I'll ask you what you asked me when I came to your grandmother's funeral, Maggie Fraser. What do *you* want here? I can't honestly say it's a pleasure to see you again.' The way she bleated, only went to show her alarm and obvious insecurity. 'I suppose you've come to gloat about Daddy's sad passing?' Millie visibly shook from head to toe. It seemed she had inherited her father's cowardly instincts.

'For your information, my name is now Mrs Stark, and I haven't come to gloat. Although for the life of me, I can't see what's sad about his death. It's not as if he was a great loss to anyone, including yourself. The reason I'm here is to give you the opportunity to do one decent thing in your life by returning to Eve and me what's rightfully ours. Now, Millie, why don't we go inside and talk about this like civilised human beings over a cup of tea?'

A face-to-face encounter alone with her stepsister was the one thing Millie always dreaded. It was not high on her list of things to look forward to. Grandma had always warned her, that common mill workers were an entirely different breed from them, uncouth, uneducated and ready to fight at the drop of a hat. Her own dear Daddy had been accosted by a mob in Charles Street when he went there to make sure Tina Fraser's children were being provided for (This was the simpering story Coutts put about to save face). Millie began frantically fanning her face with her hand, as if the confrontation had made her feel faint. 'I can't believe you have the gall to expect *me* to invite *you* in for a friendly cup of tea and a chat. Go back to your slum, for I have nothing that belongs to you.'

The hurried closing of the door in her face was something Maggie had anticipated. She stepped forward and put her foot inside. In a somewhat menacing tone, she said, 'Now Millie, I don't think you'd like to hear what I have to say out here on the doorstep: although then again, your neighbours might appreciate an earful.'

The two women faced each other, not as stepsisters but as adversaries. Millie Coutts's bulk filled the doorway barring Maggie's entry, and plump ring-laden hands rested defiantly on her fat hips. 'Like I said, you're not setting foot inside my house,' she repeated. 'Unlike some, I've nothing to be ashamed of. Say what you have to say out here, because I've got nothing to hide.' Millie's voice was like her stature, big and booming. 'My Daddy told me all about how you people stirred up trouble in the hope of getting money out of him,' she bellowed.

The quiet serenity of this exclusive neighbourhood was broken, and windows and doors began opening, although in keeping with the character of the inhabitants, no one actually showed themselves, but countless ears listened to every shameful word.

'It's fine by me if you want everyone in earshot to hear about the kind of monster your father was.' Maggie deliberately raised the pitch of her voice and watched as curtains twitched and dumbfounded faces peeked tentatively around doors. 'What I'm more interested in is if and when you intend returning the money your thieving father stole from us.'

Bright, scarlet lipstick accentuated the full, podgy lips appearance of a permanent sneer. A not too flattering look Millie had inherited from her father. She was supercilious and arrogant in the extreme, for this was the fashion in which she had been raised by doting grandparents who had instilled in Millie the concept that she was one of the elite. Giving in to her every whim was their way of compensating for the loss of her mother.

As a child, Millie was greedy and gluttonous, and instead of controlling her enormous appetite, her grandparents, all in the name of love, allowed her to gorge herself into obesity which they immodestly referred to as… cute puppy fat. She was Miss Millicent Coutts, born into a distinguished family, and by definition, this set her on a pedestal: as good as some, but better than most.

Even with such a pedigree, Millie was still unwelcome within her own society. Her constant, spontaneous flatulence disgusted the eminent socialites more than the repulsive person, who was without dignity, in either her conduct or her appearance.

Millie glared menacingly at the intruder on her doorstep and folded her arms over her chest, bringing huge breasts together until the cleavage disappeared somewhere under her chin.

'Well, what do you have to say for yourself?' Maggie shouted.

The corpulent, imposing figure moved forward and looked haughtily down her nose at Maggie. 'Unlike you, I was born into money. My Daddy had many business interests,' she sneered. 'I really don't know where you got the notion that your mother was wealthy. You live in Charles Street for heaven's sake. Surely, that speaks for itself.' Millie stepped quickly back as if she half expected Maggie to lash out. Once in the confines of her own little kingdom, she leaned nonchalantly against the doorframe and delivered her final, insulting address. 'If you're that desperate for money, I suggest you go back to the mill and work for a living like the rest of the riff-raff. What's more, if you don't stop harassing me, I'll send for the police and have you arrested.'

Far from disconcerting Maggie, the rude remarks, that were the stamp of Millie's infamous lack of social graces, only seemed to amuse her. 'You really think you're something special, don't you?' It was Maggie's turn to snigger as that look of smug contempt turned to confusion when, instead of turning and running, Maggie actually took a step forward. 'Since we're *family*, I'll tell you to your face what others say behind your back. All you are is just another silly, fat cow pretending to be something you'll never be—a lady. *Daddy* taught you well. He was a thief without morals too. I knew before I came here we'd never see a penny of our money.'

'Huh, some hope.'

'I only wanted to give you the chance to prove you weren't as dishonest as your father by doing the decent thing.' The words were spoken more with sadness than anger, but as Maggie turned to leave, from the corner of her eye, she caught Millie making an obscene gesture. Maggie spun around with a fury that only the gravely wronged could know. In a deeply sinister voice, she said, 'I saw that Millie Coutts, now hear me and know this. I have the power to curse you and this I do in my mother's name.' Dramatically, she held up her right hand. 'May you never enjoy your ill-gotten gains nor one happy day for the rest of your miserable life.'

Reeling from this omnipotent outburst, Millie gasped for breath and the hand she clasped to her ample bosom freed the locket that had been trapped within a fold of flesh and it glistened in the sunlight. Tina's locket hung like a trophy around Millie's fat neck, the sight of which incensed Maggie even more and she lunged forward, grabbing it forcibly enough to break the chain.

'Wh… what do you think you're doing? That's mine, a present from my Daddy. Give it back this instant.'

Before Millie could recover from the surprise attack, Maggie had opened the locket. She remembered how Tina had shown her the secret to opening it, something Millie obviously hadn't discovered. 'If this is yours, perhaps you can explain why it holds the pictures of *my* parents.' Maggie was victorious, it wasn't much, one small trophy, but it was her mother's, and if Millie Coutts wanted it, she'd have to fight for it.

There was no answer to this, because Millie was unaware it opened, far less held photographs. In her usual ungracious way, she admitted defeat. 'Take the damned thing and go, because that's all you'll get,' she screeched. 'You common, working-class people think you can simply take whatever you want.'

'I've said all I came to say,' Maggie spoke the words calmly but purposefully. 'Take the time to think about my curse because I promise, one day; you'll have cause to remember.'

The ugly confrontation ended there among the floribunda that edged the smooth, green lawn. With head held high, Maggie defiantly plucked a red rosebud, then steered the pram through the wrought iron gate and onto the street. She never looked back at Millie standing there on the doorstep of the Coutts's big, fancy house, alone and badly shaken. A wicked smile spread across Maggie's face. Her poor, simple-minded stepsister actually believed she had the power to lay a curse on her: just another facet of her ignorant upbringing.

The morning air smelled sweet as Maggie strolled through the park. Her mind was at last freed of the soul-destroying need to stand toe to toe with a Coutts, and allowed the deep-seated anger she had borne for the best part of her life to at last, gush out and be gone. For a time, it had weighed heavily on her conscience that she may have been too quietly accepting of the evil, which had entered her life, but that was yesterday and this was the new tomorrow. This was the day she had at last stood on Coutts's doorstep and roared her demands for the world and his wife to hear. Fruitless as her demonstration had been, at least she had given Millie Coutts a lot to think about. But best of all, she had recovered the one thing which had been her mother's most precious possession—her locket.

The rosebud's scent was strong. Maggie tittered as she pushed the stem into her rolled up hair. Maybe it was the realisation that she didn't need money to make her life rich that made her feel jaunty, and why not? She had a perfect husband, a demure, loving sister and a beautiful, healthy son. Millie Coutts's life would be one of stagnation in that big, empty house that should be filled with the laughter of children. What a waste, for she couldn't envisage Millie ever having children of her own, whereas she and Tommy... Well today, the doctor had confirmed her suspicions and tonight, she would tell Tommy they were expecting a second child.

For the rest of the day, Maggie drank countless cups of tea while impatiently watching the clock and willing the hands to turn so she could confess to Tommy what she'd done, and relate every detail about the chaotic events of the morning, simply and without frills or fuss.

The afternoon that seemed eternal, passed and daylight was fading when Tommy walked through the door. He kissed Maggie's forehead and sniffed her hair. 'You were at the park today,' he said, 'I can always tell because your hair smells like flowers.'

'I did take Billy to the park, but I was other places too.' She crossed her fingers, Tommy wasn't quick to anger, but he definitely wouldn't take what she had to say, well. 'Do you want to know where I went today?'

'You look like you're bursting to tell me, so spit it out.' Tommy sat in the armchair with the folded paper on his lap and waited.

'I went to see Millie Coutts.' The words were rushed before her bravado waned.

This was one admission that took the feet from Tommy. His wife was hot-headed and given to act impulsively at times, but this was lunacy and what's more, she was standing there looking all innocent, like he'd asked her what she did today and she'd answered, 'nothing much, I went to the grocer and the butcher, then I flew to the moon.' It would have been less of a surprise anyway.

Tommy was livid and what was more, he felt let down. 'You made me a promise that you'd washed your hands of the Coutts, and you deliberately broke that promise.' There was hurt in his voice and scorn in his eyes, because this wasn't a spur of the moment thing. Maggie had to have planned it behind his back.

'This was my mother's,' Maggie held out the locket. 'Millie was wearing it around her greasy, fat neck, so I ripped it off.' She stamped her foot in a show of defiance. 'What's more, I enjoyed doing it.'

'What were you thinking about? Don't you realise she could have you arrested?'

'I couldn't help myself. All I wanted was to tell her a few home truths, but when I saw her wearing Mum's locket, something inside me snapped. Please don't be angry with me, Tommy.' Maggie used her most cultivated, wheedling tone while hanging her head in pretence of shame. 'Women do strange things when they're expecting,' she added slyly.

'Damn it, I am angry with you...' He stopped in mid-sentence. 'Did I hear you right? For a minute there, I thought you said...' Tommy watched the slow nod of her head. 'You did say that.'

Curly tendrils of hair, damp with the perspiration of heated anger mixed with ecstatic delight, tumbled over her brow. 'I didn't want to say anything until I was sure.'

The anger left him, it was gone. Maggie's admission of guilt about her verbal attack on Millie melted into insignificance. It didn't matter anymore. Besides, didn't Millie Coutts deserve it? Didn't she get just what was coming to her? Tommy determined that if she did send the police, then he'd make a counter charge that Miss Millicent Coutts, a brawny lump of a woman, was the guilty one. It was she who had accosted her delicately-built, pregnant stepsister. See then how she liked a taste of her own medicine.

'If our family keeps growing at this rate, we'll soon need a bigger house,' Tommy quipped light-heartedly. It was all he could think of to say.

'That big house Millie lives in would be perfect, but somehow, I don't think she'd be interested in swapping with us. In fact, after the names I called her today, we'll be lucky to keep this place.' Maggie sat on Tommy's knee and in playful, quick succession, planted kisses all over his face: just her way of saying sorry.

'I suppose there's one thing I should be thankful for.'

'What's that Tommy?'

'Life will never be dull as long as you're around.'

Chapter Thirty-Two

The three years following Coutts's exit from this earth was perhaps unspectacular for Maggie and her family money-wise, but they were happy, contented years. They might now or never be termed financially well-off, but they thrived and did well in so many other ways. They were at ease in such a wealth of love and friendship in the humbleness of Charles Street.

The birth of their daughter completed Maggie and Tommy's family circle, drawing them closer and sealing their love. Baby Ann had the look of her grandmother and like Tina; she had the promise of growing into a really bonnie little girl.

Like bad dreams, that are so real in the night, but forgotten in the morning, the bitter memories no longer haunted them. Oh, there were still rare occasions when Eve woke in the night with a bad dream and Maggie quelled her fears. 'Bad things can't get to you when you're surrounded by love,' she'd say and this reasoning let Eve sleep in peace, knowing her sister spoke the truth.

From time to time, they heard snippets of information about the unfortunate Millie. By all accounts, it seemed she had become a virtual recluse. Having been shunned by the sophisticated clique, yet wary of anyone outside her own caste, she was left in a sort of limbo. Maggie had never really felt any hatred or animosity towards her step-sister, only pity. She was, after all, just another casualty of her father's corruption.

Eve was now sixteen and growing more like Tina with every passing day; petite, pretty, and her true nature so sweet. Yet, excluding Tommy and her Uncle Joe, she treated all men with suspicion, which prevented her from forming a relationship with any of the boys who showed an interest in her. Oh yes, there were many who adored and would have given their eye teeth to court the beautiful, enigmatic girl. So many handsome young men clambered to feature in Eve Fraser's life, but she shunned them all. She had also inherited not only her mother's looks, but her frugality. Tommy often made harmless fun of this trait by teasingly suggesting that she was saving up to become either a miser or a millionaire.

The secret worry Maggie nursed and shared with no one, not even Tommy, was that Coutts had damaged Eve permanently and irreversibly. She even half-expected and prepared herself mentally for the day her sister announced that she was to join a convent and become a nun. In view of the cloistered life she had chosen, it wouldn't have come as a great surprise to Maggie. The reason she squirrelled away every penny possible from her earnings at the mill was a secret Eve kept to herself and they never trespassed on her privacy.

Every Friday, pay day, Eve took money from her wage packet and gave it to Maggie as her contribution towards the housekeeping. All except for a few pennies to keep in her purse, she put the best part of her wages aside for the bank. It was what they referred to as Eve's pay day ritual. And then one Friday, Eve said she had something important to tell them and they'd best sit down. She was ready to let go the secret of what all her saving had been about. It was the last thing any of them could have imagined.

'I've saved enough to buy a one way ticket to Australia.' Eve told them in such a matter-of-fact way, it didn't register. Not right at that minute anyway.

At first, there were only blank looks, as if they either hadn't heard properly, or they didn't fully understand what she had said. And then came that moment of perception when Maggie strung together the words Eve had spoken, Australia—one way ticket and she recoiled with shock.

Maggie made frantic waving gestures with her hands, as if she were shooing this away, out of sight, out of mind. 'No, no you're not serious, you can't be,' she tried to say. Her throat was dry as a bone and her voice hoarse with dread. And then came the wailing and buckets of tears.

Eve had expected an unfavourable reaction, but not this pain and terror that creased Maggie's face. 'Please, don't get all upset or angry with me,' she cried pleadingly. 'Leaving you will be the hardest thing I'll ever do in my life, but my heart isn't in this country. There are too many bad memories for a start.' She had agonised for weeks over the best and kindest way to tell them. She knew now, there was no kind way to say what had to be said.

'Then you... you are serious? I... I can't believe you want to leave us after all we've been through.' Maggie crumpled in the anguish and heartbreak that shattered her. 'What happened to you was a terrible thing, and I'll carry the shame and the guilt for the rest of my life that I didn't see what was happening to you, but leaving us is too harsh a punishment.'

'It's not a punishment, Maggie…'

'Then what is it?' The shrillness of Maggie's scream filled the room. 'You're not talking about going to the other side of town, for God's sake. You're going to the ends of the earth and I'll never see you again.' Maggie failed to grasp the theory that leaving friends, family and the place where she was born, would wipe out all that was painful.

Eve tried to explain that memories weren't just in a place, they were within a person and no matter how far she went, they would be carried with her. With quiet dignity, she told Maggie, 'You're all here in my heart and always will be.'

In a moment of logic, Maggie said, 'Have you stopped to think where you'll go? You don't know anyone in Australia.'

'Have you forgotten our grandparents are there, Maggie? Maybe because you have your own family, you've never felt what I feel. Try, just try and see it from my point of view.'

'All I can see is stupidity.'

She heaved a great sigh of exasperation and then quietly, Eve tried to explain this compulsion that was in her heart and her soul. 'I'm drawn to the country where our father was born and don't ask me why, because I can't explain what I don't understand myself. I never knew our father, but for some reason, I've inherited whatever pull he had towards his homeland. Ask yourself, why salmon fight exhaustion to follow the strongest need to swim upstream to spawn? Does anyone know why homing pigeons find their way back?'

'You're not a fish or a bird,' Maggie argued.

'But I have instincts too, and I'm being pulled to another continent. It has nothing to do with what happened to me. Can't you understand, Maggie? It's an urge so strong; I can't put up any resistance. I've thought long and hard. I've tried to talk myself out of the idea, but it's useless. My mind's made up and I'm going.' Eve put a finger to her lips and said, 'Shush, let it rest now, Maggie. I'm going to write a letter tonight to our grandparents and ask if they'll have me to stay with them.'

Being told that her only sister was about to up sticks and move to a place distant and faraway was far from gratifying news. A visit wouldn't be like taking a tram to the other end of town. They would never, in this lifetime, afford the cost of going to Australia. This wasn't a *bye, bye see you later* situation. This would be a last goodbye.

Eve could see her family were in turmoil over what they thought to be a hasty decision, which of course it wasn't. She had carried this secret dream for all of two years.

The weeks that followed Eve's shocking disclosure were tense and Maggie found herself constantly looking for reassurance that her sister would outgrow the concept that leaving Dundee was going to solve all her problems. 'It's a silly phase,' she told Tommy. 'Wait and see, she'll meet a nice boy and give up this crazy idea.' But Maggie was clutching at straws and she knew it.

When the letter addressed to, *Miss Eve Fraser,* arrived from Australia, Maggie knew in her heart it was the beginning of the end. She also realised, that since the night Eve told them of her plans, they had degenerated from a family united to a family divided, and all because *she* had tried to dictate how Eve should live her life.

Tommy tried to tell her in the kindest way possible. 'You can't hold onto her forever. A fresh start in another country might not be such a bad thing.'

Maggie wasn't one to be told what she didn't want to hear, and lashed out with a razor tongue. '**I** know what's best for her, she's **my** sister.' It was a cruel thing to say to the man who had sheltered Eve and lived through the nightmare with them.

Logical thinking had always been Tommy's forte, and he understood perfectly the torment Maggie was going through. Of course she was irascible. She was chasing moonbeams. She wilfully blinkered her eyes to the facts Eve tried to put to them: facts that the horrors of her childhood would never really go away as long as familiar, everyday things remained a constant reminder.

'It's time to let go,' Tommy said firmly. 'From now on, you have to give all the support you can. Put yourself in her position, Maggie, maybe then you'll find it in your heart to ease the poor kid's guilt about what must be a hard thing she's going to do. *Try* to hide your own hurt and be happy for her.'

'This came for you today.' Forcing a smile, Maggie handed Eve the letter. 'We're all dying to hear what they have to say,' she chirped lightly, even though her heart was heavy.

Slowly and gently, Eve opened the letter. A money order was folded inside and the letter read,

Our dearest granddaughter,

How excited we are that you want to come and live with us, and we can't wait for you to arrive. The money order is to help you on your journey. Now, don't go bringing too many clothes with you, because when you get here, you're going to the city to buy a whole, new wardrobe, no expense spared.

One thing we do want you to bring (other than yourself), is pictures of Maggie and her husband with the kids. We long to see what our new granddaughter looks like. Will you do this for us, please?

Let us know the date you sail and the date you arrive, your granddad and I will be waiting with open arms.

Your loving grandma.

Shortly after her seventeenth birthday, Eve realised her dream and bought a ticket to Australia. A one way ticket that was to sever the ties that bind and they had only four short weeks before the final parting.

Maggie never gave up hoping against hope that Eve would change her mind, but there was no turning back. With every passing day, the pull became even stronger, so much so, that Maggie truly believed Eve would have swum the ocean to get there if need be.

And then the day of parting was upon them. The money Eve carried, although not a fortune was nevertheless more than enough to keep her until she was safely with her grandparents. Fearful that it might be lost or stolen, Maggie stitched the notes inside the lining of Eve's coat with a warning not to trust anyone.

They walked to the train station in silence. What was there to say that hadn't already been said?

The platform was cold and grimy, as dismally, they huddled together awaiting the train that would take Eve to Southampton where she would board the ship bound for Australia. Many things still needed to be said, but feelings weren't easily expressed when they came from a broken heart. The pain Maggie felt at this moment was almost unbearable. She had fought so hard to save Eve from self-destruction after the abuse Coutts had subjected her to. Together, they rode the greatest storm life could ever throw at them, and after all that, she was losing her sister and there was little or no chance they would ever meet again. How do you come to terms with that?

'Will you come back soon, Auntie Eve?' How could Billy possibly understand that this was likely to be the last time he might ever see the auntie he adored?

'I don't think so, Billy, you see, I'm going far, far away and it may not be possible for me to come back.'

The last four weeks had passed in a haze, but now, standing on the station platform saying final farewells, even amid all the grime and smoke, it was like emerging from a mist and Eve was able to see clearly. She was suddenly gripped with a feeling akin to terror. This parting from her family was no longer a pipe dream, it was actually happening and only the sheer determination to start a new life stopped her from turning back.

'Promise you'll never forget me.' She knelt down and held the little boy tightly. 'I'm going on a great adventure, Billy.'

'Can I come too?'

'I'm afraid not, but every night when you're asleep, I'll blow you a kiss,' she whispered.

'Auntie Eve,' Billy gently pushed her away, 'you're making my face all wet.'

'I'm sorry, sweetheart,' Eve said, taking a handkerchief from her pocket and wiping her tears from the little boy's face. 'The trains are making so much smoke, there was a little, sooty mark on your cheek. I was just trying to wash it off.' At a time like this, a lie was often kinder than the truth.

'I'll blow you two kisses every night, Auntie Eve, all the way to Australia,' Billy said enthusiastically.

The station master walked the platform, looking at his watch. The moment was fast approaching when the red flag would wave and the whistle blow to signal it was time to board. Eve reached for Ann and kissed the bewildered baby before handing her back to her father. 'Don't ever let anyone hurt her, Tommy.' They were but a few words with a world of meaning.

'Never,' Tommy promised, fighting back tears. His throat constricted as he held his baby girl, remembering how much pain Eve had endured and how valiantly she had overcome her fears.

'We won't let them forget you,' Maggie promised. 'Every single day, we'll remind them about their beautiful Auntie Eve and try to keep the memory of you alive in their hearts and minds.' It was too much to bear, Maggie did the one thing she promised herself she wouldn't do, she broke down and, sobbing like her heart was breaking, threw her arms around Eve. 'I love you, little sister. You'll always be in my heart and my prayers.'

The whistle came to board, there was a last emotional farewell then Eve was gone. An important chapter in their lives had ended and now, unless by some miracle, Maggie would never see her sister again. 'Damn you, Coutts,' her agonised voice echoed through the empty station, 'I hope you're suffering the torments of hell. Because of you, we've lost our darling Eve forever.' Maggie clutched Tommy's arm: the sorrow of parting had left her weak and wan. She rested her head on his shoulder and felt an instant comfort in his closeness. 'Thank God for you and our children,' she said.

In the weeks following Eve's departure to her, 'brave, new world,' as Tommy put it, Maggie shed more tears than she'd shed her entire life. She couldn't have been more heartbroken if Eve had died. At least then, there would have been a grave to visit. When the person who had always lent enchantment to your life has gone, how do you reach out and physically touch a memory?

A whole season, weeks that seemed like an eternity passed and at last, there was a letter from Eve.

My dearest family,

This is the most spectacular place in the world, and the farm, or the old homestead as Grandma calls it, stretches as far as the eye can see.

You should see our grandparents, Maggie, they're in their seventies and as fit as fleas. Granddad still insists on doing a full day's work on the land, although he never stops promising Grandma that he's going to retire one day.

Ralph Mayberry takes me everywhere. He's the grandson of Bruce and Dolly, and they're Gran and Granddad's best friends. He's really special Maggie and I like him a lot, maybe because he's so different from the boys back home.

I have another surprise for you. Grandma enrolled me in secretarial college and I'm learning shorthand and typing, what's more, the teacher says I have a natural ability, so what do you think about that?

The letter, five pages in all, went on to tell about all the people she'd met and the places she'd been to and how the grandparents loved to hear about Dundee. There were fleeting references to her classmates at college, but in every sentence, one name kept repeating—Ralph. It was as if just writing his name filled her with joy, and the intimation was there in black and white. Eve was more than a little love-struck.

'That letter's done you a world of good,' Tommy commented. 'You look happier and more contented than I've seen you for weeks.'

'Oh I am, Tommy! My prayers have been answered. Eve's found her niche in life and by the sound of things, her future husband too.'

Chapter Thirty-Three

James Coutts's death had made little or no impact on the community as a whole, except that is, for the many jokes about him which circulated around pubs. The incident with the overflowing sewer in Charles Street had become a long-standing source of laughter and also set off a whole catalogue of fun-poking gags.

It began with someone walking into the pub, sniffing the air and asking, 'What's that fucking smell? Is Coutts around?'

'No, I just stood in dog shit.'

'What's the difference between dog shit and Coutts?'

'Nothing, they both stink.'

Those and many more mocking quips became much used sayings that fell easily from tongues. The unforgettable and wholly laughable sight of him floundering in stinking mire was how Coutts would be remembered; certainly never as a saintly man with a compassionate nature. The legacy Coutts left was a haunting reminder of a heartless and merciless man.

The property in Milton Street, which James Coutts bought with Tina's money, had not only put him on the up, it completely changed his way of thinking—investment-wise. His brush with near bankruptcy had turned Coutts into an older and much wiser man. He had learned the hard way that get rich quick schemes always seemed to have a catch, and money invested invariably melted like snow off a dyke. He continued to play the stock market, only now, it was on *sound* advice and the financial tide turned in his favour.

Coutts developed a kind of genius for amassing wealth through property. He was always on the lookout for any property, maybe a block of flats which were becoming a bit dilapidated but with lots of potential. His tactic was to skilfully employ a bit of scaremongering by baffling a tight-fisted owner with science to convince him that the building might well be in real danger of collapse unless a huge amount of money was spent on it. Possibly by someone like himself who could bear the cost of renovation out of his own pocket. And then, with a swift parry and thrust of the financial sword, Coutts would cut a hurried deal with the befuddled landlord to take it off his hands—for a song, of course.

It was no problem for a man like Coutts, a man without a conscience, to then serve immediate eviction notices on sitting tenants while cunningly deceiving many small businesses into believing wealth was within their grasp if they fulfilled his orders for goods and supplies. Simple tradesmen, striving to earn a crust, were recruited for their labour with the promise of payment in full *and* a hefty bonus when the job was done. And then, once the shabby property had been given a face-lift that turned it into an elegant and desirable block of flats, Coutts commanded high rents that only professional people could afford.

But it was after completion of the work that Coutts's true badness was revealed in all its malevolence. When the due payment for goods and services became long overdue, demands for settlement were made time and time again. Of course, being a man without scruples or morals, the invoices were simply ignored. Coutts wasn't a great believer in paying his dues, not when they could be brushed aside as easily as flicking dandruff from his collar. Being accountable for the ruination of genuinely hardworking people meant nothing to an unscrupulous man like Coutts a swindler without ethics or decency.

When news of Coutts's death was heralded, it brought an assortment of shopkeepers and tradesmen (all of them carrying wads of unpaid invoices) to the offices of Mather, Crumb & Dick to demand payment of these bills out of Coutts's estate, only to be told that Mr Coutts had died almost penniless, but what little he had was to be distributed among his creditors. Many accepted a little as being better than nothing, but the more robust seekers of a fairer settlement approached Millie for payment, merely to be turned away with the stony response that she was in no way accountable for her late father's debts, therefore, it wasn't her duty to settle them.

These hardworking people, who had foolishly trusted that Coutts would do the honourable thing by settling their accounts promptly, were now left with the long overdue bills still unpaid. Now, because of her continued refusal to acknowledge that merchants and workers had a right to be paid, Millie Coutts destined herself to forever suffer the stigma and carry the shame of her father's double dealings.

As his only living relative, Millicent made a show of mourning her 'beloved Daddy,' (which in itself was laughable, since she hardly had any contact with him throughout her childhood), She went everywhere wearing the same black outfit and black hat with a heavy, lace veil over her face for effect. Millie only cast off the funereal black, and reverted to her own pretentious and tasteless style of dress when she realised people weren't offering sympathy for her loss. Instead of the normal condolences, they sniggered and openly ridiculed her.

When her grandparents died within one month of each other, Millicent had just entered puberty. Not that anyone would have noticed the change from child to adolescent, since being such a big girl, she had developed unnaturally large breasts at the age of seven. It angered Coutts that his parents' passing left him with no option but to take the daughter he had tried so hard to forget, to live under his roof. Her presence not only greatly disturbed Coutts, it infuriated him.

Coutts could not bear to dine at the same table as his daughter. Among other things, her lack of table manners repulsed him even more than Millie herself and he began to understand what Barton Brown had meant when he disowned them saying, *had she been left in their care, Millie would have gone to the finest finishing school and become a refined lady instead of being turned into a freak.*

The only way Coutts seemed able to handle the situation was by making Millie, the butt of his jokes. Laughingly, he'd tell anyone who was prepared to listen, that each time he saw her walk; he was reminded of a huge jelly with legs. Making fun of the poor girl came easily to Coutts and he excused the pitiless remarks by telling himself that if his wife had followed orders and given birth to a son, things would have been different. Obesity in a boy could have been dismissed as brawn, whereas there was simply no excuse for Millicent. Girls her age were supposed to be slim and pretty, and above all, ladylike. This one had none of these attributes.

Her father's death left Millie a sad, lonely girl, for she was now alone without kith or kin to turn to. She lived a solitary, unhappy life within the four walls that were her own self-made prison. When she looked out of the window onto her garden, Millie was still haunted by the vision of Maggie, standing on the path, hurling abuse at her. Each passing day, made Millie surer than ever that her life truly had been cursed.

At times, she wondered what would happen if she was to knock on Maggie's door and magnanimously hand over a large sum of money. It might even be worth it to see her simper and grovel in gratitude. But the thought of parting with her ill-gotten gains didn't appeal to her greedy nature, and Millie quickly told herself there was no such thing as a curse.

The big house with its fine paintings, antiques and elaborate furnishings were no consolation for her loneliness. She had everything, yet she had nothing. In complete contrast to Maggie's full, rich life, Millie Coutts was alone in a world of broken dreams, without family or friends, and every shadow, every sound haunted her. The echo of those parting words that cursed her with endless unhappiness would forever ring in her ears.

How could a family like Fraser command such respect while she, a Coutts no less, was shunned by everyone? She wasn't exactly inundated with invitations to parties. In fact, not one solitary invitation had ever dropped through her letterbox. If there was a social function, Millie was deliberately omitted from the guest list, and the fact that the income from business interests made her a wealthy woman, meant nothing to people of a social standing who were themselves rich: rich enough in fact, to banish Millicent Coutts from their circle. In truth, she was an embarrassment the socialites could well do without.

Having so much time to reflect on her lot in life, Millie grew more and more hateful and bitter against the clique of arrogant, tittering ladies. With the belligerence that only a social outcast can understand, she questioned who they were to snub her anyway. If the upper classes didn't want her company, it was their loss.

In as much as these snobbish ladies might find it demeaning to mingle with the working classes, Millie thought it might be worthwhile doing just that… if only to prove a point. The idea that it might actually be sort of exhilarating to mix with people, who congregated in public houses to swill gin and laugh heartily in the face of poverty, took root. The thing about these people, they could be bought for a few glasses of cheap gin, and she had the money to do just that.

In her desperation for company, Millie made an illogical decision to cast her net beyond the tiaras and ball gown set who only turned their snooty noses up at her anyway. She had every right to set foot inside the one place where commoners gathered—the pub, and that's what she made her mind up to do. What point was there in sitting idly by waiting for them to come to her when that could take until doomsday? She, Miss Millicent Coutts, would just have to go to them. Many times, Millie heard Daddy say there was no shame in using people for your own ends, especially the lower classes, who he laughingly referred to as, "bugs to be stepped on."

There was a certain thrill in planning and preparing for a campaign such as this. It had been so long since she'd been out of the house, Millie couldn't even remember the last time she'd sat in company and conversed about everyday things. When Daddy had friends in for a drink or a chat, it was usually about business and she was expected to stay in her room.

There was no doubt in Millie's mind that she would be welcomed with open arms once these people of simple tastes saw the colour of her money. Of course, at first, she'd have to walk into the bar unaccompanied, but once that hurdle had been overcome and there was acceptance; why, they'd be falling over themselves to accompany her. At least this was Millie's belief, although, it might be advisable to remain inconspicuous to begin with. A plain, brown dress would be the best choice, and a shawl, mustn't forget the shawl if she was to blend in with the blithering halfwits.

Feverishly, Millie rummaged through her dresses looking for something suitable that still fitted. For all of ten seconds, the thought crossed her mind that her grandparents must be turning in their graves right now. It was their belief that society was divided into two, the rich and the poor, and it was inconceivable that the different cultures could overlap, let alone form friendships. Lord Almighty, wouldn't that be like inviting the hired help to sit at the dining table with you? It was unthinkable. They had all but washed their hands of James when he married the factory girl, Tina Fraser. It was Millie who instituted the deathbed reconciliation between her grandfather and Daddy.

Turning this way, then that in front of the cheval mirror, Millie felt quite pleased with the way she looked. Even if the white, lace jabot had faded over the years into more of a grubby greyish-white, it didn't really matter, since it was only for mingling with the great unwashed anyway. Should she wear a hat? Millie took her favourite from the wardrobe, the one grandma hated. 'It's so common,' she had said with her little, squat nose in the air. But Millie loved the wide, purple brim with the festoon of pink roses. It was elegant and, oh yes, she'd seen the way Maggie Fraser gazed with envy that day in the cemetery. Millie really did believe she was rather chic and the envy of other women for her style and dress sense: but to quote the true words written by Robert Burns, "oh to see ourselves as others see us."

Millie had second thoughts, and reluctantly took the hat off and put it back in the wardrobe. It was much too grand for the pub, so instead, she unearthed a moth-eaten, old shawl that had belonged to her grandma, draped it over her shoulders and left the sanctuary of that big, yet desolate house.

It felt strange and rather eerie to walk alone through the dark, unlit street, slowly, hesitantly at first. And then her steps quickened before she lost fortitude and turned back. Breathless from the effort, Millie patted her chest and felt the large, ornate cameo brooch that, through force of habit, she'd pinned onto the jabot, it was much too ostentatious for a pub and would only draw attention to her. Millie quickly removed the brooch and dropped it into her handbag.

A few more steps, then out of the dimness, she saw directly ahead of her the door to *The Snug*. Millie hesitated momentarily and gritted her teeth. There was still time to change her mind. She now had to make the jabbing decision whether to do—or not to do. She glanced back along the lonely, deserted street, which, at that moment, seemed a reflection of her life, and the decision was made. She pushed open the door and boldly walked inside.

The stench of stale beer and smoke filled her nostrils. Millie covered her mouth with a lace-edged handkerchief and fought the urge to run from this hellish place. Because her eyes were unaccustomed to this atmosphere, they stung like hell and through a haze, she saw the barman and the menacing glower that her presence had provoked as Millie kind of tiptoed none too daintily to the bar. A dirty apron, that at one time had been white, covered the barman's equally dirty, grease-stained trousers. The remains of whatever concoction he had recently eaten, stuck to his moustache. 'What can I get you?' he growled.

'Err... D... Do you have gin?' Millie stammered, without realising the idiocy of asking if a pub had gin.

Other than a small sherry at Christmas, she had never partaken of alcohol, but she had heard it said that the women who worked in the jute mill were known to be partial to a glass or two of what they colloquially referred to as mother's ruin. It seemed reasonable, that if she intended to mix socially with these people, she must also learn to acquire their taste in beverages.

'This is a pub! Of course, we have fucking gin.' The barman muttered another obscenity as he reached for the bottle.

This first encounter with the working classes, although a little disturbing, had been comparatively painless and much less traumatic than Millie had expected. Casually, almost indifferently, she rested her elbows on the counter and then suddenly, she was aware that the loud, bawdy voices that assaulted her ears when she entered the pub, had become hardly audible whispers, and the patrons were staring in her direction.

'It's Coutts's whelp,' someone ungraciously roared.

She had been recognised!

'Well, well, would you look what the cat dragged in?' The loudening ripple of unflattering comments had begun.

'What does she want here?'

'Yeah, someone should tell her to get back to where she fucking belongs.'

Millie placed a coin on the counter and ceremoniously picked up her drink. 'Keep the change,' she told the barman, trying her best to look as provocative as was humanly possible. The barman was unimpressed.

Peering around the room through a mist of smoke, the next step was to look for a group sitting at a table with at least one empty chair. It was imperative to appear lost and lonely when approaching a company. If she played on their sympathies, so to speak, someone was bound to take pity, for wasn't it a well-known fact that mill workers were renowned for being sociable? What's more, they were neither proud nor fussy about the company they kept, especially if free drinks were on offer.

'Do you mind if I sit here?' Without waiting for a yea or a nay, Millie began settling her great bulk onto the chair, but one thing she hadn't reckoned on was the antagonism that was still carried in the minds of these people and the enmity that remained even after all this time. They were unforgiving and she was greeted with a stony silence as her plan began to fall apart.

The only one to speak was a large woman with callused hands. 'As a matter of fact, we do mind,' she answered, like a snapping dog. 'Get your fat backside off that chair and find someplace else to sit, preferably in another pub.' The woman snorted loudly then spat on the floor, narrowly missing Millie's foot, and the place erupted with laughter that ridiculed the bewildered Millie and sent her into a state of agitation.

It seemed everyone still remembered and believed the stories that had been put about of what her father was supposed to have done to the Fraser family. Now, Millie was finding out to her cost that these people were *not* mindless morons who could easily forgive and forget for the price of a drink. Her confidence had been misplaced. She'd never be made welcome in these circles. Acceptance wasn't going to be as easy as Millie had anticipated.

In desperation, Millie dipped into the beaded bag she carried over her arm and withdrew some paper money. 'I'm not looking for trouble,' she cried. 'See, I want to buy everyone a drink.'

'When you've bought the drinks, remember to close the door after you on your way out,' a muffled voice shouted and the hilarity began again as the most obscene remarks about Millie came from every which way.

The mockery and contemptuous comments, which fed to Millie's humiliation, had all been witnessed by two men sitting at a table in the corner. They weren't regulars in the pub. In terms of frequency, they were virtual strangers. One of them called to Millie, 'Sit here, darling, where it's more hospitable. We're not proud, and your money's as good as anyone's.'

Giggling nervously, Millie unashamedly sat down beside the two men whose timely intervention had stopped her from turning and running for the door. 'Thank you for your kind invitation.' She couldn't take her eyes off the man who had invited her to join them. He was sort of handsome in a rough and ready kind of way. Millie turned and looked haughtily at everyone who watched with interest, and said out loud, 'Some people can be so ignorant. All I want is a quiet drink and some company. Is that too much to ask?'

'I couldn't believe my ears! Treating a fine lady like yourself so badly after you'd generously offered to buy everyone a drink, and if you don't mind my saying, there's enough money in that pretty, little bag to keep everyone here drunk for a week. Never mind, my lovely, you're welcome to sit with us.

'It's gratifying to know there are *some* decent people,' Millie said pointedly and her fixed gaze glowered at the woman with callused hands.

'Take no heed of them, it's their loss. I'm John Adams by the way, and this handsome chap is my best pal and constant companion, Ernie Hind.' He took Millie's outstretched hand and stroked the palm. 'My, but these are dainty, soft hands.' John closely watched her reaction. She was simpering and practically swooning at his feet. Who said flattery gets you nowhere?

'I'd like to buy you two nice gentlemen a drink as a thank you for taking pity on me.' Millie dipped once more into the beaded bag, smiling at the looks on their faces at the sight of the neatly folded notes. How the underprivileged revered money. It was almost as intoxicating to them as the beer they swilled. Millie teetered over to the bar, the gin was taking effect, but so too was the thrill of being wooed off her feet by a handsome man.

'What the hell are you playing at, John?' Ernie waited until Millie was out of hearing distance. What had started as a bit of fun had gone past that and was now beginning to make him feel sick to his stomach. Ernie drained his glass and stood up. 'Whatever it is you're planning, you can count me out. I don't mind the odd scam but...' his eyes were drawn to the bar where Millie, oozing arrogance, handed the barman a generous tip and Ernie flinched with a kind of abhorrence. 'I hope I never get that desperate.'

'Sit down and think for a minute, Ernie.' John gripped his arm so tightly that Ernie was forced to sit down. 'She's loaded, and if we play our cards right, we could end up living the good life. Take a good look at her, isn't it obvious what the sad cow's doing in a place like this? She's on the hunt for a man and we'd be doing her a favour.'

'That bitch is Coutts's daughter and I'll have no truck with her kind.' Ernie strode to the door without looking back and John was left somewhat surprised by this sudden onset of moralistic values, considering Ernie had never been shy about scrounging drink in the past.

'Where's your friend gone?' Millie asked, slopping beer everywhere as she struggled with the glasses.

'He suddenly remembered a job that had to be done and asked me to pass on his apologies. Now, don't go worrying that pretty, little head, my dear, I'm still here to protect you.' John moved closer and laid his hand on Millie's thigh to see what her reaction would be. He felt her tense beneath the soft, brown cotton dress and then slowly relax. She moved even closer as her breathing became rapid and excited.

'That's very comforting, John,' Millie said in a way that was open to interpretation. Did she mean it was comforting that he had stayed with her, or that his hand was now gently stroking her inner thigh? Millie covered his hand with hers in a way that said she had no objection to him taking the liberty of being this intimate. 'I like you and you seem to like me. We have something in common, so why don't we sit here and enjoy the rest of the evening?' This was a side to life Millie had never seen, and feelings she didn't understand were stirring inside her.

As the night wore on and the gin took hold, Millie had a feeling of congeniality, like she belonged here. She had gone in search of nothing more than companionship, but meeting John was way beyond her wildest dreams. Lo and behold, she had found a man who actually seemed to not only like her, but find her desirable. In her drunken state, Millie saw the dirty, disagreeable pub in a different light. Now, it was a nice place with nice, new friends who gathered around to sing her praises every time she paid for their drinks.

The following morning, unfortunately, was not quite as exhilarating for Millie. For the first time in her life, she experienced a hangover and vowed not to drink so much next time. Still, what she set out to do had been accomplished and the worst was over. The fuzziness in her head began to clear and bit by bit, she remembered things that had happened. Things like the kiss John stole outside the pub when he whispered, 'meet me here again.'

The recreation ground of the lower classes had been successfully infiltrated, and the next visit would be much easier, providing she made a mental note of those who had rejected her with such contempt. Rebels who refused to sell themselves short, especially to a Coutts. There were many more who accepted her, perhaps not gladly, but definitely greedily into their company.

Sly like her father, Millie quickly learned from last night's lesson, that the best way to be invited to join a company was simply walk straight over and say, 'hello,' followed by, 'can I buy you all a drink?' This was the approach to make everyone shuffle around and make room for her.

As Millie was growing up, her grandparents' somewhat radical teachings had confused the rather dim-witted girl and ultimately led her to believe working class and idiocy automatically went hand in hand. This new set, with whom she had joined ranks, defied these teachings. Working class they were, stupid they were not: on the contrary, they knew a good thing when they saw it and tholed Millie for one thing, and one thing only—the contents of her purse. The frivolous way she opened her purse and freely spent money to fill everyone's belly with booze fooled no one but herself. Millie may have been willing to give, but they were more than eager to take.

The once sad and lonely girl changed dramatically. No longer a prisoner in her own home, Millie had a sense of purpose and even walked to the shops each day to buy her own supplies. In the evening, in the hope of seeing John again, it was the pub that beckoned.

It became common knowledge that Millie was searching for a mate and her sights were set on John Adams, what's more, she had adopted a new image and no longer wore dull and dowdy attire to *blend in*, but frivolous, tasteless dresses with plunging necklines that allowed her breasts to spill over.

There were some who were more principled than to humbly accept Millie's generosity; hardworking women who ungraciously refused to sup with a Coutts and gathered together in a clique to happily enjoy a drink or two while taking in everything that went on around them.

'That one's on the hunt for a man.' One of the female group watched Millie through narrowed eyes. 'She don't try to hide it either,' the woman sneered in disgust.

The woman sitting next to her, equally disgusted, answered, 'Yeah, and I don't think she'd be too particular whose man it was. Just look at her: like a bitch in heat she is,' and then she pointed a finger at John Adams and lowered her voice. 'That one's been sniffing around here a lot.'

'I was told he's a real, bad egg and she wouldn't have her sorrows to seek with him.'

The whispering and sniggering went on behind Millie's back as her mood swings became quite erratic. It didn't go unnoticed that she was the life and soul of the party when in the company of John Adams, but like a wet weekend, crying into her gin when he wasn't there.

John knew exactly how to play the mating game. He'd spend five nights a week in *The Snug* companioned by Millie, and at closing time, gallantly offer to escort her through the dark, lonely streets to her home. It also didn't go unnoticed that John was still in the house when the bedroom light went out. And then for weeks at a time, John Adams would disappear off the face of the earth, leaving Millie in a sort of half existence, each time wondering if he'd gone for good.

Like the con man he was, John had a psychological awareness of what made people tick. He was the worst kind of wastrel who had no hesitation in robbing and cheating ordinary, hardworking folk who earned their money by the sweat of their brow. Millie was different and John understood how vital it was not to rush things and frighten her off.

Chapter Thirty-Four

The Sailor's Rest was a bar near the docks used by prostitutes. It was where John Adams normally hung out, but being a born and bred opportunist, *The Snug* where Millie could be found most evenings, was more practical if he was to pursue an easy living. John didn't like that pub in particular but he did have an ulterior motive in going there, and that was to captivate the hapless Millie until he had her in the palm of his hand and then *squeeze* the wealth from her grasp. He had no problem either about squeezing the breath from her body if need be. 'One step at a time,' he told himself. 'Take it slow and easy, tease your way into her heart until she's panting for you—then pounce.'

The prostitute, who was John Adams's steady girlfriend, had taught him the fine art of seduction, how to talk his way into Millie's bed—which he'd already done—then make her feel his interest was waning by catching her eye and then turning indifferently away. Like any woman, Millie would crave the man she thought unattainable, especially if he'd given her just enough to whet her appetite. Millie already had a taste of what she'd be missing if she lost John Adams. He was the one and only man who brought ecstasy and excitement into her life. She'd do anything to hold onto him.

Millie had become a familiar face in *The Snug*, sitting in a little booth in the corner, facing the door where she could see John when he came in. She liked this little corner of the bar where she nestled her fat backside away from prying eyes. She liked the privacy for John to casually put an arm around her shoulder then allow his hand to slip down the front of her dress to fondle her breast. And there in that shady corner, where eyes couldn't see, it fairly took her breath away too when he reached under the table to run his hand up and down her thigh. She knew, that at closing time, he would invariably begin whispering in her ear the kind of sexually explicit words that roused lust the likes of which she'd never known.

Until now, it had been not only difficult, but almost impossible for Millie to gain a man's interest. Therefore, the flattery and adulation John openly displayed was like the sweetness of candy to one who had never known the taste of love. She truly believed that this one man really did desire her body, and she craved his touch. Millie longed to lie beside him on the huge, feather bed in her own room and have John say out loud all those things that set a furnace alight in her blood.

It was John Adams who had opened the door to Millie's sexuality and turned her into an even bigger whore than any of the dock's prostitutes. The seduction was complete and the web was spun.

At his usual haunt, John had become conspicuous by his absence, which brought Ernie to *The Snug* looking for him. 'Why are you spending so much time in this pub?' he asked. 'I thought you preferred *The Sailor's Rest* with what's-her-name, that red-haired tart you normally hang around with.'

'Ginger's an alright girl, but I've set my sights higher—with her blessing, I might add. It's the most beautiful scam you could ever imagine, Ernie. The fish is hooked and all I have to do now is reel her in,' he nudged Ernie and winked maliciously. 'You know what I mean?'

'You don't mean the Coutts woman?' Ernie's face screwed up in disgust and horror. He spat as if to rid his mouth of a bad taste. 'She's got to be the ugliest woman ever. Where's your taste man. Bedding her must be like fucking a pig.

'I wouldn't knock it if I were you, Ernie. Something tells me I'm about to become a very rich man and anyway, you don't look at the mantle when you're poking the fire.' John roared with laughter at this cruel innuendo. His intentions were painfully clear. 'I only have to do the needful in her bed, every filthy thing she asks and she'll do anything for me.

'I heard talk but I didn't believe it. I even argued with everyone that they'd got it wrong, that you weren't that desperate or hard up. What you're doing isn't kosher, John. The woman's simple, for Christ's sake, and she isn't to blame for what her father did.'

'Sins of the father and all that, Ernie, you see, Coutts may have been the one to do the dirty deeds, but it's his daughter that's left to pay the piper. The fat cow's fallen heir to her father's ill-gotten gains. If she needs a consort to help her spend it, I'm that man.' John openly sniggered at his pal's new-found Christian attitude and wickedly fuelled his outraged morality. 'She'll be here soon, why don't you hang around and enjoy yourself at her expense?'

'This is more than I can stomach, John! You don't want advice and you obviously don't need a friend, so don't come looking to me for sympathy when you fall flat on your face.'

Ernie had no idea why he felt this indignant. He wasn't exactly in the running for sainthood himself, since he was a born thief and criminal activities came as second nature to him. But this… this was real crime and it was nothing less than cold-blooded cruelty. It was inhuman. Whatever else she was, Millie Coutts was a living, breathing person who was about to be subjected to the ultimate humiliation at the hands of John Adams. It was Ernie's view that this poor, gullible soul didn't deserve it and he, Ernie Hind, drew the line at being party to something so dastardly.

'You don't look too happy Ernie, so let me make one thing clear. I don't want or need *your* seal of approval.'

Ernie fit his old pal's aggression and growled, 'Good, because you don't have it.'

It may have been the dim light or perhaps the smoky atmosphere, but a look of pure evil crossed John's face and it was frightening. He had always been a crook without boundaries, they both were, but something in him had changed. John Adams had sold his soul for the Coutts' fortune.

In a threatening voice that would be barely recognisable to those who knew him best, John said, 'This is my meal ticket and I have no intention of letting go without a fight, **do you understand?**' And then, he patted Ernie's back in a manner that was suddenly lighter and more congenial. 'Besides,' he added as an afterthought, 'she's not that bad—in the dark.'

That was when Ernie vowed to wash his hands off John and end their lifelong friendship. He didn't know this man any more. This avaricious thing wasn't the pal he'd committed countless robberies with. Dipping the pockets of drunken sailors or nicking a purse from the handbag of some well-to-do lady was honest thieving. Running together through back alleys to dodge the cop— that was what they'd always called a bit of fun. They were famous for living on their wits to get enough money for booze, or if they were lucky, ten minutes with one of the dockside girls for free.

'Goodbye, John,' Ernie said with sadness in his voice, for this was the end of an era. 'Don't look for me, because I won't be looking for you.'

There was no reply, no jolly voice laughingly telling him to sit on his arse and take a joke, and no more the John Adams he knew. This man was a complete stranger to him. A man who sadly had wagered everything, his happy-go-lucky way of life, his best mates and yes, even his very soul, and all for a place on the money wagon.

Chapter Thirty-Five

John Adams had given a whole lot of thought to the situation he was in. He could probably have pressurised Millie into handing over a wad of money here and there, and she'd no doubt have been only too happy to pay for the "services" he gave. But what if she opened her eyes one day and realised the novelty had worn off? What if, with nothing to tie them together, the money tree suddenly withered and died? He had too much to lose. The only way he could keep a grip on things was by marrying the silly cow. And therein lay the answer.

Adams hurried to *The Snug* while the carefully rehearsed words were fresh in his mind. Millie was there in her usual seat, waiting. He stretched an arm around the broadness of those shoulders to pull her close to him, then guzzled down a beer and threw back a large whiskey. Not that a man with the morals of an alley cat needed Dutch courage to carry out any kind of heinous or corrupt deed. Slyly, he whispered in her ear, 'I was thinking, instead of sitting here night after night, why don't we go on a proper date?' In a beguiling and seductive way, John nibbled her earlobe.

Millie's breast heaved with excitement. 'And show everyone we're going steady, you mean?'

'We could sit in the back row of the pictures and do the things courting couples do in the back row.' John had to stifle a laugh the way she quivered with expectation.

Right there and then, while the iron was hot in a manner of speaking, John suggested that tomorrow he could meet her at the cinema where they were showing King Kong, the film about a giant ape. He chuckled deviously as the thought entered his mind that he mustn't slip up and ask if Millie was related in any way to the monster on screen.

From here on, he must be the soul of discretion and play the part of a proper gentleman to the letter, for although Millie was well and truly hooked, there was still the reeling in. Tomorrow night, after they came from the cinema, the grand plan was to propose marriage.

John could have thought of a lot more pleasant things to do than rolling in a feather bed with Millie, still, needs must. Firstly though, there was someone he had to have a quiet word with.

His step was light and carefree as Adams walked south along Dock Street towards the *Sailors Rest*. The brown fedora he'd recently purchased perched jauntily on the back of his head. He'd bought the hat at a second-hand market with the idea that it might just give him a stylish appearance that would impress Millie. It worked, and she thrilled at how handsome he looked, but what he needed to get now was a bit of helpful advice from the prostitute, Ginger Gates. If Adams was capable of loving anyone, she was the one. He'd already told her that his disappearing to *The Snug* these nights and his dalliances with Millie was "purely business." He had a plan. There was no doubt in his mind that Ginger would fully understand, even applaud this plan once he got around to telling her how much *she* could benefit if he entered into an unholy union with Millie.

The smoke-filled pub by the harbour was teeming with patrons, mostly foreign sailors, as John pushed his way to the bar and had to shout at the barman to be heard above the noise. 'Has Ginger Gates been in tonight, Badger?'

The barman was known affectionately as, Badger, due to the white streak of hair that ran from the front of his brow to the nape of his neck. He put down the glass he was drying. 'She said if you came in, I had to tell you to wait. There's a Russian ship in port, or hadn't you noticed the place is packed to the gunnels with sailors? The prossies are minting it tonight.'

'Give me a beer while I'm waiting.' John put money on the counter then found a seat in a quiet corner where he could talk to Ginger. He didn't have long to wait.

'Would you look at the state of me?' Ginger dropped the money she'd just earned into her handbag then adjusted her dishevelled clothing, pulling her skirt up and her blouse down. 'Some clients get a bit carried away, know what I mean?'

'Another satisfied customer, eh,' John said, proudly.

She gave an impish, little wink then planted her full, red lips on his. Ginger had long, titian hair and was quite pretty in a lewd sort of way, which was why she was so popular with the foreign sailors. 'I hope you weren't waiting too long, because I had a bit of business to attend to. A girl has a living to earn and I tell you, my drawers have been up and down so often, today the elastic's worn out.'

'What would you say if I was to tell you it looks like I could be about to come into a lot of money?' John leaned forward until their faces were almost touching, 'legitimate money that is.'

Ginger's eyes widened and her bright, red lips parted to reveal her nicotine-stained teeth. 'Tell me more,' she said enthusiastically.

'Now hear me out before you start shouting,' he warned. 'That one I've been meeting at *The Snug* has more money than the Bank of England. All the tricks you showed me to keep a girl happy worked a treat. She's done everything but beg me to marry her and before you say anything, she's the ugliest woman I've ever met, but her money's very attractive and there's lots of it. Much more actually than I first thought.' He watched Ginger for a sign of approval.

'Hmm... well,' she tapped her fingers on the table, thinking, and then her eyes twinkled lasciviously. 'To hell with it, if the loot's good, it doesn't matter what she looks like. Just close your eyes and think of me.'

'Clever girl, I knew you'd understand. Now, I'm taking her to the pictures tonight and then afterwards, when I walk her home, I'm going to propose.'

'I suppose this means I won't see you until after the honeymoon.'

'Mm... we'll have to see about that! Right now, I need some expert advice on how to get her really worked up.'

'Then you've come to the right girl! Remember what I told you about touch? You have to make it just enough to kindle a fire, don't light the furnace just yet. Go only so far then back off and wait for her to beg for more. You want putty in your hands, not solid rock.'

'This is what I have in mind,' John said gleefully. 'I'll whisper sweet words in her ear and slip in a few hints about marriage. By the time King Kong's offed it, she'll be red-hot with curiosity and I'll have her in that bed quicker than you can get your drawers down. Then, in the heat of passion,' he clutched his heart in the pretence of being love-struck, 'I'll swear on my mother's grave I can't wait to make her my wife.'

'You mother's grave?' Ginger tittered callously. John wouldn't know his mother if he passed her on the street, let alone where her grave is. He was just another unwanted new-born left on the doorstep of the orphanage. She wiped the smile off her face and said, 'Sounds good to me, go on.'

'We'll marry as soon as possible, and I'll be the perfect husband until I have access to her money… Oh, you understand I'll have to go missing for a few weeks?'

'Of course, you can hardly leave your bride when you're still on honeymoon.' Ginger cackled gleefully. 'Just don't make the honeymoon last too long, and you remember one very important thing.'

'What's that?'

'I expect a nice, *expensive* present to ease my loneliness.'

'Once she says yes and I put a Woolworth's ring on her finger, you'll have the best of everything. A proposal will definitely come as a shock at first, she'll hesitate, and that's when I make a great show of telling her she's only been stringing me along and its best if I never see her again. How does it sound up till now?'

'Perfect! You'll have her grovelling at your feet.' Ginger licked her lips. She could almost taste the money.

That night, everything went like clockwork. Millie went on about the film and how sad the ending had been. 'The great beast died for love,' she said sadly.

And that was John's cue. He got down on one knee. 'That's how I feel about you, Millie.' John was so believable, even Ronald Coleman couldn't have played it better. 'Please say you'll marry me.'

'Tell me something first, John,' she asked hesitantly, tearfully. 'Do you think I'm too fat? I know people call me fat behind my back, but Grandma always told me it was rubbish and they were only jealous because I was… voluptuous. Do you think I'm voluptuous, John? Tell me you like my body.' She wanted flattery and reassurance, but most of all, Millie wanted to believe she was a creature of desire.

'I love every inch of your body,' he lied. 'I'd rather have a full-bodied woman like you than one of those scrawny hens.' That was the one and only time John Adams ever felt a pang of conscience, but that's all it was, one solitary moment of weakness, then it was forgotten.

Blinded by love and driven by loneliness, Millie was only too ready and willing to accept such an urgent proposal of marriage from John, this man whose very touch sent her into spasms of ecstasy. The act he put on was so perfect, never the slightest indication he felt no love for her. How could she know or even have the slightest suspicion all that mattered to Adams was her money.

'Yes, yes, yes,' she cried passionately.

She was now a betrothed lady and that meant more than anything to Millie. What fun to revel in her new-found status and walk with head held high? This turn of events was one in the eye for all the cultured ladies who thought themselves too good for her. Of course, she didn't see the real Adams the way others saw; the uncouth, illiterate rough-neck who was obviously taking advantage of her.

Just when Millie had given up all hope of ever becoming a bride, John had stepped into her life and taken her out of the gloom that, for a time, seemed like this was all life held for Millie Coutts. He swept her off her feet. There was one thing she hesitated to mention, and that was the fact John hadn't as yet produced the customary ring to seal their engagement. Purely and simply to save face, Millie took her mother's ring from the jewellery box and slipped it on her own finger. It would do for now, besides, who the hell would know it was her mother's ring.

It was somewhat farcical the way Millie flashed the expensive engagement ring. No one in their right mind believed for one minute it had been bought by John Adams, and even if he'd stolen it (which was more feasible), John certainly wouldn't have given something as saleable as this to Millie. She remained blissfully ignorant of the fact that lust for wealth was John's only motivation in romancing her.

For the first time in her life, Millie was truly happy. In her own feeble mind, she fantasised that John had gallantly placed the magnificent diamond and sapphire ring on her finger the night he proposed. She had the greatest urge to knock on Maggie Stark's door and flash the engagement ring just to prove her wrong then stand in Charles Street shouting to the world that Millicent Coutts was a happy woman.

It was quirky, and in a way, rather scary that the two men in Millie's life, her father and John, were breeds apart yet so alike. Both were corrupt, avaricious and cruel men who would stop at nothing. Two men with the same characteristics: not an ounce of love for anyone but themselves.

'I heard all about the gorgeous engagement ring you bought your lovely bride to be.' Ginger said sarcastically. 'Not bad, considering you never even gave me as much as a bar of chocolate for services rendered.'

'Well, Ginger, if you believe all you hear, you'll eat all you see. It was her mother's ring, if you want to know. Crazy bitch just needed something to show off to the la-de-da set. As long as it didn't come out of my beer money, I don't give a damn.'

'You know, of course, you'll have to speculate if you want to accumulate, and that means spending a few bob on her. It doesn't have to be that much. She knows you're not a rich man, so she won't expect expensive presents.' Ginger looked for some sign that John understood what she was trying to put to him, but there was only a look of horror on his face at the idea of spending *his* money on Millie. 'Let me explain *again*,' Ginger said wearily. 'You have to spend a few bob on her, then throw in some subtle hints about how you don't have as much as a couple of penny coins now to jingle in your pocket. She'll feel guilty and give you much more than you spent. Perhaps even a few pounds.'

'Now, I've got you,' John said, snapping his fingers. 'Give her conscience a nudge because she's so rich with all that loot and poor me, not as much as the price of a pint.'

'Now, you're learning.' Ginger had more than a friendly interest in the scam; much, much more. She had nothing to lose by orchestrating John's every move, but she had a lot to gain. 'Now off you go and play the part of a loving fiancée like a true professional.' Ginger brushed her lips across John's face, leaving a bright, red smear on his cheek and for one wicked second, she considered leaving it there, proof of ownership so to speak, then decided against it. After all, what would be the point in jeopardising her future gain? She wiped away the tell-tale smudge with the corner of her handkerchief.

Chapter Thirty-Six

Millie stood in front of the cheval mirror and slowly raised her skirt. The rash she had discovered was becoming sores that were spreading onto those intimate areas ladies didn't mention. She felt feverish. All morning, she had psyched herself up to boldly go see the doctor. 'He's a nice man,' she told herself, 'he'll understand. He's probably seen all this before.' She gave that idea more thought and it went straight out the window. Examinations were one thing, but this was far too intimate and personal, and she couldn't bring herself to make the move. Instead, she decided just to do what Grammy would have done, dab the sore bits with calamine lotion. Millie ran her tongue over the ulcers inside her mouth, Grammy always said mouth ulcers were a sure sign a person was run-down, so that's all it must be. No need to bother the doctor. All she needed was a tonic from Boots Chemist, a pick-me-up. That would do the trick.

The doorbell ringing startled her and Millie quickly gathered her composure before answering it. John stood there holding a small, blatantly inexpensive posy of flowers. As per Ginger's instructions, he was playing the part of an attentive fiancée. 'If I were a rich man, I would fill this house with a thousand red roses, but for now, this is the only token of my love I can offer,' he told her with the ardour and passion he had rehearsed with Ginger as his coach.

His silver tongue, as usual, duped Millie into believing all the love and adoration he showed her was real and true, when in fact, the words of love he spoke so eloquently had been carefully rehearsed with Ginger. She herself was adept at speaking fallacious words of endearment to clients who came to her for what she salubriously referred to as a fumble and a quickie in the darkness at the back of the pub.

Adams then delivered the punch-line. 'Instead of waiting months, I think it best if we get this shindig over in say… three weeks from now.'

Instead of being suspicious about the rush, Millie was too besotted to see the deceit, which hid behind John's crafty smile, and ecstatically, she took his word that waiting would be a waste of time.

When the wedding date was announced, there was much supposition about the haste in which it had been arranged. Although it wasn't to be as elaborate as a normal society wedding with a guest list straight out of who's who, astonishingly enough, gifts began arriving from all those upper-crust ladies Millie least expected to send presents: the very ones who in the past had shunned her. Of course, this bearing of gifts wasn't to be confused with friendship. It was merely to establish financial superiority and one-up-man-ship so that, at social gatherings, they could discuss who sent gifts to the Coutts girl. Even though her union with the uncouth Adams person wasn't to be marked with a proper society wedding, propriety must be adhered to. Those who paid handsomely for a present were able to wallow in self-esteem. Those who were more frugal in their choice of gifts said it outright. No damned way. Why should *they* throw good money away on that abomination and her loutish fiancé?

The dining room table positively groaned with the weight of gift boxes holding silverware, crystal and fine china. John's eyes bulged at the sight of this Aladdin's cave and how much it was all worth. The pocket money Millie had been so loftily giving him over the past weeks was nothing compared to this.

With little more than a week to go until their wedding day, John stepped up the pitiful inferences on what lack of finances did to a generous man such as himself. "Without a pot to piss in," was how he woefully referred to his financial state.

Finally, Millie got the message and her way of resolving his economic strife was by handing him what she said in a light-hearted way so as not to embarrass him was… her dowry?

'We can't very well have you going about town with empty pockets.' The soon to be Mrs Adams cooed like a dove as she held out this symbol of her love. Namely, a gold money clip holding banknotes. 'Oh, and you really should go to the outfitters immediately to buy a new suit. We must make every effort to keep up appearances.'

John shed a few crocodile tears as he praised Millie's generosity. 'I must be the luckiest man in the world,' he gushed, but all the while, that money was burning a hole in his pocket. There was a horse running in the two thirty at Epsom and he had it on good authority it was a sure thing. Also, unbeknown to the love-struck Millie, John had made a list of the expensive wedding presents. With Ginger's help, he'd have no bother selling them on at a bargain price to the French and American sailors with more money than sense.

The simple, cheap but not very cheerful wedding ceremony took but a few minutes, and the registrar hardly gave them time to say, 'I do.' They didn't know it, but the registrar was running late and another wedding party, who had been cooling their heels outside, were threatening violence if their wedding was held up for one minute longer.

John slipped the wedding ring on Millie's finger. Not the Woolworths' ring which he had bought at little cost, but her mother's wedding ring. Millie had taken one look at the dull, brass ring and insisted on swapping it for the broad, gold wedding band. Instead of wedding bells, Millie should have heard warning bells. She had given John money to buy a wedding ring and he came back with this cheapest of cheap item and not a penny change. He gave the excuse that it was a stupid waste of money when there was a perfectly good wedding ring in her jewellery box. Perhaps Millie did hear those warning bells, but she chose to ignore them.

The ease by which he could extract cash from his wife surprised Adams. He expected her to be like other women who grumbled and shouted when it came to dipping into their purse. 'She doesn't even have to be slapped around first. Oh yes, it pays to wed a rich bitch,' he jovially let it be known. Ginger would hee-haw at his remarks and since his wife was paying, she'd have a large gin.

It hurt Millie that only a few months after the nuptials, the only way she could keep her new husband sweet was by financing his weekend drinking sprees with his old pals. She tried every way possible to beguile him into spending time with her instead.

'Now, now,' John scolded when she complained, 'you're my little ray of sunshine, but a man needs the company of men too,' and that was all it took. He only had to call her a few pet names, and if he had wiped his feet on her, she would have thanked him for the honour of being his doormat.

'Bye-bye dear,' Millie looked every bit the dejected and deserted wife standing on the doorstep waving goodbye to a husband who didn't even take the time to reciprocate the loving farewell as he hurriedly took off towards the harbour. The solitude was creeping back into her life and Millie wept as she whispered soulfully, 'I'll miss you, John, enjoy yourself but please hurry back.'

In no more than eighteen months after the nuptials, the sugar coating wore off and the pill was becoming just too damned bitter to swallow. Millie discovered her new husband was gambling heavily and since he didn't have a steady job, he had to be using—or to be precise—*losing* her money. How stupid she had been to have put her signature on that piece of paper which gave Adams freedom to dip into her funds. Although according to bank statements, he wasn't so much dipping as diving headlong. Why, oh why had she allowed John to talk her into making the bank account into joint names?

The whole scenario was becoming impossible to tolerate. Millie was forced to accept that her wayward husband's weekend visitations to that bar at the harbour had escalated. John was now spending every night with his cronies and of course, Ginger, who greedily reaped the benefits of Millie's rapidly decreasing fortune.

For a while, the void in her life had been filled but now, Millie had time to count the cost and speculate as to whether or not she had been wise in using her heart instead of her head. For some unknown reason, she remembered something she had read at one time, how did it go? Something like, how foolish those who are too blind to see: it was as close as she could remember, and it was so apt.

It had been on the cards all along, only a matter of time until some rude and greedy bad boy came along to feed on Millie's lust.

We all make mistakes in life; some good, some bad, some are just silly... and some downright dangerous, as was the case with Millie.

Chapter Thirty-Seven

Millie decided to make their second anniversary special with a meal fit for a king. She covered the dining table with a lace tablecloth and then placed a rose bowl filled with red roses in the centre. Now was the time to use some of their beautiful wedding gifts. The exquisite crystal, silver and finest china had never been used. Such a shame they'd never seen the light of day. But there had never been a reason to set a fine table for guests or friends. She had no friends.

'I can't find the silver canteen of cutlery that Mr and Mrs Price sent us as a wedding present. The Victorian silver cruet set is missing too. In fact, there are quite a few things I can't find.' Millie frantically rummaged through drawers and cupboards. 'Did you perhaps put them away for safety, John?' It was a simple enough question. Millie wasn't making accusations; she was merely trying to ascertain where her most prized gifts had been put. Instead of an explanation, Millie only incurred John's wrath.

John stamped mean and menacing towards her with a clenched fist raised. He growled accusingly, 'What are you saying? That I stole them?'

John's incensed bellowing almost made her faint with fear. Terror and trembling were no strangers to Millie, and she cowered in an armchair. 'Of course not, dearest, I only wanted to set the table for our anniversary dinner.' She held her breath and waited for the first punch.

'How often do I have to tell you I don't eat posh food? The pub serves tasty pies and that's good enough for me.'

All Millie wanted right that minute, all she prayed for was to hear the slamming of the door and know it was safe for her to get out of the armchair.

The honeymoon was well and truly over. Looking back now, it had never really begun. Oh yes, there were those first few weeks of lovey-dovey when, all humble and pitiful, he would ask for *a little hand-out to tide him over*. After only a few short months came the grumbling and hinting, that their marriage couldn't possibly last if he constantly had to come to her cap in hand for pocket money.

And then the punch-line: wouldn't it be easier for both of them if his name was on the bank account too? It was Millie's first wedding anniversary present to John—a joint bank account and this accomplished, Adams changed from the loving husband to the husband from hell.

In an instant, John began laughing, but not in a happy, carefree way. This was the sound of insanity. 'What did you think *I'd* do with all that finery?' White froth gathered at the sides of his mouth and onto his rough, unshaven chin.

'I never accused you of stealing it, John.' She may have tried to look appalled at the suggestion, but Millie's true belief was written on her face. The belief that John was a liar and a thief with little or no morality and worse than that, Millie feared he was quite, quite mad. 'Why don't we forget all about the silly presents and I'll make us a nice cup of tea?' She forced a smile then slid from the chair and hurried into the kitchen, heart pounding in case he came after her.

The slamming of the front door brought Millie hurrying to the bay window that overlooked the front garden. John was staggering towards the gate and she sighed with relief. He would be gone until late into the night, thank God. Instead of fretting over this, as she used to, Millie was glad of the respite from his narking and bullying.

A half-empty bottle of whiskey and an overturned crystal glass lay on the floor at the side of the armchair. Millie held up the fine, crystal glass and laughed bitterly. 'Pearls before swine right enough, John dearest.' She had recently developed this odd way of speaking to herself or holding a conversation with her dead father as if he were there in the room with her. Perhaps her happiness had been so fleeting; it was a sign of discontentment, regret and disappointment. Perhaps it was something more sinister.

Millie fastidiously washed away John's greasy fingerprints in the soapsuds and the crystal glass regained its glisten. Sunlight beaming through the kitchen window made iridescent colours dance across the whitewashed walls when Millie held the glass up to the light. The beautiful colours fascinated her. How she loved pinks and purples. But this glass was now only another sad reminder of a time not so long ago when they first met. John had been content to swig cheap ale from the equally cheap, dirty glass back then. She had smiled affectionately at the way he clutched it like a trophy and drank from it in *The Snug*. But the adoration she once felt for him had turned to nauseating disgust that turned her stomach. The veneer of marital bliss had cracked.

Not long after their third wedding anniversary, Millie realised just how much of a downward spiral there was in her financial situation. She never took much interest in the money side of things, that was what accountants were paid for, and having enough to cover her needs was all that interested her. It was a visit from her accountant that put into perspective the true state of her financial affairs.

'Your ledgers show a serious shortfall, Mrs Adams. In fact, your out-goings now vastly exceeds your income.' The gravity of the situation was reflected in the way his mouth twitched and rapid swallowing made the knot in his tie bob up and down.

'I'd prefer it if you'd get to the point, Mr Wightman,' Millie said, handing him a glass of water to ease the dryness in his throat.

'Three years ago, your out-going expenses were approximately thirty percent of your income, today, it is *one hundred and ten percent*,' he almost roared as his exasperation accelerated. 'Are you not aware Mr Adams has been making large withdrawals of cash on a daily basis? At this rate of spending, you will be penniless in a few years.'

'I had no idea things were this bad! I'll speak to John and explain the situation, I'm sure he'll understand this heavy spending must be curbed.' Millie smiled confidently and muttered some inane comment about her husband being too generous for his own good.

'Right you are then! Give it a month to see if things settle down and I'll see you four weeks from now.'

It had to stop, that had been made crystal clear by the man who knew more about her finances than Millie herself did. But once you've created a monster and given it carte blanche, how do you put a stop to it? Millie felt a deep anger that the man she trusted enough to give him access to more money than he had ever seen in his life had abused the privilege… and her trust.

She sat in the lounge all that evening, fretting, wondering whether or not to stay up until John came home. Then, after giving it careful consideration, Millie decided she didn't have the stomach for a drunken confrontation and went to bed. Tomorrow, she'd say what had to be said.

It was around mid-day when John rambled into the kitchen. Millie poured a cup of tea and put it in front of him. He made a grunting sound, shoved the cup aside and reached for the whiskey bottle.

Millie sighed plaintively and silently handed him a glass. It was either that or suffer the indignity of watching him slurp straight from the bottle.

'You're spending too much money, John.' Millie had intended to be forthright while maintaining civility when she confronted him but instead, her manner was abrupt and challenging. It was purely an accidental, hurried slip of the tongue, but it took Adams completely by surprise.

'What do you mean I'm spending too much money?' He glowered chillingly and screamed a string of oaths.

The verbal attack startled Millie, although she didn't know why. Over the past few weeks, she had become increasingly alarmed by the terrifying changes in his character. There was a kind of madness about him that seemed to come out of the blue. At times, he could actually be a kind and considerate husband and then suddenly, this oppressive stranger would appear, screeching the vilest expletives and lashing out at her... like now.

Millie recoiled in terror. 'The... the... accountant, he c... came to see me yesterday.' She had a great need to say what had to be said, but an even greater reluctance to speak the words. 'You see, John, he's alarmed b... by the amount that's been spent in such a short space of time.' She gasped and wheezed in sheer terror and her head pounded as if it were about to burst. 'He says you're spending more in one night than some people earn in a month.' And then she twittered timidly, 'm... money doesn't grow on trees, dearest.'

Millie's frail attempt at levity only seemed to incense him and without warning, John slapped her so hard, she staggered backwards and fell heavily into the armchair gasping from the shock.

Slowly, menacingly, John walked towards the armchair. He leaned over her until their faces were no more than an inch apart. Millie had to turn her head away to avoid his stale, offensive breath. 'Listen to me, you stupid bitch, and listen well,' he rasped, 'don't **ever** question me about my spending.'

Fright and panic turned Millie's face a ghostly pallor and the pupils of her dark eyes dilated, giving her an unnatural appearance, like a plump snowman with eyes of coal. 'I wasn't questioning you, John.' Her eyes were now tight shut so that if he was to hit her again, she wouldn't see it coming. 'I was just telling you what the accountant told me, that money should be used wisely and respected.'

Once more, his mood changed, he smiled and gently stroked her cheek. 'I spend money on my friends and spread a little happiness, that's wise, isn't it? And I respect it too, dearest. You'd never catch me buying a drink for someone I didn't like.'

From the abysmal fear came knowledge. Millie learned one important lesson today, and that was if she were to do anything to stop John from getting to the money, it could have serious consequences. She well remembered the first time he had ever used violence towards her, and in that moment of such fear and pain, she instinctively knew it wouldn't be the last. That was the time she should have taken measures to put a stop to his brutality before it was too late. Now, it was too late.

Chapter Thirty-Eight

Efforts to reverse the financial collapse were futile. Millie had more chance of holding back the tide. As promised, Mr Wightman came to see her one month later. The first thing that struck him as he walked the path towards the front door was that the lawn and flower beds, once meticulously cared for, were now unkempt and overrun with weeds. The brass fittings on the beautiful, ornate door had become encrusted with verdigris. In truth, the entire place appeared now to be going to rack and ruin. If anyone needed help and guidance, it was this unfortunate woman.

'Over the past month, I've been working out a way to resolve your—shall we say—temporary financial problem.' Mr Wightman took some papers from his briefcase. 'I have a proposition for you whereby, if you allow me to take over all your business interests, I may still be able to salvage something and even regain the prosperity you once had. It would mean tightening your purse strings.' Then absolutely emphatic on this, he added, 'and that includes *denying Mr Adams any more access to money.*'

Unknown to them, John had been listening from the other side of the door. He came barging headlong into the room as soon as it was suggested that his own personal money tree be cut down. 'What's that charlatan doing here again? She doesn't need you or anyone else telling her how to spend her money, so get the fuck out and don't come back,' he shrieked, waving his fists in the air.

'With respect, Mr Adams, I've been explaining to Mrs Adams that you are in a dire situation and I was suggesting that...'

'Keep your fucking suggestions to yourself.' John knew this man could convince Millie to turn the flow of money into a mere trickle, unless he was stopped, and John's philosophy was, why spend one pound when you could spend twenty?

The accountant stood abruptly and picked up his folders. He had come here to help, not to be subjected to this kind of verbal abuse. 'I'm sorry, Mrs Adams,' he said solemnly, 'I won't bother you again with unwanted advice. If you're happy with the situation, well, it's your funeral.'

'Please don't go, Mr Wightman, my husband wasn't meaning to be rude...'

'Oh yes, I fucking was! Now see him out the door before I lose my temper and throw him out.' John gloated victoriously as Wightman, with Millie in his wake, scurried to the door.

'What can I do, Mr Wightman?' Millie wrung her hands in anguish. 'You see how it is. There are times John is positively maniacal.'

'If you want my personal opinion, I think he's a lunatic and you would do well to consider having him committed. I deplore squander and it pains me to see not just you, but any woman being treated so deplorably.'

It was sound advice—if Millie had been brave enough to take it. Any doctor would have readily committed John to an asylum for the mentally ill on hearing a full account of his actions. It was obvious he was verging on insanity. Had Millie acted on the advice she had been given, the reason for John's madness would have been discovered and with it, Millie's own declining physical and mental state.

After almost five years of misery, worry and pain, Millie knew what real servitude was like, for when John came home, he inevitably had one or two scroungers in tow and she was expected to serve food and drink to the kind of men decent women crossed to the other side of the street to avoid.

The final degradation came when John brought two of the roughest characters she'd ever seen into her home and ordered her to treat them like princes. One of the men, an ugly, pock-faced man they called, Chick, kept leering at Millie and pawing her when she passed, and instead of stopping the torment, John goaded the man. 'Go on,' he kept saying, 'you can have her for the price of a few drinks. She won't mind and you'll enjoy it. Trust me; it's just like bouncing up and down on an overstuffed mattress.'

Chick didn't need much coaxing. His mouth was already drooling when he pounced on the petrified Millie while John and the other man held her down and cheered as Millie cried and begged them to stop. It was the worst humiliation she had ever been forced to endure, but there was far worse to follow.

Chick bragged explicitly about John Adams's well-disposed wife in the pub and John was inundated with requests to *borrow* Millie, for a fair price naturally. Shamelessly, John saw prostituting his wife as an easy way to make money, a legitimate business venture, no less. From then on, strangers were brought into her home at any hour of the day or night. If Millie tried to fight, she was forcibly held down while the foulest dregs of humanity subjected her to the most abhorrent acts.

The Coutts' fortune was rapidly dwindling and Millie had been forced to sell most of the properties to sustain John's addictions to gambling, drink and prostitutes. The many violent arguments about her husband's costly way of life and the repercussions left Millie with constantly blackened eyes and swollen lips. It was either accept this as her fate or lose the man who had come to her rescue when solitude was all she had to look forward to. At least that was how Millie's befuddled mind interpreted this hell on earth. Or was it more feasible, the effect of the disease that was slowly ravaging her body, also destroying what little intelligence she had been born with?

It was as if Millie was trapped between two worlds, one lucid and the other nightmarish. Knowing, yet not knowing what was happening to her. Used and misused, she dreaded the sun by day and the moon by night, for neither brought solace or peace of mind. Her grandparent's love was all she remembered as being worth living for, yet even that had been misguided. They did love her, but it was a love divided between her and wealth. They instilled in Millie that, 'selfish is as selfish does,' the interpretation of this little maxim being, that it was simply good business to cheat others, especially if they were down on their luck. Only, now that she was a victim of this concept, did Millie see the badness in it and the pain it brought. John had robbed her of everything: wealth, self-respect and even the will to live. How she wished the clock could be turned back so that if Maggie Fraser were to offer once more to be not only her sister, but her friend, she would grasp it with both hands and never let go.

She was big in body but frail in mind, and if Maggie hadn't made her believe she was cursed then Millie might have kept what little dignity she had and never set foot in *The Snug.* If fate hadn't put John Adams there on that particular night, neither would she have fallen from what little grace she possessed, straight into his clutches and his seedy world of corruption.

The day inevitably came when the fear of being left penniless was greater than the fear of losing her husband. The love Millie once felt for John, had been replaced with an overpowering terror and now, she must overcome this terror and find the courage to stop the madness. At the risk of another beating, she resolved to try reasoning with him.

'Oh John, the money's almost gone!' It was an agonised, pitiful wail that burst from Millie's lips. 'There's very little left in the bank, John. You *can't* go on spending like there was no tomorrow.'

'Then sell something woman. Do I have to do all you're thinking for you?' John's outstretched hand began furiously pointing at the walls and display cabinets. 'For a start, we don't need all these paintings and ornaments. They must be worth a pretty penny.'

'I can't do that.' Millie couldn't remember a time when all these beautiful things hadn't been there. Paintings and antiques that were a delight to any eye— except the eyes of a Philistine like John Adams and the very suggestion that they be sold like unwanted junk, appalled her. 'Most of these things have been in our family for generations. I… I… can't let them go.'

'Well, the choice is yours, either stay here with your finery, *or else…*' That inference was there again, always there whenever she looked like standing up to him and refusing to obey an order.

John knew if *he* approached a dealer, then questions would invariably be raised about the true ownership of such fine items. Millie, on the other hand, could spin any kind of yarn and they'd accept it. This was one of those times when psychology was more effective than a fist. 'Take your pick, my dear,' John said almost lovingly and then, instead of another punch on her already pudding lips, John gently kissed her cheek. 'It's them or me,' he said pointedly. Without turning to look at her, he walked slowly from the room leaving a sad and wretched Millie to make choices.

The familiar slamming of the door had become synonymous with stormy confrontations. And then, those days and nights followed when she was left alone to be haunted by the dark shadows that were now her life. To be abandoned was the one thing Millie feared most. With this in mind, she had no alternative. Some things would have to be sold if she was to avoid losing John. What good were worldly possessions to her anyway without her husband?

Chapter Thirty-Nine

Millie browsed aimlessly round the antique shop. There was a certain smell that filled a room where old artefacts were stored. It wasn't a bad smell, but it was one she remembered from a time long gone when, as a child, her grandmother brought her into this very shop in search of beauty and elegance. And now, she was here to try and sell back some of these once-treasured possessions.

A shopping basket, strategically placed to hide the mend in the one and only decent dress Millie had left, was meant to make it look like she was simply a lady out shopping when something in this window had caught her eye. Millie even put on a show of admiring and appearing interested in certain items: a painting, a delicate figurine, an exquisite chandelier that hung from the ceiling. Well, she had to at least show some finesse and at least pretend to be interested in making a purchase. Millie thought it best if she purported to be redecorating. These were, after all, professional dealers in fine art. Not some under the counter shysters. It was important that a sense of propriety must be upheld. She couldn't afford to let her desperation show.

'Can I be of any assistance? You appear to be somewhat indecisive.'

It was only when this shabbily-dressed woman turned to face him that the antique dealer recognised her as no other than Millicent Coutts. The vivid memory of that obnoxious brat who answered the door when he personally delivered a painting to her grandparents was imprinted on his mind. She was a mere adolescent then, but he'd never forget that horrible child. He would have recognised her anywhere.

'I'm quite taken with that chandelier, and this.' Millie held up the figurine of a flower seller, the basket of blossoms by her side were so real she could almost smell them. This was the kind of thing that always caught grandma's keen eye, but of course, Millie was simply using the piece as an introduction to what she was really there for.

'Oh yes, a figurine such as this would be a perfect enhancement to any sitting room mantelpiece,' the dealer enthralled.

'Well, I'm redecorating,' Millie lied, 'and I'm not really sure what I want.' She pointed to the paintings and remarked casually, 'I actually have some lovely, old paintings myself, which I'm seriously considering disposing of as they won't fit in with my new décor.' Then, as if the idea had just crossed her mind, she added, 'perhaps you might be interested in buying fine works of art.'

So this was what the charade was all about? She wasn't interested in buying, she wanted to sell. Redecorating indeed, she must think he came in on the last banana boat. 'Let me see,' he said slyly, tapping his chin with a forefinger as if he were indecisive as to whether or not he should make a valuation and an offer.

With some urgency, Millie said, 'I'm not one to drive a hard bargain.'

Everyone knew the man Millie Coutts married had almost exhausted her fortune. Well, it *was* common knowledge in the businessman's club that Coutts's daughter was on her arse financially, thanks to the lout she had married. Dinner parties too positively buzzed with lurid tales of how she had fallen into utter degradation. According to the jungle drums, she was in dire straits, and from where he was standing, it looked very much like she was desperate for money: but just how desperate?

'Actually,' he gave one of those indecisive sighs, 'you might be able to twist my arm into taking some paintings off your hands.' He grinned avariciously. 'Providing of course, the items on offer *were* reasonably priced. Fine art just isn't selling too well,' he lied.

This was an opportunity not to be missed. In the world of antiques, a dealer could make a killing and a healthy profit from someone this despairing of funds. Well, if he didn't take her up on the offer, someone else would and this theory gave him a clear conscience.

Millie put on an altogether over-feigned air of prestige, fingering the figurine then laying it down with an indifferent shrug. She carried on with the sham of browsing for a few minutes in the hope a casual approach would work wonders. Finally, she ambled over to him and as nonchalantly as possible said, 'At the minute, I have some shopping to do, but perhaps you could come by the house later today.'

The casual manner didn't fool him for a minute. She didn't say later this week or next week, she said *today* and this dealer recognised real desperation when he saw it. 'Would seven o'clock be convenient for you?' Had it not been for looking overly-keen, he would gladly have shut up shop and gone immediately to her house. But this was a game of cat and mouse, which he intended to enjoy playing.

A true professional, the antique dealer opened proceedings by firstly testing the water. He offered a ridiculously low price for two paintings, fully expecting the financially strapped Mrs Adams to at least put on a show of non-urgency by haggling. To his surprise, Millie was unquestioning and without the slightest hesitation accepted the offer: an offer which was only a fraction of their true value. The dealer shook her hand vigorously as he left clutching the paintings.

The house was a veritable Aladdin's cave, and this buyer of fine antiques had a gut feeling; he just knew that before long, he would own every one of these fine items. Treasure hunters would undoubtedly come flocking to his shop once these went on display. 'If there's anything else you wish to dispense with, I'll be only too happy to deal with it personally, at a time that suits you of course.' He left a card with the inscription *Philip Ross, dealer in fine antiques and paintings.*

From that day, Mr Ross was a regular caller at the Coutts' house as, piece by piece, he bought up everything of value until finally there was nothing of value left. Ross had been just another man in a long line of men who, each in their own way, used Millie.

Alone in the big house, Millie shed bitter tears and the empty walls echoed her despair. Solitude, the thing she feared most, was the penance she paid for foolishly believing the sugar-coated words of a rogue.

John's gambling debts were mounting and still, he refused to believe, even to himself, that the flow of money had dried up. The money tree had withered and died, and even Ginger moved on once she read the signs.

On the rare occasions when John wandered home, albeit briefly, his story was invariably the same: the horses he backed had been nobbled or he had been cheated at cards. The bottom line was, he had lost everything—*again*—and needed more money to feed his indulgences. It had been two weeks since Millie last saw him. He had taken the last of the money and scuttled off to take part in a high-stakes poker game.

Now, he was back. 'I want money,' and they were the only words he spoke, no respectful enquiry as to how she was, just the usual demand.

'I have nothing to give, because there's nothing left,' Millie told him coldly and without a grain of emotion.

'Then dip into the money pot,' John ordered drunkenly, swaying towards her with clenched fists at the ready.

The adoration and love she once had for this man was gone and strangely enough, so too was the fear. Millie was an empty shell, bereft of any feeling other than hatred for the person who had systematically robbed her of her inheritance, her lifestyle, but most of all, her pride and self-esteem.

'Look, look around you, John.' Touched by the irony of it all, Millie suddenly began to laugh hysterically. 'All we have left are four bare walls. Every stick of furniture has been sold. Do you see that pile of blankets in the corner? That's my bed. Yes, John, that's what I'm reduced to. Now, do you understand? I can't give what I haven't got.'

'Are you refusing me?' He looked bewildered. The disease that left him covered in suppurating ulcers stank horribly. It was eating away at his brain and the John Adams, who had always lived by his wits, no longer had the capability to think rationally. His feeble mind had only one response to a refusal. True to form, he lashed out and his fist struck Millie's face with such force, she fell to the floor. 'If there's nothing left inside, then sell this fucking empty mausoleum.' Rapaciously, he pulled Millie back by the hair when she tried to run, and continued his tirade.

The vicious, rasping voice sent shivers through her, for Millie was in no doubt, that murdering her would be an easy option for John Adams. 'Alright, alright,' she screamed in pain, 'I'll do whatever you want.' Blood trickled from the corner of her mouth and Millie folded her arms over the bruised and battered face in an effort to protect herself from further blows. 'Please, John,' she begged, 'don't hit me again, I can't take any more.'

The day her house was put up for sale, Millie's plight was already common knowledge and the sharks were waiting to move in for a quick kill. Within an hour, the house had sold for less than half its value. It was one of those under-the-table deals between a shrewd solicitor and an even shrewder businessman. Justification nullified guilt! The easy excuse for cheating Millie being that she would only hand over the money to that scoundrel, the man she married.

It was a sad day for her, and a far cry from the life she had been accustomed to when Millie moved into a dingy, little garret in an effort to escape the man who, if he found her, would claim what little money she had managed to hide away to feed and keep herself. But even God Almighty couldn't protect her when John Adams was on the rampage for cash. There was no hiding place or anonymity. John found her and after a beating that left her more dead than alive, Millie handed over the bag containing the last remnants of the Coutts Empire.

The once cosseted and pampered girl became a bloated and miserable woman old beyond her years. Millie hid herself away in a half-lit room lest people saw her pox-marked face and turned away in disgust. She wandered the streets in the early hours while normal folk slept, scavenging for scraps of food and stealing milk from doorsteps. Misery had many forms and many names, but one name described the ultimate misery—*Millicent Coutts*.

The decline into total poverty had happened at startling speed. One man's greed, like some ferocious beast, had devoured all the things Millie valued and now, the same disease that contaminated John was raging through her and the limited faculties she possessed were already diminishing.

There were times, whatever remnants of sanity she had left, fled her ravished mind and madness took over. Millie believed that all the awful things she remembered had all been just a dream, a terrible nightmare. In the few and far days of lucidity, one thing alone haunted her, and that was the memory of Maggie's curse. That was the day Maggie Fraser came to seek justice and retribution for the wrong she claimed had been done to them by her beloved Daddy when he stole their mother's money. Oh yes, Millie knew all along her father had stolen Maggie and Eve's inheritance. Didn't he brag about it often enough?

There was one day in particular, it was hazy, but her befuddled brain recalled Daddy coming to her grandparent's house the worse for drink. He was celebrating having finalised a lucrative business deal that, in his own words, 'put him back in the big money league.' She recalled him pouring whiskey from a crystal decanter and then holding the glass aloft as if toasting someone. He raved drunkenly about parcels of money and how good it felt to watch Tina gasp her last breath. Millie also remembered joining her father in a merry toast to his wife's demise because they, the working classes that is, didn't have feelings so they didn't count in life's equation.

A solitary candle flickered, casting shadows around the small, bug-infested room and when Millie stared long enough at the dancing flame, it created hallucinations: figments of the imagination. She saw Grandma, and Daddy, then Maggie would smile and say, 'I forgive you, Millie.' Many times, Millie burned her hand reaching out to touch the images. Of course, these were only conjured visions that were in themselves conducive of a rapidly deteriorating mind. There was nothing there, she was alone.

She had no recollection of the grandeur she had at one time been accustomed to, or the lavish lifestyle that was hers before John infested it with his malice, brutality and avaricious objective. Millie simply forgot and thought that her life now was what it had always been and the memories that flashed through her mind were only dreams.

When the authorities searched for Millie's whereabouts to inform her that John Adams, her estranged husband, had died of syphilis and she too would most likely be in the advanced stages of the same disease, Millie's confused brain couldn't take it in. 'Who's John Adams?' She asked, 'I don't think I know anyone of that name.'

Perhaps Mother Nature had at last taken pity on Millie by obliterating the memory of the man she had married in desperation: a man for whom, death had come as a blessed relief from paralysis and madness. What Millie would never know was that before his death, John had raved incessantly about the Coutts and their cursed money.

Chapter Forty

On a chilly, damp autumn morning in 1943, ten years after the fateful meeting and subsequent marriage to John Adams, Millie followed her husband to the grave. John had taken everything from her and left Millie with only the horrors that untreated syphilis brings. Lying on a bed of straw, she died alone and penniless in the empty garret and no one knew or even cared how long she had lain there. The only thing that alerted neighbours was the smell of her decaying body. Death permeated the walls and when the stench became unbearable, the police were sent for to break down the door and news of Millie's death spread. She had become legendary for all the wrong reasons. Her name was now synonymous with stupidity.

The only person to witness Millie being laid to rest in her pauper's grave, and the least likely person to mourn a Coutts, was Maggie Stark. She placed rosary beads and a simple posy of flowers on the unmarked grave, then bowed her head in a silent eulogy for an unfortunate girl who had never known goodness.

'Oh Millie, you poor, little, rich girl,' Maggie's remorseful sigh was both pitying and grieving. 'Why did you have to be so uppity and class conscious? We should have been friends, and probably in different circumstances, we would have become friends, but now, we'll never know. You must have been so alone and frightened and all the time I… we were there. Tommy and I could have helped. All you had to do was ask. There was no reason to be alone when you had sisters and a brother-in-law. You had a family, and what happened wasn't your fault, Millie. The real blame was in the idiotic things you were brought up to believe.' The simple eulogy delivered in that cold and empty graveyard lifted the weight of any guilt Maggie may have felt. That day she stood on Millie's doorstep and delivered such a harsh verbal beating had lain heavy on her conscience all these years but now, her mind was clear of fault.

The tear tracks on her face told a tale. Maggie brushed away a fresh flow of tears that trickled freely down her cheeks. How strange it was to be standing in this forlorn place, grieving the stepsister she once hated, yet stranger still, Maggie wasn't grieving Millie's death. The grief she bore was for a life ruined by upper-class convention.

The ground was soggy under her feet as Maggie turned to leave, and then she was overcome by the oddest sensation. Her steps faltered as an unknown force seemed to pull her back and goose pimples rose on her arms at the feeling, Millie wanted more from her: perhaps forgiveness. In the deserted cemetery, Maggie turned to address what was nothing more than a pile of damp earth on a freshly dug grave.

'OK, I'm sorry for the way things turned out for you, Millie, but that's the way it is. You played the hand you were dealt, and lost. What comes around goes around. Your misery is over now. It's time for you to rest in peace.'

For the rest of the day, Maggie was filled with a great sadness she hadn't reckoned on. Even as she prepared the evening meal, it was difficult to detach her mind from the mockery that was Millie's funeral and the barren, soggy patch of ground that was her last resting place. Maggie couldn't stem the tears that kept falling from her red and swollen eyes.

Wearied by the events of this day and the effort of trying to put them behind her, Maggie suddenly felt drained of energy and very tired. She fell into the armchair, snuggled up and allowed her eyes to close.

The sound of the doorbell's harshness startled her from a sound sleep into sudden awareness. Maggie opened the door to the one sight that struck fear into her heart—a policeman on the doorstep.

Her whole body trembled as wounds reopened and old fears returned, but the policeman, taking in the panic on Maggie's face, smiled reassuringly and leaned forward to steady her saying, 'no need for worry, Mrs Stark, I'm not here to deliver any kind of bad news.'

It took but a few moments for Maggie to regain a sense of reality. She had already been unnerved by ghosts from the past today, so what next? She invited this very polite member of the local constabulary into her home, intrigued as to why the police found it necessary to pay her a visit.

'I'm here in connection with the death of your stepsister,' he explained. And then he took an envelope, a very tattered envelope, from his pocket.

'I'm already aware of Millie's death. She was buried this morning,' Maggie said impartially and with little interest, other than that ominous envelope he clutched. 'I attended what can only laughingly be referred to as a funeral, and that's as far as it goes.'

That dirty, crumpled envelope he kept tapping against his fingers kind of bamboozled Maggie, but since he made no reference to what it held, why should she? He would no doubt tell her, when he was good and ready. whatever significance it had to Millie's death.

'Mm,' the policeman mumbled in a vague way, as if he were trying to find the words to say something that needed to be said.

Maggie carried on explaining her association to the now-deceased Millie. 'My mother made the mistake of marrying a Coutts, but other than that, we had nothing in common. There was bad blood between us. My family wanted nothing more to do with the Coutts after my mother's death and the Coutts wanted nothing to do with us.' Maggie shrugged in a, "that's that" kind of way.

'It's a sad tale and no mistake! I've heard the stories that went 'round.'

'I lost faith in justice many years ago. I went to the police when I discovered that James Coutts had helped himself to every penny of my mother's money. I can't remember the officer's name, but he had a good laugh at my allegations before threatening to put *me* in the cells if I refused to withdraw my complaint, so you'll understand why I'm wary of police.'

'I know the officer you're referring to. Obviously, I can't mention any names, but he left the force—let's just say—under a cloud. Small talk said, he was involved in some kind of cover-up and Mr Coutts's name was mentioned at the time.'

'Well I can't say *that* comes as a surprise! I warned him to be cautious that day in his office. I told him Coutts had no scruples and he'd sell his mother to save his own neck.' Even after all this time, it felt good to know the high and mighty officer had (metaphorically speaking) fallen off his horse, but there was still the mystery of what the police wanted with her. 'That envelope you're holding, does it have anything to do with me?' Maggie finally asked.

'We found this in the garret where the body…' he quickly corrected himself, 'where Mrs Adams died.'

At that point, the policeman became ill at ease. The faces of the duty policemen and their repugnance when they described the removal of Millie's body from the scene of her death still haunted him. But most of all, it was the disgust he felt at the way his own colleagues laughed because the corpse wore a tatty, purple hat with pink roses. An article she had obviously prized and loved at some time in her tortured life.

Maggie looked questioningly at his efforts to regain some composure. She wasn't to know that he was trying hard to remind himself that deaths like this were an everyday occurrence. Yet, wasn't it still sad in the extreme that any human being could be so alone and nondescript, that they were left to lie in such squalor without love, friends, or compassion for their plight?

With some hesitance, he held out the envelope. 'Though not related by blood, it would appear from this letter, she acknowledges you as her next of kin.'

Maggie took the mysterious, grimy envelope with the words, *for my sister, Maggie Stark,* printed on the front, which alone was confusing. Why would Millie refer to her, not as stepsister, but as *my sister*? Hesitantly, Maggie turned the envelope round and round in her hands. There was un-sureness of what she'd find once it was opened, like a sort of Pandora's Box, besides, did she really want to read the last words dictated by Millie's tortured mind?

If their last meeting was anything to go by, Maggie couldn't imagine her stepsister being in any way repentant or seeking forgiveness. Still, there was only one way to find out. Unable to control her curiosity any longer, Maggie tore open the envelope, removed the single sheet of paper, then slowly and deliberately, she unfolded it to read the words that were most likely written in a moment of futility and despair. Maggie turned deathly pale and staggered back as if she had been struck.

'Dear oh dear, you've gone as white as a ghost, Mrs Stark.' The policeman was genuinely concerned that whatever was in that letter had catapulted this young woman into a state of shock. 'I can get you a glass of water, but to be honest, you look like you could do with something stronger.'

'I'm fine, really I am! It's just that today has been a strain.' Maggie held up the letter and said wearily, 'one surprise after another. You probably know the history between Coutts and our family,' she laughed sarcastically, 'if you don't, you're the only one. It was the talk of the town for years.'

'I've heard stories,' he answered reticently, 'but I'm not paid to take notice of idle gossip.'

Diplomacy was necessary in certain instances, and this was one of those instances. Of course, he had heard stories about the sudden retirement of certain officers, and the connotation that they were in some way linked to the suspicious and very hush-hush circumstances surrounding the death of the first Mrs Coutts. It was one of those stories that serve as a warning to policemen to stay on the right side of the law.

'Let me explain, you deserve that much.' Something about this policeman's gentle manner put Maggie at ease, and then she saw how ridiculously misplaced her dislike of *all* policemen had been. One bad apple had destroyed the respect for peacekeepers who deserved to be respected for the job they did, especially at times like these.

'Thank you, Mrs Stark. I appreciate your honesty and have every respect for your principles.'

'When James Coutts died, I went to see Millie in the hope she had more decency than her father, and that I could convince her to give back my mother's money. I had more chance of becoming Queen of England. Millie Coutts looked down her nose at me and we ended up having a blazing row right there on her doorstep. She wouldn't let me inside the house you see. It was a real slanging match and then before leaving; I pretended to have the power to put a curse on her.'

At first, the policeman looked at Maggie oddly, and then a strange smile crept over his face. His brawny hand tried to suppress a titter from escaping lest it sounded facetious. 'She didn't honestly believe you could do it?'

'As I live and breathe! *May you never enjoy our money or one happy day for the rest of your life*, were the exact words I spoke. She tried to act as bold as brass, but her face was pea green. Needless to say, we never kept in touch. The last time I ever saw Millie Coutts was when she turned up at my grandmother's funeral. Even then, she flaunted common decency by wearing a big, flowery hat.'

'Purple with pink roses?'

'Yes! How did you know?' Maggie asked.

'She was wearing it when she died. God help her, it must have been all she had left. Most probably something she prized because it reminded her of happier times.'

'You know what happened with the man she married?'

'Sufficient to say, John Adams was well known to the police. We were also aware he was robbing his wife blind, but without a formal complaint, no action could be taken. Anyway, you were telling me about the day you went to see her.'

'As I walked away, she started taunting me that I could never win. I was filled with anger and those words kept ringing in my ears. Never win! You see, it was her arrogance that angered me most and I wished that one day, she'd know what it felt like to have her world come tumbling down around her, but I honestly didn't want her to suffer the way she did.'

Filled with curiosity after hearing the full sad and strange story, the policeman asked, 'After all that happened, I can't understand why Mrs Adams named you as her next of kin. All the bad blood between your families, yet she called you her sister, it's a piece of jigsaw that doesn't fit. Perhaps I'd have a better understanding if I knew what she wrote in that letter.'

'*That* is what's so odd. She must have been riddled with guilt, not just for the taking of what she knew wasn't hers, but allowing a scoundrel to fritter it all away. Read it for yourself: it's only five words that sum up her bitterness.' Maggie handed him the letter.

'Before I read this, let me give you my point of view. I think when things went too far, she found it not only difficult, but consequences made it impossible to hand you an olive branch. By calling you her sister, wasn't she in her own way begging your forgiveness?' He held the scrap of paper between thumb and forefinger, shook it open and then frowned in bewilderment. Millie's last words read, *you won and I'm sorry.* 'She must have carried your words with her to the grave, but what was she trying to say? Sorry you'd won, or sorry about the money?'

'Like you say, she carried it with her to the grave, but I know what I prefer to believe. Now if you'll excuse me, my family will be home soon and there's tea to be made and grieving to be done. My sister was buried today,' Maggie said sadly. She showed him out, then wept some more.

All those years of hoping and wishing were finally ended, but there was no joy in the passing away of the last remaining Coutts, even though it felt like the blight of hostility was finally gone from their lives.

The day after Millie was buried, a letter arrived from Australia; a letter that would fulfil all Maggie and Tommy's dreams, and begin a new chapter in their lives.

My dearest family,

I have so much to tell you. Firstly, Ralph and I are to be married, but you probably expected that so it won't be much of a surprise. I have one very dear wish and that's for you, Tommy and the kids to be here, now, I know you're going to say you can't afford it, but wait for the rest of my news.

At eighty-two-years-old, Granddad is finally retiring and the farm, livestock and all the land have been sold, and for a fortune I might add. Grandma says she wants to make up for what Coutts did (I told them everything), and the bulk of the money is to be split between us. The accountant will send you a banker's draft very soon, but I warn you Maggie, you'll faint when you see the amount of noughts on the cheque.

*I love you all and **will** see you soon. Grandma and Granddad are so excited about spending time with you, Tommy and the kids, maybe even convincing you to stay.*

Your loving sister,

Eve.

It was hard to take in at first. Maggie and Tommy read and re-read the letter over and over. It wasn't until the banker's draft was actually in their hands that they believed in Divine Providence.

Just weeks away from her birthday, her thirty-fifth, Maggie found herself planning and organising a magical trip to the other side of the world. Not so long ago, she walked into town to save the tram fare.

'Who would have thought it,' Tommy said with the same incredulity he'd carried since the letter from Eve arrived. 'Years of scrimping and then, just like that,' he snapped his fingers, 'our ship comes in.'

'I don't think Billy's slept a full night since we told him he's going on an aeroplane to see his Auntie Eve.'

They had laughed so much over the past few weeks. Of course, there was so much to laugh about. The one thing that meant more to them than the unexpected wealth was seeing Eve again and knowing she was happy at last. So why amid all this joy, why did Maggie seem so pensive and troubled?

'Maggie, my darling, I think I know you better than anyone and I can tell when something's worrying you.' Tommy knew from experience, blunt talking was the only language Maggie responded to. 'It's not lack of money, not anymore, so what's troubling you?'

'Now that money isn't a problem, there's something I want to do before we go to Australia.'

'And that is…?'

'I want to put up a headstone for Millie.'

'And you thought I'd be angry, did you? Tomorrow, we'll go together and order one.' Tommy never stopped marvelling at how a woman, who'd been through so much strife, could still retain all this compassion, especially for the Coutts who caused her so much grief.

The headstone was carefully chosen, duly ordered, and was to be placed on Millie's grave the morning before the Stark family's epic journey.

They were packed and the following morning, Maggie, Tommy and the children would set off on an adventurous journey that they never thought possible. There was only one more thing to do before they left.

In the florists, Tommy joked that they could lock up the shop for the day since his wife had bought every flower; every pink and purple flower in the shop. Then they took a taxi to the cemetery where Maggie covered Millie's grave with the flowers. She positively glowed with pride as her hand caressed the new headstone of white marble with gold lettering.

'Isn't it beautiful, Tommy?' Great, big tears rolled down Maggie's cheeks. She felt so fulfilled, so proud and happy to have done this one thing, because it felt good and right. 'I don't think anyone should leave this earth without something to mark their existence.'

'You chose the right words, Maggie.'

'Oh I hope so, Tommy! I want people to come past here, admire the beautiful headstone and know she belonged to someone.'

'Oh, that they will, you've made sure of it.'

As they walked from the cemetery, Maggie experienced the same tugging feeling she felt on the day, as a solitary mourner, she came here to watch Millie being laid to rest. Maggie was filled with the urge to turn and look back at the grave resplendent in a blaze of pinks and purples. Millie loved flowers, especially these vibrant colours in particular. You could tell by that awful hat she obviously adored.

The smile on Maggie's face was one of contentment. Tommy was right, the words were perfect and she just knew Millie would be so proud of the headstone that read—

Millicent Coutts
Sister of Maggie and Eve
Rest in peace.

And the hate was gone.